READY TO SCORE

ALSO BY JODIE SLAUGHTER

Play to Win
Bet on It
To Be Alone with You
Just One More
White Whiskey Bargain
All Things Burn

READY TO SCORE

JODIE SLAUGHTER

ST. MARTIN'S GRIFFIN
NEW YORK

This is a work of fiction. All of the characters, organizations, and events portrayed in this novel are either products of the author's imagination or are used fictitiously.

First published in the United States by St. Martin's Griffin, an imprint of St. Martin's Publishing Group

www.stmartins.com

Designed by Gabriel Guma

The Library of Congress Cataloging-in-Publication Data is available upon request.

ISBN 978-1-250-82186-7 (trade paperback)
ISBN 978-1-250-82187-4 (ebook)

First Edition: 2025

10 9 8 7 6 5 4 3 2 1

For Becca, Joe, and Scoop, who had to try to teach me football from scratch

THE SPRING BEFORE

The halls of Greenbelt Senior High School were mostly empty. It was a professional development day, which meant that the students stayed home and most teachers showed their faces for a couple of hours in the morning before finding themselves free to go about their days. Jade Dunn, on the other hand, took it as an opportunity to get a bit of real work accomplished. Using the kind of focus that could be maintained only when she and the bookkeeper were the only ones in the building.

She was sitting behind the desk in her classroom, switching between grading quizzes and looking at her defensive line playbook, when the sound of something heavy rolling down the hallway caught her attention. Ignoring the instinct to be nosy had never been her strong suit, so she peeked her head out of the doorway, expecting to see someone from the custodial staff.

Instead, she saw *her.*

Ms. Lim.

Wearing a pair of slim-fit khaki pants and a button-up as she rolled a . . .

"Is that a SMART board?" Jade was incredulous.

Lim stopped in her tracks just across from Jade and smiled widely at her. "It sure is." She patted the side of the giant screen.

"Where did you get that?"

"We got a little bit of funding, and Ms. Lim here submitted a pretty great proposal." Principal Fletcher Coleman appeared like a gust of wind from one of the classrooms down the hall. "It was delivered today."

"I've been trying to get a SMART board for my classroom for a year and a half," Jade said, gritting her teeth. "She's been here five minutes, and she just gets one handed to her?"

"Well, um." The older man turned red in the cheeks. "The funding—"

"The funding was for the arts," Lim interrupted with a smile. "And I *am* the art teacher."

"And what does an art teacher need with a SMART board? What are the kids even going to do? Paint all over it?"

"Now, Ms. Dunn—"

Jade was incensed as she cut her boss off. "I'm sorry, Principal Coleman, I really am. But I just don't understand how it makes sense that her class could use that tool more than mine. One of those boards would help my students get a leg up on literal hands-on learning."

"And it would help mine too." Lim still had that little smile across her face. "This board is going to enable me to incorporate more interactive learning into my lessons. The kids will be able to learn about the new frontier of digital art."

Jade scoffed. "The new frontier of . . . Coleman, you cannot be serious."

"Ms. Dunn." The man's scolding of her was gentle but firm. "We can revisit your proposal, but there's no need to be antagonistic."

"Exactly, Ms. Dunn. We can all have things here. Me having a SMART board is a positive for all the students." Ms. Lim may as well have winked at them both.

Jade's eye twitched.

Ms. Lim turned that smile back on Jade, only it wasn't as sweet as it had been seconds earlier. Its edges had gone sharp, not quite smug, but definitely knowing exactly what she had done. It ground the ever-loving fuck out of Jade's gears.

Everyone loved Ms. Lim. She'd come to Greenbelt and the people had taken to her so fast that everyone had forgotten about a time she hadn't been there. Jade . . . had not had such an easy time. Not with the students and not with her fellow staff either. And she'd been there her whole damn life.

People tended to find her intense. Serious, even. But Ms. Lim was all easy smiles and warm kindness. People took to her immediately. In the two years she'd been in Greenbelt, Jade hadn't heard a single person say one unkind thing about her. Not even a student.

Jade didn't really understand people like that, and it was enough to make her bristle. But not enough to stoke the flames of the intense dislike she felt for the other woman now. No, that had been driven by something else.

Ms. Lim hadn't ever done anything to cross Jade. Honestly, she'd even been helpful once or twice. For a moment in time, Jade had thought that she might be able to look past Lim's sunny disposition. Then, during an end-of-the-year field day, she'd seen Ms. Lim coach her ass off during a friendly flag football game while the head coach of Greenbelt Senior High's football team watched with clear approval written all over his face.

It had taken one afternoon for that particular piece of straw to seat itself on the camel's back. A later conversation with a staff member who revealed that Lim had real coaching experience had broken that back completely. Jade could see the woman's game from a mile away. Francesca Lim was coming for her spot—Jade didn't need confirmation or threats from the woman herself, she could *feel* it. And it made her furious.

Now Lim had gotten a SMART board. A SMART board that should've been Jade's.

She disliked the woman immensely. She wanted her gone. Out of her school, out of her town, and especially far, far away from her goddamn football team.

Everything inside Jade ached to curse her out. Of course, she couldn't quite do that in the middle of a high school without drawing even more ire from her boss. So she swallowed the urge, even though it tasted like tar going down her throat.

She turned to Coleman. "Can we have a later meeting about this, Mr. Coleman?"

He sighed with all the world-weariness of a man who'd been dealing with teachers for the better part of two decades. "Yes, Ms. Dunn."

"I'll get back to papers, then."

Jade turned on her heel, making a show of ignoring Ms. Lim, hoping she would flit off somewhere so Jade could continue to pretend she didn't exist.

She was not so lucky.

"Bye, Ms. Dunn." Lim's voice was saccharine. "If you need me to help you write up a better proposal for your own board, just let me know. I know that kind of creativity might not be your strong suit."

Jade's eye twitched again. And if anyone asked, it was the wind that slammed her classroom door shut in their faces, not her own hand.

1

A year ago, Jade's best friend, Miriam, had won the lottery. Miri had a heart on her the size of an old magnolia tree, and she'd been incredibly generous with her closest friends, gifting them life-saving amounts of money. Jade spent months trying to kiss Miri's feet after, with every red cent sitting in her bank account untouched. Her best friend damn near had to kick her in the face to get her back right. But once she did, it was game time. Jade broke some off for her folks and made sure that Social Security and her teacher's pension weren't the only things she had to live on in retirement. The rest had been put into the school. Anonymous donations that helped buy new desks and repair two of the broken ovens in the cafeteria. They'd even finally managed to get a laptop for every enrolled student and then some. Somehow, even when she was the one providing the healthy funding, she still couldn't manage to find the funds for her own SMART board. Go figure.

Surprisingly, she hadn't even made sure most of the donated money went to the football team either. She was of the mind that the kids worked better when they were a little scrappy. Besides, from an economics standpoint, most of the teams they played weren't much better off than her kids. She wanted Greenbelt to win—always—but it didn't seem right to try to make that happen by throwing money their competitors didn't have on the field. So her kids got refreshed uniforms, new cleats and pads and helmets, better snacks for during practice than they'd ever had, and fresh turf on the field. This also meant that team parents wouldn't have to scrounge and scrimp to make sure their kids were able to make it to away games and tournaments.

Less-stressed parents meant less-stressed kids, which turned into players with more focus.

This was exactly why, on July 6, the first day of summer training camp, Jade stood with the brim of her cap pulled down low and her hands on her hips, looking every bit like her daddy as she surveyed the field.

Junior varsity tryouts for the upcoming school year wouldn't happen for another month, but the boys would be doing one-a-days until then.

It was hotter than usual for July in South Carolina. The Fourth had brought rain, and while the grass was no longer wet, there was plenty of moisture in the air. The only thing on their side was the overcast sky, taking some of the heat off. This meant that at least not all their time had to be spent in the weight room today.

Duncan Landry, the head coach, was a big, tall white man who'd come up playing ball in Louisiana. He'd spent four years at Louisiana State as a defensive back and somehow wound up coaching football in some nothing town in the Carolinas. In the fifteen years he'd been at Greenbelt Senior High, he'd led their team to six state championships. Unfortunately, it had also been six years since their last big win. And no matter how much red the old man still had in his cheeks—or how much fire in his belly—Jade knew he was nearing the end of his tenure.

She could just *feel* it. The same way she felt like hers was about to begin.

And it didn't matter that she was basically fifth in the line of succession. She'd been delusional in going after the job she had now, so she might as well let it carry her through to the end.

Landry had the boys running offense-versus-defense flag football drills. No tackles, pads off to try to keep the heat at bay, with water breaks every five minutes. She and Coach Carr, a stout, middle-aged Black man who kept a Bluetooth glued to his right ear at all times, watched their boys with shrewd eyes.

She squinted under her cap, scribbling in her notepad every time she spotted a weakness or an area for improvement. The boys were a bit slow, but that was to be expected during their first day back. And there was spottiness in their movement together, a kind of uncertainty in how they were supposed to work with their teammates.

The drill ended in a stalemate, no scores. But the boys were sweaty and hyped and energized. They could work with that. *She* could work with that.

After the boys were gone and the coaches were left to straighten out the field, Landry gathered all five coaches in a circle on the forty-yard line.

"We had a good first day." His Cajun accent was as thick as if he'd never left the Boot. "The boys looked good out there. They hustled hard. We got plenty of work to do, but I think we can get them all the way this year."

The Greenbelt Gators had braved a rough last few years as a team. First, a revolving assistant coaching lineup, then a string of losses that had seemed to render all their previous title wins obsolete in the eyes of their town. Just the year before, a few of Greenbelt's richest—and the other sponsors who helped make sure their largely low-income players were outfitted in fresh cleats and jerseys each season—had taken it upon themselves to call for Landry's removal as head coach. Jade hadn't been in the meeting that Landry had called to address the matter. But when all was said and done, that talk had been shut down entirely.

Now, though, there were new rumors flying around, ones that made Jade almost ashamed of how much they lit a fire under her ass. If the hushed words around town were to be believed, Landry was thinking about retiring. She could hardly believe it, to be honest. The man had been head coach when she was in high school in 2007. And he was just as spry as ever. The only things she could see that had changed since were the graying hair at his temples and his bad knees, which kept him from squatting when he talked to the players. Maybe he was just tired of all the early mornings and late nights. All the overzealous parents and teenage drama. If retirement were on the horizon for him, that left the door perfectly ajar for her.

She could see it all so clearly. Herself, looking out over the field with her hands on her hips, knowing that this team was hers to lead. Knowing that the championships she would bring them would show everyone that she belonged here.

Landry cleared his throat loudly, shaking Jade from her fantasies. He took his cap off and rubbed his hand over the short, grayed fuzz on top of his head before slipping it back on. "Well, shit . . . I'm sure y'all have been around here clucking like hens, wondering if I'm really leaving or not, so I'll just give you an answer . . . Yes, I am."

Jade could practically feel the air around them get sucked into the chests of five people all at once, each one of them heaving like they were trying to capture the bulk of it. Her own chest suddenly felt like it was full of fire as her mind raced.

This was it.

This was actually fucking it.

"Nobody knows yet but us, and I'd like to keep it that way for now. You know how the rest of the guys like to meddle," he said, referring to the other head athletics coaches at Greenbelt Senior High. "Principal Coleman has given me the power to choose who'll take over for me when I'm gone." He pointed a shaky finger around the circle. "The regular season's over in October. That's when I'm leaving, so that's when I'll make the decision."

Jerry Smith, a defensive coach and tenth-grade chemistry teacher, cleared his throat. "What, uhh . . . what are the criteria?"

Coach Landry screwed his face up a little bit the way he always did when he was thinking hard. "It ain't as simple as that," he answered. "I'll spend preseason watching y'all, seeing how you coach, how you lead, how you are with the kids. I'm not carrying around a score sheet here, people—no grades, no extra credit. I'll know when I know. And I should know by the time the regular season starts."

Jade clenched her jaw, her shoulders rolling like her body was preparing for a fight. All this would almost be easier if there were some kind of grading scale. She was good at tests, always had been, especially when the answers were straightforward. If the criteria were based on which coach won the most scrimmages or even which coach helped send the most kids off to college, she had a clear vision of how to meet both those goals. But when the criteria was just in Landry's head, all based on feelings and hunches . . . well, it was the nebulous things that Jade had a harder time with.

For a moment, she floundered. Her mind raced, trying to connect the dots, fighting to create a plan out of next to nothing.

Coach's next words never settled between her ears, but she dug her toes harder into the turf of the field, chin stubborn even amid all her anxiety. She only noticed that they'd been dismissed when Landry called out for her to stay behind as the other guys walked off.

He waited until they were completely alone to talk. "Dunn . . . you know you've got some stiff competition here."

Her eyes widened before she could steel her face. "Coach, I have every intention of showing you how right I am for this job. You know me; you know how hard I'm willing to fight for it."

Landry nodded. Jade maintained eye contact with him, despite how much more excruciating it got as the seconds ticked by.

"Of course I know. You hit that field running and haven't stopped since, but I've got guys out there who have a decade on you in terms of experience, and I can't lie and say that doesn't take precedence in times like these."

Suddenly, her heart was in her stomach. "I get that, I do. But sometimes it's better to bring something new to the table."

"This is South Carolina football, Dunn. Trying something new isn't exactly what we're known for around these parts."

"Right."

The word hung in the air between them for a few long, torturous moments before Landry sighed again.

"You know what we're up against here," he said. "I know I have the final decision, but that doesn't mean it won't be a hard sell. A woman . . . a Black woman . . . a gay Black woman . . ."

"I'm bisexual, sir," she corrected on instinct.

Landry rolled his eyes. "This is just as much about politics as it is about making the right choice for the team. The new head coach is going to have eyes all over them, all the time. The principal, the parents, hell, the damn mayor is in my office more often than I'd like to admit. I can't put anybody in this position who can't handle that."

Honestly, Jade thought she'd already been handling that. She was always strategic about the way she carried herself in both her jobs for that very reason. Hers was more of a show-no-weakness approach.

"I can handle anything, Coach. I'm not afraid of any of it. All I need is the chance to show you that I'm ready for this. I've got no problem showing anybody else who needs to see it too."

"Aw, hell . . ." He pinched his nose between two fingers. "You know how to play poker?"

"Um . . . a bit. Why?"

"You better get a little refresher, then. Thursday night, 8:00 P.M., you come to my house, all right? Bring fifty dollars and get ready to show that you know how to play the game."

The way he said "play the game" told her everything she needed to know.

"I'll be there," she said.

Landry nodded, his arm extended as if he wanted to reach out to her, but instead he tucked them both behind his back.

"This is about more than football, Dunn," he said. "And it's about more than poker too."

He was so serious, it almost sounded like she was about to sell her soul to gain entry to some secret assassins' guild. To be fair, though, South Carolina high school football might have been the more cutthroat of the two.

Her mind reeled again, thinking about how she was going to brush up on her poker skills. And by *brush up*, she meant learn completely. The only real experience she had with the game was the months she'd spent watching high-stakes poker games on ESPN after *SportsCenter* reruns went off during her all-nighters in grad school.

Jade nodded, trying to convey some type of surety. That seemed to be enough for Landry, who turned to make his way off the field.

"Oh, bring some tortilla chips too, would you?" he called out over his shoulder. "I'm making my famous Rotel dip."

She walked away from the conversation with heavy feet and squared shoulders. Jade had always been very aware of the tenuous position she held. She was a Black woman who had somehow finagled her way into a serious football coaching spot in the South. The first woman in Greenbelt Senior High's long, storied history to ever do so. Both she and her assistant coaching title were always on display in some way.

Whether it was the stares she received on the sidelines at games or the new players who—every damn year without fail—she had to coach into respecting her knowledge and authority.

She had her dreams. Ones that involved her name next to the "Head Coach" title in the trophy case. Ones that involved respect and reverence. Ones where people didn't constantly question whether she deserved to be where she was. But she'd be a complete fool if she didn't acknowledge that what she was fighting against to realize those dreams was much bigger than she was.

That didn't mean she wasn't going to work hard as hell to make them happen. Nor was she going to sit around feeling sorry for herself. Giving up or giving in were not in her nature.

Well, maybe in her logical mind she knew that. She was the youngest coach on the team, the one who'd been in her job the shortest amount of time. Neither her gender nor race were viewed favorably for a position like this. But that just meant she had something to give this team that none of the other guys did. If it took beating their asses at poker to prove it, then she had no qualms about that either.

2

Francesca Lim was good at wiggling her way into things. Remaining somewhat of an unexpected choice, using shy smiles and her quiet nature to remain unassuming until she was able to snap something up. This had been the case her entire life. With romantic relationships, with convincing grumpy ladies at the DMV to bend the rules for her, and with work too.

She hadn't even known about the weekly poker game at Coach Landry's house until two days ago. Her only real friend at work—as in someone she willingly hung out with outside the walls of Greenbelt Senior High—was Jeremy Bell. He was a tall, lanky white man who coached soccer—probably the least well-regarded sport in the entire school. As head coach, he apparently had a set place at the table, but he'd kept it a secret from her—that is, until they'd gotten drunk at the bar the other night and he'd started lamenting about how he wasn't going to attend anymore because he was tired of the other guys making fun of him.

Francesca felt for him—kind of. But he was one of the mayor's nephews and his wife was sexy as hell, so she felt confident that he'd fare just fine. Much less drunk than he was and sensing an in, she'd managed to worm her way into an invitation on the grounds that she was, one, really fucking great at poker, and two, trying to "make more connections in Greenbelt."

She'd been teaching art at Greenbelt Senior High for two years, and for roughly twenty-two months of that time, Franny'd had her eye on her own personal pie in the sky. Assistant coach—offensive line first, then head coach second, when the time came. There were only so many positions to fill, and since she'd been there, no one had left.

A couple of weeks ago, she'd been in Minnie's Diner standing in the line behind the hostess stand, waiting to order a burger and fries to go. In front of her were two assistant football coaches, ones who coached but didn't work at the school full-time. She didn't know their names, but there was a bald one and a redheaded one. She was there, minding her business, when she saw Baldy look around conspiratorially, trying to make sure no one was listening. Immediately, she knew whatever he had to say would be juicy. So the second he shot her a look and saw that she had little earbuds in, she tapped them twice to pause her music.

"I think Landry's got his eye on Dunn for his spot when the season's over," Baldy said about the team's head coach and her favorite math teacher to fluster.

"How do you figure?" Red questioned.

"Just a feeling. Pretty sure he's been eyeing her for a while, probably since she started."

"Hmmm." Red seemed to be the contemplative sort. "I figure she's the only one worth mentoring. I'm not saying the rest of us aren't good in our own right, but we're all too old for that shit."

"You're not thinking of throwing your hat in the ring?" Baldy asked.

"And drive my ass into an early grave worrying about Greenbelt's legacy?" Red shook his head. "I want us to win as much as anybody else on that team, but I've got five years until I retire and me and

Suzie can roast our pale asses on a beach down in Florida. I love this sport, but being head coach is just asking for a heart attack."

Whatever response Baldy had was interrupted when the hostess came to take them to a table. Suddenly, Franny found herself out of earshot, still reeling from the information she'd been inadvertently given.

Coach Landry was stepping down as head coach at the end of the season, and Jade Dunn seemed to be his number one replacement prospect. *Seemed* being the operative word. There was still time for Franny to do what she did best and wiggle her way in there. Into an assistant coaching job if she could get it, but head coach if she somehow found herself overrun with luck. Either way, the door was open, even if it hadn't been opened for her specifically.

She sure as hell wasn't about to let it close on her.

So here she was having to scheme. She might have been ashamed if she didn't believe she had plenty to benefit the team. It wasn't as if she didn't deserve the job. To be fair, going about it the old-fashioned way wouldn't have worked for her anyway. She wasn't an old-fashioned girl. Not in the way she coached, and not according to who she was.

When she'd found out Jade Dunn was an assistant football coach, Franny had nearly coughed up a lung. She was from Houston, and in Texas, where football was only one step under God—officially—the same misogyny that ran rampant in the church was just as prevalent on the football field. She'd met two other women high school football coaches in the entire state, of which there were still only a handful. And of those, none of them were Asian women. To be fair, though, a few of them were lesbians, so there was that.

Before she'd left home, she'd coached an Amateur Athletic Union football team, and she'd clawed her way into that position too. Aside from her parents, that job had been the hardest thing for her to say goodbye to. But she'd done it willingly because she was nothing if not a fool for love. Even the scant, flighty promise of love apparently.

She'd left her dream job and all its promise of advancement behind for a woman and had come up short, with very little to show for it. Now that she knew there was opportunity, Franny wasn't afraid to sharpen her nails and get those claws back out to make something for herself on this team.

She wasn't afraid of the guys. That required its own strategy. One that was definitely a delicate balance, but one she knew well enough how to handle. It was Ms. Dunn who had the ability to throw a rusty wrench in her plans.

Franny hoped like hell that there could be room for them both on the team. She wasn't interested in taking someone else's job, especially when she knew they'd fought for it. She only wanted a spot of her own. And Dunn already hated her. Every time they passed each other in the hall or so much as caught eyes, Dunn would give Franny a look so withering she felt it zing her nipples.

From what she'd seen, Ms. Dunn wasn't the warmest in general, but damn did she hate Franny. Which made very little sense, because Franny had never so much as sniffed wrong in her direction.

Whatever.

Ultimately, it didn't matter. Dunn could hate her all she wanted, so long as she didn't try to sabotage her. Anyway, as far as she knew, Dunn didn't have the same invitation Franny now held. If she played her cards right, she could get her in before Dunn ever even discovered she was looking for one.

Now it was Thursday night, and Franny was standing behind Jeremy on the porch of Coach Landry's Craftsman-style home.

"What am I even supposed to tell them?" Jeremy whined. He'd been trying to convince her not to come all day. "You're not supposed to be here, Fran, because my silly ass wasn't supposed to get drunk and tell you about it."

"I'll do the talking." Franny patted him on the shoulder. "Don't worry. Trust me."

The surprise on Coach Landry's face when he came to the door was almost comical.

"Hi there," Franny greeted him with a grin before he could speak.

His gaze immediately turned to Jeremy, expression accusatory.

"It's not his fault," she asserted. "I got him drunk and squeezed it out of him. He's just a sweet boy. He had no chance of keeping me away."

Jeremy, to his credit, made himself look significantly more pathetic. "Sorry, Coach, she reminds me of my big sister. I had flashbacks of being hit over the head with a Tonka truck if I disagreed."

Franny tapped her toe against his heel. She wasn't that much of a bully. She'd planned to return him safely and unharmed to his wife whether he'd coughed up the info or not.

Coach Landry sighed from the very depths of his soul before he pursed his lips and stepped aside. Then, after shutting the door behind them and with one last put-out look at Jeremy, Landry led them down to the basement.

It looked every bit like what Franny had pictured. Gray speckled carpet and off-beige walls. A pool table to one side, a giant sectional in the middle facing a huge, mounted television. And to the other side, a round table with four men seated at it, along with . . . Jade Dunn.

Her surprise at seeing the woman made her stop dead in her tracks, causing Jeremy to stumble into her from behind.

"Sorry," he muttered, moving around her to take his seat at the table.

When she, Coach Landry, and Jeremy were finally seated, the number of players rounded out to eight. She hadn't counted on the other woman being there. Franny sat across from Ms. Dunn, her brain whirling as she was immediately forced to reevaluate and change her plans for the evening.

"Looks like we've got a lot of new blood in here tonight," said Cody Ross, the head baseball coach with a baby face. He was a little younger than she was, but not by much.

To his left, the track-and-field head, an older Black man named Charles Byrd, laughed. "Don't matter how much new blood is in here, Ross, I'm still coming for that scratch, just like always."

Ross blushed, and even Jeremy laughed.

"I'm thinking not a single one of you is going to be left with so much as a penny by the time I walk out of here tonight," Franny said matter-of-factly. She figured her best way in was to be bold. She wasn't going to impress anybody by pretending she was timid. She was going to make them laugh their way into accepting her.

The men howled. Coach Landry even slapped his knee under the table. "Now that's what I'm talking about."

Across the table, she watched Ms. Dunn quietly seethe, not a single peep escaping from those full, glossy lips of hers.

There'd been a fifty-dollar buy-in for the game, and after Landry dispersed their individual chips, the rest were separated and placed on the right side of the table in neat little stacks.

"The game is Texas Hold'em. I'll start with the first deal." He laid a white chip on the table in front of him. "We'll be doing a twenty-five-cent and fifty-cent no-limit game. Jeremy, you've got the small blind to start. Ross, you've got the big bet."

After both men threw their respective chips in, Landry dealt cards for the entire table. Franny bent her cards up to take a peek. Eight of hearts and three of diamonds. An off suit. There was nothing she could do with this. But she looked over and watched Ms. Dunn scrutinize her own cards, trying to decipher the look on her face.

"I'll call." Byrd threw a fifty-cent chip onto the table, matching the big bet Ross had made.

Franny was next, which meant she needed to make a decision quickly. Her hand was pure trash, but that didn't mean everyone else's was good. Her options were limited. She could either follow Byrd's lead and match the current bet, or she could put on a big show and raise the bet in an attempt to cover her bluff. Or she could fold. Throw her shitty cards into the pile and give in before the game even really started.

But she wasn't going to start off by bowing out. If she was going to lose, she was going to do it in style.

"I'll call too," she said, making extra effort not to meet eyes with any of the other players.

Dunn was the second to last to go, right before it circled back around to Landry. The woman had a sweet voice that Franny had always felt was incongruous to her outward demeanor. It was soft and airy. Honestly, it sounded like something out of a Barbie cartoon. It didn't seem to matter how much the woman tried to clear her throat to deepen it, it was never anything less than cute as hell.

"I'll raise fifty cents." She tossed a one-dollar chip into the pile, then sat back in her chair with her shoulders squared and an unreadable look on her face. To Franny, it didn't immediately read as smug, but she didn't know Ms. Dunn well enough to decipher what it actually was.

Maybe she needed to do some studying.

Ugh. No.

Franny rolled her shoulders, the nervousness in her stomach mixing with something else that made her feel hot around the collar of her T-shirt. She tugged at it briefly, steeling herself for the flop round after Landry also threw a one-dollar chip into the pot.

Landry dealt the three community cards, and everyone was given the chance to bet or fold. Again, no one folded. The game continued in kind. Round after round, cards were dealt, bets were made. Little by little, everyone started to sweat.

Franny made work not only of studying her own hand and strategy but of the other players as well, trying to spot their weaknesses and tells.

Jeremy was easy. She knew him well enough to know that while the sweat beaded at his temples wasn't necessarily out of the norm, the way he rubbed his index and middle fingers together like cricket legs was.

Lionel Price, the head basketball coach, had a knack for cracking his neck right before he folded.

None of them were professionals, not at playing poker and certainly not at hiding their tells. And Franny was too observant to miss them. The only one she couldn't nail down was Dunn. The woman was stone-faced the entire time. She never looked smug, she never looked disappointed, she never even looked thoughtful. The woman could have had the worst hand at the table or the best, and none of them would have had a clue.

It made Franny steam in her seat. Each round, the fire in her belly was stoked as Dunn sat there, calm as you please.

Finally, after an hour of play, they took a short break. Landry went upstairs to check on the next round of appetizers, Ross and Price went outside to smoke a cigarette, and the other guys dispersed to chat about who knew what.

Franny spotted Dunn by herself at the snack table, putting a couple of mini sausages on a paper plate. Her guard was down, and Franny took the chance to strike. If she couldn't get a read on the woman from the outside, maybe she could wiggle her way into her head.

Dunn took a sip from her red party cup, baring her neck so much that Franny couldn't help but eye it. Slender and long, with smooth skin and a subtle scent that was entirely too heady for a basement poker game, she had to blink a few times to clear her mind.

"Good game," Franny said, biting into a strawberry from the fresh fruit tray on the table.

The second Ms. Dunn's eyes met hers, they narrowed. Oval-shaped, with dark eyelashes, her irises a light brown color. Not as light as butterscotch, but light enough that parts of them almost looked golden in certain lights.

"You too." Dunn sniffed shortly. "Even if you do have an awful hand."

"How could you possibly know that?"

Ms. Dunn shrugged. "I can tell."

Franny scoffed.

"I'm serious." The other woman laughed. "You make it very obvious, you know."

No, Franny certainly did not know. She'd put a metric ton of her energy into trying to remain as impassive as possible. She kept her leg from bouncing, her eye from twitching. Hell, she even made sure she didn't mess with her hair or face too much.

"What's so obvious about it?" she asked.

"Now why would I tell you that? It'll take all the fun out of demolishing your ass."

Franny leaned in, trying to put something of a sneer on her face. "You *wish* you could demolish my ass, Dunn."

The look on the other woman's face nearly made Franny trip over her own feet while standing still. Her eyes went comically wide, and her mouth dropped open. She looked like one of those singing fish nailed to wooden planks.

Dunn's eyes narrowed even more until they were basically slits on her face. Her lips curled back, revealing teeth. Franny supposed she was trying to make herself look intimidating. But the woman was shorter than she was and so soft-looking that Franny had to hold herself back from reaching out to stroke her cheek.

Which . . . no . . . absolutely not.

"Stop fucking with me, Lim," she said, pointing a finger at Franny. "I mean it. I don't know why you're here or what you're doing, but watch it."

"I'm coming for your job." It was a bold-faced lie, but damn did she love getting a reaction out of Ms. Dunn.

It was so damn easy too. Her soft-looking brown cheeks went a purply-red color, and Franny could practically see the steam pushing its way out her ears.

"I will eat you alive," Dunn said.

Landry appeared at the bottom of the stairs, clapping once to get the attention of everyone in the room, letting them know that the intermission was over.

It was time to get back to work.

Franny leaned in close to Dunn, their faces side by side. This close, she could see the dark little moles Dunn had around her sideburns. She could smell her better too. That dark, intense scent that Franny didn't think could be attributed only to perfume. So much better than the smell of cigars and corn chips in the basement that she took a split second to breathe it in.

"There's no way you actually believe I'd take that as a threat."

She was back in her seat before Dunn could even register what she'd said, but that didn't mean Franny missed the way Dunn seemed to choke on her own tongue at the words. A little thrill went through Franny at the thought that she could get under her skin like that. This was going to be fun.

Landry flagged Franny down during the postgame. He beckoned her over to a corner of the basement, and she worked hard not to view the gesture as displeased.

"Why are you really at my poker night, Ms. Lim?" The man had no time for pleasantries, it seemed.

She stammered a bit, floundering hopelessly on what to tell him. The truth didn't seem like a sufficient option—until she happened to glance over her shoulder. Dunn was right there behind her, not five feet away, resting her butt against the arm of the couch. Her head was down as she typed away on her phone, but Franny was close enough to see that she seemed to be randomly typing numbers into her calculator app. It was such a blatant attempt at eavesdropping that Franny—despite having begrudging respect for the action—simply could not abide it.

Dunn was afraid that Franny was after her job. That much had been made clear during their moment at the snack table. In an instant, telling Landry the truth felt like the perfect option.

"Honestly, Coach Landry, I'm here looking for a job. Some little birdies told me that poker night is where shit actually happens, so I figured I should be here."

"A job?" His blond brows furrowed. "You want a job on my team? Doing what?"

"Coaching."

There was a shuffling noise, followed by a thud. Jade Dunn had dropped her phone on the ground.

Landry let out a loud bark. "Jesus Christ. How in the hell did you hear about that?"

She didn't want to out herself as a nosy busybody in what was essentially a job interview, so she ignored the question. "I'm serious."

"Oh, I know you are."

"So, I can keep coming to poker night, then?"

He shook his head, mirth written all over his reddened face. "Good luck is all I can say to you, Ms. Lim. Good luck."

She took that as a yes.

3

Jade did not come out on top at poker night. But neither did Lim, so she was only marginally furious. By some ridiculous stroke of fate, Jeremy Bell made out with their money—all $400 of it. His skin was so sallow by the end of the night, Jade couldn't even find it in herself to do anything but pat him on the back in congratulations.

The ride home in her beloved rusted 1984 Chevy Silverado—named Gladys—was a bumpy one. The roads in Greenbelt weren't the best, and the truck's suspension had seen better days. Holding on to the wheel for dear life, Jade thought about nothing but the cocky words Lim had spoken to her. She didn't know if it made her angrier that Lim had said them in the first place or that she had managed to get the last word in. All she knew was that by the time she turned her engine off, her palms were red and raw.

Three days later, she was still thinking about it.

"I hate her," she grumbled to her friends as they sat around Aja Owens's dining room table. They were decorating sugar cookies, and if Jade had any talent for it, she'd have drawn Ms. Lim on one and smashed her to bits. "I've never hated anyone more than I hate her."

Olivia was sitting next to her, trying and failing to draw an intricate orange tabby on one of her cookies. "This is about the art teacher, right?"

"Yes," Jade hissed. "Ms. Lim."

Miri barked out a laugh that startled them all. "Why do you say her name like you're coming, though?"

"I do not! I say it like I hate her, which I do."

Even Aja, with her sweet self, giggled.

"Oh, Ms. Lim," Miri rubbed her hands over her breasts, throwing her head back in dramatic fashion. "Draw me like one of your French girls, Ms. Lim."

"She probably doesn't even draw real people," Jade grumbled. "She probably just paints like . . . fruit bowls or something. And not pretty ones either. Shitty ones with rotting fruit. Because she's rotten."

"Awww, she's probably not that bad," Aja said gently. "Maybe she's just shy."

"She's not shy, she's evil, and she's trying to take my job."

"The coaching job?" Miri asked.

"Yes!" Jade threw her hands in the air. "You know the poker game I told y'all about?"

The girls nodded, pausing in their decorating.

"She wound up being there the other night. I've been coaching at that school for five years, practically running myself ragged to get to where I am. She didn't even know Greenbelt existed two years ago, and she thinks she can just . . ." Jade trailed off, grinding her teeth.

"Well . . . how did she do?" Olivia asked.

"Not much better than me," Jade admitted. "But it's the principle of the thing. I just feel like I'm already over here working against so much to get what I want, and now somebody just threw a spiral straight at my chest. She's so . . . Everybody likes her. Like, everyone. Even the cafeteria staff, and they hate everybody. Y'all know how political this stuff is. People love to pretend they're impartial and only promote people because of merit, but that's bullshit. That's why they have that poker game every week. That's why Landry has to schmooze the mayor to get new helmets for the team every year. If Landry ends up liking her . . . No, you know what, it's more than that. If Landry thinks other people will like her more than they like me, she's got a real shot at beating me here."

She fell silent, the girls trading quiet glances as she watched. Finally, Aja spoke. "You know what? I don't think this actually changes anything. She may have likability on her side, but you've got experience. And you've already cultivated a relationship with the team; those are your boys. You weren't going to fight any less without her being there. You weren't ever going to pull any punches, and you're not going to now."

"Exactly." Miri pointed at Aja. "If anything, you might be at an advantage. You've told me about the other coaches, and even if Landry won't admit it, you're leagues above them, and you know it. If this girl is your only real competition, it won't be so hard to get her out of there."

"I don't know . . . Something feels different with her. It's like . . . when I talk to her, when I look in her eyes, I see the same thing I see in mine when I look in the mirror. She's not going to give up."

"And neither are you," Miri said. "You just need to do what you do best and go on the offense."

Jade sat back in her chair, cookies and frosting completely forgotten as she crossed her arms over her chest. Her mind started reeling. The head coaching job was right there, so close it was practically hers already. Jade had the ball tight in her grip, and Lim, in all her annoying, infuriating glory, was trying to take it from her.

Every bit of her wanted to sulk and grumble about it, but the reality was that she needed to scheme. She needed to figure out a way to cut Lim off at her pretty little knees.

Many people thought football was all about strength and brute force. They saw the running and hitting and assumed that everything happening on the field was pure coincidence. But Jade knew that it didn't matter how fast your quarterback was or how hard your linebackers ran through—without a comprehensive strategy, a real win was next to impossible.

This was part of the reason she liked the sport so much. It wasn't like math, where an equation had a set, specific answer. A team could employ the exact same strategy against the exact same team three times in a row and end up with three different outcomes. But each time, you'd learn something different about the players, about the game. You could search the gaps in the plan and spackle over them every time a new one appeared. It was problem-solving on a large scale. That was one of her greatest strengths as a coach.

"You're right," she told Miri, putting her elbows on the table and resting her chin in her hands. "I need to find a way to destroy her before she even knows I'm coming for her."

Olivia's eyes widened. "Could you sound any more like a villain right now?"

Jade gave the question a real ponder. "I mean, I could draw a hole on the side of a mountain and get her to try to run through it."

"You could also create an evil version of her in a lab and make the two versions fight each other," Miri suggested.

"Why don't you just convince the big boss that she doesn't know what she's doing? That she's totally incompetent?" Aja's words were gentle compared to their content and spoken quietly, her eyes still intent on her cookie decorating.

"That's so messed up," Jade said. "But perfect . . . I just need to make her embarrass herself in front of the old man so bad that she never even considers showing her face on my field ever again."

"Evil," Olivia whispered.

"Genius," Jade replied, taking an almost violent bite of cookie.

Jade's parents had been divorced for thirty years of the thirty-two she'd been alive. They'd also lived together for just as long. The family resided in a large, beautiful house in one of the nicer neighborhoods in Greenbelt. Built in 1898, the place was three stories, not including the attic. The upper stories both had balconies and pristine white shutters on every window. The house looked like something out of historical Charleston was plopped in a random neighborhood. None of the other homes looked anything like it.

It was her parents' pride and joy. Gene and Joyce Dunn had been married eleven years before they'd had their first and only child. They'd spent every bit of that time saving up for their dream home, and every red cent they had had gone into it. It was only natural for the baby to come after that. Two years into the life of their other most precious pride and joy, the two had realized that they did not enjoy being a couple as much as they'd previously thought.

Neither of them had been willing to give up the house, though. So a compromise was made.

Gene Dunn would make his life in the finished basement. His domain had started with uncomfortable carpet and a pool table and had since turned into a very lovely, if oddly decorated, apartment. Two bedrooms, a master suite, a living room and a kitchen. He even managed to keep the old pool table.

Joyce—who'd returned to her maiden name of Griggs—reigned over most of the rest of the house, under the agreement that she pay a greater sum of the mortgage.

For Jade, this had been life. She'd grown up knowing no different. Honestly, she'd grown up loving it. It was having to explain to friends and teachers and guests that yes, her parents were divorced, and yes, they did still live together that got old.

The annoyance never seemed to outweigh the easy access to her folks, though.

On Sundays, Joyce had a standing date with her "little friend" of fifteen years in Beaufort. Jade didn't know how her mother found it satisfying enough to see her boyfriend only once a week, but she didn't like to think too much about that situation anyway. This meant family dinners were on Saturdays.

At 5:00 P.M. sharp, Gene ventured up from the basement and joined his ex-wife and daughter at their grand oak dinner table. Not a single one of them was a good cook, so normally they got takeout.

This Saturday, Gene had picked up their meal from Minnie's Diner. A classic fifties-style diner in the center of town, Minnie's Diner had been a Greenbelt staple for longer than Jade had been alive. She'd spent plenty of postgame nights eating cobbler in the booths. She'd shared plenty of kisses in them too. But so had half the town. Everyone frequented the place. Even the mayor was known to heave himself off his high horse to stop by once a week for some of Minnie's smothered pork chops.

This time, her father had gotten them a whole heap of fried catfish with coleslaw, green beans, and macaroni on the side. They even had some fried green tomatoes for good measure.

"How's work been, Boo?" her father asked, covering his catfish in Louisiana Hot Sauce. It always made her feel warm to hear her childhood nickname from her parents.

"Oh, it's been all right." She picked at the coating on a fried tomato, trying to play it cool. "Coach Landry wants to give me the head coach position when he retires after this season."

It wasn't necessarily the truth, but it wasn't really a lie either, was it? Her parents sat up straighter in their seats as soon as what she said registered, and Jade couldn't help but puff her chest out a little bit at the obvious pride on their faces.

Her parents both loved the game, but her mother had been an absolute fanatic. A Clemson fan at her core, every week during Jade's childhood, her mother had decked herself out in orange and purple and commandeered the living room to watch her team. Win or lose, Joyce was right there with them. Infallible, unshakable. As a child, Jade had been awed by this level of love and dedication. And by the obvious joy the sport had brought her mother. She'd been bred into football superfandom.

When she was seven, Jade had asked her mother when she could play football. She'd watched Joyce's face fall as she told her daughter that they didn't really allow girls to play. Jade had signed up for a powder-puff game a few months later, and while that experience had been a transformative one, one that she still carried with her, something about it felt like a consolation prize. She'd wanted to play with the big dawgs, and she just knew that there were plenty of other girls out there like her who wanted the same thing.

In the end, it hadn't taken her long to realize that she wasn't a star athlete. Her sophomore year in college, she'd taken over as coach for her school's powder-puff team, and that was where she found her calling. She learned that she had a knack for leading. For encouraging players individually and teams as a whole. But while the road to coaching football as a woman may not have been as impossible as the road to playing football as one, it certainly felt like it sometimes.

Maybe it was because she was their only child, or maybe it was because they simply believed in her beyond reason, but her parents had never done anything but support Jade in her endeavors. Support, comfort, provide shoulders to sob into, Joyce and Gene had been there. The strange but beautiful united front they'd made had been one of the only things to keep Jade going when said going got especially rough.

And here she was, hopefully about to bring everything full circle for her, for them. It filled her with more hope and joy than she knew what to do with.

"Head coach?" her mother asked. "Really?"

"Yeah." Jade cleared her throat when the word came out shakily. "He told me the other day that he's been eyeing me for the position for a while. He said none of the other guys even came close."

Sure, she was embellishing, but when she saw the pride on their faces, she couldn't even bring herself to feel guilty. Her love of football had been hand-fed to her at a young age by them both. They'd been nothing but supportive of her goal of being a teacher, but the outright pride had come in heavy when she'd gotten her coaching position. She didn't just want this job for herself, she wanted it for them too.

Jade committed herself to coming out on top even more than she had before. That way, everything she was telling them now could pass as a prediction rather than a lie.

"I know that's right." Her father slapped his knee. "My baby's going to make sure they're champions again too."

"And she's going to do it as the first Black woman coach in Greenbelt's history." The buttons on her mother's satin blouse damn near popped off from how far her chest puffed out.

Jade swallowed, her throat thicker than the macaroni and cheese she'd just had a bite of. She decided not to tell them about Ms. Lim. If the plan she was formulating in her head worked, things were probably about to get nasty. And not only did she not want them to see her that way, she also didn't want them to know that she had any competition.

She wanted them to think the job was already hers. That all that was left for her to claim it was a bunch of red tape, instead of Jade having to scrape and claw her way to the top like the Disney villain her friends had told her to embody.

"I sure am," she said, jaw clenched but smiling at the same time. "I'm about to change the game."

4

No one had invited Franny to summer practice, but so what? It was a free world. The football field wasn't situated behind gilded gates, and there was nothing she could find in the school employee handbook that stated she couldn't be there just because she wasn't on the team or coaching.

She'd done some Facebook stalking and found out that Monday practice started at 8:00 A.M. Franny had shown up at 9:00. She wore a pair of running shorts and a loose-fitting tank top. Her long, dark hair was pulled back into a low bun at the nape of her neck, and her dollar store sunglasses sat snugly on her nose.

The sun was already high in the sky, beating down, making the eighty-five-degree heat even worse. Franny was happy to see that instead of being outfitted in their pads and uniforms, running drills in the sun, the boys sat on the twenty-yard line in regular workout clothes, water bottles in hand, as Coach Landry towered over them, speaking things she couldn't hear from where she stood on the sidelines.

With her, she also had a folding chair she'd stolen from her parents' house, a gallon of ice water, and a notebook and pencil. She set up her chair off-field, not far from the bleachers but not too close to the other coaches either.

Franny was situated for some time before anyone noticed her. If she'd been forced to bet on who would be the first to see her—and get incensed about her presence—she would have won a cool ten dollars on the spot.

Jade Dunn's stride toward her across the turf should have been accompanied by a war trumpet. The woman's light brown face was too emotive to be stoic. Her dark, full eyebrows quirked on her forehead, and her lips were pinched. The way she walked was probably meant to be angry and intimidating, but all Franny could see was that her wide hips swayed perfectly, even under her knee-length khaki shorts. Franny started a little hum in her head to match their rhythm. It tickled her so silly that when Dunn finally stood in front of her, Franny was grinning.

"What are you doing here?" Dunn practically hissed.

Franny tilted her head to one side, sparing a glance at her water on the ground, then at the pen and paper in her lap. "I'm trying to write the next great American novel, obviously. It's about a really mean, really lonely woman who spends all her time trying to destroy her colleague." Franny moved her pen to the paper in front of her as if she were writing instead of drawing scribbles for dramatic effect. "I hope you don't mind if I spoil the ending for you—"

Dunn cut her off. "It doesn't matter whether you spoil it or not, I doubt you'll even get the chance to finish it."

"The mean lady doesn't succeed," Franny said, continuing as if she hadn't been interrupted. "She ends up getting swallowed by a sinkhole, and her colleague takes her job and, like, wins hella awards and accolades, and everybody loves her more."

"Sounds like a shitty book."

"I figured you'd think so."

Dunn's gaze sharpened. "Plus, nobody says *hella* anymore."

Franny reared back. "Of course they do."

"No, they don't. Only people who are my parents' age say shit like that."

"You're so full of it, Dunn." Franny's eyes narrowed.

"I'm full of it? You're the one who showed up to *my* practice uninvited."

Finally, Franny stood up from her chair. She was a couple of inches taller than Dunn, so nose-to-nose was more nose-to-forehead, but still. "*Your* practice? Last time I checked, all you were was an assistant coach."

Dunn took a small step forward until their bodies were almost pressed together. Franny could feel the faintest brush of the other woman's breasts against the underside of hers, and her jaw tightened as heat flushed through her. "And last *I* checked, you were fighting way above your weight class. It doesn't matter how many asses you kiss or how much you flash those little smiles of yours. You have no shot here; I don't even know why you're still trying."

Franny's eyes moved from Dunn's face to where Coach Landry had sent the boys to run laps and was staring the two women down with scrutinous eyes from across the field. She smiled, waving a hand at the man, who then started approaching them.

"I don't know about that. It seems like your boss likes me well enough." Pointedly, she turned one of her so-called *little smiles* on him.

"Ms. Lim . . . I see you were serious the other night, huh?"

Hearing him, Dunn spun around so fast she almost lost her balance. Before she could think about it, Franny gripped her arm, steadying her. Then she snatched her hand back as if she'd been burned.

Dunn moved to stand by Coach Landry's side, as if they were some kind of united front against her.

"Serious as a heart attack, Coach." Franny made sure to keep her smile bright but not too wide. "I want my chance at a coaching spot."

"My spot?" Landry asked.

Franny shrugged. "There's no point in flying if you're not trying to get up high, is there?"

Coach Landry barked out a laugh that could have been heard from a mile away. "What experience have you got? Have you ever coached at the high school level? Where?"

"I spent three years as the head O-line coach for an AAU youth football team back home in Houston."

"Texas?" Landry raised an eyebrow.

"Yes, sir. We took home two national championship trophies in that time."

He grabbed Dunn's shoulder and gave it a lighthearted shake. "Looks like you might have some competition, after all, Dunn."

Dunn's face went so red, Franny thought she might actually pass out. Then her right eye started to twitch.

"We don't have any positions open right now, obviously," Landry said. "So I can't hire you. But this is a public school, so we definitely ain't strangers to volunteers. After this season . . . well, we'll be restructuring some things"—he glanced at Dunn—"so there might be a couple positions to fill. It'll be a long shot for you to get my job, but shit." The man chuckled. "Shoot for the stars, and you never know."

Landry turned to Dunn. "You mind showing her the ropes?"

Dunn paused, swallowing so hard it looked like she had a real frog in her throat. "Of course, Coach."

After a pat to her arm, Landry walked away, and Dunn waited until he was out of hearing distance before she looked at Franny again. She didn't say anything, though, and Franny couldn't keep herself from rubbing her little win in the other woman's face.

"Looks like that sinkhole is getting bigger, huh?"

Franny had three older brothers. Phillip, Kenny, and Will. Phillip lived and worked in South Korea—Busan, where their parents were from. Kenny had stayed near their parents in Houston, where he wrote—and sometimes sold—screenplays. But Will, her closest brother both spiritually and physically, lived with his wife and daughter in Columbia, South Carolina.

Two years ago, when she'd (ridiculously) agreed to follow her ex, Caroline, back to her home state, she'd only done so with the promise that she'd be within driving distance of her brother. Just in case.

The "just in case" hadn't come, not really. Sure, she and Caroline had broken up in just under six months of moving across the country together. And sure, Caroline had packed her shit and hightailed it out of her own hometown within a few days, headed who knew where. But the only thing that had gotten hurt or scammed was Franny's heart. And even then, it hadn't taken her as long to get over Caroline as she'd expected.

Originally, she'd planned to stay in Greenbelt just long enough to stop her head from spinning and save money. But then she'd gotten a real job and settled in, and well . . . sure, the place was tiny and unlike anything else she'd ever experienced. But she liked it. She didn't know why, but she did. There was something here that kept her from leaving.

Still, almost every week, she made the three-hour drive from Greenbelt to Columbia to see the only family she had in the state. During the school year, this time was relegated to the weekend. But with football practices happening every Monday, Wednesday, Friday, and Saturday and poker on Thursday nights, she had to squeeze the time in during the week.

She'd hopped in the car straight after practice that afternoon, still smelling like sweet sweat and grass. She had spent the first hour of her trip with all the windows in her little Prius down, trying to air herself out.

After she arrived in the city, her first stop was a gas station. Her six-year-old niece, Amelia, would refuse her entry into the family's home if Franny didn't present her with a slushie within three seconds of greeting her.

Franny had a key to their home, but she rarely used it. Instead, she rang the bell, then obnoxiously showed her open mouth to the little doorbell camera, hoping to annoy her brother.

Instead, it was her sister-in-law who answered the door. Yao was a tiny thing. A Taiwanese woman with shoulder-length black hair, an oval-shaped face, and the softest eyes of anyone Franny had ever seen.

"Franny!" Yao looked shocked to see her.

"This is not a pop-in." Franny would never have been so rude. "I told Oppa I was coming."

Yao's face went blank for a second, thinking, then the remembrance hit. "That's right . . . You know, your brother talks so much, sometimes I have to tune some of it out."

Franny snorted. Will was the most laid-back of all the Lim children, but he had a mouth like a motor. She imagined he'd probably mentioned her stopping by to his wife in rushed words somewhere between a suggestion for a new restaurant and recalling a childhood memory.

"Where is he anyway?"

Yao's family owned a local residential real estate company where she worked as an agent, and Will was the executive chef at a popular Korean restaurant in town. Neither of them worked a traditional nine to five, so it wasn't uncommon for them both to be home in the middle of the day. Especially when Amelia was out of school.

Her sister-in-law huffed, then rolled her eyes. "He took the girl-child to my parents' house to see the new little rat dog my mom got." She tapped her phone screen, then turned it toward Franny, showing her a picture of her adorable niece, her small face with her mother's eyes and her father's chin smooshed to a scraggly brown puppy. "They're trying to convince me to let them get one."

"Oh, good luck to them," Franny said, laughing. Yao was maybe the kindest person she'd ever met, but she was not a fan of animals in her space.

"Can you believe I'm actually thinking about it?" Yao crossed her arms, leaning her hip against the kitchen island. "This is what love does to you, Francesca. It makes you actually consider ruining your beautiful new carpet with dog pee. Don't do it, babe. Do. Not. Do. It."

A year ago, Franny would have cackled at that and meant it—six months ago, even. All she could muster now was a strained choking sound meant to masquerade as a laugh. She was finding herself increasingly impatient for when she would find her girl. It was so crappy to feel like you'd finally gotten your hands on something, the thing you wanted most in the world, something you were willing to change your whole life for. Just to have it completely ripped out from under you.

Caroline, her ex, had been everything Franny had thought she wanted in a partner. Passionate and smart, artistic and joyful. She danced samba and had visited every country in South America at least once. She painted when she was angry, and when they argued—which was often—she often said things that made Franny feel like she was in some screwed-up episode of *The L Word*.

It hadn't been perfect, or anything close to it, but Franny had been so tired of it all. How many first dates at breweries could a person go on before they snapped? How many "I'm in love with my ex-girlfriend's ex-girlfriend" stories could she hear before she just completely went off the rails?

Lately, she went to bed wishing her pillow smelled like someone else's hair. And when she woke up without an arm slung across her waist, all she felt was a deep, clenching loneliness.

Honestly, she felt a little pathetic. But every time she turned on her phone, she saw cute couples on Instagram. Every time she was out, she saw them walking the streets, hands clasped. Even now, at her brother's house, she was confronted with the fact that she was very much not in love.

Yao, to her credit, seemed to sense that something was up with Franny's response. She winced slightly, then placed a sympathetic hand on Franny's shoulder. "Obviously, I'm exaggerating, and you're going to be fine. You're so hot you could literally find somebody to fall in love with you today."

Franny snorted. "And yet here I am, with a zit the size of Texas on my chin and no wife. What's all this sexy mean if I have no wife, Yao?" She was being dramatic for show, but saying it felt cathartic nonetheless.

"The wife I can't help you with, not after the last time," Yao said.

"Yeah, no, your lesbian friend from high school who lives in the converted van was nice but definitely not for me," Franny said, shooting her a smile.

It was her sister-in-law's turn to roll her eyes. "But I *can* do something about the pimple. Come upstairs with me."

Thirty minutes later, she and Yao descended from the primary bedroom together. Franny's hair was pulled back away from her face with a pink terry cloth headband, and a thick, hard mask was drying on her face. Just as she reached the last step, the front door opened, and her brother and niece came stumbling into the house.

Amelia was first, looking up at Franny with brown eyes wide in surprise. Before she could think of anything else to do, Franny brought her hands up, curled them like claws in front of her face, and growled with a nasty snarl.

Two years ago, her little niece would have run away screaming, resulting in Franny chasing her around the house. But she was ten now—practically grown up, as evidenced by the glittery pink nail polish on her fingers. So she just laughed, a tinkling little sound that made Franny grin wider as the little girl flew into her arms.

"Gomo, oh my God, oh my God, oh my God. I didn't know you were coming."

"Your dad didn't tell you?" she asked, looking over the little girl's head at where her oppa was standing at the door.

"Obviously, Dad wanted it to be a surprise."

"More like, obviously Dad forgot," Yao mumbled good-naturedly before stepping around where her sister-in-law and daughter were still hugging to plant a kiss on her husband's mouth.

"Dad's got a lot on his mind," Will grumbled. "Your mom sent us home with some beef noodle soup, though."

Amelia snickered. "Ah Gong tried to tell Ah Mah that she was doing it wrong, and she hit him with the spoon."

Yao's eyes closed briefly as she shook her head. Her parents were notorious characters, but in a good way. It was a wonder that someone as generally quiet as Yao had been raised by two people who considered bickering to be a love language.

"You two sit here. We'll get this ready," Will said.

He and Amelia went about setting the table and reheating the soup while Franny and Yao waited with hungry bellies. Franny's let out a little growl, and she gave them a sheepish smile.

"You must have been doing something today to be that hungry. What are you keeping busy with this summer?" Will asked.

"Well," she said, before hesitating. "I guess I'm kinda stepping my toe back into coaching."

Will turned from the stove to flash her an impressed look, one that had his mouth turned down and smushed at the same time. "They have an AAU team down there?"

"No." Franny pulled Amelia in for a little kiss on the cheek as the girl set a glass down next to her empty bowl. "The high school team in Greenbelt, actually."

"That's surprising," Yao said.

Franny nodded in agreement. "They already have a woman coach on the team too. Isn't that wild?"

"It is," her brother said. "I was nervous about you living down there all alone, but you've surprised me with a lot of the things you've told me about it."

"I mean, you know, it's still a small town in South Carolina. I'm not saying it's all great or that everybody is perfectly understanding," Franny said with a shrug. "But it's a lot better than I expected. A lot of queer people willingly decide to live there despite there being other options, so that means something."

Will approached the dining table with a steaming pot and a ladle, then served everyone a healthy portion of food. Only when all their bowls were filled did everyone pick up their chopsticks and dig in.

"You already got the position?" Yao asked her.

"Not yet, but I'm close." Was it a lie if it was a gut feeling? "I won't find out until the school year starts, but I've been invited to help with summer practices."

"For free?" Will raised an eyebrow.

Franny didn't even bother hiding her eye roll, which made Amelia giggle. "It's a public high school football team, Oppa. Not the NCAA Southeastern Conference. Even once I get the position, it'll only pay a small stipend every year."

"It's not about the money." Yao winked at her. "It's about . . . um . . ."

"Throwing!" Amelia interjected happily.

"Yes." Yao pointed across the table at her daughter. "It's about throwing and friendship and teamwork and Gatorade."

Franny's snort would have earned her a withering look had she done it at her mother's table. "Especially the Gatorade. I may not have any money, but I'm practically drowning in Gatorade."

"Maybe you can make friends with the other woman coach," Yao offered. "I imagine she'll be happy to have you join the team. It must be really lonely for her out there."

Her first instinct was to screw her face up. Jade Dunn had made it perfectly clear that she did not want her around. Franny could tell she was serious, just like she was certain that Dunn's disdain for her had nothing to do with her being a woman and everything to do with her being a threat. She figured that if Dunn got her way, she'd be the only coach on that field anyway. Still, Yao was probably right about something. It must have been lonely. It would be even lonelier at the top.

Which meant that it was for the better that by hook or by crook, Franny was going to be right there with her. She was going to stick to Dunn's side like cold grits. She hoped that by doing that, she'd prove to the other woman that she was there to stay. It didn't matter whether Dunn kicked and screamed and scratched the entire time. Franny wasn't going to move an inch. She'd offer her help, her support, show Landry that she was formidable. Crucial. Necessary, even.

And maybe show Dunn that it didn't have to be so lonely at the top, if only she'd just move over an inch or two.

5

So, Coach Dunn, I heard you was about to be head coach next year," Vonte Wiley said, raising his eyebrows at her. He was a sophomore linebacker with a fluffy Mohawk and an ever-present wide grin.

Jade adjusted the baseball cap on her head so it blocked more of the sun from her eyes. "Who told you that?"

Vonte shrugged. "I don't know . . ."

The coach in her wanted to snuff out unnecessary gossip, but it also wanted to commend him for not turning in his teammates. It was better for them to be united, even in something as silly as this.

"Well . . ." she said with a sigh, trying to formulate the most appropriate answer possible. "You can tell whoever you heard it from that when there are announcements to make about coaching changes, we'll make them to the entire team. There's no need to speculate."

Vonte squinted up at her. "You only talk like that when you're mad or when you're trying to tell us to stay out of grown folks' business without actually saying that."

"Which one do you think I'm doing right now?" she asked.

"I don't know . . ."

Jade nodded, putting a hand on one of his shoulders. "Look, you don't need to worry about anything but doing your best this season and what your folks are making you for dinner tonight. Anything else is on us, okay? So let us handle it."

Vonte nodded. "Yes, ma'am . . . but . . . if we do have to get a new coach, I hope it's you."

Jade clenched her jaw tight to keep from grinning, before cuffing the boy on the back of the neck. "Get on back to those drills, boy. I want to see them knees up high too."

They had a friendly scrimmage coming up against some boys from across the river in Port Royal. The teams didn't get to play each other during the year, so the coaches got together in the offseason to try each other on for size. The game didn't mean anything, technically. But the Port Royal boys were good, and ever since her first season with Greenbelt, Jade had been able to gauge how their season would go by how they performed in this scrimmage.

Every single one of them needed this season to go well. She, to prove that her guidance was essential to the success of the team. Coach Landry, so that he could begin his retirement with a bang. And for the kids out on the field, this could be their return to glory. So much was on the line for so many people. It only felt right that she should take this as seriously as she would a championship opener.

"If you keep making that face, it'll get stuck like that."

The hairs on the back of Jade's neck stood up at the sound of Ms. Lim's voice coming up behind her.

"I thought I sensed a demonic presence in the air." Jade sniffed.

"Well, I do raise hell wherever I go."

Lim's smirk made Jade want to snap. "Which means . . . what?" Jade growled. "That literally no one wants to be anywhere near you? I guess that does sound about right."

Like some kind of aggressively annoying big cat, Lim moved around her, snatching the hat off Jade's head and raising it above her own. Lim was a few inches taller than she was, with longer arms too.

Jade refused to degrade herself by reaching for it like a child; instead, she just crossed her arms over her chest and tried to throw the other woman the most scathing look she could muster.

"You act like a child, Lim, and that's why you'll never succeed in life."

Lim's answering snort was loud. "You're the one standing there pouting with your arms crossed like one of my kids when I tell them they're not allowed to run the kiln."

Jade's first instinct was to uncross her arms, but she didn't want to give her the satisfaction. So she balled her hands into fists and tucked them farther into her armpits. "I don't pout," she said. "My mouth just naturally looks like this."

Lim's eyes immediately jumped to her mouth. ". . . And so it does," she said, then hummed, not looking away.

With sudden awareness, Jade realized just how close they were. She could smell the laundry detergent on the other woman's T-shirt, the light floral scent of perfume clinging to her neck. It was slender and smooth and had the slightest bit of sweat slicking the skin. Her lips were right there too, plump and red. She had this ridiculous Cupid's bow that made her look like some kind of Disney princess.

It made Jade so sick that her mouth watered, forcing her to swallow hard. Those lips curved into an even deeper smirk, and Jade drew her own back behind her teeth.

"I can't stand you," Jade hissed. "Every time I see you, I get hot."

When the air between them grew thick with tension, Jade knew immediately that that wasn't the right choice of words. Lim's eyes trailed up her body, starting from her exposed legs and thighs and working their way up until they landed on her face again. Lim was unabashed about it, her smirk slowly becoming a grin. Jade didn't mean to show any sign of being affected, but her body reacted on its own, completely betraying her as a shiver made her shoulders shimmy and her jaw tremble.

"I definitely agree with that," Lim said.

"That's not what I meant."

"Mmm, you might not have meant to say it out loud, but you definitely meant it."

"So now you're a mind reader?"

Lim shrugged. "I think I can read you pretty well, at least."

Jade kept silent, her arms still crossed tightly over her breasts, now heaving as her heart rate increased. She didn't like that. Not one bit. Had she ever met anyone as presumptuous as this woman? They barely knew each other, and yet she thought she somehow knew everything there was to know about Jade?

"You're so full of shit," Jade said, lip curling.

"It's not that serious." There was that fucking shrug again, like everything was cool and nothing mattered. "You wear every emotion on your face, Dunn. Reading you is like reading a picture book."

Lim grinned then, and Jade's heart stuttered. That was offensive, wasn't it? And wrong. Jade prided herself on being unreadable. Most people, especially those who weren't close to her, never seemed to know what she was thinking. Honestly, they just assumed she was mad all the time. That was one of the not-so-hidden truths of being a Black woman, though. Any emotion that wasn't explicitly happy read as mad to people who couldn't be bothered to examine their own bullshit.

Right now, though, she *was* angry. Or at least she thought she was. She didn't know what other emotion could cause such heat to sear through her entire abdomen or make her knees feel so close to buckling.

"What do you see now, then?" she asked, her throat dry, finally uncrossing her arms so she could shove her sweaty hands in the pockets of her shorts.

"You want me," Lim said simply.

"Bullshit."

Lim's eyes ventured to her chest, and Jade knew immediately that she could see her hard nipples through the thin material of her shirt.

"That always happens when I'm mad," Jade lied. "It definitely doesn't mean I want you."

"I don't believe you."

Jade took a deep breath. "How about I tell you what I do want, then? I want you off my field. I want you to take those stilts you call legs over to Coach Landry and tell him that you're not coming to poker on Thursday because you've finally come to your senses and realized that you're simply not qualified to coach at this level."

"Hmmm." Lim tapped a finger on her chin like she was thinking about it. "No, I don't think that's what you actually want. *I* think you kind of like having me here. I think you like my company. I also think you want to kiss me."

It was Jade's turn to snort, but it was half-hearted. "I think you are loathsome and full of shit."

"And I think your lackluster offensive line is the reason this team hasn't won a championship title in five years."

Every ember that smoldered in Jade was stoked by those words. Her upper lip curled, mouth preparing to release something viciously nasty, but before she could get the last word in, they were interrupted.

"Ms. Lim," Coach Landry said, and from the way his eyes had widened, he seemed to sense that something was happening between them. "The offensive line boys are about to run some dip-and-rip drills. You want to help us over there? Give me a chance to see how you handle running 'em."

Lim gave Jade one last long look, and this time she wasn't smirking. Jade couldn't quite read it, but she could tell the other woman wanted to say something else. She didn't, though. She gave Landry one curt nod before jogging off to where the other O-line coaches were rounding the kids up.

"You good, Dunn?" Landry coughed.

"Yes, Coach."

When she finally calmed herself enough to look him in the eye, his were concerned.

"What just happened there?"

Had she been willing to play dirty or be a snitch, she might have told him what Lim had said. But she wasn't. She was going to beat the other woman's ass at this, and she was going to do it clean too. Jade didn't need to tattle to their boss to get what she wanted. She needed to figure out how to get in Lim's head.

"Just a little friendly competition," she told him with a sickly sweet smile. "Ms. Lim's trying to throw her weight around a bit."

Their eyes turned to across the field where Lim stood, now in front of the other coaches, with a whistle around her neck as she talked to the boys.

"I'm giving her a fair shake," he said. "But that doesn't have anything to do with what you're shooting for."

His words made something twinge in her belly. It was the kind of feeling you got when you knew you were wrong about something and felt guilty, even though you were going to stand in your wrongness. All that talk of solidarity and sisterhood seemed to have flown out the window for her. Somewhere deep, deep down in her chest, she got the feeling that Landry was right. That Lim's presence on the team didn't hurt her own. But out here in the real world, she just couldn't make that truth curl all the way over for herself.

"Sure it does, Coach."

He furrowed his brows at her, confused.

"It's going to be hard enough convincing the other guys to even consider standing behind me as their leader. Let alone the parents and the school board and the damn mayor. Like you told me before, I'm a woman, a Black woman, a gay Black woman—"

"Bisexual," Landry interrupted, causing her to laugh despite the gravity of their conversation.

"Regardless," she continued, "you think they're going to allow us both to hold positions of power on this team? Next thing we know, there'll be write-ups in the paper about how the liberal agenda has come for America's favorite pastime."

"That'd be baseball," Landry corrected her yet again. "And frankly, the longer I think about it all, the less of a fuck I give about what they have to say. They can do all the write-ups they want, so long as they include the wins by whoever ends up coaching this team."

Jade swallowed. She wanted to believe that. She did. But this was Greenbelt, South Carolina. And it was far from the scene of some inspirational sports movie. She knew what people would think, what they'd say, what they'd do once they got their hearts set on bigotry.

Still, in all that muck, there had been something just as important for her to take note of. Coach Landry was an incredibly encouraging figure for the kids, but for the coaches . . . not so much. Generally, that was fine. Jade didn't need her boss to spend all his time praising her. She had herself for that. And her parents and Miri and the deep delusion that lived in her head telling her she was the best to ever do it. This was different, though. She was coming after his spot, and to hear him even insinuate that he thought she deserved it meant more than she'd realized it would.

She nodded, trying to convey her thanks with her eyes. She knew he wouldn't know what to do with any of her words.

"I'm still going to beat her," Jade said. "I don't know why she's decided to do this all of a sudden, but she doesn't deserve this. She's way too green; I think she hardly knows what she's doing. Maybe we should make some calls to verify her claims about coaching in Texas. That could be complete bull-hockey for all we know."

"Hmm . . . maybe." Landry sighed and shook his head at her stubbornness. "Looks like she's not doing too bad now, though."

Fifty yards away, Francesca Lim was demonstrating the correct stance for the O-line boys. Both of her feet were planted in the turf, one of her arms tucked against her side and the other in the grass. Her shoulders were perfectly aligned, and her ass was high and tight. Jade tried not to stare too hard at it—and failed. Watching unblinking as Lim blew her own whistle in quick succession twice before immediately charging forward and grabbing the white towel situated on the ground a few feet from where she'd started.

The towel drill was a short one, no impact, and quick to accomplish. But it taught the players how to position and move their bodies to secure the gaps between them on the field.

Lim lined two players up, facing each other but a few feet apart so they didn't run into the other when the drill began. Jade heard the whistle go off again and saw the first two boys perform the drill, only to be stopped by Lim on their second go-round. She helped one of the boys position his shoulders and get lower to the ground, and the other was told something that Jade couldn't hear. When she blew the whistle again, both players grabbed their towels up with no problem, earning pats on the back from the woman guiding them.

It was only a small showing, the type of drill the boys could coach themselves on, Jade told herself. But she saw how the boys responded to her, how they didn't give her a hard time. They respected her.

Truth was, that was more than half of it—the respect. In her mind, the logistics of the game came second to being a good leader. It was troubling to see Lim display these qualities. It was even more troubling to feel the aching, begrudging amount of respect Jade felt for them. It was fine, though; that respect didn't make Jade afraid. She might have to sharpen her claws a bit more, but she wasn't afraid. Lim could take her childish jabs, her easygoing bull, and her YouTube University coaching and shove them up her ass.

"I guess it's a good thing that 'not too bad' isn't nearly good enough," she told Landry, eyes still narrowed on her target, laser focused.

6

Greenbelt City Bingo Hall was buzzing on Thursday night. Jade wasn't sure she'd been inside the place even once her whole life, but she could not imagine the well-loved but worn-down spot was ever as popping as it was tonight. For the first football fundraiser of the year, Greenbelt Senior High had shelled out good money to rent the entire space for the evening. Vonte Wiley had suggested a bingo night fundraiser during their team brainstorm months ago. The premise was simple enough—people would buy into the game as normal, but all proceeds and possible winnings would be donated to the team.

She stood next to him now, proud to see something one of her kids had thought of become realized.

"It's a big night," she said with a smile. "Straighten your tie up a little bit."

Vonte grimaced as he pulled the collar of his shirt away from his neck. "Granny starched this shirt way too much."

Jade laughed. Vonte was being raised by his grandparents, and his granny made sure the boy had on his Sunday best for every event they had.

"Undo the very top button." She pointed at the spot way up her neck that mimicked the placement of the button. "Now twist the knot around a little until it's straight under there."

He followed her directions swiftly, then proceeded to move his head with a little more dexterity. "Oh yeahhh."

"Are your grandparents here?"

"Yes, ma'am. Granny's over there, but Grandaddy had to work tonight, so he couldn't make it."

She could hear the lilt of disappointment in his voice even when he tried to suppress it. Vonte's granny was only a few feet behind him, sitting at the end of one of the bingo tables with her purse on her arm and her daubers on the table in front of her. Jade caught the older woman's eyes and gave her a smile and a wink.

"Don't worry," she told Vonte. "Coach Carr is going to film your speech, and everyone will take plenty of pictures, so he'll get a chance to see you."

That made the boy groan. "This is about to be so trash, Coach Dunn. I hate talking in public."

"This event was your idea. We've done a car wash every year for the past two decades. This is the first time we're doing anything like this. And look at how many people showed up." She gestured around the room. "We've barely got any more seats to fill. Everyone loves your idea."

Vonte shrugged, suddenly sheepish. "My auntie Lisa used to bring me when I was little. She still comes too. A lot of people do. So I figured it probably makes a lot of money."

"You're right. It does," Jade said. "And judging by tonight's turnout, the team is going to make bank tonight too."

Vonte's brown eyes lit up in an instant. "Maybe we can get one of them buses West Beaufort has with the TVs on 'em."

"Let's focus on making sure we've got enough money for gas on the buses we have now first, okay? We can worry about ballin' out later."

"Ballin' out?" He turned his nose up. "Sometimes I forget you're an old lady."

"Boy!"

Microphone feedback interrupted them as it screeched through the room and made everyone wince. Landry stood in front of it in a white dress shirt, a pair of black slacks, and a custom Greenbelt Gators tie. The man looked red around the neck as he shoved his hands into his pockets and cleared his throat.

"Can y'all hear me?" he asked. The crowd murmured their affirmatives, their football boys belting out a few hollers. "Let's get this started, then. I'm going to keep my talking brief because someone more important than me is going to get up here and talk to y'all. But I wanted to start by thanking everyone for coming out tonight. I know this is a little different from our normal fundraisers, but—"

A hand pulled at her arm, yanking her attention away from Landry's speech. She looked over at the young man next to her. His eyes were bright and shiny, but his expression was panicked.

"I don't want to, Coach." His words were hurried. "I mean . . . I can't go up there and talk. I can't do it."

"What makes you think you can't do it?"

Sweat started to bead on Vonte's forehead, and he gulped so big his chest moved with the motion. "What if I mess up? I might say the wrong thing or—" He shook his head. "Somebody else should do it instead of me."

"Vonte, look at me." Jade's voice was quiet but serious. "Tonight was your idea. It wasn't Coach Landry's, it wasn't mine, it was yours. You worked hard on this, you prepared for this—"

"I didn't even write the speech myself," he tried to argue. "You did a lot of it."

That was patently false. "I helped. I looked over your grammar and made sure everything made sense, but you did all the heavy lifting. Which is why you should go up there and make sure all these people know it."

The expression on his young face was so open and vulnerable that she almost wanted to fold to his fears and let him off the hook. And she would have if he'd been showing signs of a panic attack or something similar. This was just good old-fashioned nerves, though, coursing through him with enough energy to make him vibrate. At one point in time, when she'd been younger and less experienced, she'd been familiar with that feeling. Being gently guided out of her comfort zone had served her well, and she thought it might do the same for Vonte.

He didn't seem so convinced. "What if I throw up?"

Jade bit back a laugh. "You're not going to throw up."

"What if people laugh at me?" The words were spoken quietly as his eyes drifted down to his shoes.

There was the meat of it, really. Possible ridicule was the thing he actually feared.

"Everyone here loves you, kid. These are your teammates, your family."

He winced. "That means they'll *definitely* laugh at me."

"How about this." Jade crossed her arms. "You get up there and do your speech like we planned, and if anybody laughs at you, I'll make sure they pay for it."

"Really?"

Jade nodded. She had no clue how she'd follow through with that promise, but she felt pretty confident that his speech would pass without incident.

"Okay," he said, before taking in a big gulp of air. "I'll do it, then. As long as you've got my back."

"I've always got your back, kid. You know that."

Landry's voice grew a bit louder as he introduced Vonte, and

Jade watched as he shuffled his way up to the stage, shoulders tight and feet dragging. His hands shook when Landry handed him the microphone. The boy sought her out in the crowd of expectant faces, and when he caught her eyes, she screwed up her face and made a show of dragging her finger across her throat in a crude but obvious murderous gesture. When he finally started speaking, he did so with a wide grin.

"I wanted to start by, um, thanking everybody for coming. I honestly didn't think this many people would show up," Vonte said, a natural on the mic. "I wasn't really sure what all to say. I mean, I guess everybody knows why we're doing this fundraiser. But just in case you don't, you should know that Greenbelt is one of the poorest towns in the county. That means that a lot of students at our school come from low-income households—that includes me."

Vonte took a brief pause, looking over the crowd to gauge their reaction to his statement before continuing.

"Football is actually one of the most expensive youth sports to play. Um . . . we have really expensive uniforms that have to be replaced a lot, and all these pads and protective gear and stuff. We also have to travel for a lot of our games, sometimes overnight. That costs a lot. Coach says that even with all that, the team's biggest expense is our snacks and stuff. Coach Landry has worked real hard to make it so that any kid who makes the team has the opportunity to play—not just the rich ones. But all that means is we need a lot of money to keep everything together."

The boy's dark hands clutched the printed paper in front of him as he read his speech off it. With every word, something lodged deeper in the middle of Jade's throat. It felt like a brick sitting there, heavy and distracting, as it made her eyes water. She'd told herself she wouldn't cry, seeing him up there, but it wouldn't be the first time she had lied to herself.

"I was the one who suggested we do a bingo fundraiser this year. The car washes and popcorn movie nights are cool, but I felt like we needed something better than all that this year. My granny always says that people love gambling because they like throwing their money away. So, I figured, why not have y'all throw it to the team instead."

Thirty minutes after Vonte's—very successful—speech, they were well into the game. The bingo hall was alight with laughter and movement. Vonte had taken well to being the night's honorary bingo caller, using the microphone to call out the chosen balls like he'd been born with it in his hand. Jade had a personal check written out to the team in her pocket, which was the only thing that kept her from feeling guilty about not playing with everyone else.

She hated bingo. She found it tedious and stupid, a complete waste of time and money. She posted up against one of the structural beams, surveying the room like a casino pit boss. When her eyes landed on Lim, she tensed instantly. The woman sat at a table near the entrance, dauber clutched in her hand and her eyes on the sheet in front of her. Her dark hair was down but tucked behind her ears, and even though Jade didn't have a clear view of her face, she could practically see the wrinkle forming between the woman's eyebrows.

A shiver made its way down Jade's spine. Lim was completely wide open, ripe for the taking. A perfect fucking target. Jade sprang into action the second the plan started forming in her brain. She stalked her way across the room, swiftly sliding into the empty chair to Lim's left.

"Hey," she whispered.

Lim looked up at her, bewildered. "Um . . . hey . . ."

"Enjoying the game?"

The woman turned to look behind her as if she couldn't fathom that Jade was speaking to her so casually.

". . . Yes?"

Jade sniffed and relaxed into her seat, eyeing the sheet on the table in front of Lim. She had a few close possible wins. She already had three filled diagonally, three horizontally, and two vertically. Lim could get a win easily if the odds turned in her favor. And Jade had a feeling they were about to do just that.

Jade tapped her finger against the 12 in the B column. "They called that one."

"Wait, what?" Lim looked up at her, confused. "When?"

"A few calls ago."

The woman's dark eyes narrowed. "How do you remember that?"

Jade worked hard to keep her body language and tone nonchalant. "B-12 like the vitamin—it's easy to remember."

Lim considered it for a few moments before putting a big blue dot over the square. Jade bit down hard on the inside of her bottom lip to keep her smile under control.

"Why are you sitting here?" Lim asked. "And why are you in such a good mood?"

"I suppose we're teammates now, in a way." It made Jade's belly burn just to say it. "I'm only being friendly."

"Literally three days ago, you looked at me like you wanted the earth to open up and swallow me whole."

"You know, I think I was being a little territorial. This team means a lot to me, and I don't trust newcomers so easily."

Something almost hopeful seemed to cross Lim's face, and she smiled. "Is this you apologizing to me?"

Out of the corner of her eye, Jade watched Vonte reach into the cage and pull out another ball, and just as he went to speak it into the mic, she leaned in close to Lim. So close that she could smell the faint traces of perfume on her skin and see the goose bumps that arose on her collarbones. Jade made a show of dragging her eyes over the skin, slowly raking her gaze up the slender column of Lim's neck and jaw and nose before finally meeting her eyes. Jade knew that had anyone been paying attention, they'd think the two women were about to kiss.

Even her own mind couldn't help but go there for a split second. Lim's pink lips pursed just the smallest bit, quick but enough for Jade to catch the movement and commit the way it looked to memory. It would be so easy to just forget where they were or who they were and lean in . . .

Jade ground her teeth together until she felt a pang in her jaw. She was being ridiculous. Absolutely ridiculous. There was a plan here. A thing to see to fruition, and here she was acting like she'd never seen a pretty mouth before. She sniffed once, lightly, getting her head back in the game.

"No apologies," she finally replied. "Just trying to be nice."

Lim's lips pursed even more before her eyes widened in realization. "Shit, I missed the call! Did you hear what he said?"

Jade tapped her finger on a square right next to the one Lim had just filled in. I-19. "Looks like you got a bingo."

Lim studied the sheet in front of her intently, running her eyes over the card, trying her hardest to verify what Jade had told her. Sure as day, right in the center of the page was a neat row of five squares, each of them centered with a big blue ink blotch.

"Oh my God." Lim looked at her with wide eyes. "I got one! What do I do? Am I supposed to go up there or . . ."

"Normally, people yell it out, I think."

"Really?"

Jade shrugged, then held her breath as she watched Lim draw air into her own lungs.

"Bingo!" she yelled. "I have a bingo."

Her words rang out through the room loud and sudden, immediately hushing all the extra noise. One of the normal staff walked calmly to where Vonte was standing at the front and took the microphone from him.

"Our first win of the night, y'all," the older woman said as she smiled kindly. "Come on up here, then. Let us check you."

Lim paused before she stood, looking over at Jade. The excitement was written on every bare inch of her face. The expression was so open and genuinely happy that Jade almost reached out to grab Lim and stop her from going up to the front. There was no stopping this, though. Jade's eyes were on the prize, and if Francesca Lim decided she was going to try to obstruct her path forward, she had to be dealt with. There could be no ifs, ands, or buts about it.

So Jade let her go, watching as Lim's long legs carried her across the room until the bingo hall employee was bent over her sheet with a grin.

"Let's see here." The older woman had a pair of wire-rimmed glasses perched on her thin nose as her eyes scanned the card. "O-49—we got that. There's your free space right there. G-52—uh-huh. Hold on here for a second." The woman paused and turned to the small table behind her to look at her notebook. When she raised her eyes back to Lim, she did not speak into the microphone. "We didn't call I-19 or B-12, honey."

Even without the mic broadcasting the woman's words to the room, they were easy to hear.

"Wait, what?" Lim looked down at her paper. "I—"

"It's okay, sweetie." The older woman patted Lim's arm. "This happens more often than you think."

Lim spared a look at the crowd. Every eye in the place was on her, and the longer the moment went on, the more the room seemed to itch for the sweet release of being able to react.

"I'm so sorry," Lim said. "I don't know how I misheard like that. Twice."

Jade sank down a little in her seat, averting her eyes from the pair trying to meet hers from the front of the room.

"Well, this is why we double-check." The older woman raised the mic to her mouth again. "But this should serve as a good reminder to y'all to make sure you've got your listening ears on. The only interruptions we want are the good kind from now on, okay?"

Kindness was peppered over each of her words, but their impact was still strong enough to cause a chorus of light laughter around the room. Jade spared a glance to where Landry was sitting next to his wife and found herself delighted to see him hiding his own laughter behind his hands.

To Lim's credit—and Jade's disappointment—the woman took the hit gracefully.

"Sorry about that again," she said behind a sheepish smile. "You won't get any more trouble out of me tonight, I promise."

Jade sat back until her legs were splayed out under the table and her arms crossed. Her chair was pushed rudely into the aisle so that when Lim tried to return to her seat, she had to squeeze past Jade to get there. The crowd seemed to get over the small interruption easily enough as the microphone was returned to Vonte, and he pulled another ball from the spinning basket.

"You're a child, do you know that?" Lim's voice was low, but she spoke her words through gritted teeth and twisted lips.

"What?"

"Don't make that goofy-ass face like you don't know what you did. You made me look like a fucking fool up there, Dunn."

Jade snorted. "First, I haven't done a single thing. Second, you made yourself look like a fool."

The look on Lim's face was pure shock. Jade suddenly realized that she'd never seen the woman look genuinely mad until this moment. Lim's dark eyes held enough fire to set the room alight. Jade made sure to keep herself frosty, though.

"Me? You're going to sit there right now and pretend you didn't tell me lies?"

"I'm not a liar," Jade said. "I'm just telling the truth. It's not my fault you went up there all gung-ho and ready to declare yourself the victor without checking your work first."

The snarl across Lim's pink lips got even nastier in response, but Jade wasn't finished.

"You wanted to play this game with me, Lim. From that very first moment, you were trying to provoke me. All I did was decide to play along. Don't blame me because you got cocky and forgot to keep your head on a swivel."

"That's how this is going to be, then?" Lim asked.

Jade shrugged. "I don't know. You tell me."

She stood up and rolled her shoulders a bit, making a big show of straightening her clothes before she bent at the waist to get close to Lim again. "Just say when if you've had enough."

Lim's nostrils flared, her cheeks flushing a pale red as she tried to hold herself back. She didn't utter a single word, just silently turned her head back to the table and picked up her dauber as if nothing had happened.

Jade took it as a capital *W* win.

7

Jeremy Bell brought some type of seafood dip to poker night. Jade was mildly allergic to shellfish, and while the stuff wasn't deadly to her, she was more concerned with having to bow out of the game because of her swelling eye sockets than she was about the fact that she didn't have an EpiPen on her. She'd politely asked the man to set the dip on a little coffee table farther away from the one they played cards at. But it was a hot summer night, and even with the air conditioner on, it was still so warm that the smell from the dip felt oppressive.

Lim was seated across from her in a loose-fitting, cropped button-down shirt. Her clavicle was exposed, as were the multiple small tattoos that covered both her arms. Jade was studying her fiercely, trying to figure out what her tell was. They'd been at the table for about an hour, and so far the only thing she could spot was that Lim seemed to rub her thumb over the tiny cat tattoo near her elbow every time she was about to fold. The observation was newly gained, though, and Jade needed a few more examples of it before she felt confident enough to officially declare it a tell.

Next to her, the head track-and-field coach, Mr. Byrd, cleared his throat and pulled a bit at the collar of his linen shirt. "I was at a roadside barbecue joint over in Beaufort the other day with the wife and ran into Joe Spencer."

Joe Spencer was something of a legend in the surrounding counties. A Greenbelt native whose parents moved him to Beaufort in high school with hopes of better chances getting scouted for college ball. They'd succeeded, and he'd gone on to play for the Gamecocks, becoming the second Heisman winner in South Carolina's history after George Rogers. A head injury during a game had resulted in a lifelong disability and stopped his chances of going pro, but it hadn't done anything to kill his love of football. The man had spent the last twenty years coaching at one of Beaufort's best schools while also appearing in plenty of local commercials. Jade had never met him formally, but from the way folks talked about him, she felt like she knew him personally.

"Oh yeah?" Coach Landry said, his teeth around a thick cigar. "What did the ol' boy say?"

"Not much, but he told me about a little rumor he heard coming out of Beaufort . . ."

Jade had to suck down air to keep from gasping. Immediately, her head turned toward her head coach, prepared for his little secret to be spilled all over the table like poker chips. Across from her, Lim cut her eyes to Landry. He had expressed multiple times that he didn't want anybody outside the team knowing about his impending retirement yet. She didn't know exactly what kind of scheming he was trying to do on the low, but Jade sure as hell wasn't about to question or needlessly step out of line—especially not now. As far as she knew, the only ones who didn't have *coach* in their official title who knew were Principal Coleman and goddamn Francesca Lim.

"A rumor about what?" Bell asked what they were thinking with all the enthusiasm of someone completely clueless.

Byrd shuffled two cards in the middle of his hand, and even with her brain on high alert, Jade made note of the movement. The man was clearly nervous, and it wasn't because of the gossip. "There's a school up in Hampton—don't think they've ever won a single state title as long as I've been around—well, they've got this kid who's apparently just running through 'em. Spencer went up there and saw him play, said he's a fucking monster, and the entire team's really shaping up because of it."

It wasn't good news. Bigger, badder competition never was. But it wasn't the news she'd expected to hear. She watched as Landry released a long breath, same as she did. It seemed like neither of them were ready to open that can of worms, though Jade figured her reasons were different from his.

"I'm not too worried about that," Landry said, his eyes back on his own hand. "One person doesn't make a team, no matter how good he is."

Byrd shrugged, small beads of sweat dotting his temples. Jade figured he either had a hand that was about to take all their money or one that was about to make him lose all of his.

She eyed her own again. Her cards were all right, a pair of aces. It wasn't the best luck she could have gotten, but it had the potential to win her something. She held the cards close to her chest, her eyes darting back to Lim as the excitement over Byrd's little purposeful distraction died down.

The other woman's face was as close to stoic as she could get it. Plump lips in a straight line. Even her posture was relaxed. She looked completely unassuming, inoffensive, and it only served to make Jade more and more annoyed as the seconds passed. She found herself unable to draw her eyes away in time, suddenly flushed with a little panic when Lim's gaze met hers.

Jade had been riding a real high from her little bingo night antics. Sometimes, when she closed her eyes before going to bed at night, she pictured the embarrassment and fury on Lim's face before she fell asleep. A win like that should have given her unshakable confidence, but Jade knew that there was more to be done. It was going to take more than one stumble to bring Lim down.

Lim smirked when she caught her staring. The same one she'd given her days before during their little spat on the field. It was infuriating, and it made an awful feeling settle in the bottom of her belly. Something fluttered there, flying around, then crashing against the size of her. It was so intense it made her queasy.

Then, to make it worse, Lim winked at her. The action was so smooth, Jade almost didn't believe it had happened. Suddenly, she felt nothing but the urge to jump across the table and . . .

She shook her head, trying to clear it of the only image that seemed to settle in her mind. For some reason, it wasn't a snapshot of her tackling Lim out of her chair and onto the floor. It wasn't her scratching the other woman's eyes out either. No, it wasn't anything violent or hateful that popped up. Instead, it was an image of her climbing across the flimsy old poker table and pressing her mouth against Lim's until that fucking smirk was nothing but a whisper in the wind.

Jade swallowed and bit down on her bottom lip, trying to force her body to forget the fucking motion picture playing in her head of her making out with the woman across from her.

Next to her, she heard a throat clear. Her head snapped up to see multiple pairs of eyes on her.

"You all right, Dunn?" Landry asked, one of his bushy blond eyebrows raised.

Jade squared her shoulders until her posture was nearly perfect, then glued her eyes back to her hand, where she planned to firmly keep them the rest of the night. It was one thing to be caught staring at someone—that you could blame on spacing out or something. It was another thing altogether to be caught staring multiple times.

"Just lost my train of thought there for a second," she assured the table with a short, nervous laugh.

Jeremy Bell nodded in understanding, but Landry didn't seem to buy it. She didn't dare peek across the table at Lim, but she could only imagine that infuriating mouth had curved into an even more infuriating smirk. Her fingers curled around her cards, bending the card stock.

"It's your turn to place your bet," Landry told her.

She looked down at the table. She'd been so caught up, so distracted that she hadn't even seen everyone else put their cards down for the river—a final round of betting that ultimately determined who won and went home with the pot.

The community cards on the table were a nine, a jack, a seven, and, thanks to the river, a pair of aces.

With the two aces in her hand, Jade was sitting on four of a kind. This was the kind of luck she'd been looking for all along, and it was definitely up there.

She took another peek around the table. Byrd still had little droplets of sweat beading at his temples, Bell looked just as clueless as he always did, and Lim's lips were still curved in that infuriating smirk.

Her mind immediately went to probability, a lesson plan she'd be teaching her freshmen in just a few months. There were 1,326 possible hole card combinations in Texas Hold'em. Among the eight people sitting around the table—including her—that made for a lot of goddamn possibilities.

She did know that none of them had any aces, though, which was something. There were no other four-of-a-kind combinations to be had using the community cards anyway. Even if she couldn't literally profile everyone at the table, she guessed that her chances of coming out on top were pretty high.

With one last peek at the two cards in her hand, she pushed every last chip she had sitting in front of her into the center of the table. "I'm all in."

Almost immediately, Jeremy Bell folded, turning over his cards to reveal a pair of twos. Cody Ross was the next to go down, followed by Lionel Price, both men folding with grace. Every other man at the table followed suit until the only two left standing were her and Lim.

Now she had a reason to stare. Jade tried to wipe every thought and emotion off her face until the only thing to be seen was her slightly curled upper lip. Lim bit down on her bottom lip for a split second before she pushed all her chips into the center as well. "I'll call," she said.

Lim laid down two jacks, the look on her face smugger than it should have been.

Something surged through Jade then, strong enough that she had to plant her feet on the floor to keep from jumping out of her chair. This time, it wasn't to kiss the other woman. She wanted to dance and gloat and be the sorest winner there ever was.

Instead, she silently laid her aces down. Four of a kind was always better than three, and more than that, she had the higher-ranking cards.

She'd won.

And from the looks of almost everyone at the table, she'd managed to impress with it as well. She outright grinned at Lim as she made a show of scooping up all the chips, collecting her winnings—all $400 of it.

"Well, look at that," Landry said, and she glanced over to see a spark of pride in his eyes. This only bolstered her mood even more. "I thought for a second there you were about to lose your shit, Dunn."

"So did I." Byrd snorted. "But you robbed us blind instead."

Jade shook her head in disagreement. "I didn't rob you, I won."

"Barely," Lim's low voice chimed in from across the table.

"How about you come talk shit to me after you come up with something better than two lazy-ass jacks."

Less than an hour later, Lim practically cornered her next to her car after leaving Landry's. It was dark out, but the lack of sun did nothing to curb the heat. The second she'd stepped outside, she'd felt like the air was sticking to her skin. She'd taken a second to shed her T-shirt in the back seat, leaving her in just a tank top. She was ready to get home and take a long, hot shower before cranking her air conditioner up high enough to damage her power bill this month.

Instead, she found herself so close to Lim that she could practically feel the other woman's breath on her face when she spoke.

"Good game tonight," Lim said, her hands tucked deep into the back pockets of her jeans.

"Uh," Jade stammered. She had not been expecting a compliment. What was it with this woman reducing her to a bumbling fool all the damn time? "Yeah, I got lucky with good cards tonight."

"I'm sure the guys were sufficiently impressed."

Jade shrugged. "I'm not trying to impress them. I'm just throwing my weight around, letting them know that they don't own this space, they don't own any of these spaces."

Lim looked at her silently for a while, so long that apprehension started to well up in the center of Jade's chest.

"Fair enough," Lim said finally. "You know, if you weren't so hell-bent on hating me, we might be able to show them that together."

"I can do it myself."

Jade was quick to answer, almost reflexively. She hadn't always been one of those people. The kind who stubbornly insist on never receiving help. There had been a time when she'd been an eager student, open and vulnerable. A veritable sponge who had never been afraid to raise her hand high enough to seek guidance. Then she'd decided to coach high school football and that girl had been forced to fall away. She'd hardened herself piece by piece with every new offense—each racist joke and misogynist macroaggression—until all that was left of her was a forced grit that made her too stubborn to ask for anything. Part of her was proud of that. Part of her resented it—though she acknowledged this part far less often for her own peace of mind.

Maybe this was why she resented Lim so much. The other woman didn't seem to have nearly as much baggage as she did. In Jade's eyes, she floated through the world unbothered, unhindered by all the expectations and by apprehension. Jade figured that the way she'd been going about it was the right way—the only way. To see Lim fall so quickly into trying to team-build with her, instead of viewing her as competition, was confusing. Had the woman been lucky enough to sidestep all the bad parts, or had she just been better at handling them? It made Jade wary.

It made her jealous.

Lim toed at a pebble, rolling it under the sole of one of her checkered Vans. Jade could practically hear the little stone being ground into dust.

"I don't know how well that rugged individuality is going to go for you this time," Lim said. "Especially if you get what you want. You'll need people you can depend on, people who know your weak spots and can make up the slack."

Jade crossed her arms over her chest tightly, immediately defensive. She didn't appreciate being talked to like she didn't know anything. Like she hadn't spent the past ten years of her life preparing for this.

"You seem to think I don't know exactly what I'm doing." She sniffed.

"I didn't say that."

"You might as well have." Jade took a couple of steps closer to Lim until she was in the other woman's face. "I don't know you, and I don't need your advice. All I need is for you to get the fuck out of my way."

Lim's dark eyes found themselves on Jade's chest for a moment before they caught hers again. The woman wasn't smirking now. Her mouth was a straight line, and Jade could see the spot in her left cheek where her tongue was trying to press through.

She looked like she was holding back words.

Good. Because Jade didn't want to hear them.

"You know," Lim said, taking several steps back, looking cooler and more casual than she had any right to. "I don't think I will. If you want to sit there and act like a little brat, I figure it's time for me to turn the heat up on you."

"Lim, you're so lukewarm, I don't think you could turn the heat up on me if you tried with everything in you."

"Lukewarm?" Lim snorted. "Look, Jade, I know you think you're, like, the first girl to ever look at a football or something, but you have no idea what type of shit I've had to eat to be here."

Jade's eyebrows went up to her hairline. "No idea? When Landry announced that he'd hired me for a coaching position, they called a town hall meeting. I sat there in a dusty-ass room in the commonwealth building and listened as people of this town—men *and* women—stood at a podium and yelled about how the boys would never listen to me, how I was ruining the sport, how I was going to drag this team to hell. To this day, every time Greenbelt loses even a game, it's my fault in their eyes. There's been a fire under my ass from the second I decided to do this. This thing. *You.* It's nothing in comparison to all that."

"It's interesting . . . You'd think going through something like that would have made you more open to sharing the space with someone who knows how it is. I could have your back if you let me."

"I don't need you at my back just so you can turn around and make everything harder for me," Jade gritted out. "I just need you *gone*."

Lim shrugged. "Well, that's too damn bad, because I'm not going anywhere. Not until Landry himself tells me to get lost."

"We'll see about that."

"That fire under your feet ain't going nowhere. You're not going to eat me alive, Dunn. I won't let you."

Jade wanted to protest and spit. But she didn't want to give Lim the satisfaction of a reaction. She'd won tonight, and she had every intention of going out on a high note. She didn't need the last word to do that.

So she opened her car door and slid in, pulling out before she even had a chance to put on her seat belt, leaving Lim standing there. The entire drive home, she pictured the other woman still in the middle of the street, her face contorted in frustration and worry. Skin glowing in the moonlight, beautiful as ever, but with her boldness turned to dust like the pebble under her foot.

Except the image didn't make her feel as good as she wanted. Instead, her stomach sank, and her throat constricted. The constant buzzing energy of anxiety welled in her chest, telling her that something wasn't right. She told herself it was just good old-fashioned worry—even though she knew that was a lie.

8

Franny walked into Lucky Leagues Bowling Alley with a shiny new ball and a pair of truly silly clown shoes on Sunday. Despite her slight humiliation during the team's bingo night and her confrontation with Jade, she was determined to be in good spirits.

There was a lesbian bowling team that met at Lucky Leagues in Greenbelt every other week. Franny had found out about it while scrolling through a local LGBTQ+ events Facebook page. She'd been looking for a way to make new friends that didn't solely involve nightlife activities. As much as she loved the surprisingly good bar scene in Greenbelt, she craved some weeknight platonic companionship too.

As always, Barb and Stella were already at their reserved lanes. They'd been married for twenty-five years, their relationship so lived-in that they practically dressed the same.

"Hey, y'all," Franny offered as she slid into one of the hard chairs, immediately going about changing her shoes. Everyone else rented a pair each time and laughed at her for insisting on buying her own. She was unmoved, though. Whatever the kid behind the counter sprayed in those things couldn't be nearly enough to disinfect them.

"Hey there, girlie." Stella gave her a grin as she sucked on something out of a Styrofoam cup.

She threw a look at Barb, who was sitting up close to the automatic scorer with her nose in a notebook. The woman kept meticulous records, had done since she and Stella had started their small bowling team a decade ago. She kept hers and her wife's scores, and it was deeply adorable to watch Stella—who clearly wasn't as into the numbers as her wife—take special pains to look after the notebook at almost all times.

A few minutes later, they were joined by the rest of the women. Janet, a Black woman who exclusively wore purple. Charlie, a tiny white woman who always seemed to be channeling Stevie Nicks. Last to arrive was Carmella, a Mexican woman who always came after babysitting her grandson on Sunday afternoons.

The chatter didn't start until they were all gathered around their two designated lanes, shoes on, food secured, waiting for Barb to give them the go-ahead to start. The woman always insisted that they go in the same order every game for structure. Everyone else seemed to be amused by it but put up no fight.

The first time Franny had shown up, she'd worn a thrifted vintage bowling shirt and a pair of cuffed khaki pants, completely expecting to be among a bunch of ironic, mullet-wearing, Diet Coke–drinking queers. She knew nothing about bowling; she could have counted on one hand the times she'd ever even been to a bowling alley. She figured they might sit around and pretend to sip on beers and shoot the shit long enough that she met her self-imposed socialization quota.

Instead, what she'd found were five sixtysomething lesbians in crewnecks and mom jeans who set the lanes ablaze. The gals were serious about bowling. And when Franny had tried to worm her way out of actually participating, they'd heard none of it.

"I had a hell of a week," Charlie said in her small, soft voice after she'd sunk seven pins. "One of my favorite girls who works at the crystal store in Port Royal quit to follow her boyfriend to Houston.

Then the health food store ran out of mullein tea." She dug an elbow into Franny's side. "I need that to clear my lungs out after my daily smoke sesh, you know. And I think there are starlings nesting in my attic."

To Franny, that didn't seem like too bad of a week, but she figured retirement came with its own special set of troubles.

"I'm sorry to hear that," Franny told her, trying to make her hand on the woman's shoulder as sympathetic as possible.

"How was yours, Francesca?" Janet asked. "Please tell us something exciting happened. I feel like I spent my week watching my lawn grow and counting the cans of soup in my cabinets."

"How many cans did you have?" Franny was genuinely curious.

To her credit, Janet's eyes lit up a bit at the question. "Fourteen cans of Progresso and twenty-five cans of Campbell's."

"That's impressive," Carmella commented.

"Not as impressive as whatever Franny's gotten up to, I'm sure."

"I hate to disappoint you ladies, but my life is absolutely boring as shit."

"That can't be true," Janet argued. "You're what, thirty? You're just getting started at this whole life thing."

"I remember when I was thirty." Charlie's eyes took on an almost mystical effect. "I had this girlfriend named Big T. She drove a motorcycle and had the biggest arms you've ever seen. The things we got up to . . ."

Franny smiled with interest. "Like what?"

Barb cleared her throat. "Francesca, please do not goad this woman into telling us about getting fisted in a river bend in South Dakota again. We've only got the lanes for two hours."

Franny turned her mouth down. "Aww, but now I really want to hear it."

Charlie patted Franny's knee. "I'll tell you after. It's a hell of a tale. She ended up leaving me for a Denny's waitress in the middle of Montana, and I had to hitchhike home."

"Yeah . . . my life isn't nearly as interesting as that. All I've got is a hot coworker who basically wants me dead. That's literally it."

"Hold on now." Stella held up a hand. "Those coworker romances are some of the best ones."

"And the worst ones," Barb interjected as Charlie left her seat for her turn at the lane.

"Me and Connie met at work," Janet said, a soft smile on her face as she spoke of her partner. "We used to complain about our supervisor at the paper mill together so much that we ended up falling in love."

Franny laughed, reflexively tightening her ponytail. "Yeah . . . I don't think Jade and I are anywhere close to falling in love. Like I said, she hates me."

"Hate and love aren't always that far off," Charlie said, almost wistfully. "People confuse the two all the time."

Janet nodded. "Exactly! Maybe it's just passion."

Franny wasn't a big enough fool to deny that there was passion between her and Jade. It was obvious. The air between them practically sparked every time they were together. But that didn't mean much of anything . . .

Nor did it mean anything that Franny's heart pounded faster in her chest every time she so much as looked at the other woman. All of that was just . . . well, she didn't know, to be honest. Sometimes it felt like they were playing some big, elaborate game of cat and mouse. Sometimes, she stood toe-to-toe with Dunn, looked in her eyes, and thought she saw the exact opposite of hatred.

In another life, maybe Franny and Jade would have met for the first time at a lesbian bar in Houston. They would have danced, shared a couple of drinks, gone home together, and put that spark to good use. Maybe it would have even led to something more.

She also knew that she didn't hate Dunn. Not in the slightest. Franny wanted—needed, even—the coaching position. As it stood, she was floundering. Her breakup with her ex, Caroline, had been traumatic in and of itself. She had spent a couple of weeks of PTO—and unpaid leave—holed up in her apartment listening to Tegan and Sara, trying to cope. But when the initial shock and awe of the abandonment had worn off, Franny had found herself surprised when the overwhelming emotion left had been a profound sense of loss. Not for the girl or the relationship they'd had but for herself. For the parts of her that she'd packed up and tucked away in a suitcase under her bed.

Her first six months in Greenbelt had been spent firmly under the wing of an incredibly flighty bird. The only people she'd known were Caroline's people, the only passions she'd cared about were Caroline's passions. It had been a total mindfuck to find herself alone in a strange place and feeling like she hardly knew who she was anymore.

Franny's first instinct had been to run back to the safety of her old life in Texas. But even that hadn't felt completely right. She had a good job and a cute apartment and just enough willpower to try to stay and make it work. Just under two years later, Franny had made a good life for herself—even if it was lacking. It was only recently that she'd started to feel that itch for more than just good again. She wanted to feel hopeful and ambitious, and she wanted all the upsets that came with those things too.

It had been right there in front of her the entire time. The thing she'd loved but had relegated to hobby status because no one else seemed to understand its importance the way she did.

She needed football again. The thrill of it. The competitiveness. The heart. Getting out on that field every day and helping coach those kids—through their wins or their losses—was something she had lived without for far too long.

And if getting all that back meant that she had to use whatever flamed between her and Dunn to completely burn the other woman, so be it. It wasn't as if the fight wouldn't be a fair one. Jade was doing the exact same thing to her.

"If good old-fashioned dislike is passion, then I suppose it is," Franny said with her tongue in her cheek.

She floundered for a moment, her mouth still open but releasing no sounds. Her argument was so flimsy that she barely had any way to argue it, even in her own head. The silence drew out until, finally, her name popped up on the display screen above their heads, signaling that it was her turn to knock down some pins.

The other girls were quiet, obviously letting her have it. But she could see by the looks on their faces that they didn't believe her.

Which was fair enough, since she was lying her ass off.

Later that night, she lay in her bed in the dark, wishing for the first time that she'd put a television in her bedroom to distract her from her thoughts.

Her mind kept replaying the conversation from the bowling alley and the conclusions she'd come to. Her mind wasn't changed in the end, but she was finding it impossible now not to focus on the other feelings she'd identified.

The spark, the heat, the passion. Whatever her rational mind was made up of completely dissolved after 2:00 A.M. Anything that was left burned and ached to the point that she didn't even see the point in pushing it down anymore. What for? There was no one here but her. The images that flashed behind her eyes were only for her to see.

Jade Dunn smiling at her. The smooth skin of her chest and shoulders extra golden because of the sunlight. Jade had a little scar above the knuckle of her index finger on her left hand. It was darker than the rest of her skin, shinier from the way it had healed. Franny imagined running her own finger over the mark, bringing it up to her mouth, and laying a kiss on it.

She sucked in a sharp breath, her thighs squeezing together tightly when the next frame in her mind became an image of her sucking on Jade's finger. Just one, then two. Her tongue swirling around the hot flesh, her lips keeping them inside.

Suddenly, she could practically feel those fingers sliding into her panties. It was so real that Franny had to put a hand on her mound to make sure it was just her imagination running rampant. She was hot there, so soaked that she could feel it through her underwear just by pressing against herself a little bit.

The motion set her body alight. Her nipples hardened to stiff points underneath her little white T-shirt; even just the fabric brushing against them felt good enough to make her hiss.

Franny settled back into her pillows, closing her eyes and shutting out everything but the fantasy.

Jade's fingers—hers—were soft as they circled her clit, and Franny's thighs clenched imagining Jade's soft, plump lips pressing kisses into her neck as she worked her over. She squirmed in her bed, trying to re-create for herself what it might feel like to have Jade on top of her, inside her.

It was a heady feeling, so much so that Franny could practically smell whatever perfume the other woman wore. As if she could feel her tongue brush against her lips. The weight of her, the sweetness.

It didn't take much to send her over the edge. She'd been so worked up recently, so much tension wrapped around her body that a few fast circles around her clit and Jade's name on her tongue were enough to make her come so hard she had to turn her head and scream into a pillow.

She kept her fingers underneath her panties, even after she was done. Feeling herself with soothing strokes and pets as she waited for shame to fill her. It was entirely unethical to think about your coworker like that, to masturbate to the thought of her. To call out her name in the darkness of your bedroom. Franny didn't know how in the hell she was supposed to look Dunn in the face after what she'd done.

Still, when she turned over on her side, finally ready to fall asleep, her brain was far too hazy to fight off the image of the other woman curling around behind her, arm over her waist, breath against the back of her neck.

Franny figured she couldn't be responsible for what her head dreamed up in such a vulnerable state. She'd had far worse nightmares than this, after all.

9

Jade hated sitting at the bar. The stools were uncomfortable and hard to sink into, and she always felt like she was being watched like a hawk perched up on one. It was a Friday evening, though, and everybody and their mama had decided to have their supper at the diner. Because Miri was the only one who she'd been able to rope out of the house, they'd been peer pressured into giving up a chance at a real table to a young family only to find themselves stuck at two of the open stools left at the bar.

The bar at Minnie's Diner wasn't actually a bar. It had the same high, rounded tabletop as one, accompanied by glossy blue vinyl backless stools. There was no alcohol to be found, though. No towering bottles of vodka and whiskey. There wasn't even a beer tap. Just vintage refrigerators filled with glass soda bottles and a ridiculously large stash of salt and pepper holders.

She knew she was ornery tonight, but Jade had seriously considered saying, "Fuck it," and just going home instead. But Miriam, being the absolute menace that she was, had taken her by the wrist and forced her into her seat.

"Mommy will buy you a milkshake after your supper if you quit pouting," her best friend said, snorting around a sip of peach tea.

Jade picked at the paper that had come off her straw. "Don't call yourself *Mommy*. It's weird."

"It's only weird because it makes your repressed ass horny."

Jade gasped. "I am not repressed! And I'm not horny either. I'm . . . I'm very satisfied."

Miri pressed her lips together and made a very unimpressed face. "When was the last time you even touched yourself?"

"I'm a grown-ass woman, Miriam; I think I have a genuine understanding of how to give myself pleasure."

"I'd agree with that. It also wouldn't matter if you never did it, if I didn't know that you're good for just straight up pretending like you don't want it."

Jade sighed and pressed her head against the tabletop. Her best friend wasn't wrong but . . . she didn't see it as repression. She saw it as compartmentalization. And, well, she supposed she was in a bit of a dry spell.

"I hit up Marley the other night, and she completely blew me off." Jade's words were muffled by the furniture under her face, but Miri still heard.

"Jade . . . Marley told you she loved you a year ago, and you were basically like 'Appreciate it. Deuces, babe.' You think she's lining up to bump pussies after that?"

Jade opened her mouth to respond but was interrupted by the clearing of a throat. Her head was off the table so fast it almost spun. Behind the bar in front of them was a young white boy with wide eyes and a face as red as a tomato.

"Um." His voice cracked. "I'm here to—to take your orders."

Miri grinned and ordered a crispy chicken salad as if she hadn't just completely embarrassed all three of them.

"I'll have the patty melt," Jade said, trying to convey an apology in her smile. "And a strawberry milkshake on her check."

The kid walked away with barely another word.

"I think he goes to Greenbelt," Jade groaned. "I'd be surprised if every high schooler in this town doesn't hear about that shit within the next ten minutes."

Miri rolled her eyes. "Oh, please. You should hear the stuff these kids say. You thought we were bad? My eight-year-old nephew used the word *bussy* the other day, and my sister-in-law almost had a stroke behind it. Trust me, that's nothing to what that kid sees every day on Snapchat."

Jade supposed that was fair. She wasn't the type of teacher who sat around talking about how much worse the kids these days were than kids in her day. It simply wasn't true. Almost everything her freshman kids did was a direct copy of the types of shit she'd gotten up to at their age. Sometimes, though, she found herself speechless at their antics. She couldn't count the number of times she'd had to look up terms they used, only to find herself rubbing her temples as she pleaded with them to at least keep that language out of her classroom.

"Either way," she grumbled, completely unwilling to lose the little spat. "Keep your damn voice down. I don't need everybody in here knowing that I get no ass."

"You could get as much ass as you want to. Stop playing." Miri's eyes cut to somewhere behind Jade for a split second before she smirked. "I think you just want one particular ass right now, and it's blinding all the others."

Jade didn't have any prospects at present. She was a bisexual with a roster as dry as the Sahara. It was a sad thing to be, but it was the truth. She'd been trying to big herself up by remembering that she was just too focused on her goals to give anything of herself to anyone else, even if the anything in question was just a bit of no-strings fun.

"I don't know what you're talking about."

Miri's eyes cut away again. This time, Jade was forced to swivel her head to see what had gotten her friend's attention.

"Aww fuck," she moaned.

Francesca Lim was standing in the packed line in front of the hostess booth. She was wearing a pair of tiny running shorts and a tank top, and Jade had to drag her gaze away from the stretch of her long legs.

"That's her, right?" Miri asked. "The art teacher? The one you supposedly hate?"

"I don't hate her."

Miri laughed. "Of course you don't hate her. You like her."

"Are you out of your damn mind?" Jade's voice came out much louder than she'd intended, and a couple a few seats down from them turned to look at them with questioning eyes.

"I mean, she's cute."

Jade took another peek at Lim, who luckily hadn't noticed their gazes on her. It was clear that she'd just come back from the gym or a run or something. Her long, dark hair was in a messy knot at the nape of her neck. Her skin was glowing, and even from feet away, Jade could see the blood pumping under her skin, making her cheeks pink.

"She's all right." Jade turned back to the bar, finger idly playing with the sweat on the outside of her cup.

Miri made a noise at the back of her throat, and Jade knew that she'd been about as convincing as a Piggly Wiggly cake at a church bake sale.

"Aaaaaand she's definitely coming over here," Miri practically singsonged.

"Fuck," Jade said, running her fingers through her week-old silk press. "I was not prepared for this today. What the hell am I supposed to even say to her?"

"You could try being nice."

Jade shot Miri a withering look that her best friend returned with a grin just before Lim came to stand by them.

"Um . . . hey."

"Hi," Jade said with what she hoped was blatant disinterest.

"Do y'all mind if I sit here?" She pointed to the stool to the left of Jade. "There's no way I'm getting a table to myself tonight."

Jade went silent, decidedly not answering. Miri sent a kick to her shin under the bar that almost made her eyes water.

"Of course you can sit," Miri answered with a smile. "I'm Miri, by the way."

Lim smiled as she took her seat. Jade could instantly smell the coconut scent of her hair, and it made her mouth wet.

"I'm Franny," she said. "I hope I'm not interrupting a date or anything . . ."

"She fucking wishes." Miri snorted. "We're just friends."

Jade couldn't pass up the chance to get her licks back, even if it meant having to give up her little show of ignoring Lim.

"She's the most insufferable person I've ever met in my life, and she won't leave me alone."

Lim's eyes seemed to light up with opportunity, one of those signature smirks appearing across her lips. "That's relatable."

Jade narrowed her eyes.

Their little red-faced waiter reappeared with Jade's and Miri's food, taking Lim's order before running off again. Jade took a knife to her patty melt, cutting it down the middle. Steam rose up from between the two sides, and because she didn't feel like completely sloughing off the skin on the roof of her mouth, she bit into a fry while she waited for it to cool down.

"What are you doing here anyway?" she asked Lim.

"Same thing as you," Lim said, raising an eyebrow. "Trying to have a meal."

"No, I mean . . . I didn't know out-of-towners even knew about Minnie's."

"I've been here two years, and my ex brought me here basically the second we crossed into the city limits."

She shouldn't have been, but Jade was nosy by nature, and the mere mention of an ex made her perk up. Luckily, her best friend was just as nosy as she was but had way fewer qualms about hiding the quality.

"Ohhh, an ex," Miri said with a wiggle of her eyebrows. "Anyone we'd know?"

Lim's mouth turned down, and she shrugged. "Maybe. I mean, she grew up here, so you must, right? Greenbelt is definitely an everybody-knows-everybody type of place."

Jade had to chuckle genuinely at that. "Not necessarily everybody. A lot of people, for sure. I'd say we *know of* more people than we actually know. The wealthy families of Greenbelt don't concern themselves much with the rest of us unless they need us to scrub their floors or check out their groceries."

"That makes sense. I think it's like that in a lot of places, just on a bigger scale."

"The ex," Miri butted in to remind them.

"Oh, right." Lim rubbed a hand on the back of her neck, and Jade spotted a small half-broken heart tattoo on her inner arm; the inside of it had been filled in with black ink. "Caroline Bailey."

Jade's head shot around to look at Miri, their eyes widening.

"You were in a relationship with Caroline Bailey?" Miri asked incredulously.

"For two years."

"We're talking about the same Caroline Bailey who had her superintendent mother fire our English teacher sophomore year for having us read *The Crucible* even though it was literally in the curriculum?" Miri asked.

"Uhhhh . . ." Lim trailed off, looking like a deer caught in headlights.

"It can't be the same Caroline Bailey who sent around a petition to declare cheerleading a civil rights offense?" Jade asked.

"Yeah, that actually does sound like her."

Jade scarfed down another fry. "How in the hell did that happen?"

"We met at a queer burlesque show my friend was performing at in Houston. Caroline was hosting, and we ended up talking backstage. Within like two months, I was convinced that she was the love of my life, and I moved here with her thinking we were going to . . . I don't know . . . get married or something. It didn't last long. A few months after that, she ran off with some girl she met during a pottery-making seminar in Charleston. I haven't heard from her since."

"Fuuuuck," Miri breathed out.

"She just left you here?" Jade asked, her heart sinking into her stomach at the mere thought of that type of callousness. She might have been a bitch, but she at least had morals.

"I literally came home to her packing her shit up into one suitcase and hopping into the other girl's car like it was nothing."

"That's so . . . fucked-up," Jade said, trying her hardest not to sound pitying.

"Why did you stay?" Miri asked. "Why not just go home after all that?"

Lim was silent for a few moments, a small wrinkle appearing between her eyebrows as she contemplated. Then she flashed a look at Jade, and it nearly knocked her out of her seat. It wasn't the sad, defeated look she'd expected from someone who'd been stepped all over. There was fire there, the kind that came from someone who was ready for a fight.

"I saw an opportunity here," Lim answered. "I still do. I'm trying to show myself that I didn't just upend my life for some girl who didn't give a shit about me. I want something good to come out of all this. Something great, actually."

"I hear that," Miri said, and she raised her peach tea in solidarity.

Lim laughed, not smug or condescending. A genuine, tinkling sound that felt in direct contrast to the smokiness that was normally in her voice. It made Jade's throat feel thick.

"That search for something great has you encroaching on dangerous territory, girlie," Jade remarked.

The condescension rolled from Lim like water off a duck's back. "I told you before, Jade, you don't scare me. I've dealt with bigger and badder than you."

"I don't believe you."

Next to her, Miri snorted but otherwise kept quiet. Lim crossed her arms, her posture immediately more defensive than Jade had ever seen it.

"I'll admit that I've never had a town hall meeting called over me, but this one time, one of the dads on my AAU team literally picked me up and carried me off the field against my will."

Jade's spine straightened in an instant. "What?"

"Excuse me?" Miri was incredulous.

"One of the kids on my team did AAU and played for his school at the same time. He had one of those dads who never made it pro himself and was pushing his kid way too hard to make it happen for him. You know the type."

Jade nodded, mouth hanging open slightly.

"He'd had problems with me all season, questioning every decision I made, complaining about me to the head coach, that sort of thing. Anyway, we were in a playoff game, down by eight points, and I pull his kid because he's clearly tired and he's moving slow. And the second I get him off the field, his dad rushes me and starts screaming in my face and shit. He starts getting progressively more furious, and I just stand there straight-faced, trying not to sock him in his big, nasty mouth. I guess he got enough of that because all of a sudden the dude just picks me up under my arms, carries me off to the side of the bleachers, and tells me I belong there and not on the field."

Now Jade's jaw dropped open so wide she was surprised her tongue didn't touch her shoes.

"What did you do?" Miri asked, her tone colored with all the shock Jade felt.

"I shrugged it off because that's what you have to do. My coach got him ejected from the game and his kid was basically banned from competing in that league, but nothing like that would have ever happened if he hadn't felt like he had a right to literally command my body because I'm a woman."

"No, it wouldn't have," Jade agreed. "His cowardly ass probably would have been too scared to get in your face at all."

"Exactly." Lim had fists tucked underneath where her arms were crossed.

Whatever her feelings were for the other woman, Jade felt horrible for Lim in that moment. She was absolutely disgusted to hear what she'd been through. This career they'd chosen for themselves could be brutal on anyone, but when it was compounded with misogyny and racism, it could become downright violent.

"I-I'm sorry, Lim," Jade said. And no matter how much she wanted to right then, she didn't reach out and touch her. "You didn't deserve that. You deserved for that guy to be taken care of the second he started singling you out."

Lim caught Jade's eyes, the look in them warm and appreciative. The palms of Jade's hands ran as slick as her mouth. She swallowed.

"You're right," Lim said, her eyes following the line of Jade's throat before flicking back to her face. "That's why I believe in solidarity now. The more of us there are, the easier it'll be to fight them."

Jade looked away from the other woman's gaze as a thing that felt suspiciously close to shame flooded her. It made its way slowly through her entire body until she was left with a chilly feeling all over. She didn't know what to say in response. The humanity in her wanted to acknowledge Lim's statement as correct, but the rest of her knew that all that hand-holding peace-and-love shit didn't work. The stakes were too high to let her guard down over one sad story.

Weren't they?

As a coach, she taught her players that good sportsmanship was imperative to being a good player. That didn't mean they couldn't get a little trash talk off from time to time or consider themselves the best in the game. It just meant that she was always there to remind them that they were only as good as their biggest loss. And those losses were inevitable.

This was different, though. Neither she nor Lim were on the field, fighting for the right to call themselves MVP. They were going after something that had the potential to change their lives. As women. As women of color. Trying to make names for themselves in this arena took an immense amount of drive and focus. It took a hell of a lot of grit and willingness to take it on the chin too. They were using kitchen knives to carve their names into institutions older and more solid than either of them could ever probably imagine. But the same stubbornness Jade saw in herself, she saw in Lim. That single-minded unwillingness to fold or give up, it was right there in the other woman's eyes. And she'd be a fool not to recognize and respect it.

That didn't mean she could fall into that well of respect, though. Not if she wanted to stay her course. Not if she wanted to win.

She hadn't anticipated how hard it would be to manufacture animosity for someone, though. Not for longer than the course of a game. Not while she saw and interacted with them so much. It made her shoulders tight and her abs ache. It was taxing.

But Jade figured that she could put their rivalry on hold for an hour or so while they finished their dinner. Then she could get right back to it.

"You should come out with us sometime," she heard Miri tell Lim.

Lim flashed a look at Jade that she couldn't quite decipher before offering Miri a small smile and a noncommittal maybe. Jade figured she wouldn't be joining the girls for drinks and dancing anytime soon. She convinced herself that this was a good thing. Ignoring the thought of Lim in a pair of well-tailored dress pants, grinding against her beneath strobing club lights.

She took a bite of her patty melt to distract herself. Three bites in, she looked over at Lim, who hadn't even gotten her drink order yet. Sighing with all the reluctance left in her body, she pushed her plate toward Lim.

"You can have some fries if you want," Jade offered. "Until your food gets here."

Next to her, she heard Miri suck in a breath. Normally, it went against every single one of Jade's instincts to share food, even with her friends. She'd sooner give someone the clothes off her back than a bite of her sandwich. And here she was, acting completely out of character, for reasons she couldn't even narrow down herself.

It was her turn to send a kick into Miri's shin.

"Thank you," Lim said, smiling at her as she ate a crispy golden fry, then licked the salt from her thumb before going back in for more.

Jade didn't find it the least bit disgusting. Not even a little bit.

10

Port Royal Academy had a lot of money. It was evident to Franny the second they pulled up to the scrimmage game in two charter buses decked out with the burgundy and white of their school colors. The boys exited the vehicles in single file, already sporting their pristine uniforms, trying their hardest to look as intimidating as a bunch of adolescent boys possibly could.

The second bus held their parents. Largely a ton of white people with coiffed hair, pearls, and Vineyard Vines' finest.

Franny supposed this obvious showing of wealth and privilege was supposed to spook them. But as she stood off to the side while the coaches shook hands and exchanged pleasantries, she couldn't help but take note of Greenbelt's side of things. Just about every child on the team had a parent or family member there to support them. Team parents made sure the snack table was well stocked. Their buses may have been yellow and their cleats may have been well-worn, but they were in damn good spirits. This team reminded her of what she loved so much about sports at this level. When it was still kids and families and community coming together to create magic.

She wouldn't knock Port Royal for what they had. But those cushy seats on the ride over didn't mean anything for their chances of winning. Greenbelt had too much to lose this season, between

Landry retiring and trying to get a championship in the process and Jade and her clawing their way toward their dream jobs, not to mention the kids working their asses off to win. They had it in the bag, Franny could feel it. And it made her feel so excited she could hardly keep the grin off her face.

"What are you over here smiling so big for?" Landry had approached her stealthily, with Dunn right on his tail.

"We're going to win this one, Coach." Her smile didn't break. "I can feel it."

"For once, I agree with her," Dunn offered.

Franny bit back the urge to say something snarky about how the other woman had agreed with her enough to share her food the weekend before. But now wasn't the time. They were on the same team, and solidarity was necessary in times like these, with the real enemy breathing down their necks.

"Their boys are looking good this year," Landry said.

All three pairs of eyes cut across the field to where Port Royal was doing their stretches on the away side of the field.

"Hmmm." Franny's tone was noncommittal.

"They can't beat us." Jade's words were so strong and sure, Franny had no choice but to believe her.

Landry's mouth curved into the tiniest smile, his eyes fiery. "How do you figure?"

"They don't want it like we want it," Jade said. "They don't need it."

Franny nodded so much, her baseball cap almost popped off. "Look at them. This doesn't mean shit to them. Their coach is over there sitting pretty. He's got years left under his belt. There's no fire in him. The kids know it."

"And we've got fire in us?" Landry asked.

"Enough to tear all this shit up, sir," Jade damn near snarled.

The words made Franny's heart pound. Half because it was, unfortunately, wildly sexy to hear the other woman so worked up, and half because she was right. There was no way they were losing this. There was no convincing her otherwise.

Landry stared Franny down for a few moments before crossing his arms over his broad chest. For a second, she thought he was going to tell her to go home. Her breath hitched with anticipation.

"Why don't you come over here with the other coaches on the sideline," he said. "Let's see how you interact with everybody in a game setting."

Franny heard Jade suck in a breath of her own, but it was completely drowned out by the blood rushing to Franny's head and making her ears feel fuzzy.

"S-sure," she stuttered out, running to catch up as the duo walked away but making sure she walked on the other side of Landry instead of behind him.

The energy was even more palpable closer to the field. Franny was welcomed with a few kind smiles and nods, but her presence wasn't treated like any kind of anomaly. All it did was bolster her. If she wouldn't have felt so silly doing it, she might have puffed her chest out because of all the pride swelling up inside it.

Twenty minutes later, they were set to begin. Franny had watched Landry put together his starting lineup with precision. Eleven boys started on the field, a showing of all different types of players who served various purposes at various levels.

She eyed the boys on the bench and sidelines, not spotting a single angry or jealous expression. Most of them were homed in, ready to make magic happen. Jaxon Myers—the kicker—was near the watercooler having a conversation with Alonzo Holton, who played left tackle on the O-line. Whatever they were talking about seemed to be serious from the way Alonzo's shoulders slumped more and more by the second. She couldn't see his face, but his body language told her that someone needed to see what was up. All the actual coaches were busy elsewhere, so she made the executive decision to run over to them.

"Everything all right, boys? The game's starting soon. Where are your heads at?"

Neither of them said a word, but Jaxon spared a long glance at Alonzo, who had his chin tucked into his chest.

"Hey," Franny said softly, moving closer to the boy. "Alonzo, is everything okay? Has something happened? You aren't hurt, are you?"

It was a lot of questions all at once, she knew, but their silence was making her worried. After the silence stretched on for a few more long moments, Jaxon finally spoke up.

"His dad is sick. He had to go to the hospital last night."

"Jax, what the hell!" Alonzo was incensed.

"Hey! None of that language." She slipped into her teacher tone instinctively. "Jaxon is just trying to help."

"Well, he's not."

"Do you . . . want to tell me what happened?"

Alonzo heaved a big sigh, the pads under his uniform puffing out with his breath. "My pops had a heart attack last night."

"Oh God, I'm so sorry. Is he—"

"He's alive." The words were choked and garbled coming from the boy's mouth. "But he could barely talk when I saw him this morning."

"Alonzo, why are you here? You should be with your family."

"I said the same thing!" Jaxon interjected. "He said he didn't want to let the team down."

"The scrimmage is important," Alonzo said, finally looking up at her, his dark eyes glistening. "Coach Dunn always says that we can't be part of the team if we don't show up."

Alonzo was taller than Franny, so there was no squatting down to try to get to his level. All she could do was put a hand on his shoulder. "Listen to me. There's not a single person on this team who would want you putting this game before your family when you need to be with them instead. Do you understand me?"

The boy didn't say anything, but he gave a small nod. Franny watched his face crumple in real time, his mouth turning down at the sides as his big eyes overflowed with tears until they started falling down his face.

She let out a sympathetic little coo. "Can I hug you?"

Alonzo nodded again, and she grabbed him up in her arms, holding him tightly as his body shook with sobs. She rubbed his back, encouraging him to let his emotions flow. Only when his sobs turned to sniffles and his frame stood mostly still again did she speak.

"I'll tell you what . . . Jaxon?" The boy was still next to them, quiet concern written all over his reddened face. "Go grab Coach Dunn for me, will you? Tell her it's very important."

"Nooo . . ." Alonzo's voice was muffled in the collar of Franny's polo.

"It'll be okay," she said. "Trust me. I've got you."

He stayed in her hold until Jaxon ran back over with Jade on his tail. Dunn eyed the scene in front of her with clear apprehension.

"What's going on? We kick off in less than ten minutes, y'all."

"I don't think Alonzo is in any shape to play today, Coach." Franny made sure to keep things professional in front of the kids.

Jade moved closer to inspect Alonzo. "Holton, talk to me."

"I'm sorry, Coach Dunn." The boy's lips quivered. He looked close to crying again. "I . . . My . . ."

It became clear that he wasn't in much of a state to communicate effectively either, so Franny pulled away from him so she could talk with Jade one-on-one. "His father had a heart attack last night. I don't know everything, but he's apparently still in the hospital."

Dunn paused, then looked past Franny to Alonzo. "Does your mama know you're here?"

She didn't coo at him or seem overly sympathetic, just laser focused.

"I don't know," Alonzo said. "She sent me and Nia home with my auntie earlier today because we had been there all night. I know we were supposed to go back to see him tonight, though."

"All right. You're not playing today. I'm going to call your mama and tell her what's going on, then I'm going to find somebody to take you home. Jaxon, take Alonzo over to the bench and sit with him until I get there."

"Yes, Coach." Jaxon nodded like a soldier who'd just been given marching orders.

"Holton," Dunn called out before the boys left earshot. "This team is your family too. We love you. You're not letting anybody down by taking care of yourself. Please remember that."

"I will," Alonzo croaked.

"And if anybody has anything to say about that, you let me know, and I'll set them straight. Now go on, sit your butts down. I'll be over in a minute."

They watched the boys until they'd made it to their destination.

"Do you need me to go look in the team files for Alonzo's mother's number?" Franny asked.

Dunn shook her head. "Nah, don't worry about it. I've got it in my phone."

There was an awkward silence between them. It was a bizarre thing too. The heaviness of the situation they'd suddenly found themselves in paired with the buzzing nature of competition in the air made it impossible for Franny not to get jittery.

Franny pulled at her earlobes a few times. "I barely knew what to do besides get you . . . It wasn't weird that I hugged him, was it?"

"No, it's all right to comfort them. But you can't let that get in the way of solving the issue. These kids need help and guidance and stability. That means knowing when to be soft and when to at least put on the mask of somebody getting down to business. I may not be the one they come to for hugs, but they should always know they can come to me to get help when they need it."

"So, what you're saying is both of our approaches were needed and we actually made a pretty good team."

Jade rolled her eyes so far into the back of her head that Franny was afraid they might stay there. "I don't have time for this foolishness tonight, Lim. Let me go call this boy's mama before you get me started again."

Alonzo's auntie picked him up from the field within minutes, and the opening kickoff started without much fanfare shortly after. Port Royal won the coin toss and decided to kick off, and the entire field erupted in excitement.

It had been so long since she'd felt this—the rush of pure energy that only ever seemed to happen when everyone decided to make a game the center of their universe. Franny's heart started to thud progressively louder, and her skin grew hot, sweat beading at her temples and along the back of her neck, the thrill of a big game day pulsing in her veins.

The first quarter of the game ended without either team scoring, but as the boys shuffled to the sidelines, sweaty and covered in dirt, the hopeful looks in their eyes hadn't gone anywhere. She moved closer to the action so she could hear what Coach Landry was saying to them.

"You're looking good out there, boys," he said. "Strong stances, good hustle. We need to tighten up on defense, though, isn't that right, Coach?" He looked straight at Jade.

She nodded, the ponytail sticking through the little hole in the back of her cap bouncing. "They're spreading their offense wide, and it's making us scramble to find an in. So, we're going to run our version of a Tite front." Jade began drawing *x*'s and *o*'s on the small whiteboard in her hand, showing each player where they'd be. "We're going to do what's called a *spill and kill*, taking up all that space on the inside. They won't be expecting this, and by the time they figure it out, they'll be scrambling. Monty and Trevor, you'll be putting in work as linebackers with this play. You be patient, wait for that ball to get downhill, then I want you to get there before they do, and I want you to make sure there's plenty of room for our quarterback to run that ball through."

When she spoke, Dunn was clear and concise. There wasn't an ounce of indecision in her voice. And it made everyone shut up and listen. She didn't even need to yell.

The boys ran back into the next quarter hydrated and, after a few changes to the lineup, with a new play.

Franny cleared her throat. "Tite front was a good choice," she said as they watched the players get into position on the field. "Heavy for a scrimmage, but it'll be good for scoring in the second down."

Franny half expected the other woman to hit her with something snarky, but Dunn seemed too enmeshed in the game to keep the rivalry up in the moment.

"What do you think of their offensive game?"

"What?" Franny couldn't keep the shock out of her tone.

"Port Royal's offense, what are your thoughts?" Jade's expression was almost impassive. "I can't focus on both when I'm in the middle of strategy. I've got to pick one, and it's defense. So, I want to know what you think about their offensive strategy."

"You want *my* opinion?"

Jade sniffed. "I could just go ask Coach Carr instead . . ."

"No!" Franny almost jumped, reaching a hand out to grasp Dunn's upper arm. Immediately, it felt like she'd been seared by something hot. "Sorry," she mumbled. "I, uh—I think they're good.

They're active out there, and they're good at finding our weak spots. But they lag a bit, and their coach puts too much energy into the star players. They're not so cohesive as a unit."

Dunn nodded, considering this. "That's their weakness, then. Their lack of unity."

"It's also our advantage," Franny offered. "Look at how our boys are communicating with one another." She gestured to the field. Obviously, they couldn't tell what they were saying, but their boys were talking.

They moved in sync, almost rhythmically, across the field. They kept tight after the snap, so close to one another that every one of Port Royal's players who tried to break through found themselves on their backs.

Franny kept one eye on the field and one eye to her left, where Jade stood with her arms crossed and eyes wide. Every now and then, Jade would put a pen to the little notepad she kept in the back pocket of her coaching khakis. Franny couldn't see what Dunn was writing most of the time, but she caught a glimpse of a few words, like *eagle front* and *radar*. She was strategizing. It almost seemed like she was thinking about the current game but also all the future ones.

Dunn was a diligent onlooker. Nothing seemed to pass by her without notice or regard.

Suddenly, there was an eruption from the crowd, even bigger than the one that had happened at kickoff. Zion Perkins, their quarterback, had the football gripped tightly as he sprinted down the field toward Port Royal's goal line.

He was yards ahead of the other players, but their opponents were gaining on him. Zion had two defensive tackles trailing and a tangling of thrown limbs and pileups behind him.

She and Jade were standing closest to Port Royal's goal line, and Zion was coming up the middle. Coach Landry flew past them, gripping the belt of his khakis to keep them up. Jade took off running behind him, and Franny followed on instinct. When somebody suddenly took off running, it was almost always in your best interest to follow.

The three of them went wild, yelling encouragements and screaming instructions, fighting to be heard over the crowd. Every bit of blood in Franny's body seemed to exist only between her ears. They rang with the force of her own screams, only growing louder as Zion crossed the line, throwing the football into the dirt and collapsing into it.

His teammates threw themselves on top of him once they made it. It was an incredible sight. All that joy and exhaustion combined into one.

"Your Tite front was a good call," she heard Landry tell Jade as they made their way a few yards back, up to where the other coaches were greeting the boys as they stepped off the field.

"Any strategy is only as good as the team seeing it through, Coach," Jade responded.

Franny trailed behind them. This down had been a win for Jade. Not just because they'd gotten themselves into the lead but because she was showing herself to be indispensable. Franny couldn't stop the twinge of jealousy that bubbled up in her chest—but she couldn't deny the admiration that was there either.

Greenbelt won the scrimmage 7-3. During the actual season, putting up seven was small numbers. But for an early-summer scrimmage . . . things were looking up.

Hours after the game ended, after cleaning up and having a coaches' debriefing that Franny had so thoughtfully been invited to, she finally made it to her car. It was close to 3:00 P.M., the sun high and unobstructed by clouds. Franny was thoroughly exhausted. She felt like she was drenched in sweat, and all she wanted was to take a long, lukewarm shower and fall into bed for a few hours.

She was rearranging things in her trunk, looking for a reasonable spot to put her bag and a small case of Gatorade a team mom had pawned off on her.

"You did well out there today." Jade's sudden presence and voice made Franny jump, immediately causing her to hit her head hard on the open trunk lid.

"Fuck!" Her hands immediately went to her head, her eyes clenched shut as pain shot through her skull.

"Oh shit." Jade ran over to her. "I'm so sorry. Oh my God."

Franny groaned, her head suddenly aching. She felt Dunn's hands on her hips, guiding her to sit down on the edge of her open trunk.

"How does it feel?" Jade asked. "Can you see? You're not bleeding, are you?"

"Too many questions."

Jade clicked her tongue. She squatted down between Franny's thighs, reaching up to take her head in her hands. Franny blinked a few times, trying to make sure her eyes weren't completely deceiving her.

Then Dunn was talking to her again. "You don't feel nauseous, do you?"

"No," Franny groaned, clenching her eyes shut again. Her head was starting to hurt more by the second.

"How about your ears? Are they ringing?"

"No," she whined.

"Head still hurting?"

"Hold on," Franny scoffed. "Please tell me you're not doing what I think you're doing . . ." Dunn went silent. "You are not giving me a freaking concussion assessment right now."

"Well, I'm not a medic, so I couldn't make that call anyway, but . . ."

"Jesus, Dunn. I don't have a concussion."

"You don't know that! You just hit your head so hard they can probably hear your ears ringing in Orangeburg."

Franny grumbled under her breath. Her eyes were still closed, but now all she wanted was to lie down even more than she had before. "Yeah, because you scared me."

"I know." Dunn's tone was dripping with guilt. "Which is why you should let me take you to the hospital."

"Oh, I—no, no, I don't . . ." Franny tried to stand up, but those hands were immediately at her waist again, pulling her back down. "I don't need to go to the hospital. Just . . . leave me here a minute and I'll be ready to drive in no time."

The hands fell away, and for a few long moments, everything was silent except for the light breeze in the trees and the distant sounds of voices. Franny began to feel like she was actually alone.

Her peace was interrupted by a heavy sigh. "You can't even open your damn eyes, and you expect me to believe you can drive yourself home?" Jade said.

"Damnit, I thought you were finally gone," Franny said, squinting at her.

"Isn't that my line?" Jade stood up. "Give me your hand."

"Why?" When had Franny turned into such a whiny little baby?

Jade huffed. "Because I said so. Let's go. Give me your keys. I'll drive you home."

Franny clutched the keys in her hand, desperate with the need to stomp her foot in frustration. "Fine. Just don't crash my car."

"Oh, you mean your tiny little Barbie car that a child could probably legally drive? Yeah, don't worry about that, babe."

Babe.

Franny's heart thumped.

Babe.

11

Jade made it through a ten-minute car ride and to the last turn in the parking lot of Greenbelt Memorial before Lim uttered a drowsy "Wait, do you even know where I live?"

She almost felt bad for what she was about to do, but she knew how serious head injuries were. So much of her job was spent attempting to prevent things like concussions for the kids on her team. Their sport was rife with injury and not enough people to take those injuries and the players who got them seriously. She was not one of those people. Anytime one of her kids took a tough hit to the head or body, she made them see a medic.

Lim was no different.

"Okay, so about that," Jade said with a grimace. "We're actually at the emergency room."

Lim gasped as if she'd been thoroughly betrayed. "Jade, noooo."

"Look . . . I'll . . . I'll go in with you if you want. I'll sit in the waiting room and drive you home when you're done. But you have to get checked, you know that."

Lim had spent the entire car ride with her eyes shut, and still Jade could feel her rolling them behind the lids.

"Lim, open your eyes, right now."

Lim crossed her arms over her chest like a petulant child. "I don't want to."

"No, you can't, because if you do, your head will start hurting even worse, right?" Jade huffed the string of words.

"No." Lim's tone could be described as nothing short of bratty. "It's because I simply don't want to."

"Right," Jade said. She threw open her door and heaved herself out of the car, moving around the front and opening the passenger-side door before Lim found it in her wherewithal to stop her. "Let's go. You probably have a mild traumatic brain injury, and if you die out of pure stubbornness, I will fucking kill you."

Lim wouldn't budge. This time, Jade threw her head to the sky and let out a screech.

"How about this," she said to Lim through gritted teeth. "If you go in there and get seen by a doctor, I'll—" She broke off, feeling flushed. Her immediate instinct had been to offer some type of physical service, like a massage or something. Not that she would have referred to *that* as labor on her part. "I'll . . . I'll big you up to Landry once," she said instead.

Lim's ears practically wiggled with the way she perked up. "What will you say?"

Jade rolled her eyes. "I don't know. I'll think of it in the moment."

"That's not good enough."

"What do you mean that's not good enough? I'm the one trying to keep you safe here."

"I already know I'm fine, so you're going to have to try harder than that."

Jade bit down on her lip, stressed. "What would you tell one of the kids, Lim? If they hit their head so hard they could hardly open their eyes. Would you tell them to walk it off?"

"Of course not!"

"Right, so how about you get out of the car before I'm forced to drag you out."

Immediately, she could tell Lim wanted to argue, but her point had been too good. She didn't know the other woman that well, but she knew enough that if she was anything like the type of person Jade thought she was, a hypocrite was the last thing she wanted to be.

"You've got a lot of nerve threatening me, Dunn," Lim groaned as she stepped out of the car. Jade was immediately at her side. She put one of Lim's arms around her neck and rested a hand around her waist, walking her the short distance toward the entrance of the hospital.

"Why don't you just hush now and focus on not passing out."

Luckily, the small emergency waiting room at Greenbelt Memorial was close to empty. There was a woman and a child sitting off in one of the corners near the loud vending machine. Aside from that, there was only one other person, filling out paperwork with his right arm secured to his chest with an old T-shirt.

Triage demanded that Lim be taken back first because of the nature of her injury and ensuing symptoms. Jade helped her complete her intake paperwork, then watched as Lim was helped into a wheelchair by a young nurse with kind eyes. She followed after them.

Before going through the double doors that led into the exam rooms, the nurse paused to exchange words with a colleague. It was only a brief moment, but Lim looked up at Jade, an expression coming over her face. Vulnerable, afraid. Jade opened her mouth to suggest that she escort her back for moral support. But nothing came out, because all she could imagine was Lim rebuking her for being inappropriate.

Just as quickly as it came, the moment was gone, and Jade was left to park her ass in one of the uncomfortable waiting room chairs.

It was almost three hours before the doors opened and Lim walked back out to the waiting room. Jade stood up to go meet her halfway to the door.

"I figured you would have left by now," Lim said. Her eyes were open and clear now, but Jade could already see the dark circles beginning to form under them.

"Well, I have your car," she said. "Is it a concussion, then?"

"No, thank God. Just a migraine triggered by the hit."

"They gave you a CT scan to be thorough, right?"

Lim rolled her eyes and started walking. "Yes, Mommy, I promise they took the little picture thingy of my brain."

Jade coughed, suddenly a little warm despite the sterile coldness of the room they were in. "Come on, let's get you home before you pass out."

The heavy-duty ibuprofen they'd given her at the hospital mixed with the anti-nausea pills seemed to make Lim drowsy from the way she leaned her head against the window the entire drive. She didn't fall asleep, but every time Jade took her eyes off the road to peek over and make sure she was all right, Lim was looking at her. It made Jade too nervous to acknowledge, so each time she cut her eyes back ahead as quickly as she could.

"Did you tell Landry to call my old team in Texas?" Lim asked quietly.

Jade choked. "Uh . . . What? Why?"

"I got a call from my old head coach asking me what I was getting into out here. He told me he'd gotten a call from Landry asking about me. I'm not trying to accuse you of anything. I just figure . . . that type of thing seems up your alley."

"Up my alley?"

"Yeah." Lim sighed and shifted in her seat so her back was pressed against the passenger-side door. "It's definitely up your alley to try to catch me in a lie, just so you can get me tossed out on my ass."

Jade's hand tightened on the wheel. Her stomach flipped like she was taking a long drop off a rickety roller coaster. "And maybe you're paranoid."

"Or maybe I'm right."

They stopped at a red light, and Jade pressed her foot down firmly on the brakes and glanced over at Lim again. She didn't look high, but she did look tired. Her eyes were heavy, drooping more and more every time she blinked. Jade took in Lim's ruddy cheeks and her chapped lips and found herself struck by how lovely she looked even still. Those eyes were hard to look away from—they were hard to lie to.

"It's just protocol, you know," Jade said. "We need to make sure we're doing reference checks on everyone. People lie, Lim. You know that."

Lim blinked at her slowly once, then closed her eyes, leaning her head back against the glass. "Sure, Jade."

When Jade put her foot on the gas to pull forward, the motion made her feel nauseous.

Lim lived in an older four-unit apartment building just around the corner from where Miri and her mother had lived for over twenty years. Whoever owned the building hadn't made any updates, but it was clear that it had been kept up well. All cherrywood floors and the original black-and-white subway tile in the bathroom. Lim didn't seem to have central heating or air, but there were two window units in the place, one in the living room and one in the bedroom. It was stuffy and hot when they walked in the front door, the living room still catching plenty of light from the dusky setting sun.

Immediately, Jade moved to crank both window units up high to get the air moving. Then she sat Lim down on the couch, helping her to get her shoes off.

"If you don't have a concussion, maybe you should have a little nap."

"Yeah, okay," Lim said, nodding with a wince. "Thank you for doing all this, but you really can go now. I'll be fine."

Jade sighed, taking the blanket that rested on the back of the couch and throwing it over Lim so that it covered her entire body. "Is this a comfortable temperature?"

"I feel fine."

Jade narrowed her eyes. "Do you?"

Lim looked at her, heavy eyes wide open for the first time in hours. But it was only for a split second before they were back to the soft, sleepy gaze. "Why do you always have to fight me, Jade?"

"I don't." She knew the words were a flat-out lie the second they left her mouth.

Lim giggled. "You're literally doing it right now."

Jade watched as she sank farther into the couch, contorting her body until she was in the perfect position. Knees bent, socked feet tucked halfway between two of the cushions until her head of dark hair was barely visible beneath the blanket. They were both silent for a few long seconds. When Jade spoke again, it was only because she figured Lim had finally fallen asleep.

"Maybe it's just easier this way."

"Uh-uh."

The quiet voice shocked Jade, but not enough to make the embarrassment of her admission fade away.

"You're just scared is all," Lim said.

"I'm not scared of anything."

There was that giggle again. "Sure you are. You're scared of what people think. And you're scared that I'm not as awful as you try to convince yourself I am."

Jade only sniffed, not allowing those words to rest in her head for any longer than it took to bully her brain into trying to forget them.

She expected Lim to reply again, this time waiting for longer than a few seconds of silence. When it was clear that she was finally asleep, Jade ventured into the kitchen.

Soon she'd call Miri or Olivia and beg one of them to pick her up and drop her back off at the school so she could get her car. But first she'd at least make sure Lim had something to eat when she woke up.

Lim's kitchen wasn't scant, but Jade could see that she wasn't much of a snacker. It was also clear that they had some very obvious culinary differences. The ingredients Lim had intrigued her, like perilla seed oil and gochujang, a red chili paste, but she didn't want to try something new to her and end up making something inedible (though she did jot down a few things in the notes app on her phone for later). Instead, she found everything she needed to make a quick pot of red rice and smoked sausage.

It would be a complete, hearty meal that Lim could get full on and still eat for a couple of days if her migraine stuck around. Jade tried not to think too hard about why she was doing this as she prepared the dish, humming to herself as she fried up some bacon and sautéed some onions and garlic. All in all, it took her under twenty minutes before the tomatoey rice dish was popped into the oven to cook.

She had about forty minutes to kill before the food was done. In lieu of sitting quietly at Lim's little two-person dining table with her eyes on her phone and anxiety in her chest, Jade decided to tackle a few of the dishes that had been left in the sink. She needed something to do with her hands to distract herself from her current reality. Jade was not supposed to like this woman. In fact, she was supposed to be trying her hardest to hate her, to keep the fire in her belly burning. Instead, here she was cooking for her and doing her dishes.

She tried to convince herself that it was guilt egging her on. If she hadn't come up behind Lim, the other woman wouldn't have nearly knocked herself out. It wasn't a theory that instilled any confidence.

She'd had no reason to approach Lim earlier that day after the game. Hell, her car was parked all the way on the other side of the lot, and there she had been, head full of some half-baked statement that she hadn't even gotten to spew out.

Except, on some level, she knew that wasn't it—and that she wasn't ready to acknowledge the truth. Because if she were honest, she'd gone out of her way the entire day for the simple reason that she liked . . .

Jade shook her head hard enough to make her brain rattle around in her skull. No. She refused. She would not entertain thoughts like that. Certainly not about the woman sleeping on the couch one room away.

Jade started humming again as she finished washing the dishes, not loud enough to disturb Lim but with enough volume that it helped her quiet her own thoughts, until finally she was relieved to hear the oven timer go off.

The sound seemed to wake Lim up, because the moment Jade pulled the hot glass pan from the oven, she heard feet shuffling into the kitchen.

"You cooked?" Lim's voice was decidedly groggy. Jade guessed that if she'd turned around, she probably would have seen the woman rubbing tiredly at her eyes. Even just the image in her head was adorable, so Jade made sure to keep her gaze fixed on the food, deciding to go ahead and serve it up before she left.

"Not much," Jade said. "I just figured you hadn't eaten in hours, so . . ."

A chair scraped against the linoleum, and then Jade nearly dropped a plate at the almost breathy groan Lim let out as she took a seat at her little dinette table.

"I just made some Charleston red rice with those smoked sausages you had in there. Have you ever had it?"

Lim shook her head, but the look in her eyes was hungry as she gazed at the steaming plate in front of her. "Did you go shopping?" she asked Jade.

"No, you had basically everything I needed."

There was a long stretch of silence as they sat across from each other in the quiet room. The tentative scraping of Franny's fork on the plate.

"This is really good," Lim murmured.

Jade nodded. "We eat it all the time around here. You've really never had it?"

"No, but I appreciate you making it for me; you really didn't have to."

Jade looked up and caught Lim's eye. Even though her face was clearly tired, her eyes remained bright. Dark brown, they were endless pools of warmth. As much as she knew that she shouldn't sit there and stare at the other woman, she couldn't help it. There wasn't a single part of her that wanted to look anywhere else in that moment.

"It's, uh—" Jade stammered a bit. "It's not a big deal. Didn't even take an hour to get it all put together."

Finally, they broke eye contact when Lim chuckled, looking down at her plate. "It's definitely a big deal," she said. "You know how everyone is always talking about their love languages?"

Jade had no food in her mouth, but suddenly her throat felt too thick to swallow. "Yeah."

"Well, I feel like mine is 'getting food made for me,' whichever one that is."

"Acts of service."

"Yeah." Lim smiled at her. "Just like you washing my dishes so I didn't have to do it later."

"I could have done that for my own benefit. Maybe I couldn't navigate the kitchen with them in the sink."

"Maybe," Lim said with a shrug. "Either way. If you didn't hate me so much, I might be inclined to kiss you after coming in here and seeing that you cooked and straightened up for me."

"I don't hate you," Jade said in a rush. A few weeks ago, she could never have made that admission to the woman herself. No matter how true it was.

"You sure act like it sometimes."

"I have to." Jade shrugged. "I've got to keep my head in the game, and you should too."

Lim turned one side of her mouth up, and her expression transformed into an unconvinced one. "I don't have to pretend to hate you in order to get what I want."

"Maybe not, but you definitely shouldn't be trying to be buddy-buddy with me either," Jade said. Jade placed her elbows on the table, leaning forward. "I'm not trying to be an asshole when I say this either, but this is a lot different from what you're used to. It's summer now and things are relatively chill, but the politics start when the season starts, and people like us have to show no weakness out there. We can't second-guess, we can't falter, and we can't fuck up."

She could tell by the look on Lim's face that she knew what Jade meant when she said *people like us*.

"I'm not saying you're wrong," Lim said. "I just . . . I think there's a way for us to both get what we want without all the animosity."

"I don't agree," Jade said plainly.

"Whether you agree or not doesn't negate the truth, Jade. I see you." Lim pointed a fork at her. "I see right there through the middle of that fragile heart of yours."

Jade didn't know why, but she was willing to play along. "And what do you see?"

Lim hesitated before continuing, "It's like I said earlier, you're just scared. You look at me and all you can see is somebody trying to take something you already view as yours. It doesn't matter how much I try to tell you that it doesn't have to be a competition; you can't see the truth through that fear."

"That's my issue—you keep using the word *truth* like you have all the answers to everything, and I'm not buying it."

Lim shook her head. "I don't have all the answers, I just know that there's a reason you were so adamant about rushing me to the hospital today."

Jade scoffed. "Oh God, don't tell me you think I'm in love with you now or something."

"No, but you do care about me," Lim said, locking eyes with her. "And I think you care about me because as much as you refuse to admit it, you realize that all this shit works better if we do it together. I mean, come on, Jade, once Landry's gone, who's going to be your biggest ally on the team? Which one of those guys is going to step up and have your back when you need it? You thought a town hall was bad, what do you think folks will do if Landry names you as his successor? They're not going to take that lightly. And this one-woman-against-the-world schtick is going to do nothing but burn you out—and fast."

"It ain't just me against the world," Jade argued. "I have people who support me, people who have my back. And plenty of them at that."

Lim's gaze softened. "Maybe so, but they don't know what it's like the way I do," she said gently. "They don't know how it feels to have people assume you're a team mom when you're trying to lead tryouts or condescend to you and pretend like you don't know the game. And that's just the half of it. I know what you've been through because I've been through it in my own way."

Jade thought back to the conversation they'd had at Minnie's, when Lim told her about being assaulted by one of the dads on her old team. She hadn't used that word, but that's what it had been—an assault. It was obvious that Lim didn't have as much coaching experience as Jade; she was good but a bit green around the gills. She still had a lot to learn in the way of leadership. But whatever experience she lacked on the field she sure seemed to make up for in trauma.

Jade wasn't sure if that knowledge was supposed to be comforting or camaraderie-inducing. Because it wasn't. Instead, it just made her sad. The thing about pretending like she was the only one was that it allowed her the ridiculous, naive hope that no other women were experiencing the things she that was—let alone worse.

"I don't know what you want me to say." Jade's words were brittle and weak, even to her own ears.

"You don't need to say anything. Just keep what I said in mind the next time you think of me as your enemy."

Lim stood up, grabbed her empty plate, and put it in the sink, leaning back against it with her arms. Jade didn't know why, but she felt called to stand up too, going to press her back up against the cold refrigerator. She was only a couple of feet away from Lim. The woman had spent all morning sweating on a football field and a lot of her afternoon in an ER; she should have smelled rank. Instead, she smelled heady, deep. No perfume or even shampoo wafted off her body. Jade bit down on the inside of her lip when the desire to bury her nose in Lim's neck rose up fierce and demanding.

Quickly, rudely, she pulled her phone out of her back pocket and sent Olivia a ping to her location and a desperate request for her friend to pick her up. "Five minutes," Olivia responded, apparently just leaving the Piggly Wiggly.

"You're incredibly obstinate. Has anyone ever told you that?" Lim asked her.

"My whole life," Jade said blandly. "I'm not trying to be, I swear.

I just know that no one is going to fight for what I want besides me. I have to go hard, or I won't get anything."

"I'm not denying that," Lim said as she pushed away from the sink and walked forward, stopping close enough for Jade to bury her nose in the little brown birthmark near her collarbone, if she wanted to. "I don't begrudge you for it either. I'm just saying . . . you've been viewing me as an enemy when I could be an ally."

Jade's mouth watered, and she had to swallow. She felt like a teenager locked in a closet with another girl for the first time, eyes wide, anticipating something she was simultaneously desperate for and ignorant of.

What the fuck was happening? How many people had she kissed? Hell, how many people had she fucked? And this woman of all people was making her sweat bullets like some kind of wet-behind-the-ears virgin.

Instinctively, Jade's body leaned in toward Lim's. Millimeters apart, their foreheads practically touched.

"We can't be allies." Jade's voice was a whisper. Anything louder felt like it might disrupt the moment. And as much as she knew they shouldn't have been having it, she didn't want it to end yet.

"Why not?" Lim inched closer until the tip of her nose brushed against Jade's cheek.

The warm flesh, the subtle touch, it made Jade's entire body ache. Her nipples hardened under her shirt. Her belly filled with heat. "Because . . . uh, because . . ."

Lim reached up slowly, putting her hand on the same cheek she'd just brushed her nose against. Her thumb, a little rough to the touch, glided over Jade's warm skin and left a path of heat in its wake.

"Francesca . . ." Jade breathed the name out slowly, enjoying every bit of it on her tongue.

Francesca's eyes sparkled. "You've never called me that before," she said. She leaned in farther, until their lips were almost but not quite touching. "Say it again, Jade. Say my name, please. I need to hear it."

Jade swallowed, her hands instinctively going to rest on Francesca's hips.

"Francesca," she said. "Francesca. Francesca. Franc—"

She was cut off by Francesca pressing their mouths together. Warm lips, a little wet from water, tasting like the dinner she'd just enjoyed. Jade shivered at the feeling, then nearly melted when she felt Francesca's tongue rub against hers.

Their hips bumped together, both of them seeking closeness, needing friction. Little grunts and moans escaped between kisses that turned increasingly frantic.

Jade bit down on Francesca's bottom lip, making her giggle so freely that Jade thought her heart might actually explode out of her chest. She tightened her grip on Francesca's hips. The other woman raised her knee between Jade's slightly parted ones. The second she felt the pressure against her clothed pussy, Jade shuddered, hard.

Their kiss broke naturally, both of them heavy-lidded and breathing hard. Francesca's knee stayed right where it was, and Jade made little effort to stop her own hips from slowly bucking against it.

"You're so fucking sexy," Francesca said to her lowly. "Even in those corny little visors and khaki shorts. How are you so fucking sexy?"

Jade groaned, her panties now completely soaked through. She wouldn't have been surprised if the crotch of said khaki shorts was as well. "Shut up," Jade breathed. "You should see yourself out there with all those tattoos and those long legs. It drives me up a wall every time I see you at practice."

Francesca trailed a few kisses along the underside of Jade's jaw. "We should have done this from the beginning. Saved ourselves the trouble."

Inside, Jade was at war. Feelings versus logic. Future versus now. Everything was gamified, and she had no clue what play to run. This, right now, felt incredible. She didn't think she'd ever had this heat with someone. No one had been able to turn her on like this in years—if ever. Everything about the woman in front of her was completely intoxicating, and she wanted to fall into it, to let herself get high and ride out the effects until she was completely blissed-out and problem-free.

She'd never been a throw-caution-to-the-wind type of person, though. Her plan Bs had plan Bs. If this turned out to be a mistake, she might as well have kissed her chance at head coach goodbye already. And as incredible as she felt here with Francesca, she'd had that dream nearly as long as she'd been alive.

"Fuck," Jade groaned. "Fuuuuck."

Francesca pulled away from where she was working a little passion mark into Jade's neck to catch her eyes. "Is that a good fuck or a bad fuck?"

"It's a . . ." Jade swallowed. "It's a this-feels-too-good-to-be-real fuck."

"It's real." Francesca grinned at her, all teeth. "It's real enough that I can feel how wet you are through your pants." She put a hand flat between Jade's breasts. "I can feel how your heart thumps every time I kiss you."

"I—"

"Tell me what you want, Jade." Francesca's tone was soft. "Just tell me and I'll give it to you. Whatever it is."

Jade had never let sex or the promise of it run or ruin her life. But this felt different. This felt like it was different from just rutting and moaning. She looked into Francesca's eyes and saw something there that made her want to both hide away and show herself.

Jade swallowed, "I want you to—"

She was cut off by the abrasive sound of her phone ringing. It was Olivia. She was parked outside, waiting.

Suddenly, the fog in her head began to clear. All that mist separated from the heat until reality flowed through her senses once more. Francesca Lim stood before her, cheeks flushed, lips swollen, more beautiful than Jade had ever seen anyone look. And she felt the resolve settle in her belly.

She couldn't have her.

Not if she wanted to have her dream too.

Infatuation . . . or lust . . . whatever it was between them was simply not in the game plan.

Jade cleared her throat and straightened her clothes, ignoring the fact that her thighs were soaked when she pressed them together. "This was a mistake, Lim."

Lim took a few steps back from her, nodding. "Right."

"I'm sorry I got all worked up, but we both know . . . this can't happen."

Lim didn't say anything this time, but she turned her head toward the little window in the kitchen, crossing her arms defensively.

"Take care of yourself, okay?" Jade stressed as she put her shoes on by the door. "Get rest. Take the meds the doctor gave you if you need them."

"I'll be fine, Dunn."

That was it. Her tone was definitive and dismissive, and Jade slipped out of the apartment without another word.

Olivia's face was full of questions when she got in the car, but Jade was trying to stop the ache building in her chest. "Later," she told her friend. "I can't—I don't want to talk about it right now."

12

There was an easily recognizable giggle in her room. A high-pitched, childlike sound she'd grown used to and very fond of over the years. One that made her smile through the fogginess of a deep sleep, only to shudder her way out of it completely when cold, sticky fingers pressed against her warm face. Franny reached out just in time to catch a tiny hand and received another flurry of giggles when she clasped it tightly in her own.

"What are you doing here, little girl?" Her voice was thick from eight hours of disuse. "How did you get in my house?"

"Waking you up," Amelia said as if it were the most obvious thing in the world. "My daddy brought me. He says you need to wake up and come make us french toast for traveling so far to see you."

Franny wrapped her arms around her niece's little torso and sat up in bed with her. "You want french toast too, huh?"

She nodded, her hair waving. "With lots of strawberries on top."

"All right, all right, let me get up and out of bed first, and I'll be in there." She laid a kiss on Amelia's forehead, then picked her up and placed her on the ground next to her bed. "Tell your daddy that he's gonna get enough of making demands of me too."

There was pure, unadulterated glee on Amelia's face as she scrambled away. Franny could only imagine how jumbled her message would be once it finally reached her brother.

Fifteen minutes later, with her teeth brushed and face washed, she walked into the kitchen to see Will and Amelia sitting next to each other at her tiny kitchen table. The six-year-old was forcing her father to watch a YouTube video and getting adorably annoyed anytime he looked away from the screen.

"What type of bread do you want me to use for this french toast?" Franny didn't bother with a greeting as she started pulling ingredients out of the fridge.

"Oh, I thought I wasn't allowed to make demands of you," Will said without looking at her. "And here I brought you a bunch of my restaurant's banchan and everything."

Apparently, Amelia *was* getting better at repeating things in their entirety.

"You only ever do that if Umma told you to because she's too far away to do it herself. You want the french toast or not? I don't have anywhere to be for hours, so I can definitely go back to bed."

He had one of those patented older-brother smirks on his face that made Franny want to chuck a loaf of bread at him.

"I think I saw some brioche in the bread box," he said before taking a sip of his coffee. "You think you can get it on the plate in under thirty minutes?"

"Probably." She was already whisking together the eggs and milk. "Hold up. You're leaving right after you eat? You're not even going to help me clean up?"

"Maybe if you'd gotten up earlier than eleven. Amelia has a birthday party she's got to get to by two, and we still have to get the kid a gift," Will said. "I don't know why I had to hear from Mom that you'd gotten hurt, but we basically just drove down to make sure your head was still attached to your shoulders since you won't answer anybody's calls."

Franny groaned, turning up the heat on her gas stove and putting a pat of butter in the skillet. "I told Umma I was fine. It was an accident."

Her brother pursed his lips, clearly unimpressed. "It doesn't matter if it was an accident or not, Fran-Fran. You're out here all alone. We're lucky I can get to you within a couple hours. When something happens, you need to tell us so we can take care of you."

Franny was silent for a few moments as she quickly chopped up a few strawberries. She thought about the situation that had taken place in this very kitchen not two days ago. Jade Dunn making her dinner, them making out, the other woman running away like a bat out of hell.

She also thought about what it had felt like to wake up in her house and feel the comfort of knowing she wasn't the only one there. Jade had fussed over her, forced her to do something for her own good, and taken care of her when it was all said and done.

It had ended like shit, pure shit. But the middle had been pretty unforgettable.

"I had someone to take care of me," she mumbled, almost hoping her brother wouldn't actually decipher the words.

Her luck, apparently, was shit.

"Please tell me it wasn't who I think it was," Will groaned, but his eyes were sharp when they looked at her.

"Who?"

"Little Miss Fair-Trade Coffee Bean, 'I spent a summer touring Southeast Asia and Thai people love me,' one step above white dreads. Please tell me she isn't the one taking care of you."

Franny winced. "No, it's not her."

"Thank God, because she sure did a hell of a number on you the last time."

It wasn't quite an I-told-you-so, but Franny couldn't help but take it as one. She spent a lot of time feeling incredibly ashamed about her relationship with Caroline Bailey. Not just because she'd completely lost herself to it and ended up making stupid decisions, but because Caroline had been a genuinely shitty person as well.

Franny had always thought hippie chicks had a certain charm. With their beaded tote bags and crystals. As it turned out, a lot of them were awful bigots. And Caroline may not have been as brazen, but it was there. In the end, all she'd been was a spoiled, rich white girl with enough money to fill a closet with expensive clothes made to look like rags.

Honestly, more than feeling sad or angry at the way things had gone down between them, thinking about it made Franny cringe.

"Who is taking care of you, then, Gomo?" Her niece apparently had not been so distracted by her tablet that she couldn't keep an ear on the adult conversation.

Franny had finished up breakfast, putting plates in front of her brother and niece while she stood at the counter to eat.

"You know, Amelia, I think now is as good a time as any to remind you that you can always take care of yourself. You don't need anyone else to do it for you," Franny said.

Amelia rolled her eyes. Luckily, Will was too engrossed in smothering his breakfast with syrup to notice and scold her. Franny grinned.

"Daddy takes care of Mommy, though," Amelia argued. "And Mommy always makes sure Daddy eats his lunches and doesn't lose his keys. That's good, right?"

"That's love, baby," Will cut in.

Amelia seemed to think for a few moments. "Why don't you have love, Gomo?"

Will snorted so hard it was a surprise bread didn't come out of his nose.

Franny floundered for a few moments, her jaws flapping like a fish. "I have love."

How was it that a child had the ability to cut so deep?

"No, you don't," Amelia pouted.

Franny walked up to her niece, tickling her in her chair. "You love me, don't you?"

"Yessss." The child giggled uncontrollably. "But you need kissy love. So somebody reminds you to take your phone and puts all the pillows on your bed so you stay sitting up when you're sick."

Franny pulled away, her food suddenly uninteresting in the face of being absolutely eaten up by a child.

She may not have needed kissy love.

But she fucking wanted it.

Franny dressed up for poker on Thursday. Not too much, but it would be the first time she'd seen Jade in a place where she couldn't avoid her since their kiss, and she desperately wanted to . . . well, impress her, if she were being honest.

The other woman had run out of her house so quickly, she'd left no impression that she felt anything other than regret for what had happened. But Franny had been there. She'd felt Jade's lips as they moved against hers, the beating of her heart, the way her skin heated. Hell, she'd come away from it all with a wet spot on her pants that she hadn't put there.

It wasn't as if Franny had expected the kiss to turn the tide on their relationship. Especially not after Jade had reacted to it the way she had. If anything, she'd thought that Jade might just carry on like everything was normal and not acknowledge that it very much was not. Instead, she'd taken to giving Franny the silent treatment. A week of practices and they'd exchanged fewer than five sentences. Jade had even gone so far as to keep as wide a berth as possible. Anytime Franny happened to move close to her, Jade would suddenly find a need to be clear on the other side of the field. It was ridiculous. It was childish. And it was maddening.

Jade Dunn could pretend all she wanted that she was unaffected by her, but Franny knew the truth. The want was mutual. There may have been other things in the way, but that foundational fact was enough to stoke the hope that had started to live in Franny's heart.

Which is why she entered Landry's basement in a short-sleeved, patterned button-down shirt, open just enough to show off her collarbones and the thin gold chain she wore. The shirt was half tucked into a pair of Dickies pants that were cuffed just above her Vans. She let her hair hang freely this time, no makeup or anything, but about a hundred nervous swipes of ChapStick across her lips.

She'd seen the way Jade looked at her every time she wore a shirt like this, and she wanted the other woman absolutely salivating under the dim basement lights.

Only . . . Jade refused to look at her. She was quieter than usual all around, only speaking when spoken to, as the dealer—Landry—doled out their cards and got the game started.

Franny had a hard time focusing on anything other than the woman across from her. She caught every single one of Jade's microexpressions, but she wasn't looking for tells or tics that would help her win the game or show her prowess. Instead, she was looking for something, anything, that would prove Jade was just as affected by Franny as Franny was by her.

Jade gave her less than nothing. She wore a baseball cap that was pulled down so far that it was nearly impossible to see her eyes. Her body shifted in her chair quite often, and Franny could see that her knee was bouncing under the table.

She fought hard not to reach her foot out to still Jade's leg or get her attention. She wasn't prepared for the rejection she might face if she did.

By the time they had a small break for the bathroom and snacks, Franny couldn't have given less of a fuck about the fact that she was nowhere close to winning tonight.

She exchanged a few words with Jeremy Bell about the possibility of having dinner with him and his wife sometime soon. Her response was kind but distracted, and she had to mumble out a quick excuse to walk away the second she spotted Jade alone at the snack table.

"Are you going to avoid me all night?" Franny used all her willpower to keep her voice low and her tone even.

"Are you out of your mind?" Jade was apparently more in the mood to whisper-yell in her direction. "We are not doing this here."

"Where are we supposed to do it, then? It's not like you'll speak to me anywhere else."

"So what? You want everybody to know about this?"

"About what, Jade?" Franny knew she was being obstinate, but so what? She figured it was her turn anyway. "You keep saying there's nothing here but then turn around and avoid me like there is."

"Just keep your damn voice down. And I'm not avoiding you," Jade mumbled, keeping her attention on spreading some chicken salad on a cracker. "I just have nothing to say."

"Oh, that's bullshit," Franny argued. "You sure had plenty to say the other day."

Finally, Jade looked up at her, a small sneer on her face. "Oh, you mean when I realized I'd rather be kissing a wooden post than you."

Franny snorted, her heart thundering. "You are so full of shit. You know just as well as I do that you were fucking gagging for it."

"Gagging for it to be over, more like," Jade snarled.

Franny leaned down until her mouth was at the shell of Jade's ear. "All it would have taken was my fingers under those pants and you would probably still be in my bed right now."

Jade turned her head with a sharp intake of breath. Whatever she was gearing up to say was interrupted by the sharp crack of two hands slapping together. Landry was calling them back to the table. Jade brushed past her without a word.

Franny sniffed, her attitude on ten as she shoved herself back in her seat to continue the game.

The rest of the night passed in a distracted haze. Franny felt like heat was rolling off both her and Jade, the anger making them sloppy. Bad bets, even worse calls. Franny had started with a decent hand but had still managed to lose every cent she'd put in the pot. In the end, it was Coach Byrd, the head of Greenbelt track and field, who had taken the pot.

But she couldn't find it in herself to care. By the time the night was over, all she wanted to do was go home and fall into a bottle of bourbon. The group was exchanging jokes and banter, all casual jabs. Then Landry and Byrd came back from the cashbox with the latter's winnings, and $400 was all it took for the man to turn into an asshole.

"We let you ladies win once," Byrd said, laughter coloring his tone, "but the boys are back now, baby."

She wasn't sure why, but Franny spared a glance at Jade, who looked at her. Slowly, their faces transformed. This time, the heated expressions weren't directed at each other.

"I wonder what it says about the boys that it took both of us," Jade said, directing her finger between herself and Franny, "being extremely distracted for one of you to win with those trash-ass hands."

A few snickers sounded around the table. Behind Byrd, Coach Landry guffawed.

"We've been doing this for weeks, Byrd." Franny laughed condescendingly. "And this is the closest you've gotten to winning since Dunn and I sat our asses down at this table."

Jeremy Bell's answering laugh was gleeful. "We played every week for six months straight last year, and he didn't win once."

"Well, look at that," Jade said as she leaned back in her chair, confident and biting. "It looks like the boys would be better off shutting the hell up."

"I agree," Franny backed her up.

Jade looked over at her, tilting the bill of her cap up just a little bit to send her a wink and a small, appreciative smile.

Franny closed her eyes, taking a screenshot in her mind. It was a small gesture, one that probably wouldn't mean a thing the next time they saw each other. But it meant something to Franny now. Losses be damned.

13

They never had practices on Sundays. Most of the coaches, including Landry, were adamant that Sunday be a day for rest, family, and watching football instead of coaching it. So when 9:00 A.M. on Sunday rolled around, Jade was surprised to find herself getting a call from Coach Landry asking for an all-hands meeting at the school.

They didn't meet on the field but instead in the gym room that had been repurposed as the football team meeting hub. Jade was, as always, the first to arrive, after Landry himself.

"Is everything all right, Coach?" she asked, leaning a hip against his desk with her arms crossed.

Landry's head was buried in a playbook, and when he turned to look at her, she could see the harried look in his eyes. "Season starts in six weeks, and I just got word last night that our first game is against West Beaufort."

For all the pomp and circumstance, Port Royal had nothing on West Beaufort when it came to sheer domination. Greenbelt and West Beaufort had something of a rivalry, dating back decades. But for the past ten years, Greenbelt hadn't won a single game against the other school. The discrepancy couldn't be chalked up to more money and better facilities either. West Beaufort came from the same type of school they did. But there was something about that team and that place and that coach that led them to the championship game time and time again—whether they ended up winning or not.

Normally, Greenbelt played West Beaufort somewhere about half-way through their season. It was about the same time morale started running low for the boys as well.

"This is a good thing," Jade argued.

"How do you figure?"

"We'll have spent months doing nothing but practicing by then, the boys will be ready, eager for a fresh kill. I think West Beaufort is the perfect opponent to win against to show everybody how we're coming this year."

"It could be." Landry put a thumb to his chin. "And if we lose, all that morale could be gone like that," he said, snapping his fingers.

"Then we won't lose." Jade shrugged.

Landry shot her an exasperated look. "Okay, we won't lose."

"No, I'm serious. Look." She bent over, gently easing the play-book from his hands. "The scrimmage showed us that our defense is strong this year. We washed Port Royal because the boys were eager and ready to run those plays into the ground. We have a good base. All we need is a tactic to take us over the edge from great to winning."

"You have one?" Landry asked.

"Not yet, but I will."

Landry kept his eyes on her, narrowing them. "After this is over, stay back for a few minutes, will you? Let's see what you and I can come up with."

"What are you two huddled over there together so close for?" Coach Carr asked good-naturedly. The rest of the coaches slowly filed into the room and took seats. Intent on showing some type of power, Jade stayed standing where she was cocked against Landry's desk until the rest of the guys were sitting.

"Wait, where's Lim?" she asked quietly as Landry stood from his chair, preparing to speak at the front of the room.

"Lim isn't a coach, Dunn," he answered. "She may be trying to get there, but she doesn't actually have what you've already got. Did you forget?"

She had to pause for a moment at the weight of those words. They were an objective truth, one that made it clear that Jade was in the lead in . . . whatever messed-up competition she and Lim had going on. The moment the words left Landry's lips, Jade found herself floating. But a wink after that, she realized that something about the truth of that statement made her feel cold.

She imagined herself on that field, just as she had thousands of times before. Hands on her hips, looking over her domain. She had always imagined herself alone out there. Not necessarily out of a desire for that but out of a belief that she'd have to be alone to make it happen. Jade figured that no one else could ever possibly stand by her side, because they could never understand the unique position she was in.

Stubborn as she knew herself to be, even she could admit that she had been shortsighted in that belief. Lim could understand her. Lim *did* understand her. And that was . . . well, that was something she'd never felt before. It was completely unfamiliar. But the presence of it almost made her ache.

Maybe the sidelines had so much room for a reason.

Jade didn't answer Landry's question. Instead, she took her seat at the front. He had already given her all the information he was sharing with the rest of them. So even though she still listened, she didn't give it all her brain space. The rest was taken up trying to formulate a game plan that would help them beat West Beaufort. But every time she felt like she might have something, she hit a wall. She didn't know what the other team looked like this year. They'd had some powerhouses on the field last year, but as far as she knew, all their starters had graduated. It left a hole in her knowledge of how they were going to play. All she could use to try to formulate a plan were the various ways they'd played in the past, and that wasn't nearly good enough. Greenbelt was beginning to feel like an entirely new team; they were shaping up for something big, and that meant that even the team they were last year had been replaced bit by bit until something better and stronger took its place.

She had no doubt that West Beaufort had been going through a rebirth of their own, and she needed to see it before she could figure out her next steps.

Jade knew what she needed to do next.

She just had no clue how she was going to manage it.

A week later, she was walking through the tight aisles of the hair store. It smelled like Kanekalon and relaxer, and it was cold enough that the dark trench coat she wore felt appropriate despite the fact that it was over ninety degrees outside.

The wall of wigs was completely overwhelming. There were so many of them. All types of colors and lengths and styles. She looked at them for so long that their stoic mannequin heads started to appear terrifying.

After nearly fifteen minutes of deliberation, she chose a wig. A short little sandy-blond bob that would fall just below her chin.

Jade had gotten word from one of her cousins that West Beaufort had a scrimmage against East Beaufort that afternoon. Her plan was to crash it discreetly, find a place on the bleachers off to the side to watch. If anyone were to ask her who she was or why she was there, she planned to mumble something about being a family member of one of the players and promptly slink off.

It was a bold move, one that would catch her a lot of heat if she got caught. But she had no intention of getting caught. The one plus she had was that Beaufort was a good deal bigger than Greenbelt. It wasn't necessarily the type of place where every single person caught every single new face.

She felt like a rogue agent as she took her seat, careful not to get there too early. She had just enough time to get the notes app on her phone up and running before kickoff.

West Beaufort started out strong. She took note of which players started—labeled in her phone by the numbers on their uniforms. Much like Port Royal, they seemed to fall victim to the curse of the "star player." This time, it was their quarterback. The kid was fast on his feet, quick with his weaving, and wily enough to get out of multiple holds. But his grip on the ball was often tenuous. More times than not, Jade watched as he lost control of the ball on his way to making a touchdown.

Sometimes, he was lucky, and no one caught him. Other times, a player from East Beaufort swooped in and turned it into a win for his own team.

Jade made sure to make note of this as well. Greenbelt could absolutely use this information to their advantage. She'd make sure to tell Landry that they needed to have people on the butter-fingered quarterback every second of the game.

The other—possibly most important—thing she learned was that they had a lot of big guys on the field. Because of this, their coach was relying on pure physicality to get ahead.

This wasn't going to work against Greenbelt. They had plenty of big boys of their own, for one. For two, they were going to win through strategy. Outsmarting your opponent was easy when they relied on brute force to win.

There were still four minutes left in the game, but West Beaufort was set to blow their opponents out of the water. Looking to avoid the rush and any suspicion, she slinked out and was in her car and headed back home before the game was even over.

Jade found herself filled with pride on the drive back. A big grin on her face, she was overcome with the knowledge that she had her ace in the hole. As promised as the head coaching position seemed like it would be for her, she could never shake the feeling that she needed some extra kind of edge to really get it.

She knew that what she had done—spying on West Beaufort—maybe toed the line between right and wrong. She hadn't taken game tape; she hadn't been attempting to steal plays or poach players. All she'd done was some field research. A few notes in her phone and a brain full of ideas were what she'd been left with. She felt as if she were on fire, burning with the possibilities of what her newfound information was going to bring her.

Her elation was brought down a bit with thoughts of Francesca Lim. Ever since their kiss, Jade had done everything in her power to avoid the other woman. She didn't know how to handle Lim or where she fit in her life. And after Landry had put certain things into perspective for her, it had become even harder for her to know.

She didn't know what to say to Lim.

Landry had been right. Jade may have been viewing her as an equal competitor, but she'd had the upper hand the entire time. But just like she couldn't shake the feeling that whatever was bubbling between them wasn't going to stop, she couldn't quite get rid of the feeling that she couldn't count the woman out on the professional front either.

There was something dangerous about Francesca Lim. And it wasn't just the way she kissed or moved her hips. Those sparkly smiles of hers held something deeper underneath. Not necessarily sinister or malicious but certainly aware. Since Lim had come to Greenbelt,

Jade had seen her get just about everything she wanted. She always managed to make sure her kids had fresh art supplies every quarter, no matter what the school's budget looked like. She'd even managed to worm her way into Thursday-night poker without much fuss.

The woman seemed to stay quiet and banked on the fact that people found her unassuming. Then, once she caught them unawares, she went in for the kill.

Jade's hands tightened on her steering wheel; she would not be Lim's next kill. Her job would not be Lim's next conquest.

It was possible that Landry had too many irons in the fire to sense when he was being played—when they were all being played. But Jade didn't. The time for avoiding Lim was over. She wasn't about to sit around like some scared little puppy, cowering over a few kisses and strawberry-scented hair.

She had a job to do and games to win. A goddamn title to claim.

She'd been too nice. And with the new information she was sitting on, she knew that she had something special up her sleeve. If she had to bite back to protect it, she would.

14

Despite its incredibly corny name, Flare was the hottest club in town. Well, maybe that was overstating it. Flare had opened only a few months ago and currently held the title of Greenbelt's *only* real club. Residing in an old warehouse, it was four stories high and had clear glass floors that made it feel like you were walking on air. The entire second floor had been decorated to look like some kind of jungle. Lush fake greenery hung in canopies all around; even the private booths and hideaway cabanas were tucked behind thick brush and swaths of gauzy fabric. And the music was loud and thumping, with bass that made Franny move her hips the second she heard it.

Briefly, she wondered who had funded it, but there seemed to be a good deal of money flowing around town these days, and she figured the answer didn't matter as long as she had a good time.

It was a Saturday night, so the space was packed wall-to-wall with people, some she knew and others she didn't. Not even two hours ago, Franny had found herself once again alone in her apartment, itching for something. This time, instead of just going to Minnie's for a slice of cobbler, she'd put on a pair of leather pants, a slinky top, and what some eighteen-year-old on YouTube had referred to as "*Euphoria* makeup." She looked sexy, and she entered the club with every intention of going home with someone.

She was horny and lonely, and it had been far too long since she'd had the company of a beautiful woman between her thighs. For a while, she'd held out hope that Jade Dunn would be that woman. But every day that passed showed her more and more how that was next to impossible. It didn't matter how much Franny wanted her; Jade was too caught up in her own shit to realize or admit that she was just as interested.

So here she was, trying to move on from a thing that had never even started.

Franny made her way to the bar and ordered a vodka cran, and after trying to mix in the heavy pour as much as possible, she leaned against the bar to survey her surroundings.

She hadn't been to a straight club in a very long time. Usually, if she was going for a club experience, she wanted to lose herself and come away with someone else clinging to her. That was a lot harder to do when the subjects of your desire weren't interested on a fundamental level.

Briefly, she considered getting in her car and going to the gay club in Beaufort. But Franny knew that the second she got behind that wheel, she would take her ass to McDonald's and back home again. Her excitement could be bolstered only so much.

She'd work with what she had and be happy about it. A few minutes into her survey of the club, a woman slid into the space at the bar next to her. A white girl with dark eyes and dirty-blond hair, she had a full sleeve of tattoos, a little lace slip dress, and a pair of combat boots.

Franny considered her for a few moments, then smiled at her when they made eye contact. She was pretty. She had a dark little mole next to her mouth and very red lips. The way she smiled, openly, told Franny everything she needed to know.

"Hi," Franny breathed out just loud enough to be heard over the music. "What are you drinking?"

“Rum and Coke,” the woman said, her voice high and cute.

“Can I buy it for you?”

The woman pondered the question for a moment. “Only if you dance with me after.”

Franny laughed, half-tickled, half-relieved. “I can do that.”

She slid some cash over to the bartender and, without even exchanging names, the two women made their way into the crowd. Sufficiently surrounded by people, half-hidden by smoke and strobe lights, they rocked and grinded to the music. The other woman had very little rhythm, but Franny found it more adorable than anything else. Their hips and chests bumped and rubbed together, and every time they got close, Franny could see that they were both breathing hard.

The song changed in a slow transition. It was something that Franny didn’t recognize, but her dance partner sure did because she threw her hands up in joy, sending a large wave of rum and soda all down the front of Franny’s clothes.

“Oh my God,” the girl said. “I’m so sorry. Oh my God.”

Franny grimaced, feeling soaked and sticky. “It’s all right. I just need to clean up.”

“Come on, I know where the bathroom is. I’ll clean you up.” The woman grabbed her hand and began leading her through the crowd.

Franny was glad that the club was still relatively new. This meant that the bathrooms weren’t horrifically gross yet. The woman pushed her back up against the sink and grabbed some paper towels. After wetting them, she started to dab at Franny’s skin, only she wasn’t really hitting the areas that had been affected by the spill, like her chest and breasts. Instead, she focused on Franny’s arms, which were almost completely dry.

In the bright lights of the bathroom, Franny could see that the woman looked much more intoxicated than she had out in the club.

Not stumbling and blackout, but far drunker than Franny was comfortable with.

Suddenly, she felt tired. Maybe this had been a bad idea. Maybe she should have just gone to Minnie's after all.

"Umm." She cleared her throat. "Are you here with anybody?"

"Mm-hmm." The girl nodded, still dabbing at a dry spot near Franny's left elbow. "I'm here with my sisters; my youngest is getting married next week."

"Right." Franny racked her brain, trying to figure out how to get out of this so she could leave without a fuss.

"They must be missing you by now. Maybe you sh—" Franny broke off with a jolt.

The bathroom had been silent and empty, so the sound of the door opening startled them both. A woman in a short bob wig came in, and Franny got a sinking feeling in her stomach as she recognized her.

Jade Dunn.

In a tight pair of cargo pants that cinched at her waist and ankles, open-toed pumps, and a bralette. Her skin was sparkling, and her mouth looked dark and luscious. She was also completely sober from what Franny could tell.

Jade eyed the scene in front of her, her eyes widening as she took in the closeness of the two women.

Franny cleared her throat and straightened up from her position against the sink. Forcing the woman who had been leaning against her to stand upright as well.

"Sorry to interrupt . . ." Jade didn't sound sorry at all.

"You didn't," Franny insisted. "We were just . . . There was a spill and . . ."

"Right," Jade said. She rolled her eyes and sauntered past them into a stall.

"I think I'm okay now," Franny told the other woman quietly. "Thank you for helping me."

The woman nodded. "You want to go back out there and dance some more? We were having a fun time before."

A thump, then a curse sounded from the stall Jade had entered.

"Thank you, but . . . I think I'm going to head home. I'm all sticky now."

The woman nodded, pondering for a second before she shrugged, blew Franny a kiss, and pushed out the door and back into the crowd.

Without thinking, Franny immediately turned the lock on the door behind her. If she had Jade in the same space as she was in, Franny wasn't letting her go without . . . something.

She turned to the sink to wash her hands, biding her time. When Jade exited the stall, Franny was leaning against the sink again with her arms crossed over her chest. Jade was silent as she washed her hands.

"Were you sitting here waiting for me?" Jade finally asked. "Like some kind of fucking stalker?"

"Yes," Franny said simply. "Because you owe me an explanation."

Jade pulled the paper towels out of the dispenser hard. "I don't owe you shit, Lim."

"You come to my house and tuck me in, you clean up, you cook for me, you drive me fucking crazy with your kisses, and then you sit across from me like I don't mean shit to you."

"That's because you don't—"

Franny was up on her in an instant. "Don't fucking lie, Dunn. You're incredibly bad at it. You think I can't tell when a woman wants me? Especially when I want her back?"

Jade's eyes were a lighter brown around the edges of her irises. More caramel than chocolate. But in this moment, they were darker. When Franny's gaze caught on them, she had to fight not to get lost inside. Jade narrowed her eyes and pushed closer until their faces were inches apart.

"I'm going to tell you this one time, Lim, one goddamn time. You don't know me. I don't know what's convinced you that you do, but you don't. So whatever you *think* it is I feel for you, you'd better go back to the drawing board and reassess. Because the only thing on my mind whenever I see you is something between contempt and boredom."

Franny had to push away the hurt that began to well up in her chest at the words. They were hard to hear, but she could see clearly that they weren't true. Jade was panicking at her own feelings—even if that feeling was only lust—and freaking out. Those dark eyes looked wild, almost frenzied. Franny realized that she wasn't going to get to the bottom of this by going toe-to-toe in an argument with the other woman. She was going to have to try a different approach.

So she shrugged. "Maybe that's what's happening in your mind, but your body tells a different story."

Jade started to shake her head, but Franny wasn't letting her get a word in.

"You're breathing all hard, like you just ran five miles." Franny didn't touch Jade, but she hovered her palm a few inches above her bare chest. "I can practically feel your lungs contracting from here. Why is that?"

Jade's lip curled up. "I get passionate when I'm angry."

"Boredom is the opposite of passion," Franny said, smirking. "No one who makes you bored should make your heart beat like this. They probably shouldn't make your nipples so hard either."

"You're fucking infuriating," Jade grunted.

"Fury also isn't a characteristic of boredom." Franny bumped their noses together, expecting Jade to jump back. She didn't. In fact, her eyes almost crossed. "It seems to me that what you really feel when you look at me is . . . want."

Franny reached out and put her hands on opposite sides of the sink behind Jade. "You want me, Jade Dunn. You want me bad."

Jade started to shake her head, the need to deny clear in her eyes, even as it battled with the desire to give in to what she really wanted.

"You want me," Franny whispered, eyes locked on the other woman's plump lips. "Just admit it. Admit you want me, and I'll walk out of h—"

Then there were hands on her waist, pushing and pulling her away and spinning her body around until she was being urged to jump up and sit on the edge of the sink. Jade maneuvered between her thighs, and their mouths were pressed together so comfortably it was as if they'd never stopped kissing in the first place.

"I don't know what the fuck you do to me," Jade said, pulling away too soon to bite and lick at the warm skin of Franny's jaw. "No one has ever . . ."

"Me either," Franny gasped as that warm tongue ventured down to her neck. She was still sticky from the rum and Coke, but Jade seemed to be lapping it up happily.

Jade nipped at the skin of her chest, just above her breasts. "Oh God . . ." she moaned, spreading her legs farther, searching for any kind of friction.

"Can I take them out?" Jade asked her.

"I'll die if you don't."

Without a bra, it was quick maneuvering for Jade to pull her tits out of her shirt; she didn't even have to take it off before her dark nipples were bare and ready. Jade's tongue was on them the second they touched the air, gently biting at one while rubbing the other with her thumb.

Franny writhed above her as if she'd never been touched. Her ass no doubt bruising from the uncomfortable porcelain sink, she still couldn't think of a single place she'd rather be.

Jade pulled back and looked up at her, eyes blazing. "You want to show me how wet you are?"

Before she could even get any words out, Franny's fingers went to the button of her pants, popping it open and shoving them halfway down her thighs. She wore a pair of little see-through black panties, very different from her day-to-day underwear. She was glad that she'd had the foresight to dress for the occasion, because Jade's reaction to them only made Franny's pussy flood even more.

"Touch me," Franny begged.

"I'm touching you now," Jade mumbled around her nipple. She'd cleaned Franny's chest completely with her tongue.

"My pussy, Jade. Touch my pussy."

Jade panted, but apparently found herself just as desperate. One of her hands slowly trailed down Franny's belly, taking a second to circle around, then dip into her belly button. By the time that hand reached the edge of her panties and slipped inside, sliding through her soft curls until they found her clit, Franny was ready to explode.

Jade's fingers had barely circled her four times before her orgasm slammed into her like a freight train. She'd been so wound up for so long that her pussy pulsed and wetted even more as she reached out to cling to the shoulders of the woman touching her.

"What the fuck," she muttered, her thighs tense as she started to come down.

"Are you always this sensitive?" Jade asked her.

"No," Franny panted. "This is all your fault."

Jade's finger stopped its circling to go farther down her slit, collecting her juices and sliding into her sensitive entrance. "I want you to give me another one, Francesca."

Franny threw her head back against the mirror, trying to spread her thighs wider but hindered by the presence of her pants. It was incredibly hot that they were doing this here, in some filthy club bathroom where anybody could find them, but she also wished that they were in bed. That way, they could take their time, spread out, touch, and taste every inch of each other.

"More," she begged, "give me more."

"You want another finger?" Jade's voice was rough.

Franny nodded.

"Greedy fucking pussy," Jade growled, sliding her index finger into Franny, scissoring the two to open her up more before she started fucking her with them in earnest.

Their mouths connected again, sloppy and rough as Franny started to move her hips against Jade's fingers. Franny bit down on Jade's bottom lip, forcing her to hiss, then curl her fingers upward in retaliation. Franny's resulting moan was loud enough to shake the walls, but Jade made no attempt to shush her. Instead, she grinned wolfishly and repeated the action.

"My clit, Jade. Please touch my clit."

"Hush," Jade said, her come-hither motions making Franny's pussy gush. She was so wet she could see streams trailing down the other woman's wrist. It was an incredible thing, to see and smell the evidence of her desire so clearly. "I know what I'm doing."

"You're killing me," Franny groaned.

"No, I'm fucking you."

Jade's mouth latched onto some skin right above Franny's right nipple. Sucking and biting the heated skin until Franny was a bumbling, wailing mess. Jade added a third finger, then, as she got wetter, another and another, until her pussy was filled to the brim with all Jade's fingers up to the knuckle. She was stretched and soaked and deliciously overwhelmed. Every moment, she got closer and closer to her finish. The coil in her belly wound tightly, and as it did, every part of her body tensed up. Her nipples were painfully hard. Her ass was clenched so tight it almost lifted off the sink. Even her toes curled.

"I'm going to come." Her words were strangled and frantic. "I'm going to come, Jade."

There was a hiss from them both as Jade withdrew her thumb from inside Franny's pussy, putting it directly on her clit, circling it at a fast, steady pace. Then her mouth left the spot she'd been focusing on to wrap around a nipple.

Franny opened her eyes and looked down at Jade between her thighs, mouth to her breast, fingers in her cunt. Sensing that she was being watched, Jade looked up, and their gazes caught.

In the end, that was all it took to finish Franny off. Her legs shook, and her pussy seized up around the fingers fucking her into oblivion. She tried to bite down on her lip to keep from being too loud, but it was unavoidable. The sounds that left her lips could have been mistaken for sobs, and from the way tears welled up in the corners of her eyes from the force of her orgasm, they might well have been.

Her teeth chattered as she came down, hissing as Jade slowly extracted her fingers and mouth, giving her overstimulated body a moment of peace.

They didn't take their eyes off each other. Not even when Jade lifted her hand to Franny's mouth, urging her to clean up the mess she'd made. And she did, slowly, achingly.

"You're so beautiful when you come." Jade's voice was still ragged, and she held her body rigid. Franny could see her nipples hard as points beneath her shirt, and she reached out, desperate to make the other woman feel good too.

Jade shook her head, leaning forward to plant a short kiss on her lips. "We've been in here too long."

"Come back to my house."

"I can't. You know I can't."

Franny hung her head, jumping off from the sink and righting her pants again. "You can. You just don't want to."

"Oh, I want to. Trust me."

"So do it, Jade. Come back with me. Let me . . . let me make you feel good."

Jade was silent for a few moments, and Franny watched as the heated lust faded from her eyes second by second. The desire was still there, but her head was obviously clearing the fog it brought.

"We can't do this again," Jade said, "Even if . . . even if it weren't for all the other shit. It's bad business to sleep with a coworker. You know how messy that gets."

Not for the first time, Franny found herself wishing that she and Jade had met under completely different circumstances. In another world, they'd come across each other for the first time in this very club, sneaking off to the bathroom to hook up after grinding too closely to each other. No rivalry, no stakes, just the two of them ready, willing, and able to sink into whatever was obviously between them.

"We can try," Franny said. Her tone was dangerously close to a whine as she reached out, hands on Jade's arms.

Jade shook her head. "I'm sorry."

That right there was a thousand times worse than any slick barb or smart-ass remark she could have made. Franny could see in her eyes that those two words were real and heartily felt. She was sorry too. Sorry that she wanted Jade so much. Sorry that she couldn't manage to convince her that whatever obstacles she thought were between them could be easily hurdled if they just tried.

"Right," Franny said, swallowing. She couldn't find it in herself to beg another woman to love her. The last time she had, she'd been crushed when it hadn't worked. She couldn't do it again, not now.

"We can't do this again," Jade said. "We have to be . . . We just can't."

Franny's throat was too thick to speak, so she nodded.

Jade used a hand to brush some of Franny's hair away from her face, cupping her cheek with that same hand, thumb stroking over her flushed skin. Franny's eyes watered, and she made no effort to hide it.

"Francesca . . ." Jade whispered, pressing the softest, most delicate kiss to Franny's lips before disappearing from the bathroom so quickly Franny was left wondering if any of it had happened at all.

15

We haven't seen you in months, Francesca. Months! The best I get is seeing photos of you on Instabook in those awful little shirts you like wearing."

"Umma, I . . . Wait a minute, how do you know what my Insta is?" Franny pulled her phone away from her ear to immediately set her profile to private. The last thing she needed right now was her mother seeing strap-on memes in her stories.

"Don't worry about all that," the older woman tutted. "Worry about the fact that your mother and father are old people. We could die tomorrow, and then what? You won't even be able to remember what we looked like."

Franny tried not to roll her eyes. Honestly, she did. Her umma, Jihae, was normally very calm and levelheaded, but she had not been happy about her only daughter moving so far away from her. Especially not when her boys had already left.

"Mom, you saw me two months ago, remember? When you came out for Amelia's birthday? I saw you every day for an entire week."

"That's not the same as you being home," she said with a sigh. "I could barely feed you because we had to eat at all those restaurants."

Her mother's voice was low, like she didn't want to admit her disquiet out loud. Franny's exasperation melted away in an instant as she imagined her umma at home alone while her father worked, worrying after a child who didn't call nearly enough.

"I'll come see you then, I promise."

"When?" The woman seemed to perk up immediately.

Franny flipped through the calendar app on her phone. "I'll fly out during a long weekend, but it might be a couple months before I can swing it."

"Why not now? It's summer, and you're a teacher. No work, right?"

"Oh . . . um . . . I don't really have the time to get away right now with football and everything."

"Mmmm."

It was a sound of great disapproval. The only sport her mother had even a modicum of respect for was tennis, and even that was mostly because she thought Serena Williams was "a very nice and talented girl." Franny's love of football had always been a mystery to her umma, and though she had never discouraged it, she'd never shown much interest in it either.

"Oh, please don't make that noise," Franny groaned.

"I just don't understand how a game can keep you away from your family for months."

"I know you don't understand it," Franny said. She rubbed at her temples. "But I need you to at least try to accept that it's an important part of my life."

Her mother was so quiet on the other end that Franny had to make sure the call hadn't dropped.

"Of course I can accept that. I just want to see you at least once before I die."

"Umma, come on now. You are not dying."

"I could be." Jade sniffed. "Then how would you feel?"

Franny ignored that. "You haven't seen Phillip in how long? A year and a half? I bet he doesn't get these talks like I do."

"That's different. Phillip lives across the world."

"And he has more money than all of us! He could afford to come see you every other month if he wanted to," Franny said.

"Well . . ." Her mother simply sniffed again. "I can't believe my Kenneth is the only child of mine who stayed near home. Houston is so big. I was always so sure that when you grew up, you'd find your place here. Now look at you, too far for me to kiss or pinch when I need to. When was the last time I got to make tteok for you all?"

"Look, Mom," Franny began. "I know I don't call as much as I need to, and I promise I will get better at that. I also promise that I will make an actual effort to come visit you and Dad more. But I really hope you don't feel like we don't love you. Because that just isn't true."

"I have good children. Each of you makes me so proud. I don't mean to be so . . . I don't know, overly emotional. I just spent half my life raising you, and sometimes it's hard to look around and see that you don't need me so much anymore."

"We'll always need you," Franny said gently. "But I think you need to find something outside of your kids to love. I mean, Appa has his bird-watching group. You need something like that."

"Maybe I should get a little dog to take care of," she said hesitantly. "Carla next door got one that looks like a little drowned rat when she got divorced, and that thing is all she cares about now."

"Maybe . . . a real hobby and not just something else to take care of."

The older woman made a noncommittal noise. "Maybe I should try to learn about football . . ."

Franny perked up immediately. "Wait, really?"

"Why not? I like learning about new things, and it seems like football is always on the television. I could do some research. Maybe you could help me."

"I . . . would love that, Mom. We could schedule a weekly call to talk about football."

"Mm-hmm, yes, every week we'll call."

"Okay, yeah, that sounds so fun actually," Franny said, meaning it. "We're going to turn you into a football fan. You just have to figure out which team you want to root for."

"I'll support your team!"

"Mom, that's—" Franny paused. She'd been about to correct her, tell her that she should go for the Cowboys or something, but it had suddenly become clear to her what this was. Her mother was trying to connect with her. "That would be great, actually. I would love that."

"Good. We'll call, and you can update me on how things are going with your team."

"And you can update me on your life at the same time."

Her umma's tone was so sincerely happy it almost made Franny's chest cave in. "I love you, Francesca."

"I love you more, Umma."

Franny was surprised that the football team's annual preseason dinner took place at the mayor's mansion. When Landry had invited her, she'd half expected to find a bunch of cafeteria tables at the school covered in white tablecloths. Instead, there was an actual formal dining space fixed up to the gills with fancy cutlery and a chandelier to boot.

The space was so nice that it was almost funny to see it filled with a bunch of teenaged boys who were clearly more comfortable on the field than in their ill-fitting suits. The dinner was a team-only affair, which meant no parents or other outsiders—aside from her. Not even the man whose home they were all in was in attendance. Just four long event tables outfitted with forty-three players and six coaches.

Then there she was, classified as neither of those things, realizing how awkward her in-between position was. And far from where Landry and Jade sat with their heads huddled together. For the first time, Franny felt something close to actual jealousy for the other woman. It was easy for her to see herself as part of the team when she was actually getting work done. Even if her task at practices was nothing but keeping the hydration station stocked, it was important and it made her useful. Here, she was left to pick at her grilled chicken thigh while the real coaches interacted with one another.

Franny stabbed her fork into a fatty piece of her chicken, watching as a hot stream of grease shot out and infected the mashed potatoes next to it. The food looked and smelled fantastic, but her appetite grew less and less intense by the second. Not for the first time that evening, she wondered why she'd even been invited. She considered standing up and leaving right then and there. She imagined she could slip out easily, without anyone even noticing. She could be at home wallowing in her bed in less than ten minutes.

She stabbed the chicken again, seething as that idea left her mind just as quickly as it arrived. She was here, and so she would stay. It didn't matter how deep in her feelings she was; she'd promised herself she would be here for the kids, and she would. Even if she was going to be a big brat about it in her head.

"Hey, Coach."

She didn't think the words were directed at her at first, so she didn't look up from her plate until she felt the sustained presence next to her. Alonzo Holton towered over her, a wide grin across his light brown face. He'd gotten a fresh cut for the night, his curly hair piled at the top of his head but taper-faded at the sides. With his crisp white button-up and tie, he looked so adorable that Franny had to keep herself from cooing in his face.

"I'm not a coach, remember?" she told him with a smile.

The boy just shrugged. "You might as well be."

Her spirits raised in an instant. "You enjoying yourself tonight?"

"The food is really good. You know they told us we can have as many plates as we want? That's crazy. My mom told me I better eat my fill because I'm not going to rummage through her kitchen when I get home," he said.

Franny barked out a laugh. "How many plates have you had so far?"

"Just three." The boy had the nerve to look sheepish.

Franny smiled. "I know we haven't had a chance to talk much one-on-one recently, but Coach Dunn told me your father is doing better. How are your folks doing?"

"They're all right. Daddy had to go back to work the other day, and Mama is mad they wouldn't give him more time, and now we're all having to eat a 'low-cholesterol diet' in support, which means Mama keeps making beans, but," he said, shrugging, "other than that, everything's pretty normal."

She stared him down for a few moments, taking in his posture and checking for any signs of anxiety. But he looked calm and pleasantly happy, even if just for the evening. This made her glad.

"You're a very strong kid, you know that, Alonzo?"

His cheeks went ruddy. "Nah, I'm not."

"You are. All of you are," Franny said, pride filling her voice. "I watch you show up for this team every day, even when you're going through very real things. This team is amazing, and you're an important part of that."

"We just care about the team is all," Alonzo said. "We want to win, and I guess that just means, like, supporting each other or whatever."

"I think supporting each other is a big part of us getting those wins."

He nodded. "That's why we're going to take it all the way this year, because we're the best this team has had in years."

Franny snorted. "What makes you say that?"

"I can feel it, Coach. Can't you?"

He was grinning again, and it was so infectious that she couldn't help but return it. "I think I feel it."

"Oh, come on, you gotta believe it more than that."

"I believe it!" She spoke with all the conviction in her heart.

"That's right." Alonzo nodded like he'd just taught her something. And maybe he had.

"Go on, boy." She laughed again. "Give this pep talk to your teammates too while you're at it."

"I just wanted to come say hi. I'll see you at practice tomorrow, right?"

"I'll be there."

It was ridiculous how much her spirits seemed to lift as she watched the boy walk back to his seat. He'd crossed the room just to talk to her because he'd noticed her sitting there. Maybe it was silly, but it made her feel incredible. If even one person on the team felt like she belonged there as much as she did, that could be enough for her.

There was a renewed sense of purpose inside her that ached for a call to action. So, when she saw the waitstaff reenter the room with carts full of cake and sparkling juice, she made her way over to help distribute. The two college kids in bow ties seemed happy for the help as Franny followed their lead, placing a plate and a long-stemmed glass in front of each person as one came behind to pour the juice. She was still feeling good by the time they got to the coaches' table. Then she made eye contact with Jade for the first time that night, and something else joined the mix of emotions swirling in her belly.

Jade kept her eyes on Franny as she helped serve Landry and the others. Her gaze was dark and hot, and the smirk across her full lips was simply wicked. Franny blinked once, and her mind immediately conjured up the image of Jade all up on her in that dingy club bathroom. Franny recalled the way the other woman's lips felt on hers—hot and dewy and powerful. And she remembered how wet she'd been, dripping all over the fingers Jade pushed in and out of her. The memory came back in full force, with enough strength to make her forget where she was for a few moments.

She dragged her gaze away from Jade's as her chest began to heat up. Once again, she felt the immediate urge to flee. This time because the space was suddenly too crowded and enclosed. Franny swallowed hard in an attempt at keeping her breaths steady. Without thinking, she glanced up again, hoping for a split second that Jade had found something more interesting than her to turn her attention to.

But the smirk was still there waiting for her, and the moment their eyes met for the second time, it turned into a full smile. With Jade's wolfish teeth bared and her eyes hot, all Franny could imagine was what it would feel like to have those teeth sink into her skin. Anywhere. Her lips . . . her neck . . . the insides of her thighs.

That last one was enough to make her body twitch involuntarily, and her bodily instincts made an attempt at extracting her from the situation. Only her uncoordinated movements sent one of her arms out, knocking into the glass of sparkling juice in front of Landry, propelling the liquid right into his lap.

"Ah hell!" The man jumped up, grabbing at his crotch in surprise.

Franny looked on in horror. "Oh my God. I'm so sorry, Coach,

I . . . Here, let me . . ." She snatched up a napkin from the table and, without thinking, tried to go about cleaning him up.

Landry scrambled back even farther. "No, no. Absolutely not," he said, taking the napkin from her. "I've got it."

He trudged off somewhere in search of the bathroom, and Franny was left there mortified as she looked up to see the entire room watching her. Her cheeks flushed, and her stomach roiled with the urge to spill the contents of her dinner out onto the floor.

The sudden screeching of a chair scooting across the hardwood seemed to grab everyone's attention. "If Coach comes back in here busting out of a pair of the mayor's running pants, I better not hear a peep out of y'all," Jade's voice boomed, and the laughter that followed was even louder.

Franny may have known logically that those chuckles weren't aimed at her, but that knowledge did nothing for her humiliation. Giving in to the urge to disappear, she sank slowly into a squat right in front of where Landry's chair had been, resting her forehead against the clothed edge of the table. She took a few deep breaths as she planned her exit. From the dining room and possibly the state.

"You know," Jade began, "I have to admit, when I came here tonight, I considered finding a way to make a fool out of you like I did at bingo that time." She shook her head, returning to her seat. "Turns out, I was thinking too hard, because all I had to do was wait for you to do the dirty work for me."

"It was an accident."

Jade shrugged. "Accident or not, it was funny."

"You know that was your fault," Franny growled.

"How do you figure?"

"You know what you did, Dunn."

"All I did was sit there." Jade smirked again. "It's not my fault the mere sight of me throws you off."

Franny hated how right she was. "You're a fucking nuisance, you know that?"

"And you're an even bigger fool than I thought if that's all it takes to fuck you up."

Franny held back her exasperated huff. Apology to Landry be damned, she shoved herself off the floor and hauled herself out of there. Her hands were clenched on the steering wheel as she drove home, all the anxiety and anger and embarrassment building until tears started to leak out the corners of her eyes. She'd felt far too many opposing emotions for one evening—hell, for one lifetime, honestly.

It almost amazed her how Jade could go from being the type of woman who fucked like she was looking for love at the bottom of Franny's throat to the type of woman to gleefully kick someone when they were down.

Franny waited for it to make her angry. It would have been so much easier to rage and rant. Maybe that way she could take that energy and put it into trying to make Jade feel like the kind of fool she felt like. But the rage didn't come, no matter how hard she tried to coax it out. And when she got home and threw her keys on the coffee table and curled up on her couch, shoes and all, it was something else entirely that she felt.

Despondence. Fear and sadness that she'd completely messed up any small chance she had at being a real part of the team. Along with straight-up despair that the woman she still couldn't help but admire showed no signs of returning those feelings.

The gloom created a fat gray cloud that floated just below her ceiling, bulging and shifting as it filled with more and more water. It was an ominous thing, one that made Franny squeeze her eyes tightly and wrap her arms around her own waist. When the cloud finally broke and the rain fell, her own cries were the thunderclap.

16

Two weeks. That was the amount of time Jade went without even attempting to speak a word to Franny. Seven practices, one car wash, and a team dinner. Two fucking weeks.

It wasn't like the time before either. Where Jade had practically turned her nose up trying to avoid her. This time, she acted as if Franny wasn't there at all—like she was a ghost that Jade could see right through. More than once, Franny had been forced to pinch herself to make sure she was still flesh and bone.

Landry hadn't bestowed any type of coaching title on Franny yet. And while she hadn't expected it so soon, it did frustrate her. Especially because Jade seemed to be thriving. She rarely left Landry's side, walking along the field with her shoulders back and her head high like she was preparing for the power she just knew she was about to gain.

To her credit, Franny was gaining a certain amount of respect herself. Carr had started consulting her on the team's offense. Asking her opinion on which kids she thought should start and what tactics she thought might benefit them most.

Franny found the man a little less than inspiring. While it was clear that he cared, Carr wasn't as enthusiastic as he should have been. He didn't push the players the way they needed to be pushed.

In turn, the boys respected him a little less. They'd started coming to her more and more for correction and advice. She was starting to feel like a real coach again, and it felt incredible. So much so that she had no qualms about whatever this little unpaid internship of hers was.

July was nearly over, and school would be starting up soon. Not long after, they would have their first game. Franny knew that everything would come to a head then. But the buildup was starting to make her itch with anticipation. Landry had begun to hunker down more and more, keeping them later for practices and demanding they came earlier. Jade was right there with him—the first to show up and the last to leave. Every time she stepped foot on that field, she was serious about it.

Franny had no choice but to respect it. She was incredible to watch in action, that woman. She provided a strong, steady presence for the players. Landry had started to lean on her more and more. Franny had even seen her holding Landry's playbook a few times.

She figured if, after the first game of the season, Landry didn't let everyone know that Jade Dunn would become Greenbelt Senior High's new varsity football coach, then he wasn't leaving.

Even the other coaches could see that there was no other competitor on her level.

Franny just didn't understand why Jade couldn't see it herself. She kept telling herself that it didn't matter, ultimately, what Jade thought or felt. The woman was hell-bent on pretending that Franny didn't exist, so why should Franny spend any of her brain space focused on her?

It was easier said than done.

These days, it felt like she spent a great deal of time thinking about Jade. The more the other woman ignored her, the more intense her longing became. She replayed her memories of their time in the club bathroom on a loop. And more than that, she fantasized about scenarios they hadn't been in. Not just sexual ones either. Things like cooking dinner together and going to the grocery store. She tried her hardest to keep the images at bay, but every now and again one slipped through and made her stomach roil.

She fought the urge to just walk up to Jade every time she saw her. Her time in the shower was spent creating scenarios in her head in which she had her chance to speak her mind. Franny imagined herself stopping Jade in her tracks, shaking her, forcing her to listen and understand as she relayed her feelings.

To her, it seemed so clear what those feelings were now. After months and months of trying to figure them out, all it had taken was one earth-shattering orgasm to put things into perspective.

Somewhere, somehow, among all the barbs and sneers, she'd managed to fall for Jade Dunn. The other woman was strong and competent, driven and focused. The shell she kept around her was hard as granite, but it had plenty of cracks. Franny saw it every time her gaze softened when one of the boys talked to her. She saw it in the way she'd lovingly joked with her friend at Minnie's.

There was passion in that woman that had been locked away and was yearning to be free. The way her hands knew exactly how to caress and squeeze and flat-out please Franny's body proved that. And Franny had wanted nothing more than to hand her own heart right over for the taking.

Now Franny stood next to Coach Carr, her arms crossed over her chest like she was trying to keep her heart stuffed inside. It was in the eighties today, but goose bumps raised along her skin. She'd caught a chill weeks ago and hadn't been able to get rid of it since, no matter how high she cranked up her heated blanket.

A few yards away, Jade and Landry were huddled over his big blue playbook. In front of them all, the players were just finishing up their drills. They'd been at it for almost three hours, and some of the earlier parents had started to arrive for pickup. Once the last whistle was blown, half the boys threw themselves onto the ground on their backs, sweating and panting.

Franny moved onto the field to check on them. Making sure their skin, even if tired, wasn't sallow or sunken. They all looked thoroughly exhausted but pleased with themselves. That seemed to be a running theme of everyone on the team—coaches and players alike. Spirits were high, and it was impossible not to feel the difference in the air. Everyone—including her—was determined to win. Not just the season opening game but the season itself. Greenbelt was going all out for the victory. Their victory as a collective, yes, but also the small victories everyone had to reach out and grab for themselves.

She thought about Alonzo, crying on the sidelines as he struggled with the way his team and his personal life would sometimes butt heads. A kid with parents forced to work too hard. A family dealing with the aftermath of a terrifying health scare for one of its members. How afraid he must have been; how hopeful he always seemed to remain above it all. A win would help show Alonzo that everything he fought for could be achievable, that he could accomplish great things. There were countless stories like his on their team, and each one of them was just as deserving as the next of a happy ending.

After helping guide the boys off the field toward their water bottles and encouraging them to hydrate for the hundredth time that day, she spared another glance at Jade. This time, she was talking to a parent. A father in a pair of shin-length denim shorts with a Bluetooth the size of her cell phone in his ear. Jade's face was impassive, but her body was full of nervous energy as she talked. Franny noticed the way her clothes shifted as she moved, the way her side profile transformed with every word.

She thought of the Jade from two weeks ago, the one whose dark eyes glinted as they delighted in Franny's humiliation. Every ounce of that woman seemed to have disappeared as she spoke to the man. Jade may have been cruel then, sure, but she'd been confident too. This version of her had her shoulders drawn inward. From the side, her face looked like she was trying her hardest not to let any hint of sourness show. The man spoke with his hands, making himself look bigger, as if he were trying to scare off a bear. Jade looked like she was staring one down.

Even if it didn't seem like Jade was in immediate danger, it was clear that the man was being unkind to her. Franny thought about going over to have her back, to say something in her defense. But she paused, unsure if Jade would have done the same for her. It made her feel awful to even think such a thing, but maybe Jade was right.

Maybe she did need to be more brutal if she wanted to get her hands on her own little victory.

Maybe Jade was wrong, and all Franny really wanted was a bit of payback for her own pain and suffering.

Or maybe . . . maybe Franny was just too wounded and sad to do anything but turn away.

"You were right," Franny said.

She and the old gals took up two tables at the little food court in the bowling alley, and Franny had just bowled a strong 120, so she was celebrating her success with a bacon double cheeseburger. "I do like her."

Beside her, picking at a veggie burger, Charlie's eyes went sparkly. "The girl you work with?"

Franny nodded. "Yeah, I . . ." She trailed off. The truth was that even through her pain, she couldn't stop thinking about Jade. All she could see were possibilities. Lives they could have with each other if things were different. But she wasn't ready to say all that yet. Saying it out loud would cement it in her head, and she needed this to be a safe delusion right now. So she cleared her throat and just said, "I really, really like her is all."

The women seemed to catch her drift, nodding.

"I hate to say 'I told you so,' but there's just something about working with somebody that helps you get to the nitty-gritty." Stella seemed completely ecstatic to have been right.

Barb grunted, just as unconvinced as she had been when they'd discussed this previously. "That nitty-gritty don't lead to nothing good. Trust me."

"Um . . ." Franny eyed the older woman. "Is there a story here I'm missing? Because it already sounds like one I want to hear."

"Oh boy, is there." Stella chuckled around her straw.

"Hush, you," Barb softly scolded her wife before pointing a finger at Franny, all businesslike. "I'm telling you, nothing good comes from shitting where you eat. That's how I ended up miserable and married to some man for fifteen years."

"I think that might have just been a delayed lesbian awakening, honey," Charlie said with a giggle.

"Well, that too," Barb agreed, sitting back and crossing her arms over her chest. "When I was twenty, I was the only woman welder at a factory in Georgia. There was one guy in the whole place who was decent to me. It started out innocent, we'd eat our lunches together, then we started getting together outside of work. When he asked me to be his damn girlfriend, I figured it made sense because I damn near already was. He was a miserable sod. I worked with him for over a decade and went home with him every day. It was awful. I was already miserable, and I could never get a break from it either. I think it ends up like that more times than not."

Janet sighed. "I'm not discounting Barb's experience, but for a different perspective, my Connie and I worked at the bank right there next to each other for three years after we got together. We moved in quick, you know how it goes, but I loved being able to spend all my time with her. When she got hired on somewhere else, I missed her every day."

"My experience is tainted because I did it with somebody I didn't love," Barb said. "But I do think you should consider how messy it can get if the shit hits the fan."

"You sure are cursing a lot tonight," Stella scolded her wife jokingly.

"Trust me, I've thought about it." Franny groaned. "I can hardly think about anything else these days."

Barb nodded. "That's all I'm saying. Don't jump into something fool-headed and forget yourself."

"So tell us how it all happened, then!" Janet clapped excitedly. "Are you going to bring her to bowling?"

"Oh, we aren't together," Franny said. She took a sip of her Sprite. "Actually, she still kind of hates me."

Charlie shook her head. "I don't understand you young people at all. She hates you. You love her. How in the hell is that supposed to work out?"

"Well, she doesn't *actually* hate me. She's just trying to convince herself that she does. I think she likes me too. In fact, I know she does."

Five pairs of eyes squinted in her direction, and Franny purposely kept hers on her food.

"You slept with her, didn't you?" Carmella choked the words out between chuckles.

Franny groaned, leaning in to knock her forehead against the table a few times. It was gross and sticky, but it felt almost deserved. "Yes."

"They refuse to learn," Barb tossed in with her grumbly voice.

"Ohhh," Stella admonished her wife. "Don't you remember being all young and horny?"

"I sure do," Carmella said. "As far as sex mistakes go, this one feels pretty mild compared to the ones I've got under my belt."

"Oh, girl." Charlie snorted. "I've got stories for days if we want to talk about sex regrets. One time in '87, I took a bus all the way to Topeka, Kansas, to go to a lesbian orgy in a converted barn house, and I ended up sleeping with a butcher's wife in the back of his shop instead."

"Here we go." Barb sighed.

Franny's brows furrowed. "How in the hell did you manage that?"

Charlie got a faraway look in her eyes as she recalled the tale. "Well, I figured I shouldn't show up to the party empty-handed, so I stopped at the butcher's to see if I could get some salami or something. The gorgeous butch woman working the counter had the most muscular forearms and she was tearing into some hunk of meat or other with a big knife, and I just about fell in love right there. It all happened so quick after that, I don't know quite how. But the next thing I know, her old man was chasing me down the street with the cleaver."

The group was silent as they tried to process the wild-ass story they'd just heard.

"Did you ever make it to the party?" Janet finally asked.

"Oh yes." The dreamy look was back in Charlie's eyes. "I ended up getting passed around like a pack of cigarettes. It was incredible."

"You . . . might have me beat there." Franny laughed. "But I've made plenty of bad sex decisions in my time, trust me. Just none that felt this bad."

"Well, how good was the sex?" Janet asked.

Franny's eyes went wide. "You'd have thought she'd pulled some acrobatic shit with the way I acted. I've never felt anything like it."

"Now look at you." Janet laughed along with the other ladies. "Crying over a few fingers."

"Allll the fingers." Franny groaned again.

"Oh yeah, that'll definitely do it." Charlie laughed even louder. "So, what are you going to do?"

"I mean . . . I was hoping y'all could help me figure it out."

The table went completely silent for a few moments, and Franny began to lose hope.

"Do you want this girl, Francesca?" Carmella asked.

She nodded.

"And do you think she wants you back?"

That gave her pause. She did, she really, genuinely did believe so. But there was still doubt inside her. A small feeling that maybe whatever she thought Jade felt for her was all in her head. The last thing she wanted was to be wrong and end up looking like a creep.

Still, her gut didn't feel like it was lying to her. She closed her eyes for a second, picturing Jade's face. A floating head, almost comical, appeared in her mind. This wasn't daydreaming; it wasn't her imagination running away with her. She was replaying the mental snapshots she'd taken of every face Jade had ever made at her. Not a single one registered as full of hatred or disinterest. The last thing she saw before she shook her head to clear the picture was the way Jade had looked at her before she walked out of the bathroom at the club. Soft, longing, regretful.

That was what she'd cling to.

"Yes," Franny finally answered. "I think she does."

"Well then, in my eyes, there's only one way to play it. You've just got to tell her," Carmella said.

"What?" Franny's voice was much louder than she meant for it to be.

"Love isn't a game, girlie." From the murmurs that sounded

around the table, the rest of the ladies agreed with Carmella's statement. "You can't win at it. There's nothing you can do to make someone give in to it if they don't want to. All you can do is sit down with the girl, tell her how you feel, and hope like hell that she's ready to jump in with you."

"That's . . ." It sounded so obvious. "There's no way that's going to work."

"You'll never know if you don't try," Charlie said with a shrug. "Besides, Carmella is right. The girl either loves you or she doesn't. But it's better to find out than spend the rest of your life wondering about it. Trust me."

Franny didn't have much to say to that, so she said nothing. And after a while, the conversation at the table resumed, switching to something else. Franny stayed silent. Her mind was whirring. Suddenly, those in-shower thought experiments she'd done had been rendered useless. The entire script had flipped, and she had to come up with something else.

It scared her shitless, the thought that she'd just go up to Jade and, instead of confronting her about her avoidance, confess her feelings. Could she handle another rejection? Could she handle a life spent not knowing?

Her burger became unappetizing as her stomach started doing flips. The old gals were right. Totally and completely. Whether she wanted to admit it or not, whatever game she and Jade had been playing with each other needed to come to an end. For both of their sakes. Franny just hadn't expected that she'd be the one throwing in the towel with so much time left on the clock.

17

For the first time in months, the halls of Greenbelt Senior High were filled with people. It wasn't development week yet, but teachers had flooded the dual-floored school for a late-summer meeting called by Principal Coleman. The meeting had been long and mostly boring, with the announcement of upcoming workshops and new changes for the year. They'd also gotten their new classroom assignments. Thankfully, Jade's room hadn't changed once in the years she'd been teaching there. So instead of seeking out the real estate of her new digs like many of her coworkers, she'd made her way to Landry's office.

Earlier that morning, she'd gotten an email—rather than a text message, which was strange—from the man, asking that she meet with him after the staff gathering. That was all the information he'd provided—nothing more, nothing less. Jade had spent all morning trying to figure out what he wanted to speak with her about. The school year started in a couple of weeks, and their season opener was only a week after that. He hadn't planned to name his successor until then, but maybe he'd decided to break the news early.

She felt like she was walking on a cloud as she floated down the hall, fully preparing herself to receive what would be the best news of her life.

Landry's small office was on the basement level of the school, next to the large utility office the groundskeeper and maintenance staff worked out of. Like always, she entered without knocking. Landry was sitting at his desk, readers perched on his red nose as he typed at his computer.

From across the room, Jade could see that the man looked unhappy. She knew that the logistics were his least favorite part of the job. She also knew that there were quite a bit of logistics involved. Planning and scheduling, communicating with other coaches as well as their own principal, making sure stipends for the other coaches were handled appropriately, and dealing with the questions, concerns, and complaints of parents.

Taking on this job in addition to her current duties as a teacher would be grueling for a good part of the year. But she was ready for it. The constant emails, the late nights, grading and playmaking. She was hungry for it, even, salivating.

"Hey, Coach," she said softly, trying not to startle him.

Landry looked away from the computer slowly, and Jade could immediately tell by the way he took his readers off and tossed them across his desk that he hadn't called her in here for the reason she'd thought.

His face was contorted in frustration—no, anger. He'd never been angry with her, not once since she'd started working under him. In an instant, she felt like a child about to be scolded for doing something bad.

Only she had no idea what she'd done wrong.

"What in the hell were you thinking, Dunn?" His tone was furious.

"I—" Jade swallowed, racking her brain. "I don't know what you mean, Coach."

Landry picked up his phone, tapped a few things into the screen, then turned it around to face her. She had to walk over to him to get a closer look. The second she started to make out the image, her stomach seized up.

It was her at the West Beaufort game, sitting on the bleachers in her wig, not looking nearly as inconspicuous as she'd thought.

"Coach, I—" She broke off, wanting to explain, but the words wouldn't come.

"Somebody sent me this clip of you snuck into one of their games dressed up like goddamn Batman."

Landry handed her the device, and her throat dropped into her stomach when she saw herself on the screen. Even with the footage blurred and shaky and the wig firmly on her head, it looked exactly like her. She was embarrassed and ashamed. She felt incredibly silly. How could she have thought that had been a good idea?

Her pain was only made worse when she saw the text message that accompanied the footage. The gray bubble on Landry's phone contained large black letters that read, "This is one of yours, right? See what happens when you let little girls on the field?"

It was a vile, disgusting string of words. So demeaning and degrading it made bile rise in her throat. She didn't recognize the name of the man who'd sent it, but an intense hatred from him settled over her.

"Who is that?" she asked.

"Don't worry about that. Worry about the fact that I'm about five seconds away from kicking your ass off my coaching staff right now. Do you have any idea how this makes us look, Dunn?"

Tears immediately sprang to her eyes, and she had to blink rapidly to get them gone. "How it makes *you* look? Do you see those disgusting things he said about *me*?"

"I got on him about that, trust me," Landry argued. "He ain't right for what he said, but . . ."

"'But'?" Jade's voice went steely. "What do you mean, 'but'?"

"Maybe you aren't ready for this after all, Dunn. This was a major fuckup. It makes me look bad, and it makes you look even worse."

"I was just trying to see how they played," she argued. "The pros do it all the time, studying their opponents' game tapes."

Landry sighed, tossing his phone on the desk next to his glasses. "This isn't the pros, Dunn. This is Greenbelt."

"I didn't think it was that bad."

"So why the disguise?"

Jade didn't have an adequate answer for that.

"Exactly," he said, heated. "Because you knew it was way out of bounds. Not only were you out of line, but you went behind my back with it."

"Coach, I may have been out of line, but I wasn't trying to go behind your back. I was . . . I was trying to show some initiative."

"So why didn't you immediately come to me with what you found?"

Jade winced. "I was waiting for the right time . . ."

When she said it out loud, it felt ridiculously insufficient. In her head, she'd had it all figured out. She was going to approach him before practice one day this week and tell him what she'd found. She imagined showing him her notes, and after he realized that they had all the tools necessary to win against West Beaufort, he'd be so overcome with joy that he'd give her the job right then and there.

Instead, Landry sat in front of her turning progressively redder in the face and neck, and she realized that she'd made a huge misstep. She started to sweat as she speculated about what he would do next. Was he going to fire her?

"Coach." Jade choked the word out. "I'm so sorry. I didn't—"

Landry held up a hand to stop her in her tracks. "Go home, Dunn. Don't come to poker tomorrow night. I'll figure out what to do with you on Friday at practice. Just—just go for now."

Throat thick and tears welling up in the corners of her eyes, Jade all but ran from the office. She didn't stop to say goodbye to any of her coworkers as she rushed to her car. Despite her lack of tinted windows, she pretended like no one could see her as she finally let her tears fall, head against the steering wheel.

This entire time, she'd thought that it would be some outside force that would ultimately keep her from her dream. Lim's mere presence, the opinions of the good ol' boys up top, even Landry himself deciding she wasn't ready. Instead, she had turned out to be the maker of her own demise.

What *had* she been thinking?

She hadn't had an answer to that question when Landry had asked her mere minutes ago, and she didn't have one now, not really.

She supposed she'd just been trying to give herself and her team an edge. She hadn't thought about the consequences. She hadn't even anticipated that Landry would react in any way other than thankful.

She banged her forehead against the steering wheel a couple of times, only stopping when it seemed like she might do actual damage to the skin of her forehead. Pulling herself up, she sniffed, wiped her nose with one of the fast-food napkins she kept in her glove box, and blinked her tears away.

Jade spent the entire drive back to her house choking on her own bad decisions.

Later that evening, she sat in the living room of her little house, surrounded by her friends. Miri was next to her on the couch, Olivia sat in the patterned chair on the other side of the coffee table, and Aja sprawled out on the floor in front of them. They'd just finished massively overeating a large Chinese food feast, and Jade was so full of dumplings and spare ribs that her tears had finally managed to dry up.

"I literally fucked my entire life up with a wig." She spoke the words into a small tub of sweet-and-sour sauce. "And then had the nerve to wear it to the club like I'd really done something."

"You did not fuck your life up," Miri argued. "Nothing's happened yet."

"You should have seen the way Landry looked at me. I've never had someone be so disappointed with me in my entire life."

Her friends exchanged a few knowing glances with one another before Miri took a big, heaving sigh. "Jade, you know you can't actually do everything right, don't you?"

Her brows furrowed. "What do you mean?"

"She means," Aja interjected, "that fucking up is a natural part of life. You can't avoid it."

"I could have avoided this."

Aja shrugged. "Sure, but the fact of the matter is that you haven't actually ruined your life; you just feel like you have. Which, to be fair, is valid. But you didn't hurt anyone. You didn't scam anyone."

"I could have hurt the team," Jade said, distressed.

"We're not saying that's not true," Miri cut in. "We're not even saying you were in the right here. We just don't want you to beat yourself to death over one little mistake."

Jade bit down on her lip, unsure of what to say but almost completely disagreeing with her friends' assessment of the situation. Her entire life, she'd been able to clearly see every option laid out in front of her. She could see the paths she would need to take to get where she wanted. Hell, a lot of the time, she could accurately predict the obstacles in her way.

Now when she closed her eyes and tried to imagine a way forward, it was dark. Nothing but blackness behind her eyes. Everything felt so bleak. Her heart had been in her stomach since early that afternoon, and she had no idea how to get it out.

Without this dream, she didn't fully know who she was or what she was doing. This had been a lifelong goal, yes, but for the past five years, she'd been so single-mindedly focused on it that she hadn't made much room in her life for anything else. She'd eschewed everything, choosing to eat, live, and breathe her dream. As a result, once the carpet seemed to be getting pulled out from under her, she was left to consider the fact that she had nothing to fall back on. Not love or romantic prospects, not even a real plan B.

It was so bizarre, when your dream wasn't tied to financial success or ruin. Money had never been the motivating factor for her, not in this. Largely because the head coach's yearly stipend would be barely enough to put a down payment on a new car. It was all pride and glory. Somehow, that made it even worse.

"I just don't know what I'm supposed to do if he fires me," she said, voice wobbly.

"Have you considered coaching for another team?" Olivia asked.

Jade shook her head profusely. "I could never. Greenbelt is my home. It's my team. I could never see myself coaching anywhere else."

The tears were back again as she thought about the boys and their sweating faces staring up at her, eager and expectant. She knew every single one of them by name. Vonte with his anxious smiles and big laughs, Alonzo with his kind eyes, Jaxon and the way he seemed to move everywhere by running.

She knew their families, what their home lives were like, what their GPAs were. Many of them had been with her for years; they had real relationships. How was she supposed to give that up?

Aja, ever sweet and optimistic, smiled at her gently. "Your boss hasn't made any decisions yet, remember? You haven't lost anything as of now."

That should have been a comfort to her, but it wasn't. Jade probably would have preferred it if he'd just cut the cord in that moment. Instead, she'd been left to wait with bated breath for the other shoe to drop. Nothing was worse than anticipation. Being as tight as a drum and left to wait and wait and wait. Especially when the thing you were waiting for was earth-shatteringly bad news.

"Yeah." Jade's voice was ragged. She didn't know what else to say.

Miri reached over and wrapped an arm around Jade's shoulders, pulling her in until Jade put her head in the other woman's lap.

"Everything is going to be okay, Jadey," she said, her fingers running gently along Jade's eyebrows. "No matter what happens, everything is going to be okay."

Jade closed her eyes slowly, suddenly feeling incredibly tired. It was as if she'd just run a mile in the summer heat with cinder blocks strapped to her ankles. And it felt like she'd been doing it for months. Briefly, an image of Forrest Gump flashed in her mind. With those raggedy tennis shoes and that big beard, he hadn't seemed nearly as tired as she felt.

Her entire body felt warm and weighed down, and the beginning of a fitful sleep started to descend upon her. She wanted to fight it, to sit up and scream and yell and cry some more. But she didn't have the strength to do anything but lie there in her best friend's arms.

"I'm scared," she mumbled before she dozed off. "I'm just so scared."

18

The thick cloud of cigar smoke wafting around Landry's basement was almost too much for Franny to handle. The guys had been puffing away since before she'd shown up. The scent was thick and sweet, and even though she'd declined to participate, she could taste the cigars in the back of her throat every time she so much as breathed in.

The past two weeks, she and Jade had sat across from each other at the round poker table, not speaking, barely acknowledging each other's presence. This time, though, Jade wasn't there at all, and Franny found herself incredibly distracted by that fact.

At first, she thought the other woman might just be late. It was extremely unlike her, but shit happened. Then the minutes kept ticking by. And once Landry decided to start the game with nary a mention of her, Franny figured she genuinely wasn't coming. That was when she started to feel uneasy.

It was weird being the only woman in the room. Especially during such a competitive game. The shit-talking seemed to be even more intense than usual, which wasn't at all a problem in and of itself, just . . . weird. She thought back to weeks before, when Byrd had tried to let off some smart-ass sexist remark and Jade had immediately called him out on it. Franny had been right there to back her up, and together they'd shown him that they were absolutely not going to take any shit.

Franny was used to being the only woman in the group. Not in her personal life, God forbid. But professionally. Jade hadn't been wrong when she'd argued that one of them being accepted on the field was something close to a miracle, but two of them . . . Honestly, Franny had never experienced it.

She used to be more familiar with the lonely nature of it, but recently, she'd gotten used to having someone else by her side. Even if she and Jade were supposed to be rivals, even if Jade was determined to dislike her, there was still a certain level of respect to be had. Whether it was on the field or at poker, having another woman around meant more to Franny than she'd realized. At least until that other woman wasn't there.

She found herself quieter than usual during the game, but she noticed that Landry was quiet as well. That was her second clue that something was wrong. She kept one eye on the man the entire time, noticing the delay in his responses when someone addressed him and his lack of enthusiasm, even when it seemed like he had the upper hand.

Winning the game was the furthest thing from her mind, but she'd been cursed with a fantastic hand. Her first win had come as such a relief; she'd felt like she was doing what she'd been there to do—show that she deserved the space she wanted to take up. Now she'd realized that she was just as competent—if not more so—than everyone at the table. After a certain amount of time, she'd only been showing up to Thursday-night poker as an excuse to be in the same room as Jade.

The pot was a little smaller today with everyone pinching extra pennies for back-to-school activities, but she'd taken it all with little fanfare. Even with her lack of excitement, she'd reveled in the disappointed, frustrated faces of the other men at the table. The only ones who seemed unaffected were Jeremy Bell and Landry. Bell probably because the dude didn't have a mean-spirited bone in his body anyway. And Landry because he was obviously too distracted to give a shit.

After the game, a few of the guys headed out immediately, but Franny lagged behind, running through the motions of helping clean up as an excuse to get Landry alone to talk. It took almost an hour of near silence before she and the coach were the only two left in the basement.

She heaved a breath as she tied up the black trash bag that held their used red plastic cups and paper plates.

"Is, uh . . . is everything all right, Coach?" Her voice was rough from lack of use.

Landry's brow quirked. "What do you mean?"

Franny shrugged. "You were awfully quiet tonight and, well, Dunn isn't here, which is definitely out of character for her. So I was just wondering if there were any developments I should know about."

Landry sighed, a ragged noise that she could tell came from the deep confines of his belly. He crossed his arms over his chest and looked at her for a few long beats. "Lim, what do you want from this?"

She was taken aback by the question. Honestly, she'd sooner expect him to tell her to fuck off than ask her something like that.

"Out of . . . playing poker, you mean?" she asked pathetically.

"Out of playing poker, out of working with the team, out of being here and asking me what you're asking me."

"I love football, sir."

"We all love football, Lim," he said. "Everybody out on that field every day loves football, probably more than they should, to be honest. But I can think of only two people who would show up on the field every day and work like you work without the promise of a title, without the respect it affords them, without the stipend they get with their paychecks. One of those people is me, and you know who the other one is."

She found herself at a loss for words. Her lips opened slightly, then pressed together as she realized she didn't know what to say. Every answer that popped into her head felt almost comically insufficient. She immediately thought that this was some sort of test or trick question. That maybe Landry was looking for her to say something specific. A response that would make him go to whatever gilded box he kept his whistle in and hand it over to her like a crown of precious jewels.

Franny looked at him—really looked at him—and saw the wrinkles in his weatherworn forehead and the way he seemed to sigh with every breath he took. He did not look like a man who was staring down the barrel of naming a successor. And if Franny were being honest, she knew that. His job had never been hers. Partly because it had always belonged to someone else, and partly because Franny had never actually been gunning for it in the first place.

"I want a place on this team," she answered finally, keeping her eyes on his. "I want the community and the camaraderie. I want to guide the kids. I want to win. I want to get my bearings and my experience in the hopes that someday I might have what Dunn is about to have."

With yet another sigh, Landry moved over to the corner of the room where the small bar was. Normally, libations for poker night were dad beers provided by "the house." Every now and again, someone would bring a bottle of bourbon to sip out of red plastic cups. They'd never been offered anything from the actual bar. The man picked up a decanter of what she assumed to be scotch and poured a few fingers into a crystal-clear glass before he looked up and offered it to her.

She had to bite down the no that rose in her throat. Not because she was against sharing a drink with him but because scotch had always tasted to her like burnt gasoline. She recognized the symbolism of his offer, though. Like something out of a coming-of-age movie, Franny was being silently invited to partake in some kind of rite of passage. So she reached out and took it, immediately knocking a sip back. Pushing down an intense grimace, she forced a small grateful smile and said, "This is a good year."

"I think I've had this bottle longer than you and Dunn have been alive." He chuckled. "Which is why I'm trying my hardest to give you both a bit of grace, but goddamn do you make it hard."

Franny's eyebrows furrowed. "What have we done that needs grace-giving?"

Landry looked at her as if she'd just walked into a glass wall. "Oh, you don't know?"

She shook her head.

"Maybe we can start with whatever the hell is clearly going on between y'all before we get to anything else."

Her lips flapped open in surprise. "Coach . . . nothing is going on between me and Dunn. Like, truly, nothing. I mean, nothing like *that* anyway."

"You believe that just as much as I do," he said. "Which means not at all. I ain't saying I understand what it is or why, but all that bickering back and forth isn't fooling anybody."

Honestly, Franny hadn't considered that other people had gotten a whiff of their . . . dynamic. She sighed, crossing her arms over her chest. "Either way, I don't really know what that has to do with"—she swished her hand around—"whatever else is going on."

"Just an observation, I guess," Landry said, stalling by deflection. "Look, here's the truth of it. Season starts in a couple weeks. I've got my lead contender running around like a chicken with her head cut off, making us look bad, I've got a bunch of parents breathing down my damn neck, I've got all these kids depending on me, and I've got a wife who keeps sending me schooners she wants me to buy in Maine. The problem is, I don't know who I can trust to hand all this over to, and I don't know shit about sailing."

"You can trust Jade, Coach." The words were out before Franny could even consider keeping them in. "You know you can. Nobody else could ever possibly do it like her."

Not even for a second did Franny regret letting that truth leave her lips. There was no denying it.

"I used to think that. I did." Landry paused and shook his head. "But now I'm not sure she's ready for it. She's young yet . . . maybe it's not her time."

That gave Franny pause. Not ready for it? . . . Jade? She'd never known the woman to be anything other than a paragon of near perfection when it came to her job. She was almost . . . above it all in a way. Dunn never seemed to mess up; mistakes were not in the woman's wheelhouse. What could she possibly have done to make Landry think that? And so suddenly too.

She almost went to ask, to dig deeper and get to the bottom of it. But Franny didn't want to be outwardly nosy. She didn't think Landry would tell her anyway. Based solely on the way his expression seemed to be closing off in real time, she knew he was done with the conversation as well.

"Well," Franny said, deciding to get one last word in. "I can't think of anyone else who could even get close to doing what you do other than her." She patted the pockets of her joggers to make sure her things were still tucked away inside. "Maybe whatever extra cooking she needs isn't going to happen until she's actually thrown into the pot."

She grimaced. It was a weird way to put it, but it made Landry's face shift, so with the words hanging in the air, she made her quiet exit, bound for somewhere that was not her own home.

Smack in the middle of one of Greenbelt's oldest neighborhoods was a small ice cream stand called Custard Castle. It was a seasonal place, only open during the warmer months, and drew crowds of people from all over the city every day. A few doors down and across the street from Custard Castle was a big, beautiful house made of tan bricks and covered with windows.

Years ago, when Franny had first arrived in Greenbelt, her ex-girlfriend had taken her to the small stand on her welcome tour. As they'd walked back down the street to where they'd parked Franny's car, they had passed that brick house, and in the yard was a woman watering flowers. She'd had on a pair of tight denim booty shorts and a bikini top, all glistening brown legs and round tits, and Franny had nearly choked on her strawberry shortcake waffle cone at the sight of her.

Months later, after Franny had been left by said girlfriend, she'd recognized that woman as one of her coworkers and had barely been able to utter any type of polite Southern greeting upon their introduction. She'd felt awful about it, but all she could see was that image of Dunn in her head. The splash back of water droplets from the hose on her smooth skin, the way her round ass looked in those shorts.

Even now, as she pulled up to the curb outside the house, she got a flash of it. She'd left Landry's with something sitting in her heart. A great need to get to the bottom of what was happening with Dunn. To warn her. To check on her. This was the only place she could think of to look for her. It was weird, maybe a little stalkerish, but the need was almost oppressive, and all she could do was follow it.

Luckily, Jade's old-ass truck was right there in the driveway. Rusted near her tires and faded blue, it stood out on the perfectly paved plot next to the S-Class Mercedes that was pulled up alongside it.

She couldn't imagine the woman living here, but what the hell did she know?

Gathering every ounce of bravery she had, she made her way up the drive and onto the porch before committing one of the greatest sins known to Southern moms everywhere—showing up at someone's house unannounced after 7:00 P.M.

A woman answered the door with obvious confusion on her face. Franny knew instantly that this woman was related to Dunn. She was a little darker, taller too, but the eyes were the same, as were her lips and cheekbones. Franny couldn't help but smile.

"Hi, ma'am. I'm sorry to bother you at this time of night," she said, though it was barely past nine. "My name is Francesca Lim. I was wondering . . . is Jade Dunn here, by any chance?"

The woman leaned against the doorframe, looking Franny up and down. "Does she know you?"

"Yes, ma'am," Franny said with a nod.

"Are you her girlfriend? She didn't tell me she had a girlfriend."

Franny coughed. "N-no, ma'am, we're just . . . We work together."

"Hmmm . . ." The older woman's lips pursed. "I sure never had a coworker show up at my parents' house in the middle of the night looking for me."

Franny had no rebuttal to that. What was it with all these people shocking her into silence today? She didn't like it, not one damn bit.

"I am sorry about that." Franny choked out the words. "It's really important, or I swear I wouldn't have . . ."

The woman had a skeptical look on her face but pushed her hip off the side of the doorframe and stepped inside the house. "Come on in, then."

Franny breathed a sigh of pure relief, flashing her a thankful smile before following her inside. "So, are you Jade's sister or . . ."

She knew that Jade was an only child, but she couldn't help but try to butter the older woman up a bit. Franny had made an awful first impression, and she was willing to do anything to soften it.

"I'm Joyce, her mama." The woman snorted.

"It's nice to meet you, Ms. Joyce."

They entered the kitchen before either of them could say anything else. Two large cherrywood pocket doors briefly blocked the view, but inside was one of the more gorgeous scenes Franny had ever seen. It was a large space with dark wood cabinets that matched the hardwood and green granite countertops. It smelled like sweet, warm apples and was outfitted with warm yellow lighting. Off to the right of the room was a full-size dining table, where Jade and the man Franny presumed to be her father sat.

Jade had her head down on the table, forehead touching the wood as her father looked over her with a mix of concern and exasperation.

"You've got company, Jadey," her mother called.

"Someone come to kill me, I hope." The words were muffled by the surface under her face.

"Hey now! Don't you put that out there, girl," her father and mother immediately snapped together.

"Definitely not here for that," Franny said. She suddenly felt shy as she said the words, but the way Jade's head lifted up instantly at her voice left all that shyness by the wayside.

Her heart contracted when she saw Jade's face. Not just in the way it always did, that immediate rush of excitement and pleasure she captured like a snapshot. This time, her chest ached for the look of sadness on Jade's face. The sheer vulnerability, the wet tear streaks on brown skin and dark, soaking eyelashes.

Franny wanted to run across the room and press Jade's face into her chest, wrap her arms around those quivering shoulders until they stilled.

"What are you doing here?" Jade's words calmed her. They weren't cruel or full of disdain, but they *were* confused.

"I . . ." Franny swallowed, her throat suddenly thick and unable to let words escape.

Thankfully, Ms. Joyce took pity on her. "Franny here said she needed to talk to you about something important."

Jade sniffed. "Like, involving the team?"

She nodded.

"You saw Landry tonight? At poker?"

Franny nodded again.

Jade's face looked like it was about to crumple all over again. Then she seemed to stop herself, pushing some of the flyaways off her forehead before dragging her hands down her face. She stood up and strode out of the room, making sure to take Franny by the arm and drag her behind.

"Um, thank you for having me," Franny called out to Jade's parents just before she disappeared around the corner.

She was silent as Jade led her through a door and then down a flight of stairs into a basement that looked nicer and more outfitted than her own apartment. Pulling a set of sliding doors open, Jade took them across a path of big, flat stones set in mulch. In the huge backyard, nestled into a thatch of greenery, was a tree house. It was built around the wide trunk of a huge willow oak, a canopy of branches and leaves almost hiding the little wooden box from the rest of the world.

"Up," Jade said simply, finally—regretfully—letting go of her forearm.

"Okay." Franny's tone was skeptical, but she gave a quick smile. "Just don't look at my ass."

It was cooler than normal for late July, though still hot, and while it wasn't humid, the air felt like it was on fire.

Franny ascended the ladder carefully, opening the door to the little house to see a silvery string dangling above her. She pulled it, letting the small bulb filter light through the space. It was very rugged inside, nothing fancy, but there were a couple of beanbag chairs, a plush rug, and a bunch of books and magazines, even a little table. She would have killed for something like this as a kid.

"So this is what being an only child gets you, huh?" she said when she heard Jade close the door behind her.

"I built it with my granddaddy when I was a kid," Jade said, crossing her arms over her chest. "I needed space for my little plots and schemes."

Franny looked over at her and smiled, relief flooding her stomach when Jade smiled back at her—small as it was.

"Did you come here to tell me that Landry is going to let me go?"

"I came to see what's going on," Franny said. "I had a little talk with him tonight after the game, and he . . . he seemed really cut up about something. He wouldn't tell me the details, but . . . he was saying some things that concerned me."

"Some things about me?"

Franny nodded silently.

"And you came here to . . . what? Rub it in my face now that you've got the upper hand?" Jade's eyes were on the ground, her jaw clenched tightly.

"I'm so sick of this shit, Dunn," Franny ground out. "You've been in some kind of one-sided competition with me all summer."

"Well, you've been playing along."

"Yeah, because it was the only way to get you to pay any fucking attention to me, dude!"

"Don't call me *dude*," Jade grumbled. "And that just . . . isn't true."

Franny shot her a look. "I'm not even convinced that I did anything to make you hate me, and I've spent literal days sitting around questioning myself on that. I don't know what it is. All I know is that you've said more to me in the past two months than you have in two years."

Jade's dark eyebrows furrowed toward each other, making a deep wrinkle in the space between them. "Why do you care so much about whether I talk to you or not?"

Franny didn't say anything as she stared the other woman down. Instead, she tried to convey everything with her expression. The exasperation, the frustration, the sheer fucking want.

Jade met her eyes for a few moments. It was the longest eye contact they'd ever maintained, even longer than when they'd fucked in the bathroom at the club. Franny's insides twisted, her guts roiling like she'd eaten something spoiled. She felt afraid of the consequences of what she had just admitted, even if she couldn't say it out loud yet. Largely because she felt no confidence that her feelings would be reciprocated.

With a heavy sigh, Jade practically threw herself down onto one of the beanbag chairs. "I have so many things inside me, Francesca."

The sound of her full given name leaving the other woman's lips made Franny shiver. Jade almost never used it. She could only recall her saying it in times like this, when they found themselves swept up in passion. In those moments, it felt like Jade forgot to keep up the walls that allowed her to at least pretend to hold Franny at arm's length.

"I know everybody else does too," Jade said. She sucked her bottom lip into her mouth for a moment before releasing it. "But my whole life, I've just felt this . . . pressure. It's like there's something sitting on my chest that won't move. The only time I get relief is when something big happens and I feel like I'm *not* fucking everything up. And right now, I know that I have definitely fucked everything up."

Franny's heart sank. To her, Jade went through it all so effortlessly. From the way her ponytail swung when she walked across the field to how she wrangled her students in during fire drills. There wasn't a single part of her that seemed anything less than perfectly put together. Always. She should have known, though. Those kinds of people always seemed to have something simmering under the surface. A jitteriness, an anxiety that came inherently with desperately having something to prove, even if only to themselves.

"I don't think you've fucked everything up," Franny said, moving to sit in the big red beanbag next to Jade. Her lower back and knees immediately protested. "Landry was, well, definitely not happy about whatever it is you did, but I tried to talk him down."

Jade's head whipped over to her so fast, Franny was almost afraid the motion had broken her neck. "You tried to talk him down . . . for me?"

Franny sighed from deep in her diaphragm, not even bothering to stop her eyes from rolling. "The only thing I did was remind him of what all of us, including him, already know. Which is that there's nobody better for this job than you."

"What did he say to that?"

"He didn't say much, but he knows it's true," Franny consoled her. "What did you do anyway?"

With a groan, Jade threw herself even farther back into the furniture. "I snuck into one of West Beaufort's scrimmages and just . . . took a few notes."

"Jade!" Franny's mouth dropped open.

"I know, I know. I-I wasn't thinking straight. All I could focus on was getting the upper hand against—" She took a skittish peek over at Franny. "Against you, and I seriously crossed the line. I didn't take any game tape, I swear. I just . . . I don't know. I knew I was toeing a line, I just figured that because I didn't technically cross it, I could skate by. The worst part is that I didn't even see that I'd done something wrong until Landry found out and reamed me out for it."

"That is not at all what I expected." Franny laughed. "I thought you'd, like, called the man an asshole to his face or got into an argument with a parent or something. Not that your ass was out there doing Espionage: Sports Edition."

Jade gave another groan. "I literally put on a church-auntie wig and everything. It's deeply embarrassing to think about in retrospect."

Franny's cackle bounced off the wood walls of the tree house.

Jade bumped her shoulder with her own, making Franny snort as she came close to losing her balance.

"I can't fucking believe I'm about to lose my dream because I decided to play Harriet the Spy for a day."

"He's going to give you the position, Jade. You know he is."

Jade shook her head, suddenly sober. "I don't know that, and neither do you. Shit, he probably doesn't either."

They were looking at each other, gazes locked, faces somber. The air between them smelled like damp wood and fresh earth.

"What will you do if he doesn't give you the job?"

Jade swallowed. "I don't know that either."

19

At Friday-morning practice, she sat in the cab of her truck in the parking lot, watching as the last few stragglers showed up not quite late to the session. The Jade she'd been a week ago would have been on the field for an hour already. Helping to set out the water and snacks, looking over her playbook, greeting the kids as they trickled in. The Jade she was today was terrified to show her face.

Jade was a lot of things. Like everybody else in the world, she was a culmination of good stuff and bad stuff. Fucked-up thoughts and generous actions. Most of the time, she made peace with it all. Largely because one thing she'd always prided herself on was not being a coward. She'd never shied away from confrontation or from the truth, and she'd certainly never been too scared to face the facts of life. But here she was, staring down the barrel of losing everything she'd worked hard as hell to get, and the only thing she wanted to do was tuck tail and run so she could avoid the inevitable.

She could imagine holding her head high, striding across the green, only to be met by stares from her colleagues who knew exactly what she'd done and were judging her for it. And Landry . . . God, she could see his face now. Reddened from the sun, with his Oakley sunglasses perched on the bill of his cap, looking at her the same way he had in his office. Frustrated, disappointed, tired.

Her stomach revolted just thinking about it, and she had to clench her eyes shut to get the image behind her lids to fade away. Maybe it would be better for her to just drive off and send some bullshit text to Landry about how she was going to miss practice because she wasn't feeling well.

It wouldn't be a lie, at least. She felt awful.

"Coach Dunn!"

She cursed inside as soon as she heard the voice. Through the glass of her driver's-side window, she watched as David Kelly came sprinting toward her car. Slowly, she used the hand crank to lower the window.

"Hey, David."

"What are you doing out here?" His little blond eyebrows furrowed.

"I, uh . . ." It was shameful, the way she couldn't come up with a single adequate answer for him.

"We need to get inside—" His voice broke in the middle of his sentence. "These last few summer practices are important, remember? You told us that."

She nodded, swallowing even though her mouth had suddenly gone dry. She *had* told them that. She'd stressed it to the kids, to the parents, and to the other coaches. Over and over, she'd drilled it into their heads. Being a coward was one thing; being a hypocrite was another.

"Move back, David," she said, opening the door and hopping out, then grabbing her water bottle and canvas bag before slamming the car door shut. "I was just running a little behind."

The duo started to walk toward the field together, and Jade wasn't sure which one was keeping with the stride of the other. David had boundless energy, and he was a little on the small side, which made him one of their better running backs.

He took off like a rocket the second he touched the edge of the field, and Jade's heart started pounding just as fast. Everything looked completely normal. The boys sitting around, talking on the field. Coaches on the sidelines doing the same. Landry was in a small huddle with a group of parents. Immediately, Jade feared that he was telling them what she had done—letting them know that their kids had been coached by a goddamn fool.

She shook her head. That was ridiculous. As much as she feared him right now, Landry would never do something like that.

Her steps toward the sideline weren't as sure as they normally were, but the greetings everyone—or almost everyone—gave her seemed to be.

Lim was there too, hip cocked against the giant orange Gatorade cooler as she downed a cup. Jade drifted toward the other woman as if she were a buoy adrift at sea.

"Hi," she choked out.

Lim made something of a grimace, all clenched teeth and pitiful eyes. "You look . . ."

"Yeah," Jade groaned, pulling the bill of her visor farther down over her face. "Sleep is for people who aren't about to get fired."

"He wouldn't let you come just to fire you, Jade."

"You don't know what he'd do."

Lim sighed and pulled away from the cooler. "Look," she said as she tossed a casual arm around Jade's shoulders, doing nothing to ease her pounding heart, and spun her in the direction of the field. "It's a beautiful day, the kids are happy, and you have not lost your job." She leaned in closer until Jade could feel her warm breath against her ear. "But if you hang around here like some kind of specter of sadness, you might. The only thing you can do now is make him remember how indispensable you are. So you might as well do just that. Don't accept your fears as truths."

Jade couldn't help but look at the woman. Her full, peachy lips and the little Cindy Crawford mole just above them. The way her dark eyes never seemed to display anything other than playfulness. She was too beautiful to look at for too long, but fuck if Jade didn't want to test the boundaries of those limits.

"Why are you doing this?" she asked once she finally dragged her gaze back to the field. "You should be over there trying to wiggle your way in."

"One-sided competition, remember?" Lim shrugged. "Maybe I'm just playing the role of kingmaker. They're the ones who actually have all the power anyway."

"Ugh." Jade shoved the other woman away, ignoring her laughs as she found a spot to put her things down and steeling herself for the coming hours.

Lim was right, damn her. The only thing she could do now was show Landry—remind him—that she was his first choice for a reason. Mistakes be damned. She was it. She had to be.

She just had to remind herself too.

Landry managed to go the entire practice without speaking to her. He'd even only looked her way a handful of times, and Jade wasn't positive those hadn't been accidents.

The silence felt like a snub. Even when she'd been a child, her parents had never punished her by ignoring her. It felt impossible not to let such a thing cloud her mind and shake her already fragile confidence.

Thankfully, Landry had the boys running laps for a good portion of practice. Hot as it was, they'd also taken a lot of water breaks. So she'd been given only about thirty minutes to run D-line drills before they'd called it a day. Seconds after he'd blown the whistle signaling the end of practice, Landry had disappeared inside the school—presumably to his office. Jade had watched him walk, tall but with his shoulders drawn, and fought back every instinct inside herself that told her to follow him. Instead, she'd gathered her things and made her way back to her truck—the only thing on her mind being whether she should go cry in her mother's lap again or go home and cry into a pint of pistachio ice cream.

But the truck wouldn't start.

"This is not happening." She turned her key and listened as the ignition made a pitiful sound for the third time in a row. "There is no way this is actually happening to me right now."

She paused and took a deep breath, rolling her shoulders and giving her lips a once-over with her tongue. Then she tried again. "Gladys, baby, please. Just . . . please . . ."

Once again, that pitiful sound.

Gladys was a 1984 Chevy Silverado. At one point, she'd been a glossy cobalt blue; now she was much duller, with more parts of her replaced than Jade could count. It had been her father's truck, and for the first few years of her life, it had been her favorite place to be. Riding down country dirt roads in the bed with her cousins or strapped into the cab with wind whipping through the windows and Curtis Mayfield on the radio. Her father had given it to her when she'd turned seventeen, and Gladys had been with her ever since.

Jade had sunk more money into the old girl than she cared to admit, but she'd never been strong enough to let her go, not even when Gladys had more than three hundred thousand miles on her and an affinity for being finicky as all hell.

She didn't know shit about cars, so there was no fixing Gladys on her own. Instead, she'd have to do what she always did and call one of her friends to pick her up. Which always included listening to them lecture her about how dangerous it was for her to still be driving "that raggedy-ass truck." She didn't want to hear it. She didn't want to hear anything but that engine finally turning over.

And it wouldn't, no matter how much begging she did as she turned the key.

Jade pressed her head against the steering wheel, teeth gritted, jaw hurting from the way she clenched it. She was so caught up in her own mess that the tap on her window didn't even faze her.

"Please go away." She spoke the words into the horn.

"Can't. I have a responsibility to make sure you're good right now." Lim's husky voice was immediately recognizable, even muffled through glass.

Jade fought the urge to scream and yell and kick. She picked her head up quickly, not even bothering to pull the window down. "Can you give me a ride home?"

Lim just nodded, and within the span of two minutes, they were buckled into the front of the other woman's Subaru hatchback with the air blowing in their faces and Syd playing through the speakers.

"I still can't believe you drive a Subaru," Jade grumbled.

"You can't?" Lim laughed. "Lesbians and their Subarus, country gays and their trucks. There's no denying it, honestly."

"Fair enough," Jade said. "Everybody hates on my truck."

"I don't know why. It's very *you*."

"Is it?"

Lim kept her eyes on the road but nodded. "Oh yeah, it's sturdy and solid, obviously breaks down every now and then, but it gets back up."

"Gladys breaks down way more than I do," she said.

"Is that her name? Gladys?"

"It was my daddy's truck, and he loves Gladys Knight."

They stopped at a light, and Franny turned to look at her. "You know what? My dad loves Gladys Knight too, actually."

"Really?"

"'Neither One of Us' is his favorite song," she said, smiling. "My parents went to Dallas to see her perform at some festival a few years ago."

"My daddy always says he hates that he was born too late to have been a Pip."

"Can he sing?"

"Not a damn lick."

They shared a quiet laugh as the car pulled forward again. "The Subaru very much does not have a name."

Jade gasped. "That's sacrilege. Every good car needs a good name."

"I don't know . . . Nothing ever felt right, honestly."

Jade ran her hand along the dashboard, then the headrest of Lim's seat. She even tickled her fingers along the buttons on the radio. "Feels like kind of a Georgia to me."

Lim pulled a face. "Absolutely not. I dated a Georgia, and she used to pick her foot skin in bed."

"Eww . . ."

Suddenly, they were jolting forward and back fast, and Lim's hand shot out across Jade's chest in some kind of attempt to keep her from shooting forward. The car in front of them had slammed on its brakes for a turn it hadn't signaled. Lim cursed, then pressed down on her horn for a few long, long seconds while the car ahead made its turn. Then they were on their way again.

"What about Nelly?" Lim said suddenly. "Like 'Whooooa, Nelly.'"

"That'll work," Jade said, laughing, as they pulled up in front of her little house. "This is me."

She pointed at the little two-story cottage home with its white brick exterior and dark shingled roof.

"It's really cute." Lim leaned over, her face closer to Jade's as she checked it out through the passenger window.

"I bought it last year. It's pretty damn cute inside too."

Jade turned her head a fraction so that she was looking at the other woman. Their faces were inches apart, and Jade could smell Lim's shampoo and the minty ChapStick on her lips. Her thighs flexed in her shorts as her mind flooded with images of their mouths pressed together, their bodies pressing into each other. Then a flash of remembering the feeling of Lim's hot, wet pussy contracting around her fingers.

"Do you want to see?" The words where whisper quiet, like she couldn't believe she was saying them.

Without so much as a word, Lim put the car in park and turned it off. As Jade led them up the small path toward her front door, her tummy started to burn. After she closed the door behind them, she froze, unsure what to do.

"Can I get you a water or . . ." Jade was suddenly skittish, shy. Why, she didn't know. She was no stranger to this—to sex—not even with Lim. She already knew exactly how the other woman tasted, and here she was acting like it was the first time she'd ever been alone with a girl.

"Did you invite me in here for water, Jade?"

Jade shook her head.

Lim took a few steps until she was right up on her, breasts touching. "Why did you invite me in, then?"

All Jade could do was swallow. Her eyes went to Lim's lips, peachy and plush, and her skin tingled as she recalled how they felt making their way across her neck and chest.

Lim took Jade's chin between her thumb and her index finger, tilting her head back a bit. Jade's eyes instantly fluttered closed—like it hurt too much to look at the woman in front of her.

"Tell me."

"You already know why." It sounded more like a whine, needy and desperate.

"I want to hear you say it."

"So you can torture me?"

"No, I just want to hear it and keep it with me." Lim's voice was breathy, and it sent a shudder through Jade.

Fuck. What a thing that was to hear. Jade wound her arms around Lim's waist, resting her palms against her lower back, just under her T-shirt. She was warm there, heated and a little slick. The fine hairs at the base of her spine felt like silk that Jade was helpless to do anything but stroke with her thumbs.

"I want you," she said, opening her eyes. The words felt ragged and not enough. "I always want you. Here in my house and at the club and in the car. Even in my fucking tree house, I want you."

"To fuck me?"

"Yes, but also . . ." Jade's mouth hung open, and she hesitated. "I don't know why this is so hard."

Lim stroked a finger across Jade's forehead, down the middle between her eyes, and over her lids, before swirling around the apples of her cheeks. "You don't trust yourself," she said. "Not right now and not with this."

The words hit Jade like a Mack truck. Head-on, knocking the wind out of her sails and leaving a dagger lodged in the middle of her throat.

"I still don't," she admitted. "I'm still scared."

"You're scared of me?"

Jade nodded wordlessly. Maybe Lim was right. Maybe she'd hit the nail right on the head. Jade felt like she were living on a wire, where every decision she made had the power to knock her off and kill her.

"Francesca . . ."

Lim stroked her finger over Jade's cheek once more. Then she pulled away. "I genuinely cannot believe I'm the one saying this, but we're not doing this, not until you're sure. Because I'm not sleeping with you again just to have you run out like your head is on fire and pretend like I don't exist."

Guilt punched Jade in the chest so hard that she took a step back too. "Yeah. I get it."

"I want you, Jade Dunn. So much. And not just for sex. Like, I want you for real. I want the kisses and the crying and you sitting in my car. Fucking Sundays at the farmers market and us trying not to get caught flirting at work. I want *you*, all of you. But I'm not willing to fall for another girl who isn't all in for me too. You understand that, right?"

Jade's eyes started to water, salty liquid pooling at the edges. The tears were on her cheeks before she could take a breath in. "I understand."

The look on Lim's face made Jade's entire body ache, and the sound of the front door closing behind her almost brought Jade to her knees. Keeping shit steady had been the only way to move forward for her. No surprises, no fuckups. Clearly, that had not been sustainable. For all her caution, for every bit of her carelessness, Jade was in the exact position she'd feared most. Adrift, unsure, completely up shit creek without a paddle. She felt just as terrified as she had when she thought about Landry's final decision. Hating Lim—or pretending to anyway—had always felt much safer than leaning into whatever feelings she knew she had.

But even still, in this moment, finally understanding the truth, she didn't know how to make things right. She didn't know how to make herself feel better.

20

"I talked to Umma earlier," Will said, pinching his dirt-covered fingers together. "Seems like she's this close to pulling one of her surprise visits, probably already has her bag packed."

Will was on his hands and knees in front of his house, clad in gardening gear and pulling weeds while Franny sulked on the porch steps a few feet away.

"I literally talked to her the other day, Oppa." Franny laughed.

She'd been making a concerted effort to call home more, especially after a particularly heartfelt conversation with her mother. They'd taken to talking about football, but the topic always gave way to other things. Earlier in the week, she'd learned that her umma had a brief dalliance with an Argentinian car salesman in her early twenties. Franny didn't really know what to do with all the new things she was learning about her umma, but she'd briefly considered writing all the stories down.

"You know she needs a lot of attention." Will grunted. "Kenny and Phillip don't call nearly enough, and there's only so much I can take. I need you to step up, Franny."

"I know. I'm sorry. I'm trying to do better, I swear. I've just been caught up with . . . a bunch of other stuff. I'll call her on the drive home and see how she's doing."

Her brother paused, leaning up on his knees to wipe a forearm across his sweaty forehead. "What's wrong?"

"Nothing," she said. She looked away with a shrug.

She didn't tend to talk about her romantic problems with her family. To be fair, they didn't tend to share theirs with her either. Whenever she talked to her parents or her brothers about a woman she was dating, she kept things as matter-of-fact as possible. Part of her had always felt like they couldn't possibly understand. The other part had just found it soul-achingly awkward.

"Something's wrong," Will said, clearly in the mood to argue. "You've been acting weird all summer. Tell me what's up."

She put a hand over her brow, shielding her eyes from the sun as she looked at her brother. He was pink-cheeked and sweaty, but she could see that he was also genuinely concerned.

"There's a girl . . ." Franny trailed off. She leaned her elbows back on the concrete step behind her, hoping that the nonchalant pose would rub off on her tone.

"Of course."

She rolled her eyes. "She's nothing like Caroline."

It was true. For all her faults, unsurety, and indecisiveness, Jade was the complete opposite of Caroline. She wasn't flighty or wishy-washy, and even if they both did share an obvious fear of diving in, Franny knew that Jade's came from someplace other than viewing people as inherently expendable.

"What's she like, then?" Will asked.

Franny tilted her face up to the sun. Feeling the warmth on her skin somehow made it easier to talk about Jade accurately. "She's incredibly fucking frustrating, for one." She laughed. "Like, deeply stubborn and a little obstinate. But I don't think I've ever met anyone who knows her who has anything but a kind thing to say about her. She's so good with the kids, and she loves football so much. She stuns me."

Will made a low *hmmm*, but Franny didn't even pause for effect—she was on a roll.

"I feel like all I do is sit around and think about what it is about her that makes me want her. I'm always trying to put it into words, but honestly, I can't. I've never been good at that anyway, but with her, it's like I never had enough words to begin with to describe it all."

"So what's the issue, then? She doesn't like you back?"

"No, she does," Franny said, her words full of conviction. "She definitely does."

"Well"—Will waved an arm around in the air—"be together, then."

"It's not that easy, dude."

"Sure it is."

"It was that easy for you and Yao?"

The question sounded sarcastic, but there was more genuine interest behind it than even she realized at first. Will had told the family that he was seriously dating someone about a week before he'd brought Yao home to meet them. It wasn't a month later that they were engaged, and then they officially married less than a year after that. To be sure, the speed and lack of formality of the whole thing had given both sets of parents a ton of strife, but everyone had gotten over it by the time Amelia was born.

Much the same way she'd never made Will privy to the inner workings of her romantic life, he'd never made her privy to his either.

"No, we had it worse," he grunted as he yanked a particularly rough weed. "She wasn't even single when we met."

Franny's eyes bulged as she forced herself back up into a seated position in response to the news. "What?"

The muscles in Will's back and shoulders tensed up immediately. "She was selling one of the houses on the same street as my restaurant and came in for lunch with a client. That's how we met. Then she told me that she'd been seeing this dude on and off for a few years. He was a fucking clown and she deserved better, and I told her so."

"Did you guys have an affair?" Her metaphorical pearls were clutched.

"Of course not. You can't start a relationship built on lies. I knew what I wanted with her almost immediately, so I just had to wait it out until she came to her senses and realized it too."

"How long did that take?"

"The longest three weeks of my life."

Franny groaned. "Three weeks is nothing compared to this."

"It's all the same torture when you can't be with them."

"I just don't know what to do to get her head out of her ass."

Will went about tying the big garbage bag of weeds closed. "Have you told her how you feel? What you want? Have you been clear about it?"

"Yes."

"Then there's nothing else for you to do," he said. "Not until she comes back ready to tell you what she wants, what she needs too."

She wrung her hands together in her lap, suddenly feeling even more defeated. The sun wasn't so warm anymore, and a slight chill ran through her despite the considerable heat index in Columbia. "So I'm just supposed to wait around?"

"I didn't say that. If you want to run around like a headless chicken in the meantime, nobody's going to stop you. But the way I see it, it can be worth the wait. That three weeks could have turned into three months, and it still would have been worth it."

"What if it isn't worth it in the end, though? What if I do all that waiting just to get left behind again, Oppa?"

Will reached out and pulled Franny up by her shoulders and into his arms. One of his large, warm hands cradled the back of her head, and she breathed in the scent of soil and sweat on his T-shirt. Her brother was warm and familiar, deeply comforting and grounding. They didn't hug very often either, but when they did, Franny was instantly transported back to light-filled memories of them in the back of their father's car, the two convincing him to play the hip radio stations instead of listening to his books on tape. She thought about footraces down their cul-de-sac and covering for him when he snuck out in exchange for unlimited rides wherever she wanted to go. She wrapped her arms around his middle and squeezed him tightly.

When he finally spoke again, she felt the vibrations on her cheek. "No one would blame you for not wanting to risk it right now, Fran. Caroline treated you like shit. She sold you a dream and cashed out the first chance she got. But that didn't have anything to do with you. You say this new girl is nothing like her, and if you truly believe that, then maybe it's worth taking a second and being patient for it. And if it turns out that it wasn't, well, I'll be right here for you, just like I was the last time and will be all the times in the future."

Franny snorted and pinched him on the shoulder. "If this doesn't work out, there aren't going to be any future fucking times. I'll officially give up on love and put all my effort into becoming one of those beekeeping lesbians."

"You hate bees."

"I'll learn not to."

He laughed. "Well, why don't we see how this pans out first before we start investing in a bunch of those space suit things they wear."

"Bee suits, you absolute fool. They're literally just called *bee suits.*"

Freshman orientation at Greenbelt Senior High was quite the event by school standards. A few weeks before the start of the new school year, the incoming freshmen and their parents were invited in to meet with teachers and staff, get important information about the upcoming year, and learn the lay of the land. Never mind that almost every kid in the incoming class had at least one parent who'd attended the school at some point; Principal Coleman was big on first and lasting impressions.

Thankfully, teachers didn't have to put on much of a show. All the admins and department heads were expected to attend the formal orientation in the auditorium with the families, and the rest of the freshman teaching staff waited in their rooms, doors open, for when the students did their first official classroom visit.

Franny had used much of her buzzing, anxious energy to get her classroom together before the event. The art room was big, with big black-top tables and paint-speckled floors. She'd covered the walls in the artworks of previous and current students and placed a bunch of printouts of her curriculum plan at the door for anyone to grab.

Wax melter plugged in, she sat back in her chair with her feet up on her desk and waited until she heard footsteps coming down the hall toward her room to square her shoulders and stand up.

Relief and annoyance flooded through her when she realized the steps belonged to one of her kids. It was Alonzo Holton, who was only fifteen but taller than she was by more than a few inches. The O-line left tackle was truly never without a smile. He was also, by Franny's estimation, one of the best student artists she'd ever encountered.

"What are you doing here?" she asked, peeking around him only to find the space empty.

"Well, hello to you too, Coach," he said sarcastically.

"I'm not a—"

"I know, I know, you're not a coach. You're just Ms. Lim," Alonzo said. "But the way I see it, if you're on the field telling me what to do, you're either my coach or my mama, and I definitely know you aren't my mama."

"And does your mama know you're running around the school?"

"My sister is a freshman this year, and she made me come," he said. "They're teaching them how to use the combination locks right now, and I told her I was going to come down and see you."

The adult in her wanted to scold him for walking around the school without a hall pass, which was not allowed for students at any time—school in session or not. But damn if it didn't feel nice that one of her students was at least halfway fond of her. Especially when that student was also on her team. They weren't supposed to have favorites, but the students who had an actual interest in art—whether they came to her that way or she coaxed it out of them—always had a soft spot in her heart.

Alonzo shoved himself in one of the chairs at the black table closest to her desk. For a moment, they looked at each other like that dueling Spider-Man meme, waiting for the other to speak. He was the one to fold first.

"Is Coach Landry leaving the team?"

Franny damn near swallowed her tongue. The question hit her out of the blue, but it wasn't surprising. Not really. She didn't know what was inside adults that made them believe kids were completely oblivious to what was going on around them, but she wondered when she herself had internalized it. Of course word had gotten around about Landry's retirement. Of course the players had sensed or heard that something was amiss.

"Where did you hear that?" she asked in lieu of an actual answer.

Alonzo made a zipping motion across his lips before tossing the imaginary key into the little trash can at the end of the table.

Franny laughed. "At least you're loyal."

"Is he?"

"Lonzo, you know I can't say anything either way. If Coach Landry wants you to know something, he'll tell you."

He narrowed his eyes and twisted his mouth up, clearly skeptical of her deeply political answer.

"If he leaves, who's going to be our new coach?"

Franny peeked at her watch, wishing like hell that Principal Coleman would suddenly release the masses and flood her classroom with enough families that she could efficiently avoid this intense interrogation at the hands of a teenager with a curly taper-fade and Nike slides. The seconds ticked by with no relief.

"I'd say," she started carefully, "that if you're worried about the team not having a leader, you shouldn't be. Everybody is going to make sure y'all are taken care of."

"It's not that, really. It's just that . . . well, you know my daddy is still recovering from being in the hospital, and we don't really have money like that right now. I wasn't going to be able to stay on the team, because we couldn't afford all the fees and our bills at the same time, but Coach Landry helped us out and made it so I still got to play even though we couldn't pay."

Alonzo kept his eyes on the desk the entire time he spoke, hands fidgeting in his lap. The shame was evident in his tone, and it made Franny's heart ache. It was moments like these that reminded her how much further she had to go before she felt secure as a leader—if security was something real leaders even felt. She didn't know if she should give him a hug and tell him that everything would be all right, because no matter what she did, she didn't have the power to change his circumstances.

"You're scared that if Landry leaves, you won't be able to play anymore." It was more of a statement than a question.

"Yes, ma'am. I'm not even trying to play college ball. I just love playing and being on the team. It makes me . . . it makes me feel like everything isn't bad all the time," he said quietly.

She pressed her tongue to the roof of her mouth, tears springing up at the corners of her eyes, which she forced herself to quickly blink away.

"How about this," she began, after clearing her throat. "You have my word that you'll always have a place on that team. Don't think about Landry; don't think about the money. Just know it'll all be handled as long as you're doing everything you need to do. You can take my word on that."

Alonzo finally looked up from the table, his round brown eyes hopeful but cautious. "How can you give me your word when you keep saying you're not a coach?"

"I happen to have an in," she said. "Don't worry about that either."

He seemed to accept that and sat back in the chair, finally getting comfortable by crossing his ankles and arms. Franny sighed, taking her seat. It was clear he wasn't going anywhere anytime soon.

"You know what, Ms. Lim? I think you should be a coach."

"Oh yeah?"

"Mm-hmm. I mean, if Coach Carr can do it, you definitely can. He barely wants to talk to us half the time."

Alonzo wasn't wrong, to be fair. Coach Carr was close to retirement age himself and had lost a lot of his luster for coaching. He always seemed more than happy to let Franny take the reins—regardless of title—at practices.

"Be careful what you wish for. I'd work you way harder than Carr does."

The boy groaned and threw his head back. "You already almost killed us with all those bear drills last week. How much harder can we work?"

"Blocking drills until you drop," she said. "Agility training like you've never seen before. The list goes on, dude."

Alonzo groaned again, this time more dramatically. "You know what? I changed my mind. Maybe you should just stick to teaching us about chiaroscuro instead. You might be too evil to coach football."

"I'd say I'm just evil enough to coach football, thank you very much."

21

Leo Vaughn had a giant, annoying-ass head, but damn if he couldn't fix up a house. Since they'd gotten back together, he and Miri had made it a point to have regular kickbacks at their home. The place was big, three floors and a wraparound porch, in addition to the few acres of land it sat on. Jade had rolled up fashionably late to see people scattered around the yard and spilling out the front door. She was sure that every Black family in Greenbelt had at least one representative from their delegation here.

It took her forever to make her way inside to see Miri. Constantly stopped by people who knew her or her parents, making small talk and giving hugs, fielding questions about the upcoming football season. She was exhausted by the time she made it into the kitchen where Miri was sitting at her kitchen table, engrossed in a loud game of spades. They were playing a classic four-person game. Aja and Miri on one team and Leo's older sister, Thea, and her husband, Ahmir, on the other.

Leo and Walker—Aja's boyfriend—were at two barstools watching the game with equal parts fascination and fear. It was a loud one, and even Aja, who was famously the quietest in their friend group, was getting rowdy, throwing a jab at Ahmir when he literally threw some card down on the table.

Jade grabbed a beer from the cooler in the corner and joined the guys at the counter, settling onto an empty stool. "Figures you can't play spades," she remarked at Leo. "Now you're stuck on the sidelines with the white boy."

Leo sighed in return, barely acknowledging her, but she still got a kick out of his reaction.

"Oh, he can play." Miri spoke up from where she sat, not even looking at them. "He's just permanently banned from playing with his sister because they fucking cheat."

"We do not cheat," Leo said, defending himself and his sister in that calm way of his.

Ahmir snorted. "They absolutely cheat. Even when they aren't on the same team."

Thea shook her head profusely. "We can't help the special bond we have. It's intuitive. We can read each other."

"Special bond, my left ass cheek," Miri practically growled. "Y'all make dirty little backdoor deals."

Thea shrugged, her chin hiked in the air. "If that's how you feel."

"That's what I know." Miri pointed a finger at the other woman. "Which is why I refuse to sit at the card table with the two of you at the same time. I'll die behind that too."

The entire group shared a loud laugh, drowned out by the sounds of the party happening around them. Truthfully, Jade couldn't play spades either. Not that she'd admit it in front of everybody. She didn't want to risk the scorn or their attempts at trying to teach her.

Relaxing back onto the barstool, she took a few big gulps of the cold beer in her hand. Truthfully, she almost hadn't shown her face. She still wasn't convinced that she'd stay much longer. Jade had spent the past few days holed up in her apartment, oscillating between self-pity and righteous indignation. Her last encounter with Lim had left her piteous and pitiful. She'd swallowed her pride and invited the other woman into her home only to find herself collapsed in a heap of tears when Lim had left.

Lim had looked her straight in her face, those dark eyes of hers searing into Jade like daggers, and told her explicitly that Jade didn't seem like she was at all ready to be in any kind of relationship with her.

And damn if that didn't seem to be the through line of her entire life right now. Not even two months ago, Jade had her chest puffed out to the world, half confidence, half ego, completely secure in the knowledge that she was *it*. Now? Shit. She could barely go ten minutes without almost crumbling under the weight of her current reality.

She recognized that she was being dramatic in some respects. There were people in the world—people within a square mile of her, even—who were suffering much more dangerous realities. Jade had her health, her friends and family, her job, she even made plenty of money. Coach or no coach, Lim or no Lim, her heart would not spontaneously combust in her chest.

But damn if it didn't feel like it. She had put all her eggs in one basket off the sheer confidence that Landry would recognize her as the best choice for his successor and reward her for it. Then Lim had come into the picture, and she'd made Jade sloppy, impulsive.

No. That wasn't true. Lim hadn't done anything, not really. Jade had gotten spooked and started to act accordingly. Even when her so-called confidence was supposed to protect her and keep her steady. All it had taken was a pretty girl with shiny eyes to make her fold like a damn lawn chair. Lim had barely had to do anything but turn that knowing grin her way, and Jade had literally risked her career in an attempt to ease the anxiety and butterflies the sight of it caused in her belly.

She was a mess.

Jade wasn't sure how long she sat there lamenting, but a ruckus coming from the table interrupted her navel-gazing. All four players were standing, shoulders tensed, eyes locked on the table in front of them. She had absolutely no clue what was going on. One second, she heard a collective intake of breath, and the next, everyone erupted as Aja slapped cards down on the table.

"Ooooh-weee," Miri said, doing the gloating for them both. "Look at that. I know you're mad. I know you are."

Ahmir rubbed a hand over his bald head, composure kept, but Thea was heated. "Y'all barely won. *Barely.*"

"A win is a win," Aja said, grinning.

Miri grabbed Aja up by the neck, squeezing her and planting a wet kiss on her forehead. She was so ecstatic, someone might have thought she'd bet the house on the odds of them winning.

Jade watched as Aja lovingly pushed Miri away and made her way over to her boyfriend, standing between his legs. Walker whispered something to her that had her smiling shyly and ducking her head. It was so sweet that Jade's teeth ached, and she made it a point to look away.

After accepting congrats from her husband, Miri grabbed the beer out of Jade's hands and took a generous swig. Her best friend eyed her for a few long moments, the kind of understanding in her gaze that only came from a long time of knowing someone so intimately. It made Jade squirm in her seat.

"What?" she whined. "Stop looking at me."

Miri did not stop. "Ms. Joyce told my mama that some pretty Asian girl showed up at her house looking for you the other week."

"My mama couldn't hold water if you strapped it to her damn back."

"You got her coming to your folks' house?" Miri laughed. "I didn't know it was that serious."

Jade grabbed her beer from Miri and tipped it back until the bottle was drained. "Please don't start. It's not like that."

"I know it ain't. I just don't understand why."

"Because . . ." She hesitated. The only answers she had were the ones she'd spent months regurgitating to herself in her head. She had convinced herself that they were solid, but the realization of how flimsy they actually were was almost embarrassing.

"Because," Miri continued for her, putting her hands on Jade's thighs and leaning in close, "you're as stubborn as a mule, and you refuse to accept that something can be simple."

"There's nothing simple about any of this."

"Because you keep making it hard, Jade," Miri scoffed, sparing a look to her left, where Leo leaned on the island counter, blowing up a balloon at the request of his nephew. "This is not me pretending like I know everything, I swear. But I do know that sometimes the best thing to do for yourself is get the hell out of your own way."

"I'm so scared of fucking everything up," Jade said, looking down at her hands. "I never feel like I'm doing enough. There's always . . . more. Something else to do. Someone else to prove myself to. It never ends."

Miri sighed. "You can't control them. Not what they want or how they feel or what they think, definitely not what they do. I think that's why you're so lost right now—you keep trying to, thinking you're going to get any outcome other than disappointment."

Jade bit into her bottom lip, not hard enough to break the skin but enough to curb the tears she wanted to shed in response to her best friend's words.

"How long have you known me?" Jade asked.

Miri's eyebrows furrowed. "Shit, longer than I've known myself, I think."

"And in all that time, have I ever been able to shake off the weight of other people's opinions that easily?"

"No."

It was a simple answer. Straightforward. And it came so quickly and without hesitation. It was more devastating than anything else Miri had said. More damning. More terrifying.

"But so what?" Miri continued. "You're not dead, girl. It's not too late to change that."

"Where would I even start?"

"If I were you, I'd start by telling your coach to get the hell over himself and go from there."

Jade snorted. "Oh, so you really want me to lose my job, then?"

"You're sitting here convinced that you're about to anyway. Falling apart at the seams and shit. What do you have to lose?"

"Literally everything I've spent my whole life working for."

"There are other teams. More opportunities. And there's definitely plenty of future left." Miri stared her down. "You're thirty-two years old, bitch. You getting head coach now would just be a stepping stone to something bigger anyway. Not getting it only means that your path is going in a different direction."

"When the hell did you get so smart?"

"When I learned that my head didn't actually have to live in my ass."

A deep, rumbly snort could be heard from across the room. Jade rolled her eyes when a few heavy footsteps followed until Leo was standing behind Miri, his hand immediately going to her waist.

"It took you long enough." Leo's tone was low but playful.

Jade expected her friend to respond with something snarky, maybe pinch the man on the ass and tell him to stay out of grown women's conversations. But clearly, Jade was projecting hard. Instead, Miri put a hand on his lightly stubbled cheek, dragging her thumb over the brown skin there, before leaning up a bit to press a kiss to his lips. The couple lingered in the moment for a few seconds, as if completely unaware they were being watched, before they separated.

When Miri spoke again, it was to Jade. "All that stubbornness ended up just being me putting off my own happiness anyway."

Jade took Miri in. Her dark brown skin glowed from the inside, and her brown eyes were just as bright. Everything about her, from the dark orange on her long nails to the white halter top she wore, was vivid. Her best friend had always been somewhat larger-than-life. Funny and outgoing. Well and truly confident. Even at her lowest, Miri had served as a beacon of inspiration. Jade had always looked up to her, no matter their lack of age difference. Miri had also been through hell and back. Life had dealt her hands hard enough to make anyone crumble. And it wasn't that Miri never had. It was just that she'd always managed to come back. She'd always managed to keep hold of who she was. And now, in the prime of her life, Miri had a loving, nurturing relationship, a beautiful home, a life. A good life. One that she'd cultivated and fought for.

All because she'd believed that she deserved it.

Jade knew she deserved that head coach spot. But she deserved more than that too. Love and connection. The very life that she'd convinced herself was better to put off to the side.

She needed to ask herself how much longer she was willing to make those concessions. Sitting there, seeing what Miri had—what she'd made—didn't make her jealous. Not in that nasty, envious way that burned hot and ugly.

It was more of a restlessness she felt. A longing.

And something that seemed an awful lot like resolve.

22

Tuesday, July 25, was a nasty day. Barely sixty-five degrees, with a dark sky and clouds that seemed to sag from the sheer amount of rain that fell from them. The sheets of water pouring onto them were endless, and it made the air thick and humid, smelling like wet grass and dirt and that distinct rain smell. It was the kind of weather that would not have deterred a professional football team from practicing outside. But as high as the standards they held themselves to were, the Greenbelt Senior High players were not professionals. As such, Landry held practice inside the school that day. Because they were days away from the start of the school year, this meant that half the boys were tasked with moving furniture in classrooms while the other half made use of their meager weight room.

Landry had relieved the assistant coaches of their duties for the day as well. Jade was unsurprised when everyone but her took him up on it. The man was still hell-bent on ignoring her, it seemed. Though, if she were forced to extend any fairness to him, he'd been quiet overall.

Jade had spent days mulling over the last few years of her life in response to the conversation she'd had with Miri. She'd even made one of those goals and accomplishments lists.

"Head coach" was at the top of her goals list, but things like "Get the team a winning season" and "Make more time for personal fun" were there as well. Her accomplishments were where she really shined, though. She'd become the first woman to assistant-coach high school football at her school, she'd managed to pay off her student loans, the family and friends who made up her community were shining stars, and at the end of the day, whatever ended up happening, she was mighty close to reaching her biggest goal. That was an accomplishment in and of itself considering the odds she was up against.

Then she'd sat there, staring down at the paper that had listed so many things that so many people wouldn't believe a little Black girl from nowhere South Carolina could do. Pride had filled her up. The good kind that reminded her of who she was and what she'd done.

Miri had been right. As much as she loved Greenbelt and was loyal to this team, and as much as she wanted to be the one leading it, her opportunities were not solely confined to this place. She was incredible at what she did, and even more than that, she loved it. The game, the mentoring, the sheer thrill of winning. This was what she'd been born to do. Or, at least, one of the things. No one could keep her from it but herself. Certainly not Duncan Landry.

And now that she knew that, she needed him to know it too.

She bided her time until lunch, when the boys were sent to the cafeteria to eat, and it was just her and Landry. He was sitting at the round table at the front of the weight room, working on his laptop, when she walked up. The room was absolute crickets with just them. The only sounds were the loud whirring of the air conditioner and the occasional click of Landry's mouse. He couldn't even be bothered to spare Jade a glance.

Whatever anxiety she might have had left over about speaking to him faded as the indignation welled in her chest like reflux. The relief she got when she finally decided to let her words spew was just as sweet.

"I'm done with this." Her tone was firm as she stood in front of him with her arms crossed.

The man looked almost startled at the sound of her voice. He cleared his throat. "Excuse me?"

"Coach, if you're unhappy with me or my performance or my presence here, I'd appreciate it if you just came right out and said it. Instead of sitting around pretending like I don't exist."

"I haven't—"

She cut him off. "Yes, you have, and you know it. I've been like a ghost to you for two weeks now, and I'm tired of it."

Landry pushed his laptop away and leaned back in his chair, crossing his own arms. The defensive stances they both took would have been funny if the tension between them wasn't as thick as cold grits.

"I don't know what to do with you, Dunn." Landry sighed, shaking his head. "You fucked up. Bad. And I've been here for weeks trying to figure out if you can handle the responsibility all this brings."

"That's not fair."

"Maybe not, but it's true."

"No, I don't agree," she said firmly. "Would you be doing all this if Carr were in my spot or literally any of the other guys? Would you be this hard on them?"

"No, I wouldn't be," Landry was quick to answer. "Because none of those other guys have even an ounce of what it takes to do this job. The standards for them are completely different."

Jade huffed. "So, what? I'm held to some kind of impossibly high standard by you that leaves me no room to make mistakes? I mean, damn, Coach, I'm not saying that I didn't mess up, but the fact that you're actually considering giving up on me for *this* of all things just doesn't make sense. Not a lick of it."

"*This* was big, Dunn." Landry groaned. "One of West Beaufort's assistant coaches caught you pulling that stunt, and if that man didn't know me as well as he did, he could have gone to the district about it instead of coming to me directly. The team's reputation could have been ruined. The boys could have lost their season before it even began."

He was right. There had never been any denying that, not even to herself.

"I know." She let out a shaky breath. "I know I was wrong. I know I could have completely ruined us. It's not that I don't know that now. It's just that I didn't really grasp it then. I was . . ."

"You were shortsighted."

"Yeah, I guess that's it. I was shortsighted. I couldn't see the forest for the trees."

"Learning how to do that is an essential part of this, Dunn." He grunted. "I'd even argue that it's the biggest part—always remembering the bigger picture. When you're staring down the barrel of low morale and losing streaks and everything it means to be a leader to these kids, that bigger picture always has to be on your mind. You cannot forget it."

Jade swallowed, nodding silently. There was nothing for her to say. Once again, he was right. Her silence wasn't even born out of feeling like a scolded child. Nor was it based on feeling sorry that she might still lose everything. It was pure shame. Sure, no one had gotten hurt by her scheming, but they could have. She closed her eyes and imagined the faces of every kid on their team. Sweaty and round-eyed, looking up at her with all the trust in the world. Then she imagined the way those same faces would turn if people unfairly labeled them as cheaters because of her actions.

It made her feel sick.

Landry kept going. "Look, I apologize for ignoring you. I'll admit that wasn't the best decision on my part. I just didn't know what to say to you, because, truthfully, I still don't know what I'm going to do yet."

"Right."

"I know that's not comforting, but maybe it'll give you a chance to get your head back on straight. Remember why you're really here and why you want this. Because I know that it isn't just so you can say you won."

Her stomach churned again. Someone might assume that, with the amount of life-draining talking-tos she'd been given in recent history, she would have gotten used to the sinking feeling in her gut that came when someone made her realize something new about herself. But she hadn't.

"I'm going to make you proud again, Coach."

Landry had gone back to his computer, but he paused and looked up at her. This time, the look on his face wasn't disappointment. It was soft. So soft it made her ache.

"The only person you need to make proud is yourself, Jade. That way you can catch up to how the rest of us already feel about you."

She and Lim had exchanged numbers the night she'd shown up at Jade's parents' house. Jade had never made use of it. But in the days following their last encounter—and Lim's justified rejection of her advances—Jade had taken up the habit of opening her phone's contacts list, finding Lim's number, and attempting to send her a message.

Every single time, she typed something out quickly. Normally, it was a few lines—an introduction—that she'd edit and agonize over forever. Then, every single time when she got that message to the best version of itself, she'd delete it because it still never felt good enough.

This night wasn't so different from the rest. Except that whatever was in her stopping her from pressing Send all those other times simply wasn't there anymore.

She kept it pretty bare-bones.

Jade:

Hey. It's Jade Dunn.

Lim:

Hi! Way to formally introduce yourself like a boomer. You literally put the number in my phone. I know it's you.

Jade:

Now I'm thinking I should block you for all this sass . . .

Lim:

Sorry, sorry. I'm just kidding, swear.

Lim:

What's up? Everything ok?

Jade:

Fine as it can be, honestly. I kind of just wanted to check in, I think. Things were weird the last time we spoke.

Lim:

Weird is an interesting way to put it. I'd say it was more along the lines of really fucking sad.

Jade:

A little pathetic too, on my end.

Lim:

I think we were equally pathetic.

Jade:

Nahh.

Jade:

You basically had me crying on the floor when you left.

Lim:

. . . I shouldn't enjoy seeing you say that, right?

Jade:

Depends on whether you enjoy it because I was hurting or whether you enjoy it because I was hurting for you specifically.

Lim:

Definitely the second one.

Lim:

Which for sure makes me a bad person.

Jade:

I guess we'll have to be bad people together, then, since I've been leading the scoreboard on that with you.

Lim:

You *have* been an asshole.

Jade:

I know.

Jade:

I'm sorry.

Lim:

How sorry?

Jade:

Like, sorrier than a sorry son of a bitch sorry.

Lim:

Hmmmm.

Jade:

Maybe we could talk about it for real, in person?

Lim:

When and where?

Jade:

Tomorrow night at Blu House.

Lim:

Is this you asking me on a date??

Jade:

Yes.

Lim:

Oh.

Lim:

Come on, Dunn, you can ask me better than that.

Jade:

Francesca. I want to take you out and sit across the table from you and watch you eat truffle fries and drink wine.

Jade:

I want to plead my case.

Jade:

Will you let me?

Lim:

Yes.

23

Blu House was one of two "nice" restaurants in Greenbelt. The other was a stalwart Italian restaurant that had been around for decades and was significantly more popular among the town's older citizens. Blu House had been open for only a few years but had grown in popularity among the younger folks in the surrounding towns eager to have something that made them feel like they were showing off on Instagram.

Perfectly befitting its name, the restaurant was deep in the center of Greenbelt's historical neighborhood, in a giant blue mansion that had sat vacant for years. Apparently, the owners had spent more than $100,000 to turn it into the type of eatery that had been featured in publications across the state.

Franny had never been. Honestly, she could think of only one or two times in her entire life when she'd been to a restaurant that had more than three of the little dollar signs next to the Google listing. She'd had to FaceTime Will and Yao from her house an hour before she left to make sure her outfit wouldn't get her turned away at the door for not being fancy enough. She went with a pair of dark blue skinny-fit pin-striped pants, a crisp white button-up, and some low-heeled boots.

She and Jade had agreed to meet at the restaurant, and Franny hadn't had it in her to sit around her house fully dressed and jittery with anticipation, so she'd decided to just show up early and sit anxiously in her car in the parking lot instead. It seemed ridiculous that she would be so nervous about this date. It was their first, sure, but in name only. They'd spent plenty of time alone together, they'd eaten together and laughed together, they'd even already had sex. But there was something about stamping the word *date* on this encounter that made it feel different.

The surprise she had felt when Jade texted her had stopped Franny in her tracks. It wasn't that she hadn't wanted her to reach out, because she had. So fucking bad. She'd damn near wished on a star about it. She just hadn't expected it. Especially not so soon. Even still, sitting in her car, wasting gas and with the air conditioner blasting, Franny wasn't completely sure that she would sit across from Jade during their fancy dinner and hear anything even close to what she wanted to hear from the other woman.

Hoping against hope was a scary, dangerous thing, and Franny didn't know when the hell she'd gotten so brave.

Three consecutive taps at her window just then had her jumping out of her skin. It was Jade, standing there bathed in the orange light of dusk. Franny took a few moments to look at her through the glass, to get her bearings and prepare herself for whatever might come next, before she opened the door and stepped out to greet her.

"You look beautiful," she told Jade, unable and uninterested in keeping the reverence out of her voice.

Jade wore a little black dress with a just-short-of-scandalous thigh-high split and a pair of strappy pumps. Her legs were on full display—thick and long and juicy—and they made Franny's mouth water.

"Thank you." Jade smiled at her softer than she ever had. Then she reached out to play with one of the buttons on Franny's shirt. "You look really good too. Very dapper."

Franny grinned, her belly immediately fluttering at that particular compliment.

One of Jade's arms rested behind her back, and when she removed it, Franny expected to receive a hug, only to be met with a bouquet of flowers. Wrapped perfectly in light brown paper, with a ribbon around the stems, the bunch of wildflowers came in all kinds of colors. Vibrant yellows and oranges, deep blues and lush reds. Franny couldn't put a name to a single one, but she loved them.

"Are these for me?"

"Of course."

Franny took the flowers gently, pressing her nose into the bunch and breathing them in, feeling the various textured petals against her face. "No one's ever given me flowers before."

"That's a damn shame," Jade said. "But I can't say I'm not at least a little bit happy to be the first."

Franny pressed a kiss to Jade's jaw, letting her lips linger on the soft, warm skin there, then smiling against it when she felt a small shiver run through the other woman's body. "Thank you," Franny whispered in her ear.

"It's—" Jade had to stop and clear her throat. "You're welcome."

"Should we go ahead in?"

"Yeah, I made us a reservation; our table should be ready by now."

Not five minutes later, the two were sitting next to each other at a little table tucked away in one corner of the dining room. They'd been given one with a booth on one side and a chair on the other. Luckily for them, the booth was big enough to accommodate them both, so they'd done the annoying thing and decided to sit next to each other. It felt cozy, intimate. The lighting in the room was low and romantic, just bright enough that they could see each other clearly and read the menu. And the little candle on their table only added to the ambience.

They shared a menu, their heads bent close, reading the listings on a big piece of fine card stock. But the words didn't mean a whole lot to Franny. She was too distracted by the woman next to her.

"Have you ever been here before?" she asked Jade.

"No, never. I just figured . . . it was nice, and I wanted to take you someplace nice. Not just like . . . Red Lobster or Minnie's."

Franny leaned back to get a good look at Jade. Grinning at her until her face collapsed into adorable exasperation. "Look at you being all thoughtful."

"What? I can't do something nice for you?"

"I'm not complaining," Franny said with a small smirk. "This is really thoughtful of you, even if I have no idea what half the things on the menu are."

Jade laughed, her soft brown cheeks pinking up a bit as the corners of her eyes wrinkled. "Yeah, I definitely feel like I need to be googling some of these words on here."

"My brother is a literal chef, and I'm still stumped."

"Everybody in here is just as backwoods as we are; they're just pretending they aren't."

"I take offense to that. I am not backwoods. Houston is, like, the fourth-biggest city in the country."

"I love how you had that fact just immediately ready to go." Jade snickered.

"I have to keep it on deck to remind y'all that I'm actually cityfolk every time somebody here tries to get me to eat boiled peanuts or go in the woods or something."

"No boiled peanuts?" The surprise on Jade's face almost made Franny howl in laughter. "Yeah, we're going to have to get you out of that if we're going to be together."

"Oh, is that the stipulation?"

"It's definitely *one* of them."

They were immediately interrupted by their waiter, bringing them a nice plate of bread and butter and then taking their drink orders. Once he left, Franny watched as Jade took the butter knife and spread some over her chunk of steaming bread, closing her eyes in pleasure as she bit into it for the first time. The delight on her face was completely arresting. It made Franny want to see it over and over. It made her want to be the one to put it there.

Was it normal to be jealous of a piece of bread? Or of the fingers that brushed her plush mouth?

"What are the other stipulations?" Franny asked, her voice significantly lower than it had been before.

Jade swallowed. "There's obviously mutual respect."

"Of course."

"And care."

"Mm-hmm."

"Definitely a lot of kisses too. An excess of kisses," Jade clarified.

"I'm definitely starting to think you didn't actually think about these stipulations beforehand."

"Is it that obvious?"

Their waiter brought their drinks to the table—a gin and tonic for Franny and one of the fancy menu cocktails for Jade—and left again with their food orders.

"I'm starting to realize that you're actually not that great at bullshitting. I don't know how I was fooled by you for so long."

Jade ran her thumb over her bottom lip, and Franny watched the movement like a hawk. "I'll have you know, I'm an expert bullshitter. Maybe just not with you."

"And why's that?" Franny asked around the rim of her glass.

"You get under my skin too much. I've always kind of felt like you could see right through it, and it just irked my soul."

"That's so weird to me because I never felt like I had any real idea of what you were thinking or feeling. Sometimes I feel like I'm just throwing shit at the wall and hoping it sticks when I talk to you."

Jade's eyes widened, the expression on her face becoming increasingly more surprised as the seconds passed. "You literally looked me in the eye and told me you knew I wanted you."

Franny shrugged sheepishly. "I mean, I had hope, for sure, but ultimately, I was bullshitting, trying to get a rise out of you. You're desperately sexy when you get worked up at me."

"The only reason you got a rise out of me was because you were right."

"Oh yeah?"

"Do you remember the first time we met?"

"Of course I do. New teacher orientation. Principal Coleman introduced us, and you barely looked me in the eye."

"I was an asshole for sure." Jade grimaced. "There's no excuse for it, I just . . . I saw you, and I immediately got spooked. Hearing you talk felt like a punch to the gut. I didn't really understand it, so I figured that whatever I was feeling must have been, I don't know, dislike or mistrust. My gut was telling me that there was something different about you, and because I'm clearly a fucking fool, I assumed it was a bad thing."

Franny swallowed; her mouth had suddenly run dry. It was a trip to get a reason, an explanation for someone's confounding behavior. Even when that reason wasn't baked into anything logical or levelheaded.

This woman was so terrified of her own feelings, it was devastating to see.

"And what do you think that feeling means now?" Franny asked.

Franny had one hand wrapped around her glass while the other rested relaxed on the table. Jade looked down intently before trailing her fingers along the thin black bracelet around Franny's wrist to deftly trace circles on the back of her hand. Her touches made the skin tingle. It was almost innocent, the way she was so gentle, so sweet.

"I don't know if I fully believe in fate or destiny or whatever you'd want to call it. But I do believe that there are things in this life that are meant for you and there are people in this life you're meant to meet."

Jade looked up at Franny finally, her eyes soft around the corners. Just as soft as her touch on the back of Franny's hand. "I want to believe that I was meant to meet you, Francesca. I do believe it."

"What about after the meeting?" Franny asked quietly. "What comes after that?"

"I think that's the part that's up to us. We control what we do with what the world gives us."

They shared the bread and the entrées. They laughed at how the pasta Jade had ordered ultimately tasted like a recipe from the back of a jar of Ragú. They salivated at Franny's perfectly seared stuffed chicken thighs. They made eyes at each other over a shared ramekin of crème brûlée. Jade had handled the bill before Franny could snatch up the check, and far too soon, they were standing around the entrance of Blu House, illuminated under the twinkling lights of the perfectly paved pathway.

"Is it awful that I'm not ready to go home?" Franny had her arms wrapped around herself, still trying to push away the desire to wrap them around the woman in front of her.

Jade shook her head. "I'm not ready for the night to be over."

"We could always keep in line with the storied tradition of queer women and the never-ending first date."

"We'd only be doing our foremothers proud, right?"

Franny laughed. "I'd say we owe it to them, honestly."

Jade put a hand on Franny's arms just where they met. The

prompting made Franny immediately unravel them and gasp in surprise when Jade interlocked their fingers.

"My house is closer." Jade's tone was gentle. "We could go there."

"I can meet you there."

Jade refused to let go of her hand. "Ride with me. I'll bring you back to your car tomorrow."

"Can't stand to be separated even for a minute, huh?" It was only half-joking.

"No."

A few minutes later, they were on the road. Franny sat in the passenger seat of Jade's old truck, listening as the noisy engine chugged along. She couldn't take her eyes off the other woman's side profile. The slope of her jaw, the wide bridge of her nose, the curves of her lips. Franny's entire body thrummed with the promise of change and the anticipation of something long desired. How long had she wanted this? How deeply had she believed it wouldn't ever happen? The feelings were so heady she almost felt as if she were dreaming. Everything felt hazy and shiny at the same time. Like this moment couldn't possibly be anything close to reality.

Instead of pinching herself to be sure, she reached out to Jade. Walking her fingertips along the exposed bit of thigh unhidden by her dress. Her flesh was hot to the touch and too soft to properly describe. Franny felt the muscles underneath tense, then relax in rhythm with her touches. Even the subtle way Jade pressed her inner thighs together for a few brief moments didn't escape her notice.

Franny slid over as much as her seat belt would allow, just enough so that she could press her lips to that soft jaw. Kissing first, then sucking gently at the skin there.

"Are you trying to kill me?" Jade's voice was ragged.

"I'm trying to prove to myself that you're real."

"If you could feel what I'm feeling right now, you'd know I am."

Franny worked her way down to Jade's neck, kissing and sucking, nipping gently as she reminded herself that they were far too old for hickeys—sad as it was.

"Tell me what you're feeling."

The circles she made on Jade's thigh became slower, steadier.

"Hot." Jade's fingers flexed around the steering wheel. "And wet."

"Can I feel?"

"Please."

She didn't need to be begged—at least not now, at this moment. As cool as she was trying to play it, Franny was just as desperate. So desperate that she couldn't even bring herself to wait until they were at Jade's to delve her fingers into the other woman's panties. Instead, she did it right there at a red light, only a few streets away.

They both cursed at the same time when Franny made direct contact with wet, searing skin.

"You are wet." She spoke the words into Jade's neck. Licking, then blowing on the skin. "And you *ache*, I can tell."

Her fingers circled Jade's pulsing clit a few times, groaning as she felt it twitch under her touch.

Jade released a long, shaky breath, shivering. The sound of her teeth chattering as audible as her breathy moans.

"Maybe I should stop," Franny said. "You're too distracted."

"Please don't. Please. I'll-I'll—"

"Shhhhh. I won't, angel, I won't. I promise I won't stop; you don't have to beg. You never have to beg me."

Franny worked her middle finger between Jade's soft folds, wetting it until it was soaked enough to slide inside her smoothly, without feeling intrusive. Immediately, her pussy began to flutter around Franny's finger, wetness sliding down Franny's palm as she pressed the heel of it against Jade's clit.

"How does that feel, baby?"

Franny removed her lips from Jade's neck just long enough to look at her face. Her plush mouth was open, and her breathing was heavy. She kept her eyes wide, on the road as the light turned green. Her hands gripped the wheel so tight the skin stretched over her knuckles was white.

"I need another one. Please, pl—"

"What did I tell you about begging? Huh?"

Franny removed her finger from Jade's pussy altogether, circling her clit again.

"That I—" Jade gasped. "I don't have to."

"That's right. Remember that. Okay, good girl?"

Jade nodded profusely, only to cut herself off with another moan when Franny slid two fingers inside her. She stroked her steadily, curling her fingers up, pressing against that spongy spot every time she moved in.

The car stopped, and Franny peeked through the windshield to see that they were parked firmly in front of Jade's house.

"Let me help you take the edge off before we go inside?" Franny spoke the words in between kisses to Jade's neck and jaw. "Let me make you come."

Jade turned her head and without hesitation or delay captured Franny's lips with her own. Every cell, every atom in Franny's body came alive at once. The small hairs on the back of her neck raised, and her pussy immediately ran even slicker.

She'd thought she had been alive before. But this . . . this was different. This was like breathing fresh air for the first time. Kissing Jade, feeling her, fucking her, made her entire being feel brand-new. Restored.

She worked her fingers faster, thrusting and rubbing, sliding through hot skin and soaking wetness until she barely knew where she ended and Jade began.

When the other woman's body seized up and her lips went slack,

Franny didn't stop. She put more pressure on Jade's clit, but kept her circling steady, stroking her from the inside until she fell over her cliff of pleasure.

Jade's orgasm was nearly silent, breathy and whiny and so delicious that Franny wanted to swallow up the sounds and keep them inside her forever.

"Oh my God," Jade panted when her body finally started to relax. "Fuck."

Franny pulled her fingers out, immediately putting them inside her own mouth. She made no moves to hide the pleasure she derived from the taste. Nor did she hide the grin that spread across her face when Jade's eyes darkened again.

"We need to go inside." Jade yanked the keys out of the ignition. "We're going to need more space than this."

24

Jade hadn't known their date would end with her bringing Franny back to her place. But she'd be lying if she said she hadn't prepared for it. She'd cleaned the way her mother would have—deeply and thoroughly, as if preparing for inspection. Dishes had been washed, floors had been mopped, even her pantry had been reorganized. She'd changed her sheets too—not just washed but changed. The normal pair of heather-gray jersey sheets, built for warmth and comfort, had been replaced with a soft, lush pair of emerald-green flax linen ones. They'd never been used before, not even by her. So when Franny guided her into her own bedroom and practically threw her onto the bed, she felt herself sink into the softness of them just as her body was covered with the delicious warmth of another.

Her dress had been hiked up to her waist, and Franny was between her thighs, pants unbuttoned, shirt untucked and half-open. Jade's hands drifted down the smooth softness of her neck to the collar of her shirt, pushing the fabric off her shoulders. Franny's dark nipples were hard behind her little white bralette. Jade's thumbs found them, reveling in the way they seemed to only get harder.

Franny shivered on top of her, grinding her body harder against Jade's. A warm thigh pressed up against her sensitive pussy, and her already soaked panties grew even more saturated.

"Francesca . . ."

"Have I told you how much I fucking love it when you say my name?" Franny's words were spoken into the skin between Jade's breasts.

"No, you haven't," Jade breathed out.

"Well, goddamn I do. Every time you say it, it drives me wild."

"Why?"

Franny shoved Jade's bra down, licking around an areola before her lips sucked the nipple in. It wasn't until Jade was squirming and whining under her that she answered the question.

"Because when you say it, I can tell you mean it. You're not just saying it because it's a name; you're saying it because it's *mine*."

Franny's mouth was on her other nipple then, warm and wet, biting at the skin until it stung, just to soothe it with her soft tongue.

"Yes . . ." Jade could barely think straight. "It's yours. It's yours."

"What's mine? The name or this body of yours? Which one is mine?"

That thigh moved against her pussy again, and Jade rocked her hips against it, greedy, humping desperately. Her last orgasm had been mere minutes ago. She could still feel the effects of it in her wrung-out body. She didn't feel finished, though, not nearly. Not even fucking close.

"Both . . ." She dragged the words out.

"You want to prove that they're both mine?"

"Anything . . . I'll do anything."

Franny chuckled—it was a dark sound, though nowhere close to unkind—and she moved off Jade completely, which caused her to ache and whine like some kind of wounded animal. Franny lounged next to her, bare feet dangling off the bed.

"Stand up, Jade."

For all her talk and pomp, Jade was naught but a bottom eager to fold under the commands of a woman with the power to wield them so perfectly. So she stood, feet planted on the floor at the foot of the bed, looking down at Franny as she lay on her back, undoing the rest of the buttons on her shirt before throwing it on the floor. Those brown nipples were tight against white cotton, pressing so hard Jade thought they might rip the fabric. Her mouth watered, tongue heavy as she bit down on her bottom lip to keep from panting or begging or worse.

"Take your clothes off."

She did not need to be told twice. Her little black dress was up and over her head before either of them could blink, leaving her clad only in the pair of panties she'd had on underneath.

"Those too, angel girl."

And so they went. And there she stood, naked and trembling as Franny took her in. That dark gaze roamed every inch of her body, from the unpainted tips of her toes to the hairs that stuck out of her bun. Jade felt completely and totally exposed. More than naked, she was bare. But somehow it didn't embarrass her or make her shy. She wanted this woman to see her, every single bit. The mole on her belly and the little hair that grew out of it. The stretch marks on her ass, the silvery scars on her shins. Even the things that were deep inside too. Both dastardly and divine.

"You're so beautiful." Franny breathed the words out so confidently that there was no arguing with her.

Jade's eyes fluttered closed. "Can you tell me again?"

She heard the sheets rustle and knew Franny was sitting up before she even reached out to take Jade's hand in hers. Franny pressed Jade's palm to her mouth, kissing the warm skin, rubbing her face against it. Jade hoped her fingertips committed the feeling of her eyes and lips and cheeks to memory, until recalling them became just as easy as breathing.

This woman had her completely gone—taken. Jade wouldn't consider floating back down to any reality where this wasn't happening.

Where she wasn't standing naked in front of Francesca Lim, being seen and feeling adored.

"You're the most beautiful thing I've ever seen," Franny said, finally giving in to Jade's request.

"More beautiful than Spanish moss," she continued, trailing kisses up Jade's wrist.

"And Carolina rain showers."

A hand replaced those lips on her wrist. "And a perfect spiral throw."

Jade laughed, the moment of levity much appreciated when it felt like her heart was likely to explode out of her chest at any given moment. "That last one is a tall order."

"It's true," Franny insisted.

That hand of hers pulled Jade forward, and the closer she got, the farther Franny moved until she was lying down on the bed again.

"Now come sit on me. I want to see how beautiful you are from down here."

Jade didn't need any more urging; she felt in tune with Franny now. She may not have known exactly what the other woman was thinking, but she knew enough to understand that when she clambered up the bed, it was Franny's face she was meant to park herself on rather than her lap.

She hissed as Franny wasted no time using her fingers to spread her pussy open, laving her tongue over Jade's pulsing, wet clit.

"Oh God . . ." Jade's hands went into Franny's hair, gripping the soft raven locks just enough to spur her on but not hurt her. "That feels so fucking good, Francesca."

Underneath her, Franny reacted with grunts and hums that only made the feeling of her mouth more intense. A quick slap to Jade's round ass almost shocked her into orgasm—almost.

"Fuck my face." The words were muffled between her thighs but clear as day. "Work that pussy against me. Use me."

Jade's hips started moving in a steady rhythm. Unabashed and joyous, she threw her head back and wailed. Thankful, not for the first time, that she didn't share walls with anyone, because the sounds of their sex were too hot to ignore. Grunts and moans, the slick slide of her pussy, even the sound of the bed frame gently beating against the wall. They were all reminders that she was there, that this was real.

Her belly coiled up tightly; something wound itself around every single one of her organs and squeezed until it felt like there was no air left in her lungs. It would be so easy to let go, to release and fall, tumbling down that hill until she found her bliss. But she didn't want that, not yet. She wanted to draw it out, make the pleasure last. Honestly, she never wanted it to stop. But from the ferocious way Franny was eating her out, the other woman seemed hell-bent on squeezing the nut out of her.

"Stop," Jade panted. "Hold on, hold on."

Franny pulled back immediately, and Jade moved down just a bit until she was sitting on her chest.

"What's wrong?" Franny looked up at her, that lovely gaze full of worry. "Did I do something?"

Jade shook her head. "I don't want to come yet."

"I can give you as many as you want. You know that, right? We don't have to stop."

"I know." Jade leaned down and pressed a sloppy kiss to Franny's lips, tasting herself. "I just can't stand not being able to touch you for so long."

Franny swallowed. "I'm right here. You can touch me all you want."

"I won't want to stop, Francesca."

"So don't."

25

Do you think it'll be weird if we show up together?" Franny asked.

"Maybe." She felt Jade shrug. "But who gives a shit. What we're doing isn't nearly as messy as half the shit our coworkers get up to."

"Fair enough. I just . . . I don't want other people's reactions to spook you."

"It's not like we're going to have sex on top of the truck."

"You know what I mean, goofy."

They were in bed, naked and entwined, legs tangled and bodies warm, the soft first light of dawn shining through the white eyelet curtains of Jade's bedroom window. Franny tucked her head farther underneath Jade's chin, planting a small kiss at the hollow to signify her affection. Jade's arms tightened around her in response. Her brown skin was still sleep-warm and free of any type of perfume. Just clean sweat and eau de Jade. It was an addictive thing to take in, and Franny never wanted to be without the comfort of it. Not now that she'd grown accustomed.

It was the first day of school for all K–12 students in Greenbelt's public school system. They had a few spare minutes to lie with each other before they were forced to get up and take the world on. Franny closed her eyes, imagining the noise and hustle that was to come compared to this peacefulness. She didn't want to give it up, not yet—not ever.

"They won't spook me. They can't. The only thing that spooks me now is fucking this up," Jade said.

The two had hardly left each other's side for a week and a half. The day after their date, they'd split long enough for Franny to go grab some essentials from her apartment and book it back to Jade's. They'd had five football practices in the time between, and each one they'd shown up to in separate cars, pretending like nothing between them had changed.

Generally, that wasn't so difficult. Tensions were high on the team with them being so close to their first official game of the season. And both she and Jade were firmly entrenched in the roles they played in getting their win and kicking the season off on a high note.

Of course, there were also their personal ambitions . . .

But every time they got in their respective cars and sped out of the parking lot, they met at the same place—Jade's little driveway. They'd cooked meals together, gone grocery shopping at the Piggly Wiggly. There had been multiple mixed loads of laundry done and bodywash sharing. Their toothbrushes had even touched heads with surprisingly little disgust on both their parts.

The shacking up had commenced, and the night before, they'd finally discussed how they might handle getting to and from work now that *this* was a real *thing*. Franny hated to admit it, but she'd been surprised with how easily Jade had taken to the idea of saying, "Fuck it," and showing up together. She had pitched it to her as an "it makes more sense environmentally to save gas" idea, but Jade had come right out to say that if others didn't go to any great lengths to hide their entanglements, they shouldn't have to either.

So they wouldn't.

They'd keep things professional. No public displays of affection during school hours. No spilling tea to any of their colleagues. But they'd let them think whatever the hell they wanted, and if some of them ran into something along the lines of the truth, then so be it.

"You're not going to fuck it up," Franny told her, believing every word.

"Well, I'm me, which means there's always room to fuck it up."

Franny pulled away until she was leaning up on her elbow, looking Jade in the eye. She soothed the wrinkle between Jade's eyebrows with her thumb and planted a kiss there when her brows unfurrowed.

"I don't accept that."

Jade chuckled, her eyes rolling fondly. "Of course you don't."

"My Jade is not a fucker-upper. In fact, she's a fixer-u—" Franny stopped, grimacing.

"A what, Francesca? A fixer-upper? I'm a fixer-upper?"

"In my defense, I didn't really think that through all that well. But you know that's not what I mean. I'm just as liable to screw things up as you, which is why we have to hold each other accountable."

"And how do we do that?"

"We call each other out on our bullshit. We listen when we get called out. We don't go running for the hills at the first sign of trouble. And we definitely"—Franny kissed her neck—"*definitely* don't give up without a fight."

"A relationship manifesto," Jade said. "They're like our team rules."

"Exactly. They give us something to remember every time we step out on that field, Coach."

Jade groaned loud and long. "I actually really hate you calling me 'Coach' in bed."

"Oh yeah?"

"I'd much rather you go back to 'my Jade.' I enjoyed that way more."

"My Jade." Franny leaned forward and kissed her, thumb moving over one of the dark nipples that became exposed as the sheets settled around their waists. "My Jade. My Jade. My Jade."

"Francesca."

A shiver ran through Franny's body, the same way it always did when she heard her name on Jade's lips.

"Maybe we've got a little time for—"

The shrill sound of two phone alarms blaring at the exact same time cut her off, and she groaned.

"Fuck," Jade whined.

"'Tis time." Franny jumped out of bed before she began to entertain the idea of convincing Jade to quit their jobs and live in bed full-time. "School's back, baby."

"I hate you."

"You so don't. You . . . opposite of hate me."

A look flashed across Jade's face that immediately made Franny's stomach flip. They didn't have time to think about that. It was too early, too hectic, too . . . She clenched her eyes shut, willing the image of it away, along with her silly desires to say things they couldn't possibly have been ready to say.

Then, when they brushed their teeth in tandem, eyes locked in the bathroom mirror, Franny pretended not to understand what the heated gaze between them was for.

The first day of classes went as smoothly as it could possibly go. There had been no fights and minimal tears, which counted as a win for Franny. By the time school was over, she was knock-down, drag-out exhausted. And by the time she made her way from cleaning up her classroom to the football field for afternoon practice, she wanted nothing more than to collapse into bed.

Jade slipped her a prebottled iced coffee and a wink as Franny slunk by her to join Carr and the O-line boys.

"We thinking barrel drills today, Coach?"

The boys had been solid with their hits recently. Their strength training and speed were coming in strong, but there were a few who needed more practice on staying in control while they were on the line. Barrel drills would help show them how to keep the right center of gravity needed to maintain speed without losing control.

"I'm thinking exactly what you're thinking, Coach," Carr answered.

She rolled her eyes, watching out the corner of her eye as Carr parked his behind in the folding chair he had on the sidelines and started reading the day's paper.

"I'm not a coach," she mumbled, thinking there was no way he could hear her.

"We'll see if that's still true in a few days, I guess," he said, chuckling.

Franny rallied the boys without a whistle, getting one of the seniors to set up the barrels while she explained the drill to the kids. It wasn't a new one for them, but it never hurt to reiterate, in her opinion. Nor did it hurt to get out there and show them with her own body how they might go about getting the desired result.

She watched them with a scrutinizing eye, arms crossed, trying to find points of correction in their forms. Every now and again, she'd interrupt the drill to show one of them how to reposition their hips or straighten their stance.

Twenty minutes in, she called for a break, slapping the boys on their heaving backs while they all lined up for the watercooler.

She lifted her own water bottle to her mouth, using the guise of drinking to take an actual look downfield at where Jade was watching her D-line do hand-fighting drills. A tactical way of play fighting that would help defensive players keep the offensive players' hands off their bodies.

Franny swiped the back of her hand across her forehead. The sun was relentless today, and she had forgotten to bring a change of clothes for practice. So she stood there in a pair of full-legged dungarees with suns and moons printed all over them and a T-shirt underneath. The air conditioner in the building was strong enough that she likely would have been cold in any fewer clothes, but it made for a brutal time out on the field. So much so that she reached down to cuff the hem of her dungarees a few times in hopes that an errant breeze might sweep across her ankles and cool her off.

Jade had not been so forgetful. In fact, she'd even made quite the departure from her normal khaki shorts and coaching polo and was fitted out in an old Greenbelt T-shirt and a pair of white running shorts that showed off her long legs. She was completely homed in on what was happening in front of her, those keen eyes watching, using her whistle every time she needed to correct someone or something.

Her D-line was in tip-top shape too, focused and strong. It was clear that Jade's word was complete and total law. Not just because she'd ordained it as such but because she'd earned the right for it to be.

Franny always loved watching her like this—in her element. As stern as she looked, as seriously as she took her job, her love for it was impossible to hide. Something special came over her every time she stepped out on the field. Franny found it indescribable, intangible. If there was a name for it, she didn't know what it was, but recognizing the spark in Jade's eyes was becoming easier for her by the day.

She made no attempts to keep herself from staring, not even when Jade blew her whistle and released her players for their water break. Almost as if she sensed she was being watched, she looked down the field, catching Franny's eye in a blink and flashing her one of those shy smiles of hers.

They started walking toward each other at the same time. They met on the sidelines, somewhere in the middle, and Franny had to shove her hands in the front pockets of her overalls to keep from reaching out to Jade. She hadn't gone this long without touching the other woman in days, and the withdrawal was brutal. The two women stood side by side, both facing the field. Franny with her hands tucked away and Jade with her arms crossed.

"I think we're going to take it," Franny remarked.

"Oh yeah?"

"Mm-hmm. They're strong, and they want it."

"That might not be enough," Jade said, facing ahead and squinting.

"No, I can feel it. Not just about this game either but the whole season. It feels like something is building."

"That could just be indigestion from the leftover pizza we had this morning."

"You don't have to believe me, Dunn." Franny laughed. "But I think luck is on our side."

"I sure as hell want you to be right," Jade admitted. "It's impossible to say, though. The last time I talked to Landry, he told me that I needed to work on looking at the big picture."

"Is this team having a good season *not* the bigger picture?"

"No, it is. But winning the first game isn't. Neither is harping on luck, unfortunately."

Franny nodded, conceding to her point. "I guess that's why you're the one in charge."

"The only place I'm in charge is when it's time to choose what we're going to have for dinner," Jade said quietly, out the side of her mouth.

"For now."

Jade made a noncommittal noise, then sniffed, dropping her arms to her sides. "Focusing on the big picture right now means that, well, it means that maybe I don't let my ambitions cloud my reality."

"Jade." Franny sucked in a breath. "You are not giving up on this. You're not . . ."

Franny couldn't fathom a version of Jade that existed without a dream—this dream. Landry was not in attendance at first-day practice because of meetings or something, but Franny suddenly felt the need to seek him out and give him a real piece of her mind.

"I'm not. You know I'm not. I never will. I'm like a damn dog with a bone. I'm not giving it up. I'm just not going to keep letting myself make awful decisions in defense of it."

They caught each other's eyes and held their gazes. Franny didn't care if anyone noticed. "One bad decision does not a fuckup make, Jade."

Suddenly, Jade looked away. "I'm not just talking about the West Beaufort thing . . . I'm talking about you too."

"Oh, Jade . . ." Franny shook her head in disagreement.

"I missed out on a lot of time that could have been spent with you. I was mean to you for no reason. I said awful things . . ."

Franny touched Jade's arm, and the muscles tensed underneath her palm. The touch was simple, but it linked them together in a tangible way, and as she kept her hand there, she could feel Jade's shoulders loosen.

"You were definitely an asshole," she said. "But I liked playing along just fine."

"Still. I want this too much to let it slip through my fingers because I didn't know when to stop bluffing and fold."

"Jade, look at me, please."

Jade's movements were reluctant, a slow turn of the head until they were face-to-face again. The tears in Jade's eyes made Franny's heart ache. The scene around them was far from quiet. Even on their water breaks, the team was loud, boisterous. Their camaraderie was evident even through their exhaustion. The heat, the artificial smell of the Astroturf, even the sounds of the people around them faded away into nothing the second their eyes met.

Franny smiled at her. "There isn't a single version of me in existence that would ever want to see you give up your dream. You might not believe in luck or destiny, but I'm silly enough to, and I believe that this is only one of many great things you're meant for. There's no need to put it on the back burner, not for me. I'm not coming to you with ultimatums, Jade. So please don't give yourself any on my behalf."

Jade looked down, sniffing and blinking away the tears Franny had seen pooling in her eyes. It honestly seemed as if they both had cried full-on rivers in recent history.

"You'll keep me honest, though, won't you?" Jade's voice was as meek as she'd ever heard it. "If I start getting buck wild again?"

"Yeah. I'll keep you on the straight and narrow, kid."

Franny's heart stuttered in her chest for what felt like the thousandth time since she'd first laid eyes on this woman. Practice be damned, she wanted to kiss her, feel the warmth of her lips and her body. Franny wanted to give Jade the comfort she knew she needed.

"We need to get back to work." Jade cleared her throat.

"Yeah, before I jump your bones."

"We'll continue at home?"

"Yes. At home."

26

Jade had been six years old when she'd gone to her first football game. Dead in the middle of November, on a misty Friday night, the temperature had dipped down into the low sixties. This meant that her mother had bundled her up in a thick sweater and scarf that made the bottom of her face too warm for comfort. Jade's father had brought her to Greenbelt Senior High School's stadium to see her older cousin play in one of their playoff games. The stands had been packed to the rafters with people, but she and her father had found seats in a middle row of the bleachers, near the fence that kept folks from falling off the sides.

Jade remembered the awe she'd felt at the sheer size of the crowd. She remembered hearing the marching band play, the way each bang of the drums thumped in her chest. The smell of popcorn and the almost blinding lights that stood tall above them all. The way the crowd roared and how the bleachers shook with the force of people's stomps. It had been a heady experience, a total overload of her senses. She had never been able to forget it. That game had been such a catalyst in her life. It didn't matter how many times she'd experienced that roar, how she'd managed to migrate from the stands to the sidelines. She never got over the overwhelming elation that filled her body whenever she was at a game. She wouldn't have admitted it to anyone else, but it was the one time she understood why people got so hyped at church.

Today was no different; Greenbelt had come out in full swing for their first game of the season. With the stands packed tightly, all she could see when she looked around the stadium was a sea of green and white. And West Beaufort had a decent turnout on the away-team side, filling it with black and gold. The energy was so palpable, she felt high just being in the middle of it.

She wore her standard coach's uniform—a pair of khaki pants and a green polo shirt. It was a mild night for August, not much humidity, with a dark sky and a high moon. Still, the fabric of her shirt clung like hell to her lower back.

She'd started sweating before she and Franny had even left the house. The other woman had forced her to drink three glasses of water and eat half a deli sandwich before she'd relinquished the keys to Gladys so they could leave.

Jade eyed Francesca, clad in a pair of skinny jeans and a Greenbelt Gators T-shirt from the student center, as she huddled with Coach Carr. She should have been wearing the same thing as the rest of them. She should have had a whistle around her neck and the actual authority to call shots for the offensive line.

Jade had never wanted to see someone clad in an ugly green polo shirt more in her life.

"Coin toss in three," Landry said as he jogged over to her, his eyes lit up and his jaw tight. "You think we're ready?"

Jade had to look over her shoulder to make sure he was talking to her. It had been weeks since Landry had spoken to her with such levity in his voice. Their talk in the weight room had eased the tensions some. At least enough that Jade wasn't on the receiving end of the silent treatment anymore. But it still hadn't been the way it was before. She feared that even if he did pass the token along to her, their relationship as mentor and mentee would be forever fractured.

So many of her thoughts had been taken up with trying to make peace with it. She'd apologized, acknowledged her wrongs, and had taken great effort in getting her shit back together. That didn't mean Landry trusted her again—or liked her, for that matter. Much the same way she'd forced herself to come to terms with the uncertainties of her life's potential outcomes, she had to do the same for her relationship with Landry. There were only so many limbs she could go out on before the tree was stripped bare.

But there he was, standing at her side with the type of energy that had inspired Jade to want to work with him in the first place. He was the only person she knew who seemed less stressed during games than he did outside of them. He bounced on his feet and surveyed the scene before him. She could almost see the kid in him. The one who'd played college ball, wearing the same pair of lucky socks, checking the sturdiness of his cup one last time, before running out on the field the way their boys were about to.

It was too endearing of a vision for her not to smile at.

"We're as ready as we'll ever be," she answered. "Their energy is high. They've spent all summer going hard, working for this. We're taking it. But even if we don't, it won't be because they didn't give it everything they had."

Landry's eyes were on her then, something thoughtful coloring his expression. She was seconds away from outright asking him what he was thinking, but a low rumbling sounded behind them. The noise built progressively until it turned to banging followed quickly by deafening cheers.

The boys descended on the field just as the sound of the screams swelled. There was no banner for them to break through, but they shot out like rockets all the same, waving at the crowd. Hooting and hollering.

"See?" She had to talk loudly over the noise. "They know it's theirs."

Landry bumped his shoulder against hers, catching her eye with a stern nod, that twinkle in his eye even more prominent. "Let's go help them take it, then."

West Beaufort came out on top in the coin toss, and instead of choosing to defer their claim to the ball until the second half, they started the game off with the ball in their hands. Immediately after kickoff, Jade was reminded that the other team hadn't shown up in their fancy coach bus with their pristine new cleats just to fuck around. They saw the win as theirs and had come to claim it.

West Beaufort kept possession of the ball at kickoff. One of their running backs had gotten the ball from the quarterback at the snap, taking off downfield in a mad sprint toward Greenbelt's end zone.

Their defensive linemen were on him, though, leaving the side of West Beaufort's quarterback to book it down the field. That wide receiver barely got five yards before a nose tackle caught him around the waist and brought him down. The ball slipped from the running back's hands and onto the turf—a fumble.

Jade's breath caught in her throat, her spine immediately straightening. On the sidelines, she could hear her colleagues yelling, screaming with excitement. The ref blew his whistle, signaling the end of the play, and at once, all the boys were in the exact spot the receiver went down, waiting for the ref to place the ball and start the next down.

She surveyed the eleven players Greenbelt had on the field. The game was early yet, so they were still spry. Not bogged down by the type of tiredness that only came with being four quarters and three downs in. There was still plenty of time for that.

Landry was standing a few yards away from her, his attention on the spiral-bound playbook in his hands. Then his eyes went back to the field. This time, they were on West Beaufort's players. The boys got into their three-point stances as normal. That's when she saw something shift.

West Beaufort's quarterback moved to the right of the center instead of behind him, and just as quick, the running back slid into his place.

Jade booked it over to Landry. "They're about to do a Wildcat formation," she said in a rush.

Normally, the center would snap the football back between his legs to the quarterback, who would then run or pass it. A Wildcat formation was a sort of trick play where instead of snapping the ball to the quarterback, a running back would situate himself in that spot to get the ball directly.

If the other team got through the snap without anyone noticing, they'd have at least a few seconds' lead time. And in a game where a few seconds could mean more than a few yards, it had the potential to be a very effective strategy. It was still early in the game, and while West Beaufort pulling this off didn't automatically mean that Greenbelt would be completely screwed, it would give the other team a hell of a head start. The points they'd gain on Greenbelt would not only sting but throw a wrench in her team's morale. And that was far too precious a thing to lose so early on.

Her heart started thundering in her chest as she hoped like hell their players caught on quickly. There was no way to talk to them, to prepare them for what was to come. It would have to play out naturally while they stood around hoping they'd taught their boys enough to be observant.

The second-down snap was as quick as any other, and just as she'd thought, their running back shot off like a rocket down the field, ball in hand. Jade ran along the sidelines, yelling as loudly as she could, hoping like hell they could hear her voice. Time always seemed to move slower in the milliseconds during plays. It felt like something out of a movie, the way they descended on the running back as he made his way toward Greenbelt's end zone.

The running back saw that his time on two feet was short, pausing to look for an opening, then sending the ball down the field to the tight end, who completed the pass.

Jade's voice went hoarse from the way she yelled when the tight end took off running. He made it far, too far. Everyone took off after him, and the kid seemed to weave through their bodies like a bat out of hell. Then, in mere seconds, he pushed his way past until he was at Greenbelt's end zone, making the first touchdown of the season in the first quarter of the first game like it was nothing.

Her heart fell into her ass. She looked over her shoulder, spotting Landry, then Carr, and, finally, Francesca. Their faces were drawn, all pinched lips and hollow cheeks. She imagined hers looked the same.

Out on the field, she watched as the boys tried to shake it off. She couldn't see their faces through their helmets, but their body language was loud. The West Beaufort players were nimble, slamming into one another in a celebration that was short-lived when their coach decided to go for a field goal kick instead of a two-point conversion.

Then, just as quickly as that *6* appeared on the scoreboard in the other team's favor, it was updated to a *7* once their kicker sent it flying through the uprights.

Jade jogged back down the sidelines, keeping an eye on the game as the players went for kickoff at the 35-yard line. They'd have a short break after this, and she wanted to talk a game plan with Landry.

"I don't want them getting any further ahead of us than this," she said. "We need to change our lineup a bit."

"What are you thinking?"

"Defense needs to be a little nastier. I figured West would come at us light and ramp up toward the end, but that's not how they're playing it. We need to keep them from gaining but make sure we've got enough energy toward the end when they tire themselves out."

"Yeah." Landry said. "We'll put Tyrie in now."

"And Joshua too. Let him send some of them to the ground."

After a few yards' gain on Greenbelt's part, they had a quick break. Just enough time for water and subbing a few players out. Jade made sure she made some room to talk to her team as well.

"Your hustle is incredible, y'all. Nice clean hits, staying on their tails—I'm proud of the work you're doing out there."

"We let them score, Coach," Ozzie Alfaro grumbled, sweat pouring down his face. "That ain't good."

The other boys hummed in agreement.

"No, it isn't," Jade agreed. "But you know what? I think that having them get one on you early won't do anything but show you that they didn't come to play, so we can't either."

Next to her, Landry nodded. She paused, waiting for him to say something of his own like he normally would, but he kept silent.

She cleared her throat. "When you get back out there, I want you to remember one thing. Repeat it over and over in your heads if you have to. But tell yourself that this is yours. That ball is yours, this field is yours, this win is yours. Nobody can take it from you, least of all them."

The boys murmured their affirmative, and she watched one by one as their shoulders squared while they put their helmets back on.

"Now what did I just say?" she yelled.

"This ball is ours!" they yelled, repeating her words.

"And what else?" Jade got louder.

The boys followed suit. "This field is ours!"

"Tell me more."

"This win is ours!"

"So go take it, then."

Fourth quarter, fourth down, twenty-five seconds left on the clock. The score was 37-43, with Greenbelt down by six.

The boys were tired, sweat staining through their pads, bodies slower under the mounting pressure of taking it all home. On the sidelines, the coaches held their collective breaths as the players lined up.

There was time for one last play, and Greenbelt had possession of the ball. This was their last shot, and everyone could feel it. Even the crowd was eerily quiet, having spent an entire quarter with bated breaths as the two teams squared off.

Jade squinted across the field, using her twenty-twenty vision to spot West Beaufort's head coach. He'd taken that ugly tan sun visor off his head, sweat pulling around his temples, face stone-cold mad.

Landry was still light on his feet, face impassive. The only indicator of his stress was the way his right fist balled up tightly in the pocket of his khakis—and even that was obvious only if you knew where to look.

"They didn't expect us to come this hard," she told her head coach.

"We haven't had a season opener this good in years." The grin on Landry's face was downright wolfish.

Her own grin stretched out, and she briefly wondered if it was just as intense. Everything inside her believed that this game was theirs, that winning today was inevitable for her team. It was the type of foolhardy delusion she forced herself to stand in. She'd keep it until the very end too—even if it ended up being a bitter one. Jade figured a little delusion was allowed, if not necessary, at times like these. And hell, even if the impossible happened and they lost, she'd do nothing but keep that spirit alive at the next game. And the one after that. And the one after that too.

Total defeat was not an option. Not for her. Not for her team.

"I know," she said. "Thirty-seven isn't an opener score. Not for us."

"Let's see about forty-four."

"Fifty-one, even."

Landry cackled, and she did too. She knew they must have looked wild as hell. Looking possible defeat in the eyes and making jokes all the while. But shit, it felt too good to be back.

They'd had a quick break moments before, enough for the boys to gulp down some water and for Jade to tell them how they were going to finish the game.

A flea flicker. The type of trick play that wasn't at all uncommon but would hopefully still work to their advantage. Greenbelt was tired, but West Beaufort was too. They hadn't expected to work as hard as they'd had to to get this far and not even be ahead. Sluggish and slower than they'd been when they started, Jade figured that getting tricky with them in the final play during the final seconds would work to Greenbelt's advantage in a major way. A winning way.

The snap happened quickly; Greenbelt's quarterback handed off the ball to the running back behind him, who took off fast and furious down the line of scrimmage.

On the sidelines, the Greenbelt coaches stood in a tight row, acting almost like a wall of excitement and anticipation. Jade's eyes were glued to the field, but in her peripheral, she could practically see them suck in a collective breath of air and hold it in their chests as their running back gained yard after yard. It would have been hilarious if it weren't so tense.

She eyed the clock, watching as the seconds ticked by faster than seemed possible.

Ten seconds left.

Their running back stopped suddenly, only to pass the ball back into the hands of their quarterback, who immediately threw it downfield to a wide-open receiver. West Beaufort's actions stuttered for just a moment, but it was long enough for Greenbelt to get a good lead after their little trick.

Suddenly, all the coaches on both sides were yelling. Red-faced, veins popping, Jade screamed as her wide receiver got closer to West Beaufort's end zone. The seconds ticked as his legs worked hard and fast. His body twisting and spinning as he evaded their players trying to tackle him.

When it happened, it was too quick to elicit a real reaction. One second left, the crowd and the coaches screaming their lungs out, and their wide receiver was taken down by a defensive tackle. The kid caught him right around the waist, wrapping his arms around tightly and bringing him to the ground so suddenly and hard that he fumbled the ball. It bounced once, then landed right there on the turf a few feet away from the boys on the ground.

The players scrambled to dive for possession of it, but before they could even formulate a plan of action, the clock reached zero, loud buzzers sounding throughout the stadium and signaling the end of the game.

There would be no overtime. There would be nothing to bring them back from the edge. They'd lost. It had been the first game of the season, and they'd lost.

But damn if it didn't feel the way a loss usually felt. On the field, their boys looked downtrodden. Shoulders dropped, limbs heavy, faces to the ground. They'd fought hard—anyone watching could see that. But it still hadn't been enough to earn them their win. Jade knew they were crushed. Her position along the sidelines had allowed her to see that they'd played a hell of a game and had nothing to be ashamed of. But they were still deep in it.

She turned to Landry, who was standing at her side, clapping. She wasn't sure what she'd expected to see, but the look on his face was a pleasant surprise. He wasn't smiling, but his expression was awash with pure pride. His eyes were damn near glistening, shining brightly as he looked over his team.

It put things into perspective even more. This wasn't a win, but it wasn't quite a loss either, not truly.

The boys started to make their way off the field as the crowd in the stands slowly filed out. All the coaches stood in a line, slapping them on the backs as they made their way toward the locker rooms. They'd go in after them, letting them get a few minutes to themselves before they did their duty and came in with a pep talk. Any focus on what could have been done better would be saved for another day. On this day, they'd be celebrated.

Once the last kid was off the field, Jade put a hand on Landry's shoulder. "Well, look at that, Coach. You've done your boys good."

His eyes were still shining when he glanced down at her. The look in them felt like a bottle rocket taking off. It felt like kissing Francesca square on the lips once they got in the car together every afternoon. It felt like when her daddy had given over the keys to Gladys that fall morning.

It felt like winning.

His big hand reached out to squeeze her shoulder. "Just make sure you keep doing right by them, yeah, Coach?"

Something welled in the middle of her throat, and she had to wrap a hand around her own waist to keep from falling over. She'd come to realize over the past few months that this moment hadn't actually been everything she'd ever wanted. There were other things too. A full, happy life. A lightness in her body. Mostly, right now, what she wanted was to run up to the woman a couple of yards away pretending not to snoop on the conversation they were having.

Still, she couldn't discount that this felt fucking incredible. Her heart was racing, and she was shuffling her feet. Sweat started beading on her forehead. Her body didn't seem to know whether it wanted to throw up the contents of her dinner or do a bunch of backflips until her legs followed suit.

In lieu of making a mess all over Landry's pristine windbreaker or taking off down the field screaming bloody murder, she pushed every ounce of reactive energy down into her chest until a slow smile stretched its way across her face.

"You know I will."

27

"Lim, can I get a word with you in my office?"

Franny looked up from her notebook to see Coach Landry standing at the doorway of the classroom they used for team debriefings and indoor practice days. The game had ended over an hour ago, and every player had been patted on the back and sent home to mourn their loss with their folks. Most of the coaches had already split too. But she'd come with Jade, and well, Jade Dunn was not known for being the first out of anything. The woman had flitted off somewhere fifteen minutes ago, muttering something about game scheduling. So Franny had made herself as comfortable as she could in one of the old wooden desks and started making O-line notes.

Landry's sudden request both thrilled and terrified her. She could think of only two things the man could possibly want to say to her. One of which would crush her and the other of which could make her goddamn life.

"Sure, Coach," she said. She wiped her sweaty hands on her pants and stood up. Taking an awkward second to waffle between bringing or leaving her notebook, she decided at the last minute to tuck it into her arms before falling into step beside him. At the very least, it would give her something to clutch on to if he told her to fuck off.

"You can have a seat." He pointed to the cushy chair on the other side of his desk as he sat in his chair.

They stared at each other silently for what felt like forever. Every beat that passed made Franny's tongue heavier in her mouth. Her body didn't seem to know whether it wanted to go as dry as the Sahara or flood with sweat.

She felt completely ridiculous, but there was nothing for it.

"You did very well out there tonight," Landry complimented her.

"Thank you, Coach. I, uh . . . I just followed Carr's lead."

"No, you didn't," Landry said. "You took the reins with the O-line today, same way you've been doing all summer. The boys listen to you, and they respect you, which is important. Just as important as, if not more than, knowing all the technical stuff."

Franny nodded.

"You've still got a ways to go now. You need to ramp up your confidence, and you need to build up stronger bonds with the players than you already have. You know the game well; there's no denying that. But there's a lot that goes into coaching at this level."

"Yes, sir, I realize that," Franny said. "I'm working on connecting more with the players and their parents. I know that being a true leader to them will come with time, but I'm more than willing to spend it."

"You sound like somebody else I know." He chuckled.

"Unfortunately, she's right more often than either of us would like to admit." Franny smiled just thinking about it.

"She speaks highly of you as well," he continued. "She thinks that you deserve a real chance on this team."

Franny was immediately conflicted. It felt incredible to hear that Jade had spoken kind words to Landry about her. It felt good to know that Jade had almost certainly meant them too. The woman was practically allergic to lip service. But Franny wanted to succeed on her own merit and nothing else, and she needed him to know it.

"I appreciate that, Coach. I really do. But I'd rather your opinion of me be based on your own observations."

"Lim, I've spent twenty years raising this team. It might as well be my child at this point. I promise I don't make decisions about it based on what other people want." He leaned forward on the table, clasping his fingers together. "That said, I also need to make sure the team is stacked well for the person who comes in behind me. They need people they can trust and rely on. Maybe some people they can grow with too."

Her heart almost seemed to stop pumping blood completely. Her breath followed, halting the flow of air in her lungs as her body seized up in anticipation.

"In the spring, Carr will take over responsibilities as the D-line coach, and I'd like you to step in as the head of O-line." He slid a stack of papers across the desk toward her. "Until then, we'll bring you on with the assistant coach title, and you'll shadow Carr. We've already got your background check and necessary credentials, but this should tell you a bit more about additional pay and stipends. Look this over and get it back to me by the end of next week, and we'll get your info in to payroll."

"Are you serious right now? Like, for real? I got it?"

"You got it."

"I'm a coach?"

"You're a coach."

"Holy shit!"

On the way home, Gladys broke down. They'd taken the truck to the game to soothe one of Jade's game-day superstitions. A few weeks ago, Jade had taken Gladys in for an oil change and had come home with heartbreaking news about the old gal's transmission. Franny had held her girl in her arms for over an hour while they talked through options. Only to end on the one that made the most sense for their lives right now—Jade would use some of her riches to just rebuild the damn thing. She'd had a lot of change recently and they anticipated more to come, so keeping this one constant seemed reasonable.

In the in-between time, though, they were sitting on the side of the road in the pitch-black, waiting for someone to come scoop them up.

"C'mon," Franny said. She grabbed her water bottle and opened the door on the passenger's side. "It's too hot to sit in here."

They ambled out of the truck and into the bed, laying down some tarp as makeshift protection against the hard ridges. It was still hot outside. The air was thick and wet, and the heat clung to their skin. But it was better than sweating up a little tin box.

Jade put a hand on Franny's knee, her thumb rubbing against the warm skin. "I'm sorry the truck broke down . . . again."

Franny shrugged. "It's all right. This is pretty romantic, honestly." She squeezed Jade's hand, and they tilted their heads up to look at the sky.

On any given night, she could look up and see stars. It was one of the things that made Greenbelt so intoxicating for her. Some were twinkling and bright, others farther away and duller. But they were there. Not hidden behind a thick haze of pollution or obstructed by buildings. Even the suburbs back in Houston weren't far enough away from it all to get a view like this.

Jade giggled. It was light, almost girlish, and Franny immediately looked over at her, taking in that beautiful profile. The curve of her jaw, the way her eyelashes were so long they brushed against the tops of her cheeks every time she blinked.

Franny could hardly believe where she was or who she was with. She had to run a finger along the apple of Jade's cheek just to make sure she was real. It was soft, supple, and warm. There was so much life in the woman next to her. Franny didn't want to be absorbed into her or make their bodies one and the same. She didn't want to experience it through Jade's eyes. She wanted to be right there next to her, watching, learning, admiring. She wanted to watch from the outside as her body came alive. Acting and reacting, she wanted a front-row seat to it all.

Maybe *front-row seat* wasn't the best way to put it, actually. *In Jade's lap* was probably a more accurate description.

"There's nothing romantic about this heat," Jade said, wiping her forehead.

"Oh, I don't know . . . Isn't there a song about hot summer nights and how sexy they are?"

Jade turned her amused eyes on Franny. "You're in a good mood tonight, huh? Usually you'd be cursing Gladys to hell by now."

Franny shifted, leaning back and resting on her elbows. The ridges from the truck bed dug into her skin. She wouldn't be able to stay in the position long, but it felt good for now.

"It's been a good night!"

"We lost."

"Sure, but I watched you finally get what you've been working so hard for, and that makes it a good night. The *best* night, even."

It had taken everything in Franny not to blurt out her own news the second she'd left Landry's office. She was on cloud nine, and nothing could change that. He'd asked her to keep her new position on the down-low until he "moved some other things into place." Franny assumed that meant until Jade officially got the job. She was more than happy to bide her time and keep her own win close to her chest, even if it would be difficult. Besides, there was something a little thrilling about being on the other end of a secret agreement with Landry for once.

Jade's knees drew up to her chest, her arms wrapping tightly around them. "Nothing's official."

"Jade." Franny rolled her eyes. "It's high school football. It's not like there's going to be a literal torch-passing ceremony. You got it, Jade. You got the job. You're allowed to celebrate."

Jade's face disappeared in the space between her knees for a few moments. Franny kept quiet, letting the crickets fill the silence. When Jade pulled her face back up, there were tears in her eyes.

"I am?"

Her voice was small as it asked the question, and Franny's heart wanted to break into a thousand pieces right there. She scooted behind Jade, so that her legs bracketed her hips, and wrapped her arms around Jade's middle, pulling her close. Jade leaned back into her as naturally as breathing.

"My poor girl," Franny murmured into her hair. "You're not just allowed to celebrate your wins; you need to."

"You have no idea how silly I feel right now. I've been waiting for this for so long, and yet . . . I don't even know what to do with myself."

"Well, what do you want to do?"

There was another stretch of silence. Jade ran her hands up and down Franny's arms, her fingertips leaving gooseflesh in their wake despite the heat.

"I kind of just want to sit here forever," Jade said.

Franny pressed a kiss to the side of Jade's head. "How are you supposed to coach games from the side of the road, huh?"

"It's 2023. Don't we have access to a hologram version of me or something?"

"Maybe if we had quadruple our current budget." Franny snorted.

Jade turned a bit, wiggling so she could look at Franny head-on.

"In all seriousness, thank you for being there for me today and . . . all the other days too."

Franny's cheeks heated. "Jade, you know—"

"Don't discount it," she cut Franny off. "After everything we've been through, everything I've said and done, you being here holding me might as well be a miracle."

Franny tried to blame allergies for the way her eyes watered. She sniffed and blinked, coughed a couple of times. Nothing would clear the feeling in her chest. Nothing would dampen her emotions.

"It's not a miracle. It's just . . . Shit, I don't know what it is, to be honest."

"It's forgiveness," Jade said. "You forgave me."

"Because you showed me who you actually are. You let me see the real you, and you haven't gone back on your word once."

"I won't ever. Not if I can help it."

"I'll hold you to that," Franny said, pressing another kiss to Jade's skin, this time in the warm space underneath her jaw.

"All these responsibilities." Jade's tone was light, dreamy almost. "I'd better not fail."

"You won't."

"So sure, aren't you?"

"Just as sure as you were about us winning going into tonight's game."

"We lost, though."

"You know as well as I do that a single setback isn't even close to meaning it's over."

Jade made a humming noise in the back of her throat. "I might need you to remind me, every now and again, that fucking up is a part of this."

Franny laughed gently in her ear. "We'll probably have to remind each other."

Jade held out her pinkie, and Franny wound hers around it until they were tightly linked. "Promise."

"Promise."

Jade shuffled her body around then, all but forcing Franny to lean back on her hands as Jade climbed up over her, her thighs on either side of Franny's, straddling her lap. Franny breathed in deeply. Jade still smelled like the soap she'd used in their tandem shower earlier in the day. Like the scent of her fruity lotion, whatever sunscreen was left on her skin, and faintly of grass clippings. No doubt the first thing they'd do when they got back to Jade's was shower, but Franny quite liked the scent that clung to her now. Wild and natural, every part of her day was evident on her flesh, and it made Franny's stomach hot.

"Francesca," Jade said slowly, her eyes alert but hooded.

Franny bumped their noses together playfully. "What?"

Jade's hands went to Franny's cheeks, thumbs rubbing over warm skin. "I can't believe I can just do this now."

"What? Park your perfect ass in my lap?"

Franny put her hands on said ass, squeezing the flesh. Ample even through those unforgiving khaki pants.

"Mm-hmm." Jade nodded. "And this," she said as she planted a kiss on her lips. "I can touch you and kiss you."

"You can do more than that."

Jade bit gently into the middle of Franny's plump bottom lip. "I plan on it too, just as soon as I get you home."

"Celebrations *are* in order. Maybe we should skip the waiting part, though."

Jade leaned back, looking around them. Aside from the stars and a few streetlights down the road, it was completely dark. They were parked under a canopy of tall, dark trees that very well may have hidden them completely. Franny had never had sex outdoors before. It was damn near a bucket list item. Sex with an incredibly sexy woman beneath the stars, warmth seeping into their bones at every touch.

"As hot as fucking you in a semipublic area would be, that's a hell of a risk."

Franny sighed. Jade was right. Neither of them were necessarily pillars of the community, but getting caught could have far greater consequences than simple embarrassment.

"You're right, you're right. A bit of necking can't hurt too much, right?" Franny tried. "Just while we wait for our ride."

"'Necking'?" Jade snorted. "Since when did you start talking like my granny?"

"Don't blame me; blame this town. Greenbelt has turned me all inside out."

She pressed her lips against Jade's. Gently at first, as delicately as the first time. Savoring the feel of her, the way her soft lips moistened almost instantly, the heat they emanated. Jade's hips moved up until their chests were pressed more closely together. They were so connected, Franny could feel Jade's heart beating through her rib cage. The fast staccato thumping against Franny's flesh until her own heart matched its rhythm.

Their kisses were slow, as languid as the Sunday mornings they spent in bed together. Each brush of the tongue or sweet little nip felt like the first rays of sunshine hitting their faces through the curtains. The weight of Jade in her lap provided more relief than the hottest cup of coffee first thing in the morning ever could. She felt so alive even as her eyes became heavier. Her body felt both weightless and firmly grounded at the same time. It was entirely too heady to handle, but damned if she didn't try.

Franny tucked her hands underneath Jade's shirt, feeling her way up the curvature of her back. There was a spot, just in the middle, that made Jade go wild, and the second Franny pressed her fingers into it, her girl pulled away with a groan, throwing her head back, exposing her neck as she released her pleasure into the night.

"You are unreal." Franny made no effort to keep the awe out of her voice.

Jade looked down at her. She ran her tongue over her lips, then swallowed. "I love you."

Stunned, Franny reared back suddenly. "What?"

"I love you." There was no hesitation.

"Jade, you don't have to . . . Wait, are you serious?"

"I don't care how much of a cliché I sound like. I don't need six more months just to know that I love you. I need six more months to keep learning how to love you properly."

Franny wrapped her arms tightly around Jade's waist, her throat thick again. "I love you so much."

"You mean it?"

"I've never been so excited to be in love before. So hopeful. So—so happy," Franny said. "Whatever I imagined it would feel like to finally find my person is nothing compared to what I feel every time you so much as look in my direction."

"Francesca."

"My Jade."

Jade's eyes were glistening, and from the stinging Franny felt along her lash line, hers were too.

"You know, I never actually understood people who cried because they were happy," Jade said.

"Yeah?"

"I just didn't get it. It didn't make sense to me at all, how something that made me happy could make me cry too. But you've got me out here boo-hooing like a baby with not a negative thought on my mind."

A few tears tracked down Jade's cheeks, and Franny used her fingers to smooth away the wet streaks they left behind.

"You're so sensitive, angel," Franny told her. "Tough-ass coach. Sweet, sensitive girl. They're the same person. You've just been keeping one side in the dark a little too much."

"Not anymore." Jade shook her head. "Not with you."

Franny pressed their foreheads together, grinning at her. "That's right, because we're in love."

Jade returned her grin, eyes still watery. "Hell yeah we are. And I—"

She was cut off by a sudden flash of light, followed by a loud beep. They looked up but made no moves to untangle their bodies.

"M. M. Butler's Taxi Service, here for a pickup. Would you two fornicators happen to know where I can find two gals and an old truck?"

Jade groaned, immediately rolling her eyes as she finally lifted herself out of Franny's lap. "That husband of yours is making you corny, Miri."

Miri beeped her horn twice more in response, a shit-eating grin on her dark face. "Be careful, Jadey-wadey, before I scoop up Ms. Franny here and leave you to hitchhike your ass home."

"She wouldn't leave me behind." Jade opened the back door for Franny to slide in, but before she sat, Franny leaned up for one last cheeky peck on the lips.

"Never."

28

One day, they would have a giant clawfoot tub made of brass like the ones they had in the horny historical dramas. They'd fill it up with steaming water and sit on either side, watching each other in comfortable anticipation as they soaked.

Until then, they had the small porcelain one in their little bathroom. The one with a big surface crack down the center that Jade had covered with a plastic bath mat. It was just deep enough and wide enough for one of them to cradle the other between their legs. There was very little room to move around or do anything at all, really. But maybe that was something of a treat all on its own.

Francesca sat with her back to the tub, and Jade squeezed in the space between her thighs. They'd filled the tub with Epsom salt, eucalyptus bubbles, and water that was probably far too hot for most other people. It was perfect for them, though. Franny slid her arms around Jade, cradling her pert breasts gently as if they were the most precious things in the world.

"We should go to Costco tomorrow," Franny said quietly in Jade's ear. "We need laundry detergent, and I want to see about getting new pillows for the bed."

"We should get a chicken too."

"Oh yeah, angel," Franny growled. "And after that, we'll get the tires rotated on my car."

"Keep going, please."

Franny bit at one of Jade's earlobes, sucking the flesh into her ear to ease the sting after. "And when we get home . . ."

"Mmmm, tell me what's going to happen when we get home, baby."

Franny's thumbs slid over Jade's nipples, which turned up the heat in the tub by about ten degrees.

"When we get home, we're going to change all the knobs on the cabinets in the kitchen."

"I love knobs," Jade moaned.

"I know you do."

"You know, if you keep doing that, this is going to go from fake sexy to real sexy very quickly."

Franny wasn't the slightest bit concerned with Jade's little warning. Her thumbs continued their circles around the hard brown buds of Jade's nipples, and Jade pressed back into her, and that soft, warm skin felt incredible against her own hard nipples.

"I take your sexiness very seriously, Jade. You know that."

"We're playing pretty fast and loose with space here, then."

Franny flexed her thighs, trying to test the bounds of the bathtub.

"Up, up." Franny tapped Jade's arm then. "We're getting out."

"But we just got in."

"Do you want to eat my pussy, or do you want to sit in this water?"

There was no hesitation in her answer. "I want to eat your pussy, obviously. Like, what kind of question is that?"

A couple of minutes later, they were silently laying towels across their bed, tangling their damp bodies on top in a tangle of arms and legs and lips. Jade's hands immediately went to Franny's ass, pulling their hips together in a slow bump and grind that was too delicious for words. She squeezed the warm, pliant flesh between her fingers, reveling in the way Franny moaned.

"This never gets old." Jade pulled away from Franny's lips and spoke the words into the damp skin of her neck. Jade smelled of fresh water and clean sweat, and Franny's mouth ran wet as the other woman bit and licked her way across her collarbones.

Franny maneuvered until she was lying flat on her back and looking up at Jade as she made a show out of worshipping Franny's small breasts. Light brown areola, slightly puffy around her hard little nipples. She'd never liked how they looked more than the way they looked between Jade's lips. She spent ample time on them too. Tweaking one while her lips sucked the other. She made no move to reach between Franny's legs. Jade seemed to want her squirming and begging beneath her. It worked too, because the insides of Franny's thighs were quickly covered in slick the second her girl worked them open.

"You're killing me, angel," Franny gritted out. "It's been forever."

"It's been three days." Jade giggled. "And only because I was out of town."

"Three days is forever when it comes to you."

"What a compliment."

"I need your hands on me, always. It's hard enough going a full school day without being able to kiss you or feel me against you."

Jade gave her right tit one last nip with her sharp teeth before she paused, looking at her. "Is that right?"

Her fingers trailed down Franny's flat stomach, straight to where her tummy turned into her pussy. But just before delving inside, she moved them back up to make torturous circles around her belly button. Her tongue following into the deep little indent.

"All day." Franny sucked in a breath. "All fucking day, I have to stop myself from finding you and dragging you into a supply closet somewhere to get a piece of you."

"Ms. Lim, what a scandalous thought."

"It's depraved, I know. But I can't help it. I just need you. I need you all the time."

Jade sank her teeth into Franny's right hip. It was possible that she should have been concerned about all this biting. It must have signaled something concerning, right? The way Franny almost felt like she was being consumed. What may have been more concerning was how she welcomed it—*yearned* for it.

"And what do you think about doing to me when we're all alone in this dark closet?" Jade whispered.

"All kinds of things . . ."

Jade spread Franny's thighs then. The scent of her own arousal was heady and intoxicating.

"How about this? You tell me what you want to do to me in that work closet, and after I'll give your hot little pussy what it wants. How does that sound?"

Franny groaned and lifted her hips a bit off the bed. Her body searching for the ecstasy it knew was on the horizon.

"I want to push you against the shelves," Franny panted. "And I want my hands down the front of your pants, playing with your clit until you cream all over my fingers. I want to make you shove your fist in your mouth as you scream, desperate to stay quiet while I'm making you come your brains out. And then I want us to run home and do it over and over and over again, until the windows of this room are foggy and you no longer remember your name."

"Depraved girl," Jade admonished her lightly. "Look at how wet you are at the thought of having me wherever you want."

Finally, after what felt like forever, Jade lightly ran her fingers over Franny's pussy. Franny knew it must have been hot to the touch, and it was so wet that when Jade lifted her fingers away, Franny's juices clung to them.

"Remember the first time?" Franny's voice was strained—almost like she was moments away from sobbing.

"In the club?" Jade answered.

"You fucked me against the sink," Franny bit out. "You looked at me in the mirror as I came around you . . ."

"If I didn't know any better, I'd think you had a public-sex kink, Francesca."

"What gave it away?"

Jade slid two fingers inside her with ease, and Franny sighed like she'd been offered water in the middle of the desert. Jade fucked her fingers inside fast, curling them up. The loud squelching sounds rang through the room.

"That gives it away," Jade said.

"Please," Franny whined. "Please fuck me, angel."

"I will. You know I will. Just tell me how you want to be fucked."

"What are my options?"

"I can keep giving you my fingers," Jade answered. "I can give you my tongue." She leaned down, running her tongue over Franny's hard little clit a few times before taking it between her lips, sucking until the other woman's hips were bucking against her face. "Or I can give you dick."

That made Franny pause. She leaned up on her elbows, her chest rising and falling rapidly as she looked down at Jade. They didn't use their strap-on that often. And usually when they did, Franny wanted to top.

"Is that what you want, Francesca? Do you want me to give you dick?"

"Yes," she gasped. "Yes. Please, God, please."

"You want to choose which one you want while I get it on?"

Franny rolled to standing quickly, going for their toy box under the bed while Jade rummaged around in her bedside drawer for their shared harness. By the time Franny was back on the bed, lying on her side, dildo of choice in her hands, Jade had the harness on. The dark black straps were snug against her skin, and seeing Jade outfitted in the fabric was so delicious Franny could hardly stand it.

"Can I put it on you?" Franny asked.

"Please."

Jade walked up to the edge of the bed and ran her fingers through Franny's long hair as she put the dildo into place on the harness, securing it with a little silicone sleeve bumper that would keep the toy from ramming into Jade uncomfortably every time she thrust.

Franny stared up at her with wide eyes, heavy with lust. Jade looked down at her, squaring her shoulders.

"Get on your hands and knees, and back your ass up to the edge of the bed."

Franny took her time doing as she was told. Laying her face into the comforter and curving her back into a deep arch that raised her ass to the perfect position in front of Jade's hips.

"Thighs open," Jade said.

When her pussy was revealed, Jade dove in face-first. Tonguing Franny's clit while pushing two fingers back inside her, scissoring them in tandem until Franny was begging to be fucked. When Franny finally felt the tip of the toy at her entrance, she shivered. Jade made slow work of her hips at first, working the dick in and out of Franny at a gentle steady pace, keeping rhythm. It wasn't until Franny started to move her hips back against her that she even considered speeding up.

"You want it faster?" Jade asked.

"Please . . ."

"Please, what? Use your words, pretty girl."

"F-fuck me, Jade. Please."

Jade kept her pace. "Fuck you how?"

"Faster!"

Jade gave her four quick, deep pumps before resuming her original speed. She was a bastard for the dark chuckle that left her lips when Franny started to whine in earnest.

"Jade, please, I need it so bad."

Jade put her hands on Franny's hips, making sure her grip was tight enough for Franny to feel it. Then she worked her hips hard, fucking deep into Franny's body.

"I need you to tell me how it feels, Francesca."

"G-good, so good." Franny's voice was muffled and strained. Her skin was hot, and she was damn near drooling onto the bed.

"Good how? Where do you feel me?"

"Deep in my pussy!" Franny cried. "I feel you fucking everywhere."

Jade tightened her grip on Franny's hips to drive her back as she powered forward. The wooden bed frame creaked under their weight, and even though it wasn't literally Jade inside her, Franny felt the connection between them come alive. She took a quick peek over her shoulders to catch a glimpse of her girl. Eyes wide, hair messy, nipples hard. She looked wild and free and so beautiful Franny grew even wetter around the toy.

Jade's breaths started to come faster, but she seemed to have no intention of slowing her pace. Not until she saw Franny's hips start to stutter against her, at least. Instead of throwing her ass back in time with Jade's thrusts, Franny started grinding against the toy. Jade knew exactly what that meant.

"Are you going to come, Francesca?"

Franny made a guttural keening noise in the back of her throat, unable to answer with words.

"Can you play with your clit?" Jade asked her.

The only response she got was seeing Franny's hand go between her thighs.

"You think you can come all over this dick?" Jade asked. "It's okay, you don't have to talk. Just nod yes or shake no for me, baby."

Franny's nod was frantic.

No more words were spared as Jade found her rhythm again, sending the dick deep and hard into Franny's soaked pussy. Franny's body shook as she tumbled slowly over the edge. Then, suddenly, she went stiff as a board, a silent scream leaving her lips as the ecstasy of her orgasm overtook her completely. Jade fucked her through it, only pulling out when Franny started to yank herself away.

In a move that surprised them both, Jade grabbed Franny by the thighs and flipped her over immediately. Face back in her pussy in an instant, Jade licked and sucked her twitching insides. Cleaning up the big mess Franny had made and trying to prolong her orgasm at the same time.

"Please," Franny gasped after a while. "Oh my God, please, I need a minute. Fuck. What the fuck . . ."

Jade pulled back and up to standing until she was looking down at Franny again.

"What the fuck . . ." Franny repeated.

Jade grinned. "How's that for coming your brains out?"

"Pretty damn good."

"I figured. Can I touch you?"

"Please."

Franny scooted over to make room for Jade, who crawled into

bed next to her, immediately taking Franny's shivering body into her arms. She laid a kiss on her forehead and another one on each of her eyelids.

"You're so beautiful when you lose yourself like that," Jade said.

"That's nothing compared to the way you look when you're commanding me like that."

Franny's body was still alight, buzzing like a current through a live wire. Still, she wanted nothing more than to be right where she was. Curled up with Jade, covered in her sweat in their bed.

"How do you feel?" Jade asked. "Do you need water or a snack or anything? Are you comfortable?"

Franny smiled up at her. "Look at my top, offering me such sweet aftercare."

"You're so silly after you come, you know that?"

"I'm always silly."

"That's true," Jade agreed. "And I always love you."

"Always? Even when I put the toilet paper roll on wrong?"

"Even when you eat all the leftovers my mama sends home."

Franny's arms went tightly around her, and she pressed a wet kiss into the hollow of Jade's throat.

"That's a lot of love, Jade Dunn."

"So much love, Lim."

"Mmmm . . . that's good to hear because I definitely ate the rest of the cobbler in the fridge."

"You menace," Jade growled.

"A menace who loves you." Franny made her way across Jade's chest with kisses.

"You're evil."

"And loves you."

"For real!"

"And loves you."

"This is my payback, isn't it? I pay for my sins by spending my life with a woman who has no respect for common leftover etiquette."

"And loves you even more beyond that . . ."

Franny had been an awful league member the past few weeks. Her responsibilities with the football team had increased, and with the start of the school year and Jade taking up every spare minute outside of that, she hadn't made it to Lucky Leagues for the past three meetups. She missed her old gals, though, so much so that she'd managed to convince Jade to tag along with her to bowling night. It would be a cute date, and she'd finally get to introduce her woman to the friends who'd heard so much about her. Somehow, Franny felt more nervous about this than she had when she'd introduced Jade to her parents over FaceTime.

"Just as a warning, I'm incredibly good at bowling," Jade said as she leaned against Franny's car in the parking lot of Lucky Leagues, waiting for Franny to dig her ball out of the mess in her trunk.

"Is that right?" Franny heaved the ball from beneath a mountain of jackets and jerseys. "You've never said."

"It never came up, I guess. I just wanted to warn you before we get out there. Don't want to accidentally embarrass you or anything."

They started walking across the lot toward the entrance, and Franny spared a look at Jade. Her girlfriend was practically strutting, shoulders back, chin up, hips moving deliciously—if far too much for the setting. It was deeply adorable how competitive Jade got.

"You know, this is much less about winning at bowling than it is about the gals just getting together."

Jade paused. "So you don't bowl?"

"No, we bowl. We just pay more attention to one another," Franny clarified.

Jade's face fell almost comically as she continued walking. "So y'all will be easy to beat, then."

"Probably."

"I don't like it when people are easy to beat."

Franny snorted. "You are such a brat, you know that?"

"You love it."

They'd shown up a bit late, and Franny could see that all the girls were already seated around their usual lanes when they walked in. She'd had the brilliant idea to surprise them with her presence instead of sending Barb a message letting her know she'd be there. It was an absolute joy to see the shock and awe on their faces when she smoothly slid in front of where they were sitting, Jade trailing not too far behind.

"Well, look who decided to show her face!" Charlie's bubbly little greeting was followed by a tight hug around the neck.

"We figured you'd moved on to greener pastures," Barb grunted, using a cloth to polish the ball between her legs.

"Never!" Franny said, passing out hugs. "I'd never leave y'all behind. Things have just been hectic lately. I've barely had time to breathe."

"I can see why," Janet said slyly, cutting her eyes to where Jade was standing with her hands on her hips.

"Is this her?" Charlie gasped.

"This is my girl." Franny laughed through her clarification.

"Uhhh . . ." Jade ground out.

She was far less cocky than she had been when they'd come in. Franny understood her completely. All the women were incredibly kind, but they made a formidable group of queer elders. Especially Barb, with her grumbling and surly disposition.

Franny wrapped an arm around Jade's waist, tucking her thumb into one of the empty belt loops of her jeans. Making sure she kept a hold on her, showing her that she was right there beside her and wouldn't be going anywhere.

"Girls, this is Jade Dunn, my girl. Jade, this is Barb and her wife, Stella. They started the league. And this is Janet, Charlie, and Carmella."

"Hi, y'all." Jade's tone was as close to shy as it could be. "It's nice to meet you. Thank you for having me."

"We didn't know you were coming." Barb's words were so matter-of-fact, they earned her a light cuff on the shoulder from her wife.

"Don't pay her no mind," Stella said. "We're happy to have you."

"We need to recruit more baby gays anyway," Janet said, laughing. "We won't be around forever, and we've got to keep the league going."

Carmella rolled her eyes. "I, for one, am not going anywhere. But we've heard a lot about you, Jade."

"You have?" Jade looked at Franny.

"Oh yeah. Plenty."

"Good things?"

Carmella grimaced. "Well . . ."

Jade laughed good-naturedly. "Yeah, I figured. We had a bit of a rough go of it. Mostly my fault."

"We told Franny you were into her," Charlie offered. "She was stubborn about believing us, but we told her."

"We'd never even met you, but we could see it from a mile away. And look at you now." Janet was lacing up her purple bowling shoes and kept her eyes on her laces as she spoke.

Jade leaned in and pressed a kiss against Franny's jaw in response. Franny guided them to two open seats, where they began to get their own shoes on.

The group was quiet, the sounds of the bowling alley the perfect distraction. The lane to their left was occupied by a small family. A mother, father, and their two kids. The kids had small bowling balls and bumpers up against the sides of the lane and every time one of them sent one flying down the glossy wood, sweet peals of childish glee floated through the air.

Franny finished tying her shoes and sat back in her seat, getting comfortable despite the hard plastic underneath her. She'd underestimated how much she had missed this. The smell of stale pretzels and cheap pizza, the sound of balls rolling across the wood. Happy bowlers, serious bowlers, and the ladies surrounding her. She watched with a full heart as Jade struck up a conversation with Janet and Charlie. Her brain and ears found themselves disconnected; whatever words they were sharing flowed in one ear and out the other. All she retained was the soothing timbre of their voices as they all melded together.

She wanted to label this a perfect night, but that gave her pause. How many nights had she had recently that she'd called *perfect*? More than seemed fair, surely. They had all been different too. Her first date with Jade. Once when they'd taken a late-night trip to Minnie's for some cobbler after a bout of hair-pullingly-hot sex. Even one nighttime football practice where it had started to rain and the kids made the executive decision to keep going. Was all this perfection possible? Was it sustainable?

Maybe she'd been using the wrong words to describe them. Maybe all those nights hadn't been perfect at all. Maybe she'd just been happy. Consistently and deliriously happy. Not just with Jade but with her life in general. She was a coach again, she was a part of something big, she was building connections. Hell, she was even calling her mother more. Franny had spent the past two years wading through, biding her time until the work she was doing actually paid off.

She was there now, and it felt incredible. So much so that she hardly knew what to do with herself. Honestly, maybe there was nothing to do but live it. Enjoy it. Let the good times bolster her for when the more difficult parts of life circled back around. There would be no focusing on that, though. Not while she had her woman at her side and some pins to knock down.

"Are we bowling or what?" Barb stood up, flexing her ball in her arms a few times. "You might be Franny's girl, but don't expect us to take it easy on you, newbie."

Jade's answering grin was positively wolfish. It slid across her face slowly, transforming her from sweet conversationalist to competitive hellcat. Franny shook her head with a laugh.

"Those are fighting words," she told Barb. "This woman's got a competitive streak like no other, Barb."

"I do," Jade said. "I don't know how to play for anything but the win."

Barb grinned back, and it was genuinely the first time Franny had seen so many of her teeth. "I suppose you're up first, then. Show us how you roll."

"Oh lord," Stella groaned.

Charlie reached out and patted Franny's hand after Jade got up to choose her ball. "You done good, Franny girl. You done good."

And she knew it was true.

THE SPRING AFTER

I told Landry that he was going to have to carry on this tradition without me. If I never see another deck of cards in my life, it'll be too soon."

Jade was sitting, bent over the edge of her bed, tying the laces of her sneakers. Franny was in the en suite, cleaning a new tattoo she'd gotten that afternoon.

"It won't be so bad," Franny said, her voice muffled. "It'll be all the same guys as before."

"That definitely doesn't make it any better," Jade grumbled.

She threw herself back on the bed, staring up at the ceiling with a pout on her face. She was being ornery, she knew it. But she'd managed to get out of going to those damn poker games ever since the school year had begun. They hadn't had anything close to a perfect season. The Greenbelt Gators had taken their fair number of losses and setbacks. They hadn't ended the season with a championship trophy the way everyone had hoped they would. But they'd made it far in the playoffs. Further than they had in the past four years. The disappointment among her players had been palpable, but so had the hope for next year.

Their loss this season had been a major upset for the kids, especially the seniors who'd left for greener pastures with no championship titles holding them up. Greenbelt had closed out the season with a spot in the championships. They'd lost in the semifinals to Oakbridge High but finished with twenty-eight wins and six losses for the year. The only comfort was that West Beaufort hadn't even managed to make it past the first round of the playoffs.

They had put a lot of work into keeping the players energized. Tryouts were just around the corner, and Jade had a lot of hope, not only for all the new blood coming in but for their upcoming season in general. They were taking it all the way this year. There was no other option; she wouldn't allow it. Jade felt that familiar fire in her belly swell every time she thought about the work that needed to be done to get them there. Their most recent upset was like gasoline on the flames, and the way it engulfed her completely was all the motivation she needed.

In the meantime, Landry hadn't fought her on her absences at the poker games. Jade figured he had too much on his plate to worry about whether she was up for a weekly game of Texas Hold'em, but now all of a sudden, he was insisting on it? It was weird. And annoying.

"Why couldn't he just let us take him to Red Lobster or something, like a normal person?"

"I think Red Lobster is more of a graduation dinner place. Shellfish isn't the meal for retirement."

That made Jade laugh. She hoisted herself up and made her way into the bathroom, wrapping her arms around Franny's waist from behind as the other woman rubbed some kind of thick gel on the tiny Betty Boop tattooed on her hip.

"What exactly is a retirement meal?"

Jade pressed her face into the back of Franny's neck. She smelled clean, fresh from the shower. The woodsy cologne she sometimes wore was even more delicious on her skin, and Jade made sure to take the time to breathe in deeply.

Franny caught her eyes in the big mirror in front of them. That smirk was back on her face. The one Jade had spent two years cursing and praying to see in equal measure. For so long, Jade had purposefully interpreted that look as being malicious or nasty. She could see it clearly now, though. The twinkle in Franny's eye. The way her cheeks flushed the slightest bit red. Her pretty pink lips curved ever so slightly. She didn't look like she was being spiteful. She looked coy. Jade checked the smartwatch on her wrist, cursing when she realized that they needed to be out of the house in less than five minutes. If her ideas around timeliness were even a little laxer, she'd be sliding her fingers into the unbuttoned pants Franny wore and transforming the look on her face from coy to blissful.

"Apparently, chips and salsa are a pretty decent retirement meal," Franny joked.

Jade groaned again, burying her face into Franny's shoulder. "Yeah, and cigars."

"Come on, angel." Franny patted Jade's arm. "Let's go before you end up miserable in the squeaky chair."

"Are you sure we can't call it off? I feel like I might be getting sick all of a sudden. It could be the flu. I heard that's going around."

"Mmm," Franny hummed, turning to press her lips to Jade's forehead. "The sooner we go, the sooner we can come back and watch some gay shit on TV."

"Fine. But only because I love gay shit on TV so much."

Sometimes it seemed that when she was out in public with Franny, her brain was almost completely turned off. She held her girlfriend's hand and trailed behind her with nary a care in the world, following along like the inside of her head was filled with multicolored cotton candy or something. This must have been why she didn't notice all the cars parked outside Landry's house. And why, when Landry opened the door surrounded by a large swath of her closest friends yelling, "Surprise!" at her, the only thing she could think to say was, "It's not even my birthday!"

That garnered an inordinate amount of laughs from the crowd, which in turn made her cheeks heat up. She clasped on tighter to Franny's hand as they made their way inside. The normal poker-night guys were there, sure. But so were the rest of the Greenbelt football coaches and some coaches from the other sports teams.

"What the hell is going on?" she asked Franny in a low mumble after shaking hands with the tennis coach. "I mean, Principal Coleman is here with his wife."

Franny looked at her like she was a fool, yanking on her hand and stopping her in her tracks right there in the middle of Landry's nautical-themed living room. "You cannot be serious, Jade."

"What?"

The look on Franny's face went even slacker. "This is your party. It's for you."

"No, it isn't."

"Oh, no? Well, why did everyone yell surprise when you came in?"

"That was just a prank."

"You think your parents came here just to see you get pranked?"

"Wha—"

Franny spun her around by her upper arms, sending her toward the kitchen, where her mother and father were standing in the doorway talking to Miri and Aja.

"You didn't think we were going to let your big moment pass by without a little fanfare, did you?" Landry's voice sent her spinning around again. She was suddenly dizzy, though not solely because of the sudden movements. "It's like you don't know me at all, Coach."

"Landry . . ." Her throat was suddenly thick, and it made her words come out all wobbly. Franny grabbed her hand and squeezed.

"I wanted to throw a pep rally at the school. Bring out the players and the mascots and all that. You're lucky your girl here suggested something more intimate."

She looked at Franny, who smiled softly at her. Jade's belly flipped the way it did the first time their eyes met.

"You didn't need to do this," she said.

"Yes, we did," Landry said, his gaze incredibly soft. "I don't want there to be any doubt that you're getting this position, because no one else is better fitted for it than you."

"Coach, I don't even know what to say right now."

"You'd better come up with something quick because our speech is in ten minutes." He was off then without a word, disappearing into a small crowd of some of the more involved team parents.

"'Speech'?" She looked at Franny again. "What does he mean, 'speech'?"

Her girlfriend grimaced. "I couldn't talk him out of it. I'm sorry."

"I'm not doing a speech, Francesca. You know I hate public speaking."

"Let's go talk to your folks, so you can distract yourself and just speak on the fly."

Jade pouted but allowed herself to be pushed into her mother's arms. She breathed in the fresh floral scent of her mother's perfume, fighting back the urge to cry. She sniffed when she pulled back, going to hug her father, then Aja, and Miri last. Clinging on to her best friend like she was adrift with only a life raft.

"I can't believe y'all kept this from me!"

Her father snorted. "Now what kind of surprise would it be if we'd told you about it?"

"One I could have prepared for," she grumbled.

Miri pinched her on the arm. "It's your special day. Be nice."

"I know, I know. I'm just nervous, I guess. All this really wasn't necessary."

"It was, though, baby," her mother said. "This is monumental. Let it be that. Let us celebrate you."

Jade sucked in a deep breath, her eyes moving around her immediate vicinity as she took in some of the people she loved most in the world. It was overwhelming to see their faces, proud and joyous, and all for her. Shining eyes and lips curled up, each one of them seemed like they were actively restraining themselves from letting their excitement explode fully out of their bodies. In their defense, she was doing the exact same thing. Every time she sucked in air, her chest caved so much, she felt like her pounding heart would slam right through it. Every cell in her body felt activated. It wasn't so much fight-or-flight as it was sheer elation on a level she'd never experienced before. Jade had thought she knew how this would feel, but she hadn't. Not by a long shot. And now that she was in it, she barely knew how to act like a human, let alone convey her happiness.

As if sensing her overloading brain, Franny slid an arm around her waist. She was an anchor both literally and figuratively. Holding Jade up in more ways than one. Jade eyed her loved ones again.

"He's going to make me give a speech." Her voice was tiny when she spoke.

"You'll be fine," Miri tried to assure her. "Remember that DARE speech you gave junior year? You did great."

"We literally had to smoke a joint before that speech."

"Excuse me?" her mother asked.

Jade's cheeks heated, but she pointedly ignored the older woman, hoping to avoid a lecture that was over a decade too late.

"I mean, we could . . ." Miri clutched her purse and pointed to the front door.

Jade considered it. Liquid courage had never meant much to her, but a little hazy courage had gotten her through a few of her tougher moments.

She sighed and shook her head. "I can't be stoned with all these team parents here."

"And *your* parents," her father said mildly.

"Look, just parrot whatever he says," Franny said. "Keep it short and sweet, say your thank-yous, and you'll be done in a few seconds, okay?"

Jade nodded. A few seconds. She could do that. She could do almost anything for a few seconds. Take a needle in her gums, choke down liver and onions, even give a speech.

Thankfully, she had very little time to fixate on it further before the sound of Landry's signature obnoxious whistle was ringing through the crowded space. He beckoned her over to the center with a big grin, and Jade waded through the crowd like she was on her way to the gallows. When she reached him, he slung an arm around her shoulders.

"Hey! Hey!" His voice carried loud and strong over the room without any help from a microphone. Within seconds, it was almost completely silent as the crowd turned their attention toward them.

Sweat started to bead at Jade's hairline, taking its time as it slowly descended the sides of her face. She absolutely loathed public speaking. It was one thing to speak to a crowd of students or to put her coach face on and command her players—or even their parents. But staring out at a sea of people she knew so intimately made her feel downright queasy.

Jade put an arm around Landry's waist, not to return his hug but to keep herself upright as sweat began to pool behind her weakening knees.

Landry was determined to keep going. "By now, everybody here knows that this season was my last as a Greenbelt football coach." The crowd murmured. "Twenty years is a long time to spend anywhere, let alone coaching one team. But I've enjoyed every minute of it."

He stopped suddenly and cleared his throat a few times. Jade looked up at him and saw his eyes blinking rapidly, shining under the big lights above them. As if she were a child watching her mother cry, her own eyes started to well up in response. In all the years she'd known the man, she'd seen him cry all of two times. Once, years ago, after the sudden and tragic death of one of the players on their team. And another, when she'd accidentally walked in on him watching *Field of Dreams* in his office.

She tightened her arm around his waist, hoping to provide some type of support during his emotional moment. He smiled down at her—eyes watery and so sincere it took her breath away.

"Hell," he huffed, laughing to himself. "This team has given me more than I have the words to speak about and damn sure more than I deserve. But it's time for me to move on . . . It's time for some new blood to come in and shake shit up."

There was a sudden whoop that came from the crowd, and Jade recognized it immediately. Cutting her eyes to where her small group was standing, she saw Miri screwing her face up in some type of goofy, contrite look. Next to her, Aja looked mortified. It was an incredibly ridiculous exchange, but something about it immediately made Jade relax a little. In an instant, she was reminded that she wasn't actually up there alone. Not physically or spiritually. Her people were right there, all around her. Her eyes flitted around the room, full of faces that she may have only been vaguely familiar with but who looked at her with nothing but pride in their eyes. The man with his arm around her most of all.

"I know y'all have spent months speculating on my retirement, trying to guess who was going to fill my spot when it happens. But what are the kids saying now? If you know, you know, right? Anybody who's paid any attention the past few years can see the choice clear as day," he said, looking down at her again. "The second Jade Dunn walked into my office and told me she wanted to coach football, I knew she was going to do great things. And once I saw her on that field with those players, I knew she was going to take my job one day. She's strong and driven, she commands respect, and most of all, she loves those kids. It's been an honor to mentor her and an even bigger one to pass my torch along."

By now, Landry was clearing his throat in an effort not to cry in earnest, and Jade was blinking her own tears back rapidly.

"Thank you, Coach," she said through shaky breaths. "Thank you so much."

"Give us a speech!" someone yelled in the crowd, prompting everyone else to chant, "Speech, speech, speech!" until she sighed deep and conceded.

"Um, I'm not good at giving speeches," she said. "Definitely not as good as Landry is, so don't expect too much from me, please."

"We believe in you!" This time, it was Franny's voice that rang out through the crowd.

Jade immediately locked eyes with her girlfriend. Her gaze was lusciously brown and deeper than anything else in the world, and Jade let herself get lost in it until her heartbeat began to slow and her hands stopped shaking. Even when she finally started speaking, she kept her eyes on Franny. Using the other woman as an anchor.

"Honestly, I don't even know what to say. My heart is so full right now, I just . . . I can't possibly express it all. I'd be lying if I said

I haven't been working toward this. Anybody who knows me knows that I've been trying to take Landry's job for years now." Thankfully, that garnered her more than a few laughs. "But wanting something can only do so much when there are systems at play not built with you in mind. Or maybe even ones that are built to keep you out. I'm the first woman to ever hold a coaching position on this team, and I'll be the first Black woman to hold the title of head football coach in this county. That means something to me. It means everything, really.

"I used to think that it was enough for me to get what I wanted, but I've realized recently that it isn't enough. Not nearly. It means the world to me to be given this opportunity. And I'm going to seize it by leading our team to many more wins. But I'm also going to foster an environment where the good ol' boys club doesn't dictate who participates in this beautiful sport. I don't know exactly what that's going to look like yet, or even how we're going to get there. But I see the vision, and I believe in it. And one thing you should know about me is I'm stubborner than a mule and a harder worker by far. I'm going to work hard for these players and this team, and I expect you all to hold me accountable to that. That's . . . that's all."

She went to move to the side but remembered herself. "Wait, one more thing . . . Francesca, I know you think I don't know, but I cannot wait to keep sharing those sidelines with you. You're a hell of a coach, and watching you work inspires me every day. You always have a place with me on my team. *Our* team."

When Jade finally dragged her gaze away from Franny's so she could see all the faces in the room, she noted plenty of apprehension along with joy. That was to be expected. She'd just announced some big shake-ups, and even the people who weren't necessarily "good ol' boys" tended to feel more comfortable with the way things had always gone.

That was all right. She'd already shown them once that she could get the job done. She had no problems showing them again. And again. And again. And again, if that was what it took. She was here now. She had her team, and she had her title. Which meant that she also had plenty of time.

In an instant, she was up in Landry's arms, taking in the scent of Old Spice and Astroturf.

"Who said you were bad at giving speeches, huh?" he asked when he finally pulled away. "You might have missed your calling. You could write for the president or something."

Jade curled her top lip. "I'd rather clean cleats for the rest of my life than do that."

"Oh, trust me, girl, you'll spend plenty of time doing that too with this job."

"I'll just make one of my underlings do it now that I'm in charge."

Landry laughed deep in his belly. "Good luck with that. You're going to get someone just like you who won't let your shit slide."

Jade peeked over her shoulder to spot Franny talking to her parents. Her heart filled even more, and the smile on her face grew to show it. "I might have already found her."

"Mm-hmm." Landry smirked. "I'm so proud of you, kid. You have no idea."

"I think I do, Coach. I wanted to thank you again for holding me accountable, for giving me all the support I could possibly handle. Honestly, I don't know how I'm going to do this without your guidance."

"You won't have to," he said, tone firm. "I'm right here, Jade, right across town. I may not be a coach anymore, but I'm still Greenbelt's biggest fan. I told Carla we had to hold off on the schooner until we know what we're doing, but we got ourselves a little dinghy we're taking up to Rhode Island in a few weeks. I don't know when we'll be back yet, but if you need me, call me. I mean that. You hear me?"

"Yes, sir," she said. "I will. I promise. Just try to enjoy being retired, all right?"

"Enjoy being retired, my ass," he scoffed, putting a hand on the side of her head. "Go kiss your girl, Coach. You've earned it."

She didn't need to be told twice either. Ten steps forward and she was taking Franny in her arms, dipping her at the waist, and laying one on her that was a mite inappropriate for mixed company.

And who could blame her? She was on top of the world.

EPILOGUE

"Vonte, look at me." Jade squatted so she could be eye level with the boy.

His helmet was on the bench next to him, and his face dripped with sweat. She didn't need to take in the way his shoulders slumped or the stains coloring his uniform to know that he was knock-down, drag-out tired. But when he caught her eye, there wasn't even a glimpse of the same exhaustion his body showed. They were up against West Beaufort again, this time fighting for the title of season champions.

"I'm good, Coach," he nearly growled around his mouth guard. "I'm good to go back."

"You're looking tired, boy."

"Coach, I'm telling you I'm good. I've got this."

Jade spared a glance at where Sam Coleman, their best JV line-backer, was waiting in the wings to be put in the game. The kid was good, but he was a newly recruited freshman and not nearly as strong with his tackles as he could be. They were working on it. Jade had faith that he would get it. She just wasn't sure if now was the time to test that theory.

"We've got twelve seconds left on the clock and we're up by six. We could take this whole thing, but not if they make it to the line.

Not if we let them past. You're telling me right now that you have the energy to make sure that doesn't happen?"

Vonte's breaths were still coming in deep. His chest pads moved with every single one. There was doubt in his eyes when he caught hers again. "I . . . I don't know."

"Tell me how you're really feeling, then."

"Tired," he said. "My legs are burning, and my lungs are on fire. I feel like I can keep pushing, but I . . . I don't know how hard I can actually go."

Jade swallowed, her heart thudding even harder in her chest than it had been the past few hours. "Jaxon," she called out, and within seconds, the lithe red-haired kicker was at her side.

"What do you need, Coach?"

"Run over and find Coach Lim for me. Tell her I need her over here immediately."

It was a request that felt incredibly familiar, and Jade made a quick note in her mind to look into getting some walkie-talkies. That was a thing that could be handled for next season, though, not while they were trying to finish this current one as champions.

Lim and Jaxon were jogging toward her within moments. Franny's cheeks were flushed from the cold, and her fingers were clutched tightly around her clipboard. Franny was her offensive line coach, but Sam had grown close to Alonzo Holton, which meant that he'd grown close to Franny as well. He might have been on defense, but she trusted Lim's opinion on the matter—whatever it was.

"We've got one minute left on this time-out," Lim reminded her. "We've got to get them back out there."

Jade rose out of her squat to speak more closely with her. "What do you think of Sam Coleman?"

The boy in question was sitting on the bench, biting at his lips and shaking his knee like there was something trapped under his pants. She watched Lim look him over.

"He's a solid lineman. Vonte's been helping him a lot this season. Every time we've put him in to sub, he's done a good job."

"I've watched him in practice, though he misses a lot of his tackles."

Lim nodded. "This is his first year as a linebacker. He needs to have his fundamentals drilled into him, but he can do it."

"We don't have time to waste, not even a second."

Lim looked past her, expression pensive. "Sam, come over here a second."

"What? Coach?" Vonte's tone was alarmed, but when he tried to stand up, he hardly made it a few inches off the bench before his own weight forced him back down.

"Yes, Coach Lim?" Sam was incredibly soft-spoken, and his voice cracked on every word. He was big for his age, but Jade didn't know if what she saw in his eyes was determination or apprehension.

"How are you feeling tonight?" Lim asked him.

"I'm feeling great."

"Do you think you can handle subbing in for Vonte?"

The kid swallowed hard. "There's only twelve seconds, right? I can handle that."

"That's going to be the longest twelve seconds of your life," Lim said, beating Jade to the punch. "They've got the ball, so we're going heavy. A four-three defense, something classic, no tricks. But we need you tight out there. We need you on your game and ready. And when it's time for you to take some of them to the ground, I need you to do it right. I need to be able to trust that you can get out there and make it happen. Can I?"

Sam looked back and forth between his two coaches, the stadium lights glinting in his hazel eyes.

"You can trust me."

He sounded sure, and Jade knew that she had no other choice, so she took a deep breath of her own and nodded once. "Get your guard in and your helmet on, and get out there. Tell them what I said about four-three."

The boy barely had time to get himself together before the referee blew the whistle, signaling that the time-out was over.

"Vonte," Jade called out. "You keep an eye on him out there. No matter what happens tonight, that boy is your responsibility from now on. Think of him as your own little mentee."

Vonte's grumbling was an agreement, but Jade knew she'd be hearing an earful about this from him later.

She and Lim stood side by side with their arms crossed.

"You scared?" Franny spoke just loud enough for her to hear.

"Terrified. If we lose after all this . . ."

"We won't."

"We'd better not."

"We won't."

A 4-3 defensive strategy called for four down linemen and three linebackers. The players were aligned so they could try to control the gaps in West Beaufort's offense, which would allow Greenbelt to aggressively keep them from moving up the field with the ball. This type of play was less popular these days in favor of showier ones, but Jade figured that just meant the other team wouldn't expect them to use it.

They'd spent months running this defense in practice, but she'd never had them bring it out in a game before. It was a risky move, and she was betting everything on her boys having it down to a T.

The second the scrimmage started, West Beaufort's quarterback took off with the ball tucked. Greenbelt's two outside linebackers spread to protect their gaps, and the down linemen in the middle spread just enough for coverage. West Beaufort's QB stalled for a moment, his feet skidding on the turf as he attempted to decide which way he was going to try to run the ball.

This was all the time Sam needed to charge forward, an unexpected force taking over the field. The seconds ticked by, the number on the clock growing smaller and smaller. Jade held her breath as Sam sprinted closer to the quarterback; any sudden movements or changes and the kid's trajectory could be thrown off. If he missed this tackle, it could mean missing out on their last chance to keep West Beaufort from scoring again.

They were only one touchdown away from Greenbelt's lead becoming a tie, and they damn sure did not want a tie. They wanted a win.

The sound of the bodies impacting seemed to process faster than actually watching it happen. One moment, Sam was throwing himself into the air, taking the other player down to the ground, and the next, the final buzzer was going off.

Jade's heart thundered in her chest, and her stomach heaved like she was about to throw up.

"Jade!" Lim's voice was frantic. "Oh my God, Jade. They did it. They did it, Jade."

Jade couldn't speak. Her head was filled with static as blood rushed to her ears. All she could do was nod.

The players ran onto the field, but she couldn't follow them. All she could do was stand on the sidelines and watch as the joy overtook her team. All the sounds of the world faded out as she watched them jumping through the air, arms wide, mouths grinning. They had all worked so hard for this. Grueling hours on the field practicing in the cold and heat until blisters formed on their hands and their bodies were too tired to stand upright.

Coaches who had forgone family dinners and time at home to

travel the state for games all season. Folks who had worked tirelessly with her to foster strength and camaraderie among these kids. All of them watched on as their players were unabashed in their exuberance.

She couldn't help but think about herself too. All those years of waiting and hoping and pushing. The fighting and clawing she'd had to do to prove to everyone that she was fit to coach football at all, let alone as head coach. Just for her to bring the team to their first championship win during her first year as head coach. No, she hadn't done it alone—and she would never claim that she had. But this win was hers too.

All her senses flowed back into her body slowly, and the first thing she heard upon coming back to herself was the announcer's tinny voice through the booming stadium speakers.

"And there you have it, folks! Greenbelt is our new 2024 South Carolina state champion."

It was one of the most beautiful things she'd ever heard.

Jade had been coming to Minnie's for the better part of three decades and never once had she gotten to sit in the giant half-circle booth in the back. That table had always been reserved for large parties and, well, she'd never been part of a party large enough to earn a seat at it.

Until now.

It was a Saturday night in January. Too hot for the time of year in Greenbelt but still beautiful out. Instead of being out at a bar or hanging around someone's backyard, her friend group was sitting around a table at Minnie's Diner eating peach cobbler like it was their last meal. Truthfully, she wouldn't have had it any other way. She was sandwiched between Franny and Miri, with Aja and Walker

Abbott on Miri's other side. Across the table, Olivia and Leo Vaughn sat in chairs. In the center of the table were two whole cobblers and half a gallon of ice cream. Their waitress had simply left them with the scoop and told them to go nuts. Which they had, judging by the tightness in Jade's belly.

In one week, Olivia would be moving. Not just from Beaufort either but out of the country completely. She'd taken a teaching job in South Korea with a contract that would keep her away from them for an entire year. They'd spent the past few weeks shedding their tears and reveling in their sadness. Now it was time to send their girl off in style. With good company and Greenbelt's finest.

Truthfully, it had been a while since they'd all gotten to spend time together at once. Work was hectic, and everyone trying to cultivate their own relationships took time. They still made sure to get together plenty, but it often meant that all their schedules didn't align and someone was left out. They'd all made time for this, though, and it felt incredible to have everyone together in one place. Even Leo with his big-ass head made her heart feel full enough to burst.

"I will never forget the first time I had this cobbler," Aja said, giggling. "Walker brought me here and made me try it."

"Mm-hmm." Walker's voice was calm and quiet, like it always was. "Now she knows all about them peaches. Ain't that right?"

"I've still never had any better than this."

"I have," Walker said quietly, and judging by the way Aja tucked her face into his chest and laughed, they were being too horny for their own good.

Jade decided to let it go without ragging on them. She was in too good a mood.

"Nothing's better than Minnie's," Leo said. "And I've been to a lot of damn diners."

"I have to agree," Franny added, prompting Jade to throw an

arm around her bare shoulders. "I don't know what it is, but there's something about this place that just won't let up."

"Well, that's because Old Minnie was on her witchy shit," Miri said.

Everyone else at the table groaned, and Miri just cackled.

"I'm serious as a heart attack too. My mama said that before she opened this place, Minnie put all kinds of wards and shit around the property for protection. I mean, when was the last time you saw anybody get into a fight at Minnie's? Or even try to get nasty with one of the servers?"

They all went silent for a few moments, thinking.

"Well, never," Olivia huffed. "But that doesn't mean Minnie cast spells on all of Greenbelt."

Miri shrugged. "People in this town fight at church picnics, girl. But somehow, they never fight at Minnie's. The vibes are always right, the food is always hot, and the cobbler always hits. That feels like witchcraft to me."

"Wait a minute. When did this place open?" Walker asked.

"My folks came here when they were in high school," Leo said. "So . . . a long time."

Walker's blond brows furrowed. "My granny always told me Minnie herself was back there cooking. How old could she be?"

"Wait, I thought Minnie's was just named after someone's mama," Jade interjected. "I didn't think there was actually a woman named Minnie behind it all."

"Mama said that it's owned by a Black woman named Minnie and that these are all her original recipes." Miri's tone was incredibly sure.

Leo chuckled, not unkindly. "Well, if Ms. Patrice said it . . ."

"Oh, hush," Miri said, smiling. "She's right most of the time."

"I don't know if she's right about this one," Olivia said, phone up to her face. "The website says Minnie's was opened in 1962, but it doesn't say anything about who opened it or where it got its name."

"That's weird." Franny pulled her own phone out, tapping on the screen. "This website looks like it was started in 1962 . . ."

"Ooh," Jade said, pulling her arm from around Franny's shoulders and putting her elbows on the table, leaning forward. "Maybe we should investigate. Let's get to the bottom of the Minnie's mystery."

The entire table went silent for a few moments, and Jade's excitement grew as she assumed they were all taking her idea into real consideration.

"You want us to run around town like Scoob and the gang?" Leo laughed. "What happens if we find out the place is just an old chain restaurant run by an evil conglomerate or something?"

Jade pouted, throwing herself back against the booth, arms crossed. "Is it your life's goal to ruin all my fun, Leo?"

Leo's dark eyebrows shot up his forehead in an instant. "Oh, it's *me* ruining *your* fun now?"

"Yes, just like always."

Miri reached across the table, putting one hand on her husband and one hand on Jade. "Behave, babies. You know Mommy has plenty of love for you both."

Across from her, Leo swallowed hard at the words, immediately averting his gaze and shifting in his seat some.

"Maybe we should just let the lore stay lore," Aja offered, ever the diplomatic one. "Maybe Minnie is back there right now rolling out pie dough, or maybe she died and left her recipes to her family. Hell, maybe she was never a real person in the first place."

"Yeah," Miri interjected. "And maybe she's the greatest witch Greenbelt has ever seen."

"Anyway," Aja continued. "All I'm saying is that, maybe Minnie is whoever we need her to be. As long as we can come in here, sit down, and eat food in this place, that's what matters."

"Keeping the mystery alive." Olivia nodded. "I respect that."

While they all mulled it over, Jade took her spoon, scooping up a big hunk of cobbler and ice cream, and offering it to the woman next to her. Franny's eyes were soft like dandelion buds when they landed on her. Jade let the warmth of her gaze float over her skin. It was hot but gentle, and when Franny opened her lips, Jade didn't hesitate to feed her.

She watched as her girlfriend savored the flavors of the dessert, swallowing it down and running a tongue over her pink lips for just one more taste once it was done.

"The cobbler abides," Franny said to the group but didn't take her eyes off Jade's.

"Damn right it does." Jade grinned.

ACKNOWLEDGMENTS

Angel, who is always on the other side of a text, call, or the couch. I will never get tired of thanking you for all the ways you have enriched my life. I wish everyone could have a sister like you.

Mom, thank you for always supporting me, always asking me questions, and bragging about me to your friends. I wouldn't be here without you.

Becca, for giving me a roof under which to write this book and filling my heart with enough love to see it through. I owe you everything, least of all this acknowledgment and dedication. Your friendship transforms me and keeps me going.

Rhonda, my favorite and only auntie. My number one girl. I will never love anyone the way I love you. Thank you endlessly for hyping me up and staying on my ass!

Andrea, for opening up your office, your heart, and your mouth. One podcast episode was all it took to bring us together, but the binding glue is the care and support you have shown me. Thank you, friend.

Joe and Scoop, I hope this surprises you both. You were instrumental in quite a few parts of my writing process here. Beyond that, I am exceptionally glad to have met you and to be able to call you friends. Here's to many more late-night calls and laughter-filled meals.

Kim, my agent, who worked hard to make this happen for me. I definitely won the lottery with you. Thank you!

Vicki, I couldn't have asked for a better editor, truly. You took a chance on me and let me change things up with this one. Even through scant first drafts and tear-filled emails you kept me going. You rock my world!

Vanessa, for always chasing after me and being forgiving when it takes a little too long. Thank you for your kindness and patience that you have shown me in droves.

Marissa, Meghan, and the rest of the St. Martin's Griffin team, thank you all for the incredibly hard work you do, not just for me but for every other author on your roster. We owe you the world, truly.

To anyone else I've missed by name but have loved all the same, my gratitude is endless and undying.

ABOUT THE AUTHOR

Madison Van Zile

Jodie Slaughter is a traditionally and indie-published romance author with one major goal: to make readers completely immerse themselves in the stories she writes. Whether she's making them laugh with witty one-liners or swoon over magical first kisses, she wants her novels to be so full of passion and complexity that they're impossible to put down. When she isn't writing, she can be found baking or trying to convince her loved ones to start a commune. She has been publishing since 2019.

She is represented by Kim Lionetti at BookEnds Literary Agency.